RICOCHET

"No one does steamy suspense like Brown, as shown by this expert mix of spicy romance and sharply crafted crime drama. . . . Tight plotting, a hot love story with some nice twists and a credible ending help make this a standout thriller."
—*Publishers Weekly* (starred review)

"A great, entertaining read, with lots of surprising twists and turns, credibly flawed characters and a love affair that's as steamy as a Savannah summer."
—*The Washington Post*

"[A] taut Southern thriller . . . delectable."
—*Life* magazine

"Gripping and absorbing . . . a must-read." —*Booklist*

CHILL FACTOR

"Races along with the passion and verve that are the hallmarks of a Brown novel." —*Orlando Sentinel*

"Compelling characters, sexual tension and stunning plot twists . . . a page-turner that will keep readers guessing until the end." —*The Sunday Oklahoman*

"Virtuoso plot twists. . . . Brown's thriller engages the primal senses." —*Kirkus Reviews*

"This creepy tale puts [Sandra Brown] in a remarkable class of her own." —*Ottawa Citizen*

"Brown has done a skillful job in blending two genres— romantic suspense and serial killer—into a homogeneous whole that should please the devotees of both."
—*The San Diego Union-Tribune*

SANDRA BROWN

PLAY DIRTY

POCKET BOOKS

New York London Toronto Sydney New Delhi

Pocket Books
An Imprint of Simon & Schuster, Inc.
1230 Avenue of the Americas
New York, NY 10020

This Pocket Books paperback edition October 2019

POCKET and colophon are registered trademarks of Simon & Schuster, Inc.

For information about special discounts for bulk purchases, please contact Simon & Schuster Special Sales at 1-866-506-1949 or business@simonandschuster.com.

The Simon & Schuster Speakers Bureau can bring authors to your live event. For more information or to book an event, contact the Simon & Schuster Speakers Bureau at 1-866-248-3049 or visit our website at www.simonspeakers.com.

Manufactured in the United States of America

10   9   8   7   6   5   4   3   2   1

ISBN 978-1-9821-2111-2
ISBN 978-1-4165-4541-5 (ebook)

PLAY
DIRTY

CHAPTER

1

"HAT IT?"

"That's it." Griff Burkett tossed a small duffel bag onto the backseat of the car, then got into the front passenger seat. "I didn't bring much with me. I'm sure as hell not taking souvenirs." He wanted no memorabilia from his stint in BIG—official code name for the Federal Correctional Institution in Big Spring, Texas.

He made himself comfortable on the plush leather, adjusted the air-conditioning vent to blow straight at him, then, realizing they weren't moving, looked over at the driver.

"Seat belt."

"Oh. Right." Griff stretched the belt across his chest and latched it. Tongue in cheek, he said, "Wouldn't want to break the law."

As lawyers went, Wyatt Turner was okay. But if he possessed a sense of humor, he kept it under lock and key. He didn't crack a smile at Griff's wry remark.

"Come on, Turner, lighten up," Griff said. "This is a special day."

"Unfortunately, we're not the only ones commemorating it."

Turner drew Griff's attention to an ugly, olive green car parked in a handicapped space. Illegally it seemed, since there was no tag hanging from the rearview mirror. Griff didn't recognize the make or model of the car because it was younger than five years old. Nothing distinguished the no-frills sedan except the man sitting behind the wheel.

Griff cursed under his breath. "What's *he* doing here?"

"It's been all over the news that you were being released today, but I don't think he brought champagne."

"So why'd he come all this way to see little ol' me?"

"I assume he wants to pick up where the two of you left off."

"Fat chance."

The object of their conversation, Stanley Rodarte, had parked where he couldn't be missed. He had wanted Griff to see him. And Griff would have recognized him anywhere, because Stanley Rodarte was one ugly son of a bitch. His face looked like it had been hacked out of oak with a chain saw, by a carver too impatient to smooth out the rough edges. Cheekbones as sharp as knife blades cast shadows across his ruddy, pockmarked skin. His hair was the color and texture of dirty straw. Behind the lenses of his opaque sunglasses, his eyes—yellowish, as Griff recalled—were no doubt trained on Griff with an enmity that even five years hadn't blunted.

Griff shrugged with more indifference than he felt. "It's his time he's wasting."

Sounding like the voice of doom, Turner said, "Obviously he doesn't think so."

As they pulled closer to the other car, Griff flashed Rodarte a big grin, then raised his middle finger at him.

"Jesus, Griff." Turner accelerated toward the prison gate. "What's the matter with you?"

"He doesn't scare me."

"Well, he should. If you had a lick of sense, he would scare you shitless. Apparently he hasn't forgotten about Bandy. Steer clear of him. I mean it. Are you listening? Do not cross him."

"Am I gonna get billed for that unsolicited advice?"

"No, that advice is on the house. It's for my protection as well as yours."

Despite the blasting air conditioner, Griff lowered his window as Turner drove through the gates of the federal prison camp that had been his home for the past five years. The area in which he'd been incarcerated was classified minimum security, but it was still prison.

"No offense to the folks in Big Spring, but I don't care to ever enter the city limits again," he remarked as they left the West Texas town and headed east on Interstate 20.

The air was hot, dry, and gritty, perfumed by diesel and gasoline exhaust from the well-traveled highway, but it was free air, the first Griff had tasted in one thousand, eight hundred, and twenty-five days. He gulped it.

"Feel good to be out?" his lawyer asked.

"You have no idea."

After a moment, Turner said, "I meant what I said about Rodarte."

The sand-bearing wind scoured Griff's face and flattened his hair against his head. "Relax, Turner," he said, speaking above the noise of a foul-smelling cattle truck roaring past. "I won't wave red flags at Rodarte. Or at anybody else. That's in my past. Ancient history. I took my punishment and paid my debt to society. You're looking at a rehabilitated, reformed man."

"Glad to hear it," the lawyer said, heavy on the skepticism.

Griff had been watching Rodarte in the car's side-view mirror. He'd followed them out of Big Spring and now was matching their speed, keeping at least three vehicles between them. If Wyatt Turner realized that Rodarte was on their tail, he didn't mention it. Griff started to say something about it, then figured there were things his lawyer didn't need to know. Things that would only worry him.

Three hundred miles later, Griff stood in the center of the apartment's living area, which was a laughable misnomer. A person might exist here, but you couldn't call it living. The room was so dim it bordered on gloomy, but the poor lighting actually worked in its favor. A crack as wide as his index finger ran up one wall from floor to ceiling like a jagged lightning bolt. The carpet was gummy. The air conditioner wheezed, and the air it pumped was damp and smelled like day-old carryout Chinese.

"It's not much," Turner said.

"No shit."

"But there's no lease. The rent's paid month to month. Consider this only a stopover until you can find something better."

"At least Big Spring was clean."

"You want to go back?"

Maybe Turner had a sense of humor after all.

Griff tossed his duffel bag onto the sofa. Not only did it look uncomfortable but the upholstery was stained with God-knew-what. He remembered fondly the high-rise condo he used to live in, in the ritzy Turtle Creek area of Dallas. Suffused with natural light during the day, a spectacular view of the skyline at night. Outfitted with countless amenities. Half of the gadgets and gewgaws he hadn't even known what they were for or how to work them. But the important thing was that he'd had them.

"When you sold my place, weren't you able to keep any of my stuff?"

"Clothes. Personal items. Pictures. Like that. It's all in a storage unit. But the rest . . ." Turner shook his head and nervously jiggled his keys as though anxious to get back in his car, although the drive had taken them nearly five hours with only one stop. "I liquidated everything in the Toy Box first."

That had been Griff's pet name for the extra garage he'd leased in which to store his grown-up toys—snow skis, scuba equipment, an Indian motorcycle, a bass fishing boat that had been in the water exactly once. Stuff he had bought mostly because he could.

"The Escalade and Porsche went next. I held off selling the Lexus until I had no choice. Then I began emptying the apartment. I had to sell it all, Griff. To pay off your fine. Consulting fees."

"*Your* fee."

Turner stopped his bit with the keys. Under other circumstances, the combative stance he took would have been humorous. Griff was more than half a foot taller, and he hadn't slacked on workouts during his incarceration. If anything, he was harder now than when he went in.

Wyatt Turner had the pallor of a man who worked indoors twelve hours a day. A workout for him amounted to eighteen holes of golf, riding in a cart, followed by two cocktails in the clubhouse. In his mid-forties, he had already developed a soft paunch in front and sagging ass in back.

"Yes, Griff, my fee," he said defensively. "I get paid to do my job. Just like you do."

Griff looked at him for a moment, then said softly, "Did. Just like I *did*."

Turner backed down and, looking slightly embarrassed by his momentary testiness, turned away and laid another set of keys on the stick-furniture coffee table. "Our extra car. It's parked outside. Can't miss it. Faded red, two-door Honda. Not worth anything as a trade-in, so when Susan got her Range Rover, we kept it for emergencies. It runs okay. I had the oil changed and the tires checked. Use it for as long as you need it."

"Will the daily rental fee be added to my bill?"

Again, Turner took umbrage. "Why are you being such a prick about everything? I'm trying to help."

"I needed your help five years ago to keep me out of fucking prison."

"I did everything I could for you," Turner fired back. "They had you. You do the crime, you do the time."

"Gee, I need to write that down." Griff patted his pockets as though looking for a pen.

"I'm outta here."

Turner moved toward the door, but Griff headed him off. "Okay, okay, you're a prince among lawyers and I'm an unappreciative prick. What else?" He allowed Turner a few moments to fume in righteous indignation, then repeated in a more conciliatory tone, "What else have you done for me?"

"I put some of your clothes in the closet in the bedroom." He gestured toward an open doorway across the room. "Jeans and polos haven't gone out of style. I picked up some sheets and towels at Target. You got toiletries?"

"In my duffel."

"Bottled water, milk, eggs are in the fridge. Bread's in there, too. I thought there might be roaches in the pantry."

"Safe guess."

"Look, Griff, I know it's no palace, but—"

"*Palace?*" he repeated, laughing. "I don't think anyone would mistake this dump for a palace." Then, to keep from appearing ungrateful, he added, "But as you said, it's only a stopgap. Do I have a phone?"

"In the bedroom. I put down the deposit for you. It's in my name. We can have it disconnected when you get your own."

"Thanks. What's the number?"

Turner told him. "Don't you need to write it down?"

"I used to carry a couple hundred plays inside my head. I can remember ten digits."

"Hmm. Right. Don't forget to check in with your probation officer. He'll need to know how to contact you."

"First item on my list. Call Jerry Arnold." Griff drew a check mark in the air.

Turner handed him a bank envelope. "Here's some walking-around money until you can get a credit card. And your driver's license is in there, too. Address is wrong, of course, but it doesn't expire until your next birthday, and by then you'll have a new place."

"Thanks." Griff tossed the bank envelope onto the table beside the keys to the borrowed car. Taking handouts from his lawyer was almost as humiliating as the first day of prison, when he'd been told the rules as well as the punishments for breaking them.

"Well, then, I guess you're good to go." The lawyer clapped him on the shoulder, which seemed an unnatural and awkward gesture for him. He turned away quickly, but at the door he paused and looked back. "Griff . . . uh . . . folks are still pissed at you. To a lot of people, you committed a cardinal sin. If someone gives you flak, don't let it bother you too much. Turn the other cheek, okay?"

Griff remained silent. He wouldn't make a promise he couldn't keep.

Turner hesitated, looking worried. "Getting out . . . It's a tough transition."

"Beats staying in."

"Those classes they have for inmates about to be released . . ."

"The Release Preparation Program."

"Right. Were the sessions helpful?"

"Oh, yeah. I learned how to fill out a job application. Was urged not to scratch my ass or pick my nose during an interview."

Looking chagrined, Turner asked, "Do you have any idea what you're going to do?"

"Get a job."

"For sure. What I mean is, do you have any prospects lined up?"

"Do you know an NFL team looking for a starting quarterback?" Turner's face went so flaccid, Griff laughed. "That was a joke."

The estate was enclosed by an ivy-covered, twelve-foot-high brick wall.

"Holy shit." Griff pulled the red Honda up to the call box at the gate. He'd known by the address that this was an affluent part of Dallas, but he hadn't expected it to be *this* affluent.

Instructions on how to contact the house were printed on the box. He punched in a sequence of numbers on the keypad, which he supposed rang a telephone inside. In a moment, a voice came through the speaker.

"Yes?"

"Griff Burkett to see Mr. Speakman."

Nothing else was said. But the iron picket gate opened and he drove through. The brick lane was bordered by cultivated beds of low shrubbery and flowers. Beyond them the tree-shaded lawn looked like a carpet of green velvet.

The mansion itself was as impressive as the landscaping. Older than Griff by several decades, it was constructed of gray stone. Some of its walls were ivy covered like the estate wall. He followed the curving driveway and parked directly in front of the entrance, then got out of the borrowed Honda and approached the front door. It was flanked by urns containing evergreen trees. Idly Griff wondered how in hell they got a tree to grow in the shape of a corkscrew.

No cobwebs clinging to the eaves. Nary a stray leaf anywhere. Not a smear on any of the windows. The house, the grounds, the whole place was freaking perfect.

When he'd told Wyatt Turner he didn't have any prospects, he'd lied. Not that job offers were pouring in. Right now, Griff Burkett was arguably the most detested man in Dallas, if not the entire Lone Star State. No, that was still limiting: He was despised in the whole football-loving country. People sneered his name, or spat after saying it as though to ward off an evil spirit. Nobody in their right mind would want him on their payroll.

But he did have this one prospect, however slim.

A few days before his release, he had received an invitation to be in this spot, on this date, at this time. The stiff card had been engraved: Foster Speakman. The name was vaguely familiar, although Griff couldn't remember why it would be.

As he depressed the doorbell, he couldn't imagine what a guy who lived in a place like this could possibly want with him. He had assumed the appointment portended a job offer. Now, seeing this spread, he thought maybe not. Maybe this Speakman had been a die-hard Cowboys fan who only wanted his own pound of Griff Burkett's flesh.

The door was opened almost immediately. He was greeted by a waft of refrigerated air, the faint scent of oranges, and a guy who looked like he should be wearing a breechcloth and carrying a spear.

Griff had expected a maid or butler—someone in a white apron, with a soft speaking voice and polite but aloof mannerisms. This guy didn't come close. He was dressed in a tight black T-shirt and black slacks. He had the wide, flat features of Mayan royalty. His skin was smooth and beardless. Straight hair black as ink.

"Uh, Mr. Speakman?"

He shook his head and smiled. Rather, he revealed his teeth. You couldn't really call it a smile because no other feature of his face changed, even moderately. He stood aside and motioned Griff in.

A vaulted ceiling loomed three stories above. Oriental rugs formed islands of subtle color on the marble floor. Griff's image was caught in the enormous mirror that hung above the long console table. The curving staircase was an architectural marvel, especially considering when the house had been built. The space was vast, and as hushed as a cathedral.

The speechless man motioned with his head for Griff to follow. Again it occurred to Griff that Foster Speakman might be lying in wait. Did he keep thumbscrews and whips in the dungeon?

When they reached a set of double doors, the butler—for lack of a better word—pushed both open, then stood aside. Griff stepped into the room, obviously a library, the walls on three sides consisting of floor-to-ceiling bookcases. The fourth wall was almost entirely windows, affording a view of the sweeping lawn and flower gardens.

"I wondered."

Griff turned at the unexpected voice and got his second surprise. The man smiling up at him was in a wheelchair.

"Wondered what?"

"How physically imposing you would be in person." He sized Griff up. "You're as tall as I expected, but not as . . . bulky. Of course, I've only seen you from the distance of a stadium box, and on TV."

"TV adds ten pounds."

The man laughed. "To say nothing of shoulder pads." He extended his right hand. "Foster Speakman. Thank you for coming." They shook hands. Not surprisingly, his hand was smaller than Griff's by far, but his palm was dry and his handshake firm. He pushed a button on his fancy wheelchair and backed away. "Come in and have a seat."

He motioned Griff toward a grouping of comfortably arranged pieces with appropriate tables and lamps. Griff chose one of the chairs. As he sank into it, he experienced a pang of homesickness for the furnishings of similar quality he used to own. Now he had to keep his bread in a fridge with an irritating hum.

Taking another glance around the room and the acreage beyond the windows, he questioned again just what the hell he was doing *here,* in an ivy-covered mansion, with a crippled man.

Foster Speakman probably had five years on

him, which put him around forty. He was nice looking. Hard to tell how tall he would be standing, but
Griff guessed just shy of six feet. He was wearing
preppy clothes—navy blue golf shirt and khaki
slacks, brown leather belt, matching loafers, tan
socks.

The legs of his trousers looked like deflated bal-
loons, not much flesh to fill them out.

"Something to drink?" Speakman asked pleasantly.

Caught staring and speculating, Griff shifted his
attention back to his host's face. "A Coke?"

Speakman looked over at the man who'd answered the door. "Manuelo, two Cokes, *por favor.*"

Manuelo was as square and solid as a sack of
cement but moved soundlessly. Speakman noticed
Griff watching the servant as he went to the bar
and began pouring their drinks. "He's from El Salvador."

"Huh."

"He literally walked to the United States."

"Huh."

"He tends to me."

Griff could think of nothing to say to that, although he wanted to ask if Manuelo, despite his
smile, kept a collection of shrunken heads under his
bed.

"Did you drive from Big Spring today?" Speakman asked.

"My lawyer picked me up this morning."

"Long drive."

"I didn't mind it."

Speakman grinned. "I guess not. After being
cooped up for so long." He waited until Griff had

taken his drink from the small tray Manuelo extended to him, then took his own cut-crystal glass and raised it. "To your release."

"I'll drink to that."

Manuelo left through the double doors, pulling them closed behind him. Griff took another sip of Coke, becoming uncomfortable under Speakman's blatantly curious stare.

What was this? Invite a con for drinks week?

The whole scene was beginning to make him uneasy. Deciding to cut to the chase, he set his drink on the end table at his elbow. "Did you ask me here to get an up close and personal look at a has-been football player? Or a convicted felon?"

Speakman seemed unfazed by his rudeness. "I thought you might be in the market for a job."

Not wanting to look desperate or needy, Griff gave a noncommittal shrug.

"Any offers yet?" Speakman asked.

"None that have interested me."

"The Cowboys aren't—"

"No. Nor is any other team. I've been banned from the league. I doubt I could buy a ticket to an NFL game."

Speakman nodded as though he had already determined that was the way things were with Griff Burkett. "If you can't do something related to football, what did you plan to do?"

"I planned to serve my sentence and get out."

"Nothing beyond that?"

Griff sat back, again shrugged as though he didn't give a shit, reached for his Coke, and took another sip. "I've toyed with some ideas but haven't settled on anything yet."

"I own an airline. SunSouth."

Griff kept his features schooled, trying not to show that he was either surprised or impressed, when actually he was both. "I fly it. Or rather, I used to fly SunSouth often."

Speakman flashed an unself-conscious smile. "So do a lot of people, I'm pleased to say."

Griff looked around the beautiful room, his gaze stopping on some of its treasures, then came back to Speakman. "I bet you are."

Despite his drollness, Speakman's smile remained in place. "I invited you here to offer you a job."

Griff's heart did a little jig of gladness. A man like Foster Speakman could do him a lot of good. Now he remembered why the name had sounded familiar. Speakman was an influential force in Dallas, owning and operating one of the region's most successful enterprises. An endorsement from him, even a minor nod of pardon, would go a long way toward winning back some of the favor Griff had lost five years ago.

But he tamped down his bubbling optimism. For all he knew, the guy wanted him to strain the shit out of the sewage tanks on his airplanes. "I'm listening."

"The job I'm offering would give you immediate financial relief. I understand that your assets were liquidated to pay the fine the court imposed on you."

Hedging the truth, Griff said, "Most of them, yeah."

"Those proceeds were also used to cover substantial debts. Is that correct?"

"Look, Speakman, since you seem to know anyway, stop fishing. I lost everything and then some. Is that what you wanted to hear? I don't have a pot to piss in."

"Then I suppose a hundred thousand would come in handy."

Taken aback by the amount, Griff felt his irritation turn to suspicion. He'd learned the hard way to be wary of anything that seemed too easily come by. If it seemed too good to be true, it probably was. "A hundred thousand a year?"

"No, Mr. Burkett," Speakman said, smiling, enjoying himself. "A hundred thousand to seal our deal. Using a term you're familiar with, it would be like a signing bonus."

Griff stared at him for a count of ten. "A hundred grand. U.S. dollars."

"Legal tender. It's yours if you say yes to what I propose."

Griff carefully removed his ankle from his opposite knee and set both feet on the floor, buying time while his mind spun around the amount of money and how badly he needed it. "Are you thinking about using me to advertise your airline? Billboards, commercials, ads? That kind of thing? I wouldn't cotton to posing naked, but it could be negotiated."

Speakman smiled and shook his head. "I realize that endorsements were a significant part of your income when you were the starting quarterback of the Dallas Cowboys. That Number Ten jersey sold a lot of whatever it was advertising. But now I'm afraid an endorsement from you would repel customers, not attract them."

Even knowing that was true, Griff was pissed off

to hear it. "Then what did you have in mind? Who do I have to kill?"

Speakman actually laughed out loud. "It's nothing that drastic."

"I don't know anything about airplanes."

"This isn't airline related."

"You need a new yardman?"

"No."

"Then I'm fresh out of guesses. What do I do to earn my hundred thousand dollars?"

"Make my wife pregnant."

CHAPTER

2

E XCUSE ME?"

"You heard correctly, Mr. Burkett. An-other Coke?"

Griff continued to stare at his host until his question sank in. At least the crazy bastard was a courteous host. "No thanks."

Speakman rolled his chair over to the end table and picked up Griff's empty glass, carried it along with his to the wet bar, and placed both in a rack beneath the sink. He used a bar towel to wipe the granite countertop, although from where Griff sat, he could see that it was highly polished, not a single drop of liquid or streak of moisture on its glassy surface. Speakman folded the towel, lining up the hem evenly, and threaded it through a ring attached to the counter.

He rolled back to the table at Griff's elbow and replaced the coaster he'd used in its brass holder, gave it three taps, then put his chair in reverse and resumed his original place a few feet from where Griff sat.

Griff, watching these maneuvers, thought, *Courteous and* neat.

"Let me know if you change your mind about another drink," Speakman said.

Griff stood up, rounded his chair, looked back at Speakman to see if his lunacy could be detected at this distance, then walked over to the windows and looked outside. He needed to ground himself, make sure he hadn't fallen into a rabbit hole or something.

He felt as he had those first few weeks at Big Spring, when he would wake up disoriented and it would take several seconds for him to remember where he was and why. This was like that. He felt detached. He needed to get his bearings.

Beyond the windows, not a Mad Hatter in sight. Everything was still there and looking perfectly normal—the emerald grass, stone pathways winding through the flower beds, trees with sprawling branches shading it all. A pond in the distance. Blue sky. Overhead a jet was making its final approach into Dallas.

"One of ours."

Griff hadn't heard the approach of Speakman's chair and was startled to find him so close. Prison would do that to you, too. Make you jumpy. Linemen topping three hundred pounds used to charge at him bent on inflicting injury and pain, teeth bared behind their face guards, eyes slitted with malice. He'd been prepared for them and was conditioned to take their abuse.

But even in the minimum-security area of the

prison, where the inmates were white-collar criminals, you stayed nervous twenty-four/seven. You kept your guard up and other people at arm's length.

Of course, he'd been that way before prison.

Speakman was watching the jet. "From Nashville. Due to touch down at seven oh seven." He glanced at his wristwatch. "Right on time."

Griff studied him for several seconds, then said, "The hell of it is, you seem perfectly sane."

"You doubt my sanity?"

"And then some."

"Why?"

"Well, for starters, I'm not wearing a sign that says sperm bank."

Speakman smiled. "Not the kind of job you thought I'd be offering, huh?"

"Not by a long shot." Griff glanced at his own wristwatch. "Look, I've got plans tonight. A get-together with some friends." There was no get-together. No friends, either. But it sounded plausible. "I need to get going to make it on time."

Speakman seemed to see through the lie. "Before declining my offer," he said, "at least hear me out."

He extended his hand as though to touch Griff's arm. Griff's flinch was involuntary, no way to prevent Speakman from noticing it. He looked up at Griff with puzzlement but pulled his hand back before making actual contact. "Sorry," Griff muttered.

"It's the wheelchair," Speakman said blandly. "It puts some people off. Like a disease or a bad-luck charm."

"It's not that. Not at all. It's, uh . . . Look, I think we're finished here. I gotta go."

"Please don't leave yet, Griff. Do you mind if I call you Griff? I think this is a good point at which to shift to first names, don't you?"

Speakman's eyes reflected the bright light from the windows. They were clear, intelligent eyes. Not a trace of madness or the kind of wild glee that signaled insanity. Griff wondered if Mrs. Speakman was aware of it. Hell, he wondered if there *was* a Mrs. Speakman. The millionaire might have been completely delusional as well as compulsively tidy.

When Griff failed to reply to the question about his name, Speakman's smile relaxed into an expression of disappointment. "At least stay long enough for me to finish making my pitch. I would hate for all my rehearsing to be for naught." He gave a quick smile. "Please."

Fighting a strong urge to get the hell out of there, but also feeling guilty for the physical rebuff he'd given the man, Griff returned to his chair and sat down. As he settled against the cushions, he noticed that the back of his shirt was damp with nervous perspiration. As soon as he could gracefully make an exit, he would *adiós*.

Speakman reopened the dialogue by saying, "I can't father a child. By any method." He paused as though to emphasize that. "If I had sperm," he added quietly, "you and I wouldn't be having this conversation."

Griff would just as soon not be having it. It wasn't easy to look a man in the eye while he was talking to you about losing his manhood. "Okay. So you need a donor."

"You mentioned a sperm bank."

Griff nodded curtly.

"Laura—that's my wife. She and I didn't want to go that route."

"Why not? For the most part, they're reputable, aren't they? Reliable? They do testing on the donors. All that."

Griff knew little about sperm banks and wasn't really interested in how they operated. He was thinking more about what had happened to Speakman to put him in that chair. Had he always been paraplegic, or was it a recent thing? Had he contracted a debilitating and degenerative disease? Been thrown by a horse? What?

"When the male partner is incapable of fathering children, as I am," Speakman said, "couples do use donor sperm. Most of the time, successfully."

Well, apparently he wasn't embarrassed by or self-conscious about his condition, and Griff had to give him credit for that. If he was in a situation like Speakman's, needing somebody like Manuelo to "tend" to him, he doubted he could be as accepting of it as Speakman appeared to be. He knew he wouldn't be able to talk about it so freely, especially with another man. Maybe Speakman was simply resigned.

He was saying, "Laura and I desperately want a child, Griff."

"Uh-huh," Griff said, not knowing what else to say.

"And we want our child to have physical characteristics similar to mine."

"Okay."

Speakman shook his head as though Griff still wasn't quite getting it. And he realized he wasn't when Speakman said, "We want everyone to believe that the child was fathered by me."

"Right," Griff said, but there was a hint of a question mark at the end of the word.

"This is extremely important to us. Vital. Mandatory, in fact." Speakman raised his index finger like a politician about to make the most important statement of his campaign. "No one must doubt that I'm the child's father."

Griff shrugged indifferently. "I'm not going to tell anybody."

Speakman relaxed, smiling. "Excellent. We're paying for your discretion as well as your . . . assistance."

Griff laughed lightly and raised both hands, palms out. "Wait a minute. When I said I wouldn't tell anybody, I meant I wouldn't tell anybody about this conversation. In fact, I'm not really interested in hearing any more. Let's consider this . . . uh . . . interview over, okay? You keep your hundred grand, and I'll keep my sperm, and this meeting will be our little secret."

He was almost out of his chair when Speakman said, "Half a million. Half a million dollars when Laura conceives."

Arrested in motion, Griff found it easier to sit back down than to stand up. He landed rather hard and sat staring at Speakman, aghast. "You're shittin' me."

"I assure you I'm not."

"Half a million?"

"You have blue eyes, light hair. Like mine. It's hard to tell now, but I'm taller than the average five feet eleven. We have similar genetic makeups, you and I. Similar enough anyway for a child you sire to be passed off as mine."

Griff's mind was spinning so fast it was hard to hang on to a thought. He was thinking dollar signs, Speakman was talking genes. "Those sperm banks have books." He pantomimed leafing through pages. "You go through them and find what you want for your kid. You pick out eye color, hair color, height. All that."

"I never buy anything sight unseen, Griff. I don't shop from catalogs. Certainly not for my child and heir. And there's still the risk of disclosure."

"Those records are kept confidential," Griff argued.

"Supposedly."

Griff thought of the gate with the disembodied voice, the high wall surrounding the property. Apparently privacy was a real issue with this guy. Like neatness. The psychologist at Big Spring would have had a field day over the obsessive way Speakman had removed the drinking glasses from view, folded the towel, and replaced the coaster.

Intrigued in spite of himself, Griff studied the millionaire for a long moment, then said, "So how would it work? I'd go to a doctor's office and jerk off into a jar and—"

"No office. If Laura was inseminated in a doctor's office, there would be talk."

"Who would talk?"

"The people who staff the office. Other patients who might see her there. People love to talk. Especially about celebrities."

"I'm a fallen star."

Laughing softly, Speakman said, "I was referring to Laura and me. But your involvement would certainly add another element to a delicious piece of gossip. It would be too tempting even for people bound by professional privilege."

"Okay, so I don't go to the doctor's office with you. You could take my semen in and claim it as yours. Who's to know?"

"You don't understand, Griff. That still leaves room for speculation. My condition is obvious. A specimen I claimed as mine could have come from the pool boy. A skycap. Anybody." He shook his head. "We're emphatic about this. No nurses, no chatty receptionists, no office open to the public. At all."

"So where? Here?" Griff envisioned taking a dirty magazine and a Dixie cup into one of the mansion's bathrooms, the mute manservant standing outside the door, waiting for him to finish and deliver the specimen.

No way, José. Or rather, *No way, Manuelo.*

But for half a million bucks?

Everyone had their price. He'd proved he did. Five years had decreased it considerably, but if Speakman was willing to pay him five hundred grand for doing what he'd been doing for free for the past five years, he wasn't going to let modesty stand in the way.

He'd walk away with six hundred thousand, counting the "signing bonus." The Speakmans would get the kid they desperately wanted. It was win-win, and it wasn't even against the law.

"I assume you'd have the doctor check me out first," he said. "For all you know, I could've taken up with a lover in prison and have HIV."

"I seriously doubt that," Speakman said drily, "but, yes, I would require you to undergo a thorough physical examination and bring me back a clean bill of health, signed by a physician. You could say it was for medical insurance."

It still seemed too easy. Griff wondered what he was overlooking. Where was the catch? "What if she doesn't get pregnant? Do I have to return the first hundred grand?"

Speakman hesitated. Griff tilted his head as though to communicate that this could be a deal breaker. Speakman said, "No. That would be yours to keep."

"Because if she doesn't conceive, it might not be my fault. Your wife may not be fertile."

"Who negotiated your contract with the Cowboys?"

"What? My former agent. Why?"

"A piece of advice, Griff. During a business negotiation, once you've won a point, drop it. Don't mention it again. I've already conceded that you could keep the initial hundred thousand."

"Okay." They hadn't covered that in the release preparation sessions.

Griff weighed his options, and they boiled down to this: he didn't have any options, other than saying no and walking away from mega cash. To turn this down, he'd have to be crazy. Crazy as Speakman and his old lady.

He raised one shoulder in a negligent shrug. "Then if that's all that's required, we have a deal.

One point, though. I want to do my thing in the privacy of my own bathroom. The doctor will have to come to my place to pick up the stuff. I think you can freeze it, so I could give him several samples at one whack." He laughed at the inadvertent double entendre. "So to speak."

Speakman laughed, too, but was serious as sin when he said, "There won't be a doctor, Griff."

Just when he thought he had this figured out, Speakman hit him with something like a linebacker coming around on his blind side and knocking him on his ass. "What do you mean, no doctor? Who's gonna . . ." He made gentle thrusting motions with his hand. "Put it where it needs to go."

"You are," Speakman said quietly. "I'm sorry for not making this clear from the beginning. I insist on my child being conceived naturally. The way God intended."

Griff stared at him for several seconds, then he began to laugh. Either somebody had set him up for a whopper of a practical joke or Speakman was out of his frigging mind.

Nobody in Griff's life cared enough to play an elaborate joke on him. No one in his present life would go to the trouble. No one from his past would give him the time of day, much less invest the time it would take to set up this bizarre scenario and talk Speakman into going along.

No, he was betting that Speakman went beyond being an eccentric millionaire and neat freak and was, in fact, certifiable.

In any case, this was all one huge waste of time, and he'd lost patience with it. Flippantly, he said, "My job would be to fuck your wife?"

Speakman winced. "I don't care much for the vernacular, especially in—"

"Cut the bullshit, okay? You're hiring me to play stud. That's basically it, right?"

Speakman hesitated, then said, "Basically? Yes."

"And for half a mil, I guess you get to watch."

"That's insulting, Griff. To me. Certainly to Laura."

"Yeah, well . . ." He didn't apologize. Kinky sex was the least offensive factor of this whole interview. "About her, does she know your plan?"

"Of course."

"Uh-huh. What does she think about it?"

Speakman rolled his chair toward an end table where a cordless phone stood in its charger. "You can ask her yourself."

CHAPTER
3

UPSTAIRS, IN HER HOME OFFICE, LAURA Speakman checked the clock on her desk. Only half an hour had elapsed since Griff Burkett's arrival. *Punctual* arrival. Being on time would definitely have won him marks with Foster. But of the other impressions he was making, were they good or bad?

For thirty minutes she'd been reading a new flight attendants' contract proposed by their union. She retained none of it. Giving up the pretense of working, she left her desk and began pacing the width of the office. It was a bright and airy room. There were drapes on the windows, carpet on the floor, crown molding at the ceiling. It was designated an office only by the desk and the computer setup concealed in an eight-foot-tall French antique armoire.

What was being said downstairs in the library?

Not knowing was driving her mad, but Foster had insisted on meeting with Burkett alone.

"Let me test the waters," he'd said. "Once I get a sense of him, I'll ask you to join us."

"And if your sense of him isn't good, if you don't think he's suitable, then what?"

"Then I'll send him on his way, and you will have been spared an awkward and unproductive interview."

His plan made sense, she supposed. But it wasn't in her nature to delegate decision making. Certainly not on something this important. Not even to her husband.

Of course, if she and Foster weren't in complete accord about Griff Burkett's suitability, he would be rejected. Nevertheless, she hated to miss seeing his initial reaction to their proposal and gauging that reaction for herself. How he reacted would tell a lot about him.

She looked across at the closed door and, for a moment, considered going downstairs and presenting herself. But that would violate Foster's careful planning. He wouldn't welcome the interruption to his schedule.

The pacing was only making her more agitated. She returned to her desk chair, reclined in it, closed her eyes, and utilized relaxation techniques she had taught herself while still a university student. After going days without a break from her studies, when her head was so packed full of information it couldn't tolerate any more, she would force herself to lie down, close her eyes, do her deep breathing exercises, and rest, if not sleep. Practicing the technique helped. If nothing else, it slowed her down, made her admit to the limitations of mind and body.

Difficult as it was for her to accept, right now there was nothing she could do but wait.

As her agitation gradually abated, her thoughts drifted back to the events and circumstances that had brought her to this point in her life, to this day and hour, to hiring a total stranger to make a baby with her.

It had begun with the color of the uniforms . . .

Headlines on the business pages had blared the news when Foster Speakman, last in line of the prominent Dallas family who'd been made wealthy by oil and gas, bought the distressed SunSouth Airlines.

For years the mismanaged airline had been teetering on the brink of total collapse. It had suffered a lengthy pilots' strike, followed by a blistering media exposé on its slipshod maintenance practices; then a disastrous crash took fifty-seven lives. Declaring bankruptcy had been the airline's final hope of recovery, but unfortunately that last gasp hadn't saved it.

Everyone thought the Speakman heir was insane when he spent a huge chunk of his fortune to buy the airline. For days the story dominated local business news: COSTLY HOBBY FOR MILLIONAIRE? SUN-SOUTH'S SALVATION, SPEAKMAN'S RUIN? The acquisition was even mentioned with mild derision on national broadcasts. It was implied that yet another rich Texan had gone and done something crazy.

Foster Speakman further surprised everyone by immediately grounding the airplanes, laying off thousands of employees with a promise to rehire them once he'd had time to conduct a thorough analysis of the airline's situation. He closed the doors to all media, telling frustrated reporters that they would be notified when he had something newsworthy to tell them.

In the ensuing months, Foster sequestered himself with financial and operational experts and advisers. Upper-echelon executives of the old regime were given the option to retire early with fair retirement packages. Those who didn't opt to do so were fired outright.

The firings weren't vindictive, only sound business acumen. Foster had a vision, but he also realized that, in order to bring it about, he would need people around him with knowledge equal to or greater than his. With his enthusiasm, charisma, and seemingly bottomless bank account, he lured the best in the industry away from cushy positions with other airlines.

Almost three months after taking over, Foster called all the new department heads together for the first of many roundtable discussions. Laura was there, representing the flight attendants. It was at that meeting she saw the man in charge for the first time.

She knew what he looked like from all the media coverage he had received, but photographs and television images had failed to capture his crackling vitality. Energy radiated from him like an electric aura.

He was lean, handsome, confident, personable. He strode into the conference room dressed in a perfectly tailored pin-striped suit, soft gray shirt, conservative tie. But soon after the meeting was called to order, he removed his double-breasted jacket, draped it over the back of his chair, loosened his tie, and literally rolled up his sleeves. By doing so, he indicated that he intended to do what needed to be done, that he didn't consider himself above applying elbow grease, and that he expected the same work ethic from everyone in that room.

The date had been set for the airline to resume operation. It was circled in red on the large calendar placed on an easel where all could see. "Target date," Foster announced happily. "Following our review of the budget, each of you will get a chance to tell me why I'm out of my mind and that there's no way in hell we'll make that deadline."

Everyone chuckled as expected. The meeting commenced.

The new CFO—hired because he was a notorious penny-pincher who had won his reputation by saving an American auto manufacturer from going under—was asked to talk them through the proposed budget item by item.

In his monotonous drone, he went on uninterrupted for a full ten minutes, then said, "Flight attendant program, the allotment remains the same. Next is food and beverage. Now here—"

"Excuse me."

The CFO raised his head and, looking over his reading glasses, surveyed the table to find the voice that had interrupted him. Laura raised her hand to identify herself. "Before moving on, this figure begs discussion."

He lowered one bushy eyebrow into a near scowl. "What isn't clear?"

"It's perfectly clear," she replied. "What needs discussion is how sorely underbudgeted this department is."

"Everyone at this table thinks his department is underbudgeted." He squinted at her, referred to the agenda for the meeting, and then squinted at her again. "Who are you, anyway?"

Before she had a chance to answer, Foster Speakman spoke from the head of the table. "Ladies and gentlemen, for those of you who haven't met her, this is Ms. Laura Taylor."

Her lips parted wordlessly. It came as a shock to her that Foster Speakman knew she existed.

The CFO removed his reading glasses and, after giving Laura a glance of consternation, asked Foster, "Where's Hazel Cooper?"

He said, "Ms. Taylor, will you do the honors?"

She rose to the challenge, saying evenly, "Ms. Cooper tendered her resignation day before yesterday."

"She did, that's right," came a voice on the other side of the table. The man was director of Human Resources. "I sent a blanket e-mail. Didn't y'all get it?" His gaze swept around the table, but there was a unanimous shaking of heads. "Oh, well, Hazel took early retirement. Said as long as there was a major shake-up, she might just as well make the move now, 'cause she planned on retiring next year anyway. I asked Ms. Taylor to sit in for her until another director for the department can be hired."

The CFO coughed behind his hand. "All well and good then. Once a new director is in place, I'll take up the budget for that department with him."

"Or her," Foster said.

The CFO turned red-faced. "Of course, I was speaking generically."

"As long as we're here, let's discuss the budget for this department," Foster said.

The CFO gave Laura another irritated look. "No offense to Ms. Taylor, but is she qualified to conduct that discussion?"

Foster riffled through a stack of file folders he had carried in with him. He found the one he wanted, stacked the others precisely, leaving no edge overlapping another, then opened the one he had withdrawn.

"Laura Eleanor Taylor . . . hmm, I'll skip down to . . . Here we go. Graduated with honors from Stephen F. Austin State University. Two years later she earned an MBA from Southern Methodist's business school. Again with honors.

"Applied and was accepted into the flight attendant program for SunSouth Airlines in 2002. Advancement, advancement, and another advancement," he said, consulting her employee record in the file.

"Promoted to do training and performance evaluation in 2005. Was a thorn in the side of the previous management and has made a nuisance of herself with Ms. Cooper by writing memo after memo, copies of which I have," he said, holding up a handful of sheets, "criticizing standards and practices now in place and suggesting ways in which the department could be vastly improved." He read directly from one memo. " '*But*'—which is underlined—'not without insight, intelligence, and plain common sense on the part of the new owner.' Who happens to be . . ." He paused for what seemed to Laura an eternity. "Me."

He replaced all the sheets in the file folder, then set it on the top of the stack. Only after lining them up to ruler-edge exactness did he stand. "Will you accompany me outside, Ms. Taylor? Bring your things."

She sat stunned, cheeks flaming, feeling every eye in the room, except Foster Speakman's, on her. He was already at the door of the conference room, going through it, expecting her to follow.

With as much dignity as possible, she retrieved her handbag and briefcase, then stood up. "Ladies, gentlemen," she said. Some, embarrassed for her, averted their eyes. Others gave her nods of sympathy. The CFO, with whom this had started, opened his mouth as though to apologize, then thought better of it and gave a regretful shake of his head.

She stepped through the door and pulled it closed behind her, then squared her shoulders and turned toward Foster Speakman, who was standing in the empty corridor. "You're not nearly as ferocious looking as your memos led me to expect, Ms. Taylor."

Her cheeks still burned with humiliation, but she maintained her composure. "I didn't realize my interdepartmental memos were being forwarded to you."

"In view of her impending retirement, I suppose Ms. Cooper felt the issues you raised were no longer her problem but mine."

"I suppose."

"Would knowing I was reading the memos have changed your opinions?"

"Not at all. But perhaps I would have softened the tone and language in which I expressed them."

He folded his arms across his chest and studied her for several moments. "Satisfy my curiosity. Why, with an MBA from SMU's highly regarded business school, did you become a flight attendant? It's an honorable profession, but you were over-qualified."

"Four times I applied to SunSouth for an entry-level management position and was passed over each time."

"Were you told why?"

"No, but the positions went to men."

"Gender discrimination?"

"I'm making no accusations, only telling you what happened."

"So you settled for a flight attendant's position."

"I accepted it, but I didn't settle for it. I thought that once I got my foot in the door—"

"You would distinguish yourself and work your way up to the level for which you had applied in the first place."

"More or less."

He smiled. "Having studied your file, I thought as much. For all I know, you have your sights set on my job, Ms. Taylor. In a way, I hope you do, because I admire ambition. But today I'm offering you Ms. Cooper's position as director of the flight attendant program. Add to that the title of vice-president in charge of . . . et cetera."

For the third time since she'd laid eyes on him, he had stunned her. First, just by knowing who she was. Second, by calling her out of the meeting for what she thought would be immediate dismissal. Now this. "Just like that?"

He laughed. "I never do anything 'just like that.' No, this offer comes after careful analysis of your employment record. I also ran credit and criminal background checks, as I did with every person in that room. You passed, but you have an outstanding parking ticket that hasn't been paid."

"I mailed the check yesterday. Grudgingly. There was no sign posted, but it would have cost more to contest the ticket than simply to pay it."

"A practical decision, Ms. Taylor. I believe your drive, ambition, and talent have been wasted by managers who lacked 'insight, intelligence, and plain common sense,'" he said, his smile widening as he quoted from her memo. "I assume you accept this position?"

Still shaky, but with relief instead of the humiliation of being summarily terminated, she said yes.

With no more ceremony than that, he said, "Good. Now, shall we return to the others?" He reached for the door, then paused. "A word of warning: You'll have a fight on your hands over that budget. Are you up to it?"

"Absolutely."

Murmured conversations ceased when they reentered. Foster startled the others by introducing her by her new title, but most seemed more pleased than not. "Mr. George," Foster said, addressing the human resources director, "following this meeting, I, you, and Ms. Taylor can go over the contract I prepared in advance and with the hope that she would accept my offer. I think you'll both find it satisfactory." He slapped the table lightly. "Now,

Ms. Taylor, it's your first official duty to tell us why the budget allotment for your department is inadequate."

Out of the frying pan. Laura took a deep breath, knowing this was an acid test and hoping she didn't blow it. "While we've been grounded, we've lost a lot of flight attendants. Some have gone to other airlines. Others have left the industry altogether. Now I'm faced with hiring replacements. I can't entice the best applicants if I can't offer them starting salaries and benefits equal to those offered by our competitors. I'd like to offer them better, but I'd settle for equal. Second, the uniforms are ugly and drab."

"I thought attendants paid for their own uniforms."

"They do," Laura said. "But there's no budget for a new design. Which brings me to another point."

"The 'look of the airline'?" All heads turned toward the head of the table. Foster tapped the top file folder on the stack. "To quote from your latest memo, Ms. Taylor. Will you please elaborate?"

Things were moving along too quickly. She hadn't counted on being elevated to an executive this suddenly. Nor had she planned on being placed immediately in the hot seat. But she had been dwelling on this topic for weeks. In her idle time, she had thought long about what she would do if she were running the show. Now the new owner of the airline had invited her to elaborate on the bullet points of her many memos. She was ready.

"Days ago, Hazel, Ms. Cooper, gave me a copy of the proposed budget so I could familiarize myself with it in advance of this meeting. You're spending a lot of money to make drastic changes in the infrastructure and in total reorganization of the airline's operation," she said, addressing Foster directly. "You're making it brand spanking new. But you've stopped short at conveying its newness to consumers."

"Changing the color of the flight attendant uniforms is easy," someone remarked. "Ticket and gate agents, too."

Laura acknowledged the comment with a nod. "Their appearance is important because they deal one-on-one with our customers. So the impression they make is vital. But we're aiming for an about-face in public opinion of SunSouth Airlines. With that as our goal, I don't think changing the color of the uniforms is sufficient." Her gaze moved around the table, ending on Foster. "But as the most recently appointed department director, I don't want to overstep my bounds."

"No, please," he said, indicating she should continue.

Holding his gaze, she said, "When we relaunch SunSouth, if we look the same, consumers will figure we *are* the same."

Another of the directors said, "It's been suggested that we change the name of the airline."

"That suggestion was voted down by the new board of directors," someone else contributed.

Laura said, "I agree we should keep our name. It's a good name. An excellent name."

"But?" Foster said.

"But it suggests light. Sunny days. Bright skies and open landscapes. Our planes are the color of storm clouds, and so are the uniforms." She paused, knowing the proposal she was about to make was destined to raise a chorus of protests. "Even if it means making cuts in other areas, including the flight attendant program, I propose we budget to retain a first-rate design company to revamp the entire look of the airline."

"Hear, hear!" This from the well-liked head of advertising and marketing, a genial young man named Joe McDonald. He always wore an outlandish bow tie and suspenders. Everyone at SunSouth knew him because he made it a point to know everyone. He was an equal-opportunity teaser, from executives to the janitors who came in after hours to clean the offices. "Thank you, Laura, for putting your butt on the line, thereby saving me from having to place mine there."

Everyone laughed. The discussion continued but in a more lighthearted mode.

Laura's proposal, seconded by Joe McDonald, was ultimately acted upon, although not without many lengthy meetings and hours of debate. Cost was the major factor. Designers of the caliber she proposed didn't come cheap. Then, revamping a fleet of airplanes inside and out was exorbitantly expensive. Every coat of paint on an airplane added weight, which required an increase in the fuel needed to fly the aircraft, and therefore an increase in operational costs that was passed on to passengers in the form of ticket prices, which Foster Speakman had gone on record saying were going to be the lowest in the industry.

With that in mind, the design company suggested stripping the planes of paint and applying the newly designed logo to the silver metal. Eventually the shade of red used in the logo became the signature color of the new flight attendant uniforms. They were tailored and professional looking but conveyed a vivacity and friendliness that the media picked up on and extolled. The pilots' uniforms went from navy blue to khaki with red neckties.

The first flight of the renovated airline departed at six twenty-five the morning of March tenth—its scheduled relaunch date. That evening, Foster Speakman and his wife, Elaine, hosted a lavish party in their home. Everyone who was anyone in Dallas had been extended an invitation to the black-tie event.

Laura's escort for the evening was a friend with whom she played mixed-partners tennis. Their friendship was uncomplicated and unromantic. He was divorced, owned his own accounting firm, was at ease with strangers and consequently someone she didn't have to cater to, worry about, or look after.

Indeed, shortly after they arrived at the mansion he excused himself to go look at the billiard room. Once featured in an issue of *Architectural Digest,* it was reputed to be a guys' fantasy room. "Take your time," she told him. "I'll be busy mingling."

Mrs. Speakman, Elaine, was a gorgeous woman, impeccably turned out in an understated designer gown and breathtaking jewelry. But hers was a frail beauty, fragile, like that of a character F. Scott Fitzgerald might have conjured. Like her husband, she was blond and blue eyed, but hers was a water-color version. Standing arm in arm with him, she paled in comparison, literally.

"It's so nice to finally meet you," she said to Laura warmly when Foster introduced them. "I serve on the board of SunSouth—one of the few to survive the shake-up when the new owner assumed control." She gave her husband a nudge in the ribs.

Leaning in, Foster lowered his voice to a whisper. "I understand he can be a real bastard."

"Don't believe it," Elaine said to Laura.

"I don't. My experience has been that he's tough and knows what he wants, but he's a pleasure to work with."

"And a sweetheart at home," his wife said. The two smiled at each other, then Elaine turned back to Laura. "We on the board have heard about your excellent ideas and innovations. On behalf of the board members, the investors, and myself, thank you for your valuable contributions."

"Thank you, but you give me far too much credit, Mrs. Speakman."

"Elaine."

Laura acknowledged that with a slight nod. "Foster has made it known that the new SunSouth is a team effort. Every employee has a voice in the company."

"But some voices offer substantially more than others," Elaine said, smiling.

"Thank you again. However, I still maintain that our success will be attributed to your husband's motivational and management skills."

"Am I blushing?" he asked.

Elaine regarded him adoringly, then to Laura she said, "The gentleman I saw you arrive with, is that your—"

"Good friend," Laura said, cutting her off and hoping to avoid having to explain her single status. Although thousands of women in their thirties remained unmarried, it seemed an explanation was still required.

The truth of it was that no one, not even the occasional lover—and there hadn't been many—had been as important to Laura as the pursuit of her career. But somehow that simple explanation fell short of satisfying people's curiosity. "He's dazzled by your billiard room. I may have to drag him out."

They chitchatted for a while longer, but Laura was aware of others who wanted time with the couple. She shook hands with both and moved away.

Later, as they were leaving, she let her friend deal with the parking valet while she looked for an opportunity to thank her hosts. She spotted them across the room, their heads together, talking privately. Foster leaned down and said something that caused Elaine to laugh. He pressed a kiss on her smooth temple. Laura was struck again by what an attractive and obviously enamored couple they were.

"He's devoted to her."

Laura turned to find a co-worker standing beside her. She, too, had been observing the Speakmans.

"And she to him," Laura said.

"She's lovely."

"Inside as well as out. A real lady."

"Yes," the woman sighed. "That's what makes it so tragic."

Laura turned toward her. "Tragic?"

The co-worker, realizing her mistake, touched Laura's arm. "I'm sorry. I thought you knew. Elaine Speakman is ill. In fact, she's dying."

The sudden laughter coming from downstairs was muted by distance but loud enough to rouse Laura from her reverie. She didn't recognize it as Foster's familiar laugh, so it had to have come from Griff Burkett. What could Foster possibly have said to bring on a laugh?

A few moments later, the telephone on her desk rang. *Finally,* she thought. She picked up the phone before the second ring. "Foster?"

"Can you join us, darling?"

Her heart bumped. His summons meant that, at least so far, it was a go. "I'll be right down."

CHAPTER
4

WHILE WAITING ON SPEAKMAN'S WIFE to join them, Griff had been studying the globe. Suspended within a polished brass stand, it was as large as a beach ball and made of semiprecious gems. It was quite a trinket. He speculated you could buy a damn good car for what it cost.

Funny how having money, or not, changed your perspective. Recalling the rarely used, superfluous items in his Toy Box, he couldn't think too badly of Speakman for having a fancy globe he could well afford.

Griff turned toward the library doors when he heard them open. He expected to get his first look at Mrs. Speakman, but instead the stolid Manuelo came in.

He went straight to Speakman and extended a small silver tray. On it were a prescription bottle of tablets and a glass of water. Speakman took a pill, washing it down with three sips of water. They had a brief conversation in Spanish, then Speakman said to Griff, "While Manuelo is here, can he get you anything?"

Griff shook his head.

Speakman looked up at the Central American and dismissed him with a soft *"Nada más. Gracias."*

Manuelo and Mrs. Speakman met in the open doorway. He stepped aside so she could come into the room, then he left, pulling the double doors closed behind him. But Griff was no longer interested in Manuelo. He was focused on Mrs. Speakman. Laura, her name was.

She didn't give off crazy vibes. In fact, she seemed perfectly composed and in control of her faculties. She didn't look toward Griff, although he created a sizable silhouette even in a large room like this one. Instead, she crossed to where her husband sat in his wheelchair. She placed her hand on his shoulder, leaned down, and kissed his cheek.

When they pulled apart, Speakman said, "Laura, this is Griff Burkett."

Since she had ignored him up till now, he was surprised when she walked toward him, right hand extended. "Mr. Burkett. How do you do?" He met her halfway, and they shook hands. Like her husband's, her handshake was dry and firm. A businesswoman's handshake.

Griff limited his greeting to a simple "Hi."

She dropped his hand but maintained eye contact. "Thank you for coming. Didn't you get released just this morning?"

"We've been over that," Speakman said, humor in his voice.

"Oh, sorry. I would ask you about the long drive, but I rather imagine that topic has been exhausted, too."

"It has," Griff said.

"Small talk sounds even smaller in this particular situation, doesn't it?"

He wasn't going to touch that with a ten-foot pole.

She said, "I'm sure you were offered something to drink."

"I was. I'm fine."

"If you change your mind, let me know."

They might have been missing critical marbles, but their manners remained intact.

"Please sit down, Mr. Burkett." She took the chair nearest her husband's wheelchair.

Griff hadn't had time to speculate on what Foster Speakman's missus would be like, but if he had to define his initial reaction, it would be surprise. There was nothing in her handshake or straightforward gaze that could be interpreted as nervous, flirtatious, or coy. Nor did she seem embarrassed by the topic they now had in common. He could have been there to talk about cleaning their carpets.

She didn't act submissive or browbeaten, either, like this was something her husband had cooked up for his own gratification and she had agreed to go along with it under duress.

Hell, he didn't know what he had expected, but whatever it was, Laura Speakman wasn't it.

She was wearing a pair of black slacks and a white shirt, sleeveless, with pleats—he thought that was what they were called—stitched in rows down the front. Like a tuxedo shirt. Low-heeled black shoes. A serviceable wristwatch, a plain wedding band. Some of the players on the football team had worn diamonds in their ears much bigger and flashier than the ones in hers.

Her hair was dark and cut short. Sort of . . . swirly. He figured it would curl if it were worn longer. She was on the tallish side of average, slender, and, judging by her bare biceps, fit. Tennis maybe. A couple of times a week, she probably did yoga or Pilates, one of those women's workouts for toning and flexibility.

He tried to keep from staring, tried to avoid looking at the features of her face too closely, although his overall impression was that if he had spotted her in a crowd, he probably would have done a double take. She wasn't a babe, not like the kind of silicone-fortified Dallas dolly who used to hang out in the nightclubs frequented by him and his teammates, single or not. But Laura Speakman wasn't homely. Not by any stretch.

And another thing, she looked healthy enough to have a baby. Young enough, too, if she didn't waste time. Mid-thirties, maybe. Around his age.

He felt awkward, standing there in the center of the room, the two of them looking at him as though waiting for him to entertain them.

"Mr. Burkett? Griff?" Speakman nodded toward the chair facing them.

He'd told himself that the first chance he got, he was going to say "Thanks, but no thanks" and bolt. But he felt compelled to stay. Hell if he knew why.

Well, there was the six hundred grand. The figure had a nice ring to it that was pretty damn compelling.

He walked over to the chair and sat down. Looking directly at Laura Speakman, he said, "Your husband told me you're all for this. Is that true?"

"Yes."

No hesitation. Not even a blink. "Okay. But, excuse me for saying, it's . . ."

"Unorthodox?"

"I was going to say it's freaking nuts. A guy asking another guy, *paying* another guy, to sleep with his wife."

"Not sleep with, Mr. Burkett. Not in the context that implies. Impregnate. As for the freakiness of it, it's not unprecedented. In fact, it's scriptural. Genesis. Remember?"

In the household where Griff had grown up, there'd been no Bible. When he went to school and learned the Pledge of Allegiance, he was shocked to hear that it had the cussword *God* in it. He soon realized that *God* wasn't always used in combination with *damn*.

In any case, it came as shocking news to him that anything like this was in the Bible.

"We want a baby very badly, Mr. Burkett," she said.

"There are other ways to get pregnant."

"There are, yes. Our reasons for doing it this way are personal and shouldn't concern you."

"They do."

"They shouldn't," she repeated.

"We, uh, do our thing, I go home and sleep with a clear conscience. Is that it?"

"That's what it amounts to, yes."

He looked at her, wondering how she could speak so calmly about the two of them getting it on, when her husband was sitting right there holding her hand. Griff looked from her to Speakman, and the man seemed to read his mind.

"Before you joined us, Laura, Griff suggested that . . . well, that I would be observing the two of you while you perform."

She'd been looking at her husband as he explained. Several seconds passed before she turned her gaze back to Griff, and he took exception to her affronted frown. "Hey, don't look at me like *I'm* the pervert here."

"You think this is perverted?"

"What do you call it?"

"Would you think it was perverted if we were asking you to donate a kidney? Or give blood?"

He laughed. "There's a big difference. To donate a kidney you don't have to . . . touch," he said, quickly substituting the word he'd been about to say. "You never even have to meet."

"Unfortunately, the reproductive physiology is such that *touching* is necessary."

The hell it was. He didn't have to plant the seed personally to yield the crop. But he'd already argued that point with her husband. Speakman was determined for her to conceive naturally. She didn't seem to have an ethical or moral problem with it, so why was he making an issue of it? Mentally shrugging, he reached a decision: They wanted him to fuck her, he could fuck her. It wasn't like she had three eyes or something.

He addressed Speakman. "A handshake and I get a hundred grand?"

Speakman rolled his chair over to a desk and opened the lap drawer. He took a manila envelope from it, and when he came back and extended it, Griff was reminded of having to accept a cash loan from his lawyer like a kid getting an allowance. The sooner he was no longer obligated to anyone, the better.

He took the envelope.

Speakman said, "Inside is a key to a safe-deposit box and a signature card. You sign it. I'll see that the card gets returned to the bank tomorrow, where it will remain on file. While I'm there, I'll deposit your cash in the box. You can pick it up, um, say anytime after two o'clock tomorrow afternoon. Laura and I have a meeting in the morning with representatives of the flight attendants' union to discuss their new contract."

Hiring a stud was just another entry on their busy agenda.

Fine with him, so long as the money made it into that box.

Griff removed the signature card and glanced at it. "What about the physical? What if I flunk?"

The couple glanced at each other, but Foster spoke for both of them. "We'll take it on faith that you won't."

"That's a lot of faith."

"If we anticipated a problem, you wouldn't be here."

"Okay, I get my advance, and you get my clean bill of health. And then?"

"And then you wait to be notified of where you need to be and when. Laura's next ovulation."

Griff looked at her. She was gazing back at him calmly, apparently not caring that her ovulation was being discussed. He would have liked some clarification on exactly what ovulation entailed, but he wasn't going to ask. He didn't need to know. He knew how to fuck, and that was all they were requiring of him.

"You'll meet once a month for as long as it takes to conceive," Speakman explained. He lifted his wife's hand to his mouth and kissed the palm. "Hopefully it won't take too many cycles."

"Yeah, I hope that, too," Griff said. "I'll be half a million dollars richer."

Feeling restless again, he got up and moved to one of the bookcases. He read a few of the titles, those that were in English, but they didn't register with him. They sounded like philosophy and boring stuff. Not an Elmore Leonard or Carl Hiaasen among them.

"Something troubling you, Griff?"

He turned back to the couple. "Why me?"

"I explained that," Speakman replied.

"There are a lot of blond, blue-eyed guys around."

"But none with your particular genetic makeup. You have everything we could wish for our child. Strength, amazing stamina, speed, agility, even perfect eyesight and uncanny coordination. I could go on. There were articles written about you, published not just in sports magazines but in medical journals, about what an incredible specimen of the human male body you are."

Griff remembered the articles, written by trainers and sports medicine experts, one of whom had dubbed him "a biologic masterpiece." He'd caught hell over that in the locker room, his teammates taunting him about his so-called perfection and wanting to test it with the crudest physical contests they could devise. It was another matter when he took chicks to bed. They really got off on screwing a "masterpiece."

But he also remembered the scathing editorials that had followed his fall from grace. In them he had been lambasted not only for his crime but for squandering his God-given attributes.

God-given, my ass, he thought.

Those who had marveled over him wouldn't have thought he was so bloody perfect if they'd known the two who'd spawned him. If Mr. and Mrs. Speakman could have seen what he'd come from, they would have had second thoughts, too. Did they really want the blood of his parents flowing through the veins of their kid?

"You don't know anything about my origins. Maybe I just lucked out, got a few good genes that stacked up right by sheer accident. My gene pool could be mucked up with any number of bad seeds."

"We would take that chance no matter who the sperm donor was, even myself," Speakman said. "Why are you trying to talk us out of this, Griff?"

"I'm not." Actually, to some extent, he was. He'd spent five years in prison thinking about the bad choices he'd made. If he'd learned nothing else, he'd learned not to jump in headfirst until he knew exactly how deep the water was.

He said, "I just don't want to get into the middle of this and then have something go wrong that I'll be blamed for."

"What could go wrong?" Laura asked.

He laughed bitterly. "You haven't been around

much, have you? Believe me, things can go wrong. For instance, what if I fire blanks?"

"You mean, what if you have a low sperm count?" Speakman asked.

Griff gave a brusque nod.

"Do you have reason to suspect that's the case?"

"No. But I don't know. I'm just asking, What if?"

"When you go for your medical exam, have it tested." Speakman paused, then said, "I believe you're experiencing a carryover of prison paranoia."

"You're goddamn right I am."

A heavy silence followed. Speakman rubbed his jaw as though sorting through words to find the right ones. "Now that the subject has been broached, let's talk about your incarceration."

"What about it?"

"I'll admit that it factored into our choosing you."

Griff covered his heart with his hand, pretending to have had his feelings hurt. "You mean there was more to it than my being the ideal physical specimen?"

Speakman ignored his sarcasm. "You cheated your team, the league, and most of all your fans. Making you a persona non grata, Griff. I'm afraid you'll be subject to insults."

"I haven't had any confrontations."

"There hasn't been time for any," Laura said.

Her reasonable tone irritated him. "I'm not expecting to win any popularity contests, okay? I cheated and broke the law. I was punished for my crime. All that's behind me."

"But there's also the matter of the bookmaker who died."

Griff had wondered when that would come up. If they had any smarts at all, and he believed both did, they would inevitably have asked about Bandy. He was surprised only that it was the wife who had cracked open the delicate topic.

"Bill Bandy didn't *die*, Mrs. Speakman. He was murdered."

"You were a suspect."

"I was questioned."

"You were arrested."

"But never charged."

"Neither was anyone else."

"So?"

"So the murder remains unsolved."

"Not my problem."

"I hope not."

"What the hell—"

"Did you do it?"

"No!"

Their exchange was heated and rapid, followed by a tense silence that Griff refused to break. He'd said what he had to say. He didn't kill Bill Bandy. Period. The end.

"However," Speakman said in the soft and conciliatory tone of an undertaker, "the shadow of suspicion *was* cast on you, Griff. You were eventually released for lack of evidence, but that doesn't vindicate you."

"Look, if you think I killed Bandy, then what the hell am I doing here?" He flung his arms wide to encompass the room, the house. "Why would you want me to father your kid?"

"We don't think you committed murder," Speakman said. "Absolutely not."

Griff shifted his angry gaze over to Laura to see if she shared her husband's belief in his innocence. Her expression remained impassive, not accusatory, but sure as hell not exonerating.

Then why was she hiring him to go to bed with her? Did he really need this kind of abuse?

Yeah, unfortunately he did. He needed the money. He had to get back on his feet, and six hundred grand was a better than fair shot at doing so. To hell with them, with her, if she thought he'd clobbered Bandy. They must not have felt too ambiguous about it, either way, or he wouldn't be here. On top of being crazy, they were hypocrites.

"The matter of Bandy's homicide as well as the federal crimes for which you were convicted remain black marks against your name, Griff," Speakman said.

"I'm aware of that."

"So how realistic is it that someone around here will hire you? How realistic is it that someone will hire you for any amount, much less for what Laura and I are offering?"

The answer was obvious. When Griff declined to waste his breath on it, Speakman continued. "Your prospects are bleak. You can't play football. You can't coach football. You can't write about or talk about football, because none of the media outlets will hire you to do so. You admitted having to liquidate all your assets to pay your debts, indicating to me that you didn't save for a rainy day."

Speakman seemed to enjoy highlighting his shortcomings. Maybe, Griff thought, he should challenge him to a footrace. See who was better at that. "I made three million a year from the Cowboys, plus endorsements," he said tightly. "Everybody got a chunk of it, starting with my agent and the IRS, but what I got to keep, I spent, and had a whale of a great time doing it. What's your point?"

"My point is that you seem to have no head for business or you would have appropriated your income differently. It also appears you had no talent for larceny, or you wouldn't have got caught."

"A trap was laid for me. I walked into it."

"Nevertheless." After a beat, Speakman said, "I'm not trying to insult you, Griff."

"Really?"

Again Speakman ignored his caustic tone. "You asked why you were chosen."

"I'd almost forgotten the question."

"It required a long explanation. And I wanted to be brutally honest about our reasons for extending you this offer. Primarily, you have the genetic makeup to create the child we desire. Second, for reasons just discussed, you're in urgent need of the money we're offering to pay. Last, you're totally independent.

"You have no family, no real friends, no attachments, no one to whom you must account, and that is a tremendous benefit to us. We've emphasized the confidentiality this arrangement demands. We're the only three people who will ever know that I didn't sire the child Laura will conceive."

Griff was somewhat placated. Besides, he couldn't afford to get huffy. Especially over the bald truth. He moved to the desk, picked up a crystal paperweight, weighed it in his palm. "You're putting a lot of trust in me to keep my mouth shut."

Speakman chuckled. "Actually, we're not. We're putting a lot of trust in greed."

"Six hundred thousand?" Griff set down the paperweight and grinned at Speakman. "Not all that much when you think about it. Not what I'd call greedy."

Laura looked at her husband. "You haven't told him the rest?"

"We hadn't got that far," Speakman replied.

Griff said, "The rest?"

Speakman rolled his chair over to the desk and picked up the paperweight. Taking a handkerchief from his pants pocket, he used it to polish the crystal as he smiled up at Griff. "It's not that we question your integrity."

"Bullshit. You'd be fools not to question it."

"Right," Speakman said, laughing softly. "We would." With the handkerchief still wrapped around the paperweight, he replaced it on the desk, moved it an eighth of an inch to the left, then slowly withdrew the handkerchief, which he refolded into a perfect square before returning it to his pocket.

"So, for my and Laura's peace of mind, and to ensure your silence, you'll be paid one million dollars upon the birth of our child. Additionally, you'll receive one million dollars each year on his birthday. And all you have to do in return is forget you ever knew us."

CHAPTER
5

GRIFF TOSSED THE HONDA'S KEYS TO THE valet parking attendant and walked briskly into the sleek lobby of the upscale building. A swank hotel occupied the lower twelve floors, condos the top twelve.

The lobby bar was relatively quiet on this midweek evening. A pianist was playing Sinatra-type standards on a white baby grand. Most of the tables were occupied by businessmen, nursing cocktails while they played one-upmanship.

The bar accessed a lighted patio where seating was available, but Griff chose to stay indoors, where he could enjoy the air-conditioning while keeping an eye on the entrance. He claimed a free table, signaled the waitress, and ordered a bourbon.

"House or label?"

"House is fine."

"Water?"

"Rocks."

"Want to start a tab?"

"Please."

"Will anyone be joining you?"

"No."

"I'll be right back."

Although the occasion—getting out of prison—and the day he'd had—his bizarre meeting with the Speakmans—seemed to call for a highball or two, Griff didn't really like to drink. Since he'd had to mop up regurgitated booze so often as a kid, he'd never really developed a taste for it.

But the drink the waitress delivered to him looked and smelled good. The first sip went down smoothly, although he could tell by the instant fire it ignited in his belly that it had been over five years since he'd had spirits of any kind. He cautioned himself to go slowly. He wasn't sure how long he'd have to wait.

A million dollars.

"You'll be paid in cash," Speakman had told him. "It will be placed in the safe-deposit box, and only you, I, and Laura will be signatories. There will be no records kept, no paperwork of any kind. Once Laura conceives, absolutely no connection can ever be made between you and us. If our paths happen to cross, which will be unlikely, you won't recognize us. We'll be meeting for the first time. Understood?"

"Understood."

Conversation was suspended when Manuelo came in to deliver a phone message to Mrs. Speakman. She read it, then excused herself, saying she would be back shortly. She left, Manuelo trailing her.

Speakman noticed Griff watching the manservant as he silently closed the double doors behind himself. "Don't worry about Manuelo," he said. "He speaks only a few words of English. I told him that you were an old school chum who was passing through. He wouldn't have recognized you from your football days. By the time he reached the U.S., you were in Big Spring."

Laura Speakman returned almost immediately. Her husband asked, "Anything important?"

"Joe McDonald with a quick question that he didn't think could wait till morning."

Foster laughed. "That's Joe. Always in a hurry."

While they were chatting about the impatient Joe, Griff thought of another problem. "Cash will be hard to spend," he said abruptly.

After a slight hesitation, Foster said, "Yes, I'm afraid that will present some difficulties. I imagine that you'll be under close scrutiny by the IRS and the FBI, since there was some speculation about your empty bank accounts at the time of your arrest."

"It was assumed you had money tucked away somewhere."

Beneath Laura Speakman's cool statement, he heard an implied question mark. "Just like it was assumed I knocked off Bandy," he said tightly. "I didn't, and I didn't."

She held his stare for several moments, then said, "All right."

But she said it like she was only half convinced,

and that pissed him off. Even though he was going to bed her, he didn't think he would ever like her. She was good to look at, but he'd never been attracted to the ball-breaker type. And why was she busting his when they were vital to what she needed him for? He considered bringing this irony to her attention, then decided not to. He doubted she would see the humor in it.

He said, "I need the money, Mrs. Speakman. The money is the only reason I would even consider doing this. At least I've been honest about it."

His implication was clear—that they were being less than honest about their reasons. She was about to take issue when her husband intervened. "You haven't asked me for financial advice, Griff, but I'll offer some. Get a job that earns you a paycheck. Have a checking account, credit cards. Normal things. If you do get audited, how you'll explain your millionaire's lifestyle will be up to you. Probably for the rest of your life, they'll be looking for a source of your income."

He raised an eyebrow, adding, "Perhaps some of your former business associates can assist you with the matter. I'm sure that on occasion they use banking facilities abroad that don't question the source of great sums of cash."

"I wouldn't know," Griff said. "But even if they do, I won't be associating with them anymore." He looked over at Laura and added, "Ever." He emphasized it with a curt bob of his head.

Speakman asked Griff if he had any more questions. They cleared up some minor points. And then Griff raised one that turned out to be major. It concerned a potential problem with the long-term payout. Ten, fifteen, twenty years down the road, he didn't want to encounter a dilemma for which a solution hadn't been worked out ahead of time.

A heated discussion ensued. No solution was reached, but Speakman promised to think hard on it and get back to Griff with a resolution as soon as possible. Could Griff live with that? he asked. Grudgingly, Griff said he could. That settled, Speakman suggested they seal their deal with a handshake, which they did.

Speakman then invited him to stay for dinner.

Before Griff could accept or decline, Mrs. Speakman said, "Oh, darling, I'm sorry, but I didn't notify Mrs. Dobbins that we'd have a guest and she's already left for the day. I thought the idea was to keep Mr. Burkett's visit here a secret. Manuelo is one thing, but . . ."

Looking flustered for the first time since she joined them, she searched for excuses not to sit at the table with him. Apparently she had no qualms over having carnal knowledge of him, so long as she didn't have to eat with him. "Besides," she added lamely, "I've got a massive amount of work waiting for me upstairs."

"Doesn't matter," Griff said. "I've got plans. In fact, I'm already late."

"Then don't let us keep you any longer," Speakman said.

Laura Speakman stood up. She seemed relieved that he was leaving, and possibly just a bit ashamed over her inhospitality. "You should be hearing from me in about two weeks, Mr. Burkett. How can I reach you?"

He gave her his phone number, the one Turner

had connected in the shabby apartment. She wrote it down on a slip of paper. "I'll call and tell you where to meet me."

"In two weeks?"

"Thereabouts. It could vary a day or two either way. I'll be using an ovulation predictor kit to test for an LH surge."

"LH . . . ?"

"Luteinizing hormone."

"Ah." As in "I see," when actually he didn't have a clue.

"Hopefully I'll be able to predict the day, but it might be short notice."

"Fine. Whatever."

Her eyes skittered away from his, and that was when Griff figured her out. She could play hardball with the big boys up to a point. She could have her menstrual cycle, and ovulation, and his sperm count talked about freely in technical and practical terms. But when it came down to the nitty-gritty, to actually climbing into bed with a stranger, she turned pure female. Which to him was reassuring.

She said good-bye and excused herself. Speakman offered to escort him to the front door. When they reached it, he said, "I'm curious, Griff."

"About?"

"What you'll be thinking about as you leave here. Will you be considering what to buy first?"

Actually, what he'd thought as he'd driven away from the gray stone mansion was that, even though they looked like reasonable and intelligent people, it was probably a good thing that Foster and Laura Speakman couldn't reproduce, because both of them were fucking nuts.

Who would do this? Nobody, that's who. Not when there were scientific methods of fertilization available. Not when you had the money to pay for those methods. Maybe in Bible days this was the way to go when you couldn't have a kid. But not today, when there were options.

By the time he'd reached his destination, he'd almost convinced himself that he would never hear from the couple again.

Almost.

"Another?"

He glanced up. The cocktail waitress had returned. He was surprised to find the glass of bourbon empty. "No thanks. A Perrier, please."

"Sure. I'll be right back."

I'll be right back. She had used that expression twice, not knowing that the seemingly harmless phrase was like salt on an open wound to him.

His mother had said those words to him the night she left. For good that time.

She'd often stayed away for days at a stretch, leaving without so much as a "so long," returning without explanation or excuse for her absence. He never got too upset or worried when she wasn't around. He knew that when she got tired of the current boyfriend or vice versa, and the guy either kicked her out or simply moved on, she would come home.

When she did, she never asked how he'd been, or what he'd been doing while she was away. Was he okay? Had he gone to school? Had he eaten? Had he been frightened by the storm? Had he been sick?

One time, he had been. Sick. He got food poisoning from eating an opened can of beef stew that had been left out too long. He puked till he passed out, then came to on the bathroom floor, lying faceup in diarrhea and vomit, a knot as big as his fist on the back of his head from the fall.

He was eight years old.

After that, he took more notice of what he ate when his mother was gone. He learned to fend pretty well for himself until she reappeared.

On the night she left for good, he knew she wasn't coming back. All day, she'd been sneaking things from the house when she thought he wasn't looking. Clothes. Shoes. A satin pillow a guy had won for her at the state fair. She slept on it every night because she said it preserved her hairdo. When he saw her stuff that pillow into a paper grocery sack and take it out to her present boyfriend's car, he knew this absence would be permanent.

The last time Griff saw his father, he'd been in handcuffs, being shoved into the back of a police car. A neighbor had called the cops, reporting the domestic dispute.

Dispute. A polite name for his father beating the shit out of his mother after coming home and finding her in bed with a guy she'd met the night before.

His mother went to the hospital. His daddy went to jail. He was placed with a foster family until his mother had recovered from her injuries. When the case came to trial, the DA explained to the six-year-old Griff that maybe he would be called on to tell the judge what had happened that night because he'd witnessed the assault. He lived in dread of that. If his old man got off, he would make Griff pay for tattling on him. The retribution would include a beating with his belt. It wouldn't be the first, but it promised to be the worst.

And he honestly couldn't say he blamed his dad. Griff knew words like *whore, slut,* and *cunt* meant ugly things about his mom, and he figured she deserved to be called those bad names.

As it turned out, there was no trial. His father entered a guilty plea to a lesser charge and was sentenced. Griff never knew when he got out of jail. Whenever it was, he didn't contact them. Griff never saw him again.

From then on, it was just his mother and him.

And the men she brought home. Some moved in for extended periods of time, a week, maybe two. Others were guests who hit the door as soon as they got their pants back on.

Griff remembered, not long after his dad had been put in jail, crying because his mom had locked the door to his bedroom and he couldn't get out, couldn't get away from the spider that had crawled onto his bed. The guy she was with that night had finally come into his room, killed the spider, patted him on his towhead, and told him it was all right, he could go back to sleep now.

When he was old enough to be sent outside to play, some of his mother's men friends had looked at him with apology, even guilt. Especially if the weather was bad. Others didn't like having him around at all. That was when his mother told him to get lost and stay lost for a few hours. Sometimes he was given money so he could go to a movie. Most often when banished from the house, he would wander the neighborhood alone, looking for something to occupy him, later looking for mischief.

Some of his mother's friends had given him no more notice than they would a seam in the faded wallpaper. Not many, but a few, were actually nice to him. Like the guy who'd killed the spider. But, unfortunately, he'd never come back. One guy, Neal something, had stayed a month or so. Griff got along with him okay. He could do a couple of magic tricks with cards and showed Griff how they were done. He came into the house one day with a shopping bag and handed it to Griff saying, "Here, kid. This is for you."

Inside the bag was a football.

Years later, Griff wondered if Neal had recognized him when he got to be a pro player. Did he remember giving him his first football? Probably not. He probably didn't remember Griff or his mother at all.

Men came and went. Years passed. His mother would leave. But she would always return.

And then that day came when she was covertly packing the car that belonged to a guy who'd shown up with her a few weeks before and had stayed. His name was Ray, and he'd taken an instant dislike to Griff, who would snort skeptically whenever Ray launched into a story about his phenomenal record as a rodeo cowboy before a bronco stepped on his back and ruined him for the arena. Apparently the bronco ruined him for everything else, too, because as far as Griff could tell, Ray had no visible means of support.

Ray didn't like Griff, and he made no bones about it. But Griff wasn't very likable, either. By the time Ray appeared on the scene, Griff was fifteen, full of himself, full of anger and rebellion. He'd been busted for shoplifting and for vandalizing a car, but mercifully got probation both times. He'd been suspended from school twice for fighting. He carried a chip on his shoulder that begged to be knocked off. Over the years, his hair had darkened, and so had his outlook on life.

So that evening when his mother followed Ray to the front door and turned back to tell him goodbye, Griff feigned indifference and kept his eyes trained on the TV. It was secondhand, and the picture was snowy, but it was better than nothing.

"See you later, baby."

He hated it when she called him baby. If she'd ever babied him, it was so far back he couldn't recall it.

"Griff, did you hear me?"

"I'm not deaf."

She heaved a dramatic sigh. "Why are you being so pissy tonight? I'll be right back."

He turned his head, and they looked at each other, and she knew that he knew.

"You coming, or what?" Ray bellowed from the front yard.

The look Griff exchanged with his mother lasted a few seconds longer. Maybe she appeared a little sorry for what she was about to do. He wanted to think she was. But probably she wasn't. Then she turned quickly and left. The door slammed shut behind her.

Griff didn't leave the house for three days. On the fourth day, he heard a car pull into the driveway. He hated himself for feeling a surge of hope that he'd been wrong and she'd come back after all. Maybe she'd seen through Ray and his bullshit. Maybe Ray had seen her for the whore she was and was bringing her back.

But the footsteps on the porch were too heavy to be hers.

"Griff?"

Shit! Coach.

Griff hoped he couldn't be seen where he was slouched on the ratty sofa watching TV. But no such luck. The door squeaked when it was pushed open, and he cursed himself for not having locked it. In his peripheral vision, Coach appeared at the end of the sofa. Hands on hips, he stood looking down at Griff with disapproval.

"I missed you at practice. School office tells me you've been absent from classes the last three days. Where've you been?"

"Here," Griff said, continuing to stare at the TV.

"You sick?"

"No."

A pause. "Where's your mom?"

"Fuck I know?" he grumbled.

"I'm gonna ask you again. Where's your mom?"

Griff looked up at him then and with exaggerated innocence said, "I think she's at the PTA meeting. Either that or the church ladies' sewing group."

Coach walked over to the TV. He didn't turn it off; he yanked the plug from the wall outlet. "Get your stuff."

"Huh?"

"Get your stuff."

Griff didn't move. Coach walked toward him, his footfalls rattling the empty cereal bowls and soda cans littering the TV tray Griff had placed in front of the sofa. "Gather up your stuff. Right now."

"What for? Where am I going?"

"To my house."

"Like hell."

"Or cop an attitude with me, and I'll call CPS." Coach placed his meaty fists on his hips again and glared down at him. "You've got one second to choose."

Laughter from a nearby table jerked Griff back into the present. At some point during his reverie, the waitress had brought his Perrier. He drank it like a man dying of thirst. He was covering a soft belch when the woman he'd been waiting for came through the revolving entrance door. He stood up and waved at the waitress to bring his check, and by doing so attracted the woman's attention.

Upon seeing him, she stopped suddenly, obviously surprised.

He signaled for her to wait while he took care of his tab. He did that with dispatch, then walked toward the woman where she still stood halfway between the entrance and the elevators.

"Hey, Marcia."

"Griff. I heard you were getting out."

"Bad news travels fast."

"No, it's wonderful to see you." She smiled and looked him over. "You look good."

He drank in the sight of her, from the top of her tousled auburn hair to her high-heeled sandals. The curvy terrain in between made him light-headed with lust. Laughing softly, he said, "Not as good as you."

"Thank you."

He held her gaze for several moments, then asked, "Are you available?"

Her smile faltered. She glanced around the lobby, her unease showing.

He took a step closer and said in a low voice, "It's been a long five years, Marcia."

She considered a moment longer, then, reaching a decision, said, "I have someone at midnight."

"It won't take me near that long."

He took her elbow, and they walked to the elevators, saying nothing until they were inside one of the mirrored cubicles. She inserted a small key into a discreet slot in the mechanical panel. Responding to his quizzical look, she said, "I've moved up a couple of floors, into the penthouse."

"Business must be good."

"I have three girls working for me now."

He whistled. "Business is *really* good."

"The market for my product never goes soft." Laughing, she added, "So to speak."

Griff was even more impressed by her success when they stepped out of the elevator into a lobby with a marble floor and a clear skylight for a ceiling that provided a view of a quarter moon and a sprinkling of stars bright enough to defy the skyline lights.

Three doors opened into the private lobby. "Are you friendly with your neighbors?"

"One is a Japanese businessman. He's rarely here, but when he is, he finds the proximity very convenient."

Griff chuckled. "He comes over to borrow sugar?"

"At least once while he's in town," she said demurely. "The other is a friend, a gay decorator who envies me my clientele."

She unlocked her front door. Griff followed her inside. The interior looked like a picture in a magazine, probably would be her gay neighbor's wet dream. Griff gave it a cursory glance, said a polite "Very nice," then reached for her and pulled her against him.

He hadn't kissed a woman in five years, and the sex was going to have to be damn good to top the pleasure he derived from pushing his tongue into her mouth. He kissed her like a horny kid whose prom date was easy. Too eager, too greedy, too sloppy. His hands were everywhere at once.

After a minute of his mauling her, she pushed him away, laughing. "You know the rules, Griff. No kissing. And I'm the initiator."

His sports jacket was fighting to stay on while he was frantically trying to shake it off. "Give me a break."

"This once. But some rules must apply."

"Right. I pay up front."

"Hmm."

The sleeves of his jacket were turned inside out when he finally was able to fling the thing to the floor. He dug into his pants pocket for the money clip of cash Wyatt Turner had given him. The tight-ass would have conniptions if he knew his client was spending his food and gas money on a prostitute. Speaking for himself, Griff didn't begrudge a penny of Marcia's fee. If he had to, he'd skip a few meals.

"How much?"

"Two thousand. For an hour. Straight sex."

He gaped at her and swallowed the golf ball now lodged in his throat. "Two *thousand*? You've gone up. A lot."

"So has the cost of living," she replied coolly. "And business expenses."

He expelled a gusty breath of disappointment, then bent down and retrieved his jacket from the floor. "I don't have it. Maybe tomorrow night," he said wryly.

"How much have you got?"

He held out the money clip. She took it and pulled out two hundred-dollar bills, then gave the clip back to him. "Don't tell anybody."

Griff thought he might weep out of gratitude. "I'll be eternally in your debt."

Marcia was the most select prostitute in Dallas, and it was strict business practices that had put her there. She was a businesswoman all the way. Through the grapevine, Griff had heard that she, acting on tips from clients, had invested wisely in real estate. She'd bought up farmland north of Dallas, and when the city expanded in that direction, she had scored huge. It was also said she had a stock portfolio worth millions.

All that could have been rumor, but he wouldn't have been surprised if it was true. It was said she'd started "escorting" to help finance dental hygiene school but had soon realized that she was better at polishing knobs than she was at polishing teeth. And she could make a hell of a lot more money at it.

Soon after he'd signed with the Cowboys, Griff had learned of her through a teammate, being told that Marcia was the best if you could afford her, because even then she'd been expensive. He preferred a professional to the team groupies who threw themselves at him and, once he'd slept with them, inevitably caused hassles he didn't need.

Marcia was discreet. She was clean. She was scrupulous when it came to prequalifying her clients, making sure they were disease free, financially stable, and safe. She never took walk-ins. She'd made an exception for him tonight.

She had the wholesome face of a church choir soloist, paired with a voluptuous body that invited sin. Somehow, despite her occupation, she managed to remain a lady, and if a client didn't treat her as such, he didn't remain a client.

Five years hadn't left any noticeable damage, Griff was pleased to discover as she undressed. She was lush, but firm where she ought to be. He couldn't get his clothes off fast enough. Knowing him, remembering his preferences, she didn't assist him but idly touched herself while she watched him peel off garments and toss them aside. When her fingers disappeared between her thighs, he made an involuntary gurgling sound but was too far gone to care how gauche he seemed.

When he was undressed, she went to him and gently pushed him back until he was seated on the edge of the bed. He pressed his face into her deep cleavage, mashed her heavy breasts against his cheeks. She handed him a condom; he rolled it on. "What do you want to do, Griff?"

"At this point . . . Doesn't matter."

She lowered herself to her knees between his thighs and bent her head toward him, whispering, "Enjoy."

"Griff?"

"Hmm?"

"It's after eleven. You need to go."

He'd been sleeping on his stomach, his head buried in the soft, scented pillow, virtually comatose. He turned onto his back. Marcia had showered and was wrapped in a robe. "You went out like a light," she said. "I didn't have the heart to wake you sooner, but you have to go now."

He stretched luxuriantly. "Felt good, sleeping naked, sleeping on sheets that don't smell like industrial-strength detergent." He arched his back and stretched again. "Do I gotta?"

"You gotta."

She said it with a smile, but he knew she meant it. He couldn't argue after she'd already been so charitable. He sat up and swung his feet to the floor. She had his clothes waiting for him, actually hurried him along without seeming to as he pulled them on. She held his jacket for him, then placed her hand on the center of his back and propelled him toward the door.

When they reached it, he turned to her. "Thank you. You made a huge concession, and I appreciate it more than you know."

"Coming-home present." She kissed her finger, then pressed it against his lips. "But next time, it has to be by appointment and full fare."

"My financial situation should improve substantially by tomorrow." But remembering how uneasy she'd been to be seen with him in the lobby, he added, "If you still want me for a client, that is. I could be bad for your business."

"Every business requires a little finessing now and then." She was making light of it, but he knew the thought had crossed her mind. "You might want to try one of the new girls. They're young and gorgeous, and I trained them personally."

"Satisfaction guaranteed?"

"Always. Want me to set something up for you?"

A mental image of Laura Speakman flashed through his mind. "I'm not sure what I'll be doing, where I'll be. Let me call you. But I tried the old number. Got a recording that it had been disconnected."

She passed him a business card. "I have to change it periodically. To keep the vice cops honest," she added, smiling.

He kissed her on the cheek, thanked her again, and they exchanged a good-bye. She closed the door, quietly but firmly. Getting into the elevator, Griff met the gay decorator getting out. The man looked him up and down, then closed his eyes and gave a soft, swooning moan. "Too, too cute," he murmured as he glided past.

The lobby bar was doing less business now than earlier. The girl who had waited on him was chatting with one of the idle bellmen. The pianist had been replaced with canned music.

The doorman was greeting an arriving guest when Griff pushed through the revolving doors. Outside, the air had softened, but it was still hot enough to steal his breath until he acclimated. He stood there, sweating, for a full sixty seconds, waiting for the parking attendant to show. When he didn't, Griff went looking for him. He walked the length of the porte cochere and rounded the corner into the parking garage.

Where he ran into a fist.

It connected with his cheekbone like a jackhammer. One jab. Two. Then another.

He staggered back, swearing loudly, swinging wildly in uncoordinated self-defense, trying to bring his assailant into focus.

Rodarte.

CHAPTER
6

RODARTE'S GRIN TURNED HIS FACE INTO A halloween mask. "Oh, I'm sorry. Did that hurt?"

Griff's indrawn breath whistled through his teeth, which were clenched in pain. He dabbed at his cheekbone, and his fingers came away red. *"Son of a bitch!"*

Rodarte lit a cigarette, laughing as he fanned out the match. "That's what I heard, too."

Griff glowered at him.

"I heard your mother would screw a dog if nothing else was around. Poor little Griff. You had it rough, didn't you? Till Coach Miller and his wife took you in."

When Griff had been indicted, overnight going from poster boy to pariah, a lot of his ugly past had been exposed. Neither Coach nor Ellie had been a source of information. Griff would have bet his life on that. But a hotshot reporter from the *Morning*

News had dug until he'd excavated just enough facts to hold together his speculations. They made for a sensational exposé. In conclusion, the writer had implied that Griff Burkett's fall had been predestined from birth, that he'd been bred to transgress, and that the crime he'd committed should have been foreseeable.

Rodarte leered at him. "Tell me, how did it feel to throw the big game? Honestly, now. Just between us. Did you have any twinge of conscience? Or not?"

Wyatt Turner's warnings rang in Griff's ears. *Do not cross him. Turn the other cheek.* Which seemed an ironic admonition at this particular moment, when his cheekbone was throbbing and the entire side of his head was hurting so bad he thought he might throw up.

Griff wanted to grab Rodarte by his greasy hair and smash his face against the concrete wall of the parking garage, again and again until his ugly features had been pulverized to mush.

But Griff couldn't do a goddamn thing without bringing trouble down on himself, and Rodarte knew that. Nothing would have given the bastard more pleasure than seeing Griff locked up again on the very day he'd been released.

Muttering an invective, Griff turned away, but Rodarte grabbed him by the shoulder, brought him back around, and shoved him up hard against the wall. "Don't turn your back on me, you cocky fucker."

More than the name-calling, being manhandled like that cleared Griff's head of sharp pains and made his anger as brittle and cold as glass. He could kill this bastard. Easy. Being tackled in a game was one thing. Being touched by Rodarte was quite another. "Take your hands off me."

Either his steely tone, or maybe his eyes, telegraphed the murderous fury he felt, because Rodarte let go and shuffled back several steps. "You were owed that," he said, hitching his chin up toward Griff's bleeding cheekbone. "For flipping me off today. I drove all the way out to jackrabbit country to commemorate your release, and that's the thanks I got for my thoughtfulness."

"Thanks. Now we're square." Griff brushed past him.

"I had an interesting conversation with some former associates of yours yesterday."

Griff stopped and turned.

Rodarte took a deep pull off his cigarette, then dropped it on the garage floor and ground it out with the toe of his shoe while he blew smoke upward. "I don't need to name names, do I? You know who I'm talking about. Your former business partners."

"They went slumming?" Griff asked.

Rodarte merely grinned.

The three bosses of the organized crime group— the Vista boys, as Griff thought of them. That was who Rodarte was talking about. The men in the five-thousand-dollar suits. The trio Bill Bandy had introduced Griff to when he needed a quick fix to a big gambling debt.

The Vista triumvirate had been obliging, and then some. They'd opened wide the doors of their luxury offices in the high-rise building they owned in Las Colinas overlooking the golf course. And that was just the beginning. There were lavish dinners in the private dining rooms of five-star restaurants. Private jet trips to Vegas, the Bahamas, New York, San Francisco. Limousines. Girls.

Seduction in its purest form.

The only thing he'd turned down was the drugs, although at any given time, he'd had access to any and all he wanted.

"Those guys know you're out," Rodarte was saying. His smile was dangerous and insinuating, a jackal's grin. "They're not all that glad about it. They thought for sure you'd get nailed for doing Bill Bandy."

"I had nothing to do with Bandy."

"Riiiight."

Griff would be damned before he stood here pleading his innocence to this asshole. "You see the Vista boys again, tell them I said they can go fuck themselves."

Rodarte winced. "Oooh, they're not gonna like that. First you kill their key bookmaker—"

"I didn't kill Bandy."

"See? I don't think they buy that, Griff. You were so pissed at him for ratting you out to the FBI, of course you killed him. You had a right to. Almost an *obligation*. Look, I understand. And so do they. A rat's a rat. If you hadn't snuffed him, Bandy might have given them up next."

"So what's their gripe?"

"They'll never know for sure whether or not Bandy would have betrayed them. While you," he said, poking Griff in the chest with his index finger, "you actually named names to the FBI. *Their* names. You see the problem? Their thinking is that

Bandy would have remained loyal to them if it hadn't been for you. Regardless of how it all came down, they blame you for fucking up their smooth operation."

"Gee, this is a sad story."

Ignoring the remark, Rodarte went on. "You were bad for their business. For years after you got sent to Big Spring, they found it harder to entice a professional athlete anywhere in the southern United States. Players of every sport were nervous, afraid that if they cheated, they'd get caught like you did."

Rodarte took a breath, and when he spoke again, his voice was softer. "The Vista boys, as you affectionately call them, haven't fully recovered from the grief you caused them."

"The grief *I* caused *them*?" Griff finally gave vent to the angry pressure that had been building inside him. "None of them served a day of time."

"Only because the FBI was building their racketeering case around your testimony alone." Rodarte gave a rueful shrug over the flaws in that strategy. "Your story didn't fly with the federal grand jury. They figured you were trying to point the finger at others to take the heat off yourself."

He poked Griff again. "That's the only reason the Vista boys weren't also indicted. But they came close. They haven't forgotten how close. And all thanks to you. They're sorta holding a grudge."

"The feeling is mutual. Now, get out of my way."

When Rodarte failed to back away, Griff tried to go around him. Rodarte sidestepped, blocking him. "But basically these are nice guys we're talking about. They might welcome you back into the fold—on one condition."

"Are you their recruiter now?"

Rodarte winked. "Let's just say a word from me could grease the skids for you."

"I'm not interested in getting back into the fold."

"You haven't heard me out."

"I don't need to."

Rodarte dusted an imaginary speck off the lapel of Griff's jacket. If the man touched him again, Griff thought he might have to break every bone in his hand.

"Take a piece of advice, Griff. Think about it."

"I had five years to think about it."

"So you won't be working with them again?"

"No."

"What about their competitors? The Vista boys are businessmen, after all. They're nervous—just a little—over what you might do now that you're out."

"I'm thinking of opening a lemonade stand."

Rodarte's frown said that crack was unworthy of him.

"It's none of their goddamn business, or yours, what I do," Griff said.

"They beg to differ. Especially if you're planning to link up with one of their competitors."

"Relieve them on that score. They've got nothing to be nervous about. See ya, Rodarte."

Again Griff moved away, but Rodarte scrambled and planted himself in his path. He moved in close and lowered his voice again, this time to a conspiratorial whisper. "Then there's the matter of the money."

"What money?"

"Come on, Griff," he said in a singsongy, wheedling tone. "The money you stole from Bandy."

"There was no money."

"Maybe not cash. A safe-deposit box key, maybe? Foreign bank account numbers? The combination to a safe. Stamp collection."

"Nothing."

"Bullshit!" Rodarte stabbed Griff in the chest with his finger once again, harder, angrier.

Griff saw red, but despite his wish to break bones, he couldn't touch the man. One touch would be all the provocation Rodarte needed to engage him in a fight. If he got into a fight with Rodarte, even if he won, he'd spend the night in the Dallas County Detention Center. Bad as his new apartment was, he preferred it over a jail cell.

"Hear me, Rodarte. If Bandy had any money squirreled away, the secret died with him. I sure as hell didn't get it."

"Pull my other leg." Rodarte slammed him back against the wall and moved in close, baring his teeth. "A hot hustler like you would have made sure he didn't come away empty-handed. You've got expensive tastes. Cars. Clothes. Pussy. If you didn't tuck away some of Bandy's money, how are you going to finance all those luxuries?"

"Don't worry your pretty head about it, Rodarte. I've got it covered."

"Yeah?"

"Yeah."

"Doing what?"

Griff didn't reply.

Rodarte said, "I'll find out, you know."

"Good luck. Now get the fuck out of my way."

They shared a long, hostile stare. It took every ounce of willpower Griff had not to knee the guy in the balls and throw him off. But he stood his ground and his gaze didn't flinch. Eventually Rodarte dropped his hands from Griff's shoulders and took a step back. But he wasn't admitting defeat.

"Okay, Number Ten," he said softly. "You want to make this hard on yourself, fine by me. In fact, I prefer that you do." He whispered as though making a malevolent promise.

Griff went past him and had made it to the corner of the garage when Rodarte called him back. "Hey, answer me one question."

"Yes, I think you're ugly."

Rodarte laughed. "Good one. But, seriously, when you snapped Bandy's neck, did you come? I know that happens sometimes."

"What do you think?"

Laura didn't have to ask *About what?* She and Foster hadn't talked about Griff Burkett yet, but he might just as well have been the centerpiece on the dining table. His presence between them seemed almost that tangible.

She set down her fork and reached for her wineglass. Cradling the bowl of it between her hands, she thoughtfully stared at the ruby-colored contents. "My first impression is that he's angry."

"At?"

"Life."

The formal dining room, which accommodated

thirty or more, was used only for entertaining. The first twelve months of their marriage, they'd hosted numerous dinner parties. In the past two years, there had been only one—at Christmas for Sun-South's board of directors and their spouses.

This evening, as on most evenings, they were having their dinner in the family dining room. Much cozier, it was separated from the commercial-size kitchen by a single door. The housekeeper-cook got off at six o'clock each day. Her last duty was to leave dinner in a warming tray. Since Laura had assumed much of Foster's workload, she usually stayed at the corporate offices until seven-thirty or eight, making their dinner hour late. Foster refused to eat before she got home.

Tonight their dinner had been delayed by the interview with Griff Burkett. Laura had lost her appetite, but Foster seemed to be enjoying the beef Wellington. He cut off a bite and chewed it exactly twelve times, four series of three, swallowed, took a sip of his wine, blotted his mouth with his napkin. "Spending five years in prison would put any man in a bad humor."

"I think Mr. Burkett would be angry under any circumstances."

"That anger having been ingrained into his personality?"

"Well, you read the newspaper story about how he grew up," she said. "Granted, his early years were a nightmare. But that doesn't excuse what he's done as an adult. He broke the law. He deserved his punishment. Possibly more than he received."

"Remind me never to get on your fighting side, Mrs. Speakman. You're ruthless."

She didn't take offense, knowing he was teasing her. "I just have no tolerance for grown-ups who blame their shortcomings, even their lawlessness, on a disadvantaged childhood. Mr. Burkett alone is accountable for his actions."

"For which he has atoned," her husband reminded her gently. Lightening the mood, he added, "I promise to do my part to see that our baby doesn't have a disadvantaged childhood."

She smiled. "Left alone, I think you'd spoil him rotten."

" 'Him'?"

"Or her."

"I'd love a little girl who looks just like you."

"And I'd be over the moon to have a boy."

Their smiles remained in place, but the unspoken words hung there above the dining table. Neither a son nor a daughter would have Foster's features. Similar, perhaps, but not his.

Laura took another sip of wine. "Foster . . ."

"No."

"Why 'no'? You don't know what I'm going to say."

"Yes, I do." He indicated her plate. "Finished?" She nodded. He laid his knife and fork at a precise diagonal across his plate and folded his napkin beside it.

She stood up as he backed his wheelchair away from the table. "I'll ask Manuelo to clear the table while I get the coffee."

"Let's have it in the den."

In the kitchen she filled a carafe with coffee, which she'd set to brew while they were having dinner. She placed it on a tray with cups and saucers, cream pitcher, and sugar bowl. She carried the tray into the den. Foster was washing his hands with bottled sanitizer. When he was done, he placed the bottle in a drawer.

She fixed his coffee and carried it to him. He thanked her, then waited until she had hers and was seated on one of the leather love seats, her feet tucked beneath her.

He continued the conversation as though there hadn't been an interruption. "You were going to say that we could take the more conventional route. Have artificial insemination with an anonymous donor."

That was exactly what she'd been about to say. "They keep sperm donors anonymous for a very good reason, Foster. We would never know his identity, never have a mental image of him. The child would be ours. We'd never be studying his or her features, looking for similarities to . . . to someone we'd met."

"Do you object to Griff Burkett's features?"

"You're missing the point."

He laughed and rolled his chair over to the love seat. "No I'm not, I'm teasing you."

"I guess I'm not in a teasing mood tonight."

"I'm sorry." He reached up and ruffled her hair. But she wouldn't be placated so easily. "This is probably the most important decision we'll ever have to make."

"We've already made it. We've been over this a thousand times, studying it from every angle. We've discussed it for months. We talked it to death, and then talked it some more, and finally agreed it's the right path for us."

For *you,* she started to say but didn't. "I know I agreed, but—"

"What?"

"I don't know. In theory . . ." She let the sentence trail. What worked in theory didn't necessarily translate well into flesh-and-blood reality. Particularly since it was *her* flesh and blood that would be affected.

"I'm only asking for one child," he said, stroking her cheek. "If I could, I'd give you the three or four children we planned on. Before."

Before. There it was, that giant qualifier. That six-letter word was weighty with its significance to them. It was the line of demarcation in their lives. Before.

His eyes moved over her face lovingly. "I still dream about making love to you."

"You do make love to me."

He smiled wanly. "Of a sort. Not the real thing."

"It's real to me."

"But it's not the same."

She leaned forward and kissed him intimately on the mouth, then nuzzled her face into his neck. He held her close, smoothing his hands over her back. During her busy workdays, hours would go by when she would forget his condition and the drastic effect it had had on their lives, their marriage.

Mean reminders of it would strike her unaware, coming from nowhere like blow darts, giving her no warning, making them impossible to dodge. During a meeting, or while she was on the telephone, or when she was conducting a brainstorm-

ing session, one would hit, numbing her for a
millisecond before the pain set in.

But these quiet evenings at home were the worst.
When they were alone, like this, each remembered
how it used to be, how they used to make love when
the mood struck them, laughing at their passionate
haste, collapsing in happy satiation afterward.

Now she occasionally went to the room where
he slept in a hospital bed, rigged with every modern
contrivance to maximize his comfort. She would
undress and lie with him, her body pressed against
his. They kissed. He caressed her, and sometimes
just the intimacy of that was enough. Other nights,
she would reach orgasm, which wasn't really satisfying because she always felt selfish afterward.
When she expressed this, he comforted her by saying that his completion was derived from knowing
that he could still give her physical pleasure.

But if she left his bed feeling like an exhibitionist,
she knew he must feel like a voyeur. Because it
wasn't mutually fulfilling, it was . . . well, as he'd
said, it wasn't the same.

They rarely talked about their life together before the night it was turned upside down. Memories
of that first year of their marriage were indulged
privately, neither wanting to cause the other heartbreak by reminiscing aloud. The memories were
agonizing for her. They must have been even more
terrible for Foster. She was still whole and healthy.
He wasn't. He didn't seem to harbor any resentment
or bitterness toward fate, or God. Or her.

But how could he not?

Taking her shoulders between his hands now, he
eased her away from him. "Do you have any mis-

givings, Laura? About using Burkett or anyone else. Any hesitation at all? If so, we'll call it off."

Did she have any misgivings? She had thousands. But this was the way Foster insisted it be done, so this was the way it must be done. "I want to see the results of a complete medical checkup."

"He promised to act on that quickly and mail us the report. As soon as we've looked it over, we'll burn it."

"I don't think there will be a problem. He appears to be as physically ideal as we believed."

"What about his character?"

She scoffed at that. "Less than ideal. He proved that five years ago."

"His crime doesn't concern me. What I meant was, do you think we can count on his discretion?"

"I think the money will be incentive for him to keep our confidence."

"I made the conditions as simple for him as I could."

He had explained to Griff Burkett that he was never to make any claims toward the child, never to contact them, never to acknowledge their existence. If Griff kept to those conditions, he would receive one million dollars a year.

Burkett had asked, "For how long?"

"For the rest of your life."

He'd divided an incredulous look between them. "Seriously?"

"Seriously."

Regarding them as though they had both lost their minds, he said, "Having a kid, and keeping its conception a secret, is that important to you?"

The question sounded like a prelude to extortion. Laura wouldn't have been surprised if at that point he'd demanded twice the amount they were offering. But when Foster said, "Yes, it's that important to us," Burkett chuckled and shook his head, as though finding such an ideal incomprehensible. Obviously he had never felt that strongly about anything or held anything that dear. Not even his career.

"Well, it's not like I want a kid," he said. "In fact, since puberty I've been damn careful to guarantee that I didn't father one. So you can relieve yourself of the worry that I'll show up someday to claim him. Or her," he said, addressing that to Laura.

"What about the confidentiality issue?" Foster asked.

"There is no issue. I get it. I keep my mouth shut. We run into each other by accident, I look right through you with no recognition whatsoever. For a million dollars a year, I can lose my memory. Like that." He snapped his fingers. "One thing, though."

"What?"

"What happens if you . . . if I outlive you?"

"Laura would uphold our obligation to you."

"What if she's not around?"

That was one question they hadn't anticipated. They'd never considered the possibility that he would survive both of them. She and Foster looked at each other, and she knew they were thinking the same thing. If Griff Burkett outlived them, they were leaving their child and heir vulnerable to extortion, financial as well as emotional. They had agreed that their child would never know how he came to be. They would let him assume, as everyone else would, that Foster had fathered him.

"That's a scenario that hadn't occurred to us," Foster admitted.

"Well, now that it's occurred to me, it needs to be addressed."

Laura said, "By that point in time, you would be extremely well off."

"You're well off now," Griff retorted. "You wouldn't enter into a contract with a contingency as important as this left unsettled. Would you?"

He was right, but she was reluctant to concede the point. "I'm sure that over time we can work something out."

"Un-huh. Not over time. Now."

"He's right, Laura. The timeliness is critical. I'm proof that our lives can change in a heartbeat. It's better that we resolve this issue now, rather than leave it dangling." Foster thought on it for a moment, then said, "Unfortunately, every solution that comes immediately to mind would involve paperwork, and it's essential that we avoid that." He spread his arms, palms up. "Griff, either you'll have to trust me to come up with a workable solution, or—"

"When?"

"I'll give it top priority."

Burkett frowned as though that weren't good enough. "What's the *or*?"

"Or, what I'm reading from you is that it's a deal breaker."

Laura noted that he didn't have to think about it

for long. "Okay, I'll trust you to work something out. After all, you're putting your trust in me, and I'm the convicted felon."

"I'm glad you're the one who cited that, Mr. Burkett."

Laura had spoken before thinking, but she didn't regret saying it. He'd needed to be reminded that the risk they were taking far outweighed his. He moved nothing except his eyes, but she felt their angry impact when they connected with hers.

"You mean so you wouldn't have to," he said. "So you wouldn't have to point out that if anybody in this room is untrustworthy, it's me."

"Laura meant no offense, Griff," Foster said.

Continuing to hold her stare, he said, "No. Of course not. None taken."

But she knew he didn't mean it, just like he knew that she *had* meant what she'd said.

"Risk on both sides is inherent to any business partnership." Foster spoke from experience. He was also an excellent mediator, who always tried to defuse a disagreement before it got out of hand. "I think shared risk is a positive thing. It leaves everybody vulnerable to some extent and keeps everyone honest." He turned to Laura. "Anything else?"

She shook her head.

"Excellent," he said, slapping his hands on the arms of his chair three times. "Let's shake on it."

Now Foster was saying, "You told him you'd be in touch within two weeks."

"I'll be monitoring my cycle, taking my temperature each morning, so that hopefully I'll know the day I ovulate."

"And how long after that before you'd know if you conceived?"

"Two weeks."

"I get giddy thinking about it."

"Get giddy when I pee on a stick and it turns pink. Or blue. Or whatever it's supposed to turn."

Laughing, he kissed her soundly, then by tacit agreement, they headed for the elevator tucked discreetly under the stairs. "Race you to the top," he said as he rolled his chair into the metal cage.

She jogged up the curving staircase and was there to meet him when he arrived. "You always win," he grumbled.

"Those sprints up the stairs keep me in good shape."

"I'll say." He reached around and smacked her on the butt.

Hearing their approach, Manuelo opened the door from inside Foster's bedroom. "Can we skip the therapy tonight?" Foster asked. The aide smiled and shrugged, indicating he didn't understand the question. "He's faking that. I know he is. He knows damn well I'm talking about the therapy he puts me through and how I feel about it." He clasped her hand tightly. "Spare me, Laura. Please."

"Hey, I've got it just as tough tonight. I've got to review that union contract again. But I'll come and tuck you in." She kissed him lightly on the lips and continued down the wide hallway to her office.

But an hour later, when she went into Foster's bedroom, Manuelo had done everything that needed doing. The drapes were drawn. The thermostat was set to his preferred temperature. There was a carafe of ice water and a drinking glass on his nightstand. The call button was within reach. He was sleeping, a book resting on his lap.

She turned off the bedside lamp and for the longest time sat there in the darkness, in the chair beside his bed, listening to his breathing. He didn't stir, and she was grateful that he was able to sleep so well.

Eventually, she left him and went alone to the bed they used to share, wishing that her sleep could be that sound.

CHAPTER
7

THE FOLLOWING MORNING, GRIFF HAD A hitch in his back from sleeping on the soft mattress, which sagged in the middle. He denied that the chronic pain was a holdover from thirteen years of getting slammed into by tacklers— eighth grade through his years with the Cowboys.

His right shoulder also bothered him more than he wanted to admit. Over the course of his playing days, he'd had four fingers broken, one of his small fingers broken in the same place twice. The second time, he hadn't bothered to have it set, so it had healed crooked. Assorted other gridiron mishaps and melees made getting out of bed every morning a slow process.

Fondly recalling the comfort of Marcia's perfumed and silky sheets, he limped into the drab kitchen, boiled water for instant coffee, toasted a piece of bread, and washed it down with a glass of milk to chase the bitter pseudo-coffee taste from his mouth.

Before he forgot, he called the probation officer assigned to him. Jerry Arnold's voice-mail recording had made him sound like a likable enough guy, and now his live voice sounded even friendlier and non-threatening. "I was just calling to make sure you got the message I left yesterday," Griff said after an exchange of hello-how-are-yous.

"Sure did. But let me repeat the info back to you, check to see I got it right." He recited the address and phone number Griff had left.

"That's right."

"How about a job, Griff? Anything yet?"

"I'm seeing about that today."

"Good, good. Keep me posted on any progress."

"Will do."

"Well, you know the conditions of your probation, so I won't bore you with them again."

"They're etched onto my brain. I don't want to go back to prison."

"And I don't want you to." The bureaucrat hesitated, then said, "You were a hell of a ballplayer, Griff. A thrill to watch."

"Thanks."

"Well, good luck today."

That chore out of the way, Griff headed for the shower. It had furry black stuff growing on the tile grout, but to his surprise the hot water was plentiful. He dressed quickly but carefully, choosing the best from the clothing Wyatt Turner had left in the apartment for him. He made a mental note to ask his lawyer where the rest of his stuff was being stored and how he could go about retrieving it.

Then he remembered that if the Speakmans came through with their down payment, he could go out and buy all new stuff. The thought made his gut purl with happy anticipation.

However, he wouldn't know until after two o'clock today if they'd come through as promised. In the meantime, he had other errands to run.

He got to the walk-in medical clinic at eight-thirty and was out in under an hour. "How soon before I can pick up the lab results?"

"Three to five days."

"Make it three," he said, giving the nurse a wink and his best smile. Simpering, she promised to try. Obviously she didn't follow Cowboys football.

From the clinic he drove to a branch of the public library—the one nearest his former Turtle Creek address. He doubted there was one in the neighborhood of his present apartment, doubted many of the residents in the area could read.

He arrived at the library only to discover it didn't open until ten. A cluster of toddlers and young mothers—when had young mothers got so damn good looking?—had congregated at the doors waiting for them to open.

Moms and kids alike regarded him curiously. At six feet four he towered over all of them. The cut and bruise on his cheekbone, Rodarte's contribution, drew their attention, too, making him feel particularly conspicuous among the Thursday Morning Story Time at the Library crowd.

Once the doors were unlocked, the moms herded their children to a far corner while he went to the information desk. The librarian smiled pleasantly and asked what she could do for him. "I need to use a computer. And I'll probably need some help."

Five years of advancement in computer technology equaled aeons. But the librarian patiently showed him how to access the Internet and do a Google search, and soon he was knee-deep in information on SunSouth Airlines and, more specifically, its owner.

First, he got an overview of Foster Speakman's background. Starting in the 1920s with his great-great-grandfather, his family had amassed a fortune from oil and natural gas. As sole heir, Foster was bequeathed megamillions in addition to vast parcels of land in New Mexico, Colorado, and Alaska.

He held an MBA from Harvard Business School and was a polo player of renown. He had received countless citations and awards from business and civic groups for community service. Economic analysts lauded his courageous takeover and turnaround of the foundering airline.

If he'd been a football player, Speakman would have been the starting quarterback for the Super Bowl champs and voted MVP.

He and Mrs. Speakman—not Laura—were photographed attending various charity and social functions. One photograph accompanying an article in *Forbes* showed Foster standing tall and proud in front of a SunSouth jet, arms crossed over his chest, looking like a man who'd just conquered the world. He appeared robust and strong.

Which meant that somewhere between the time

he'd bought the airline several years ago and now, he'd become paraplegic. Illness? Cataclysmic event?

While pondering the possibilities, Griff came across Elaine Speakman's lengthy obituary. She had died after a valorous and lengthy battle with leukemia. No children had come from the marriage.

The widower had married Laura Speakman one year and five months following Elaine's death.

Foster and Elaine had been well represented in the press. But Foster and Mrs. Speakman II were featured nearly daily—which explained his allusion to their being celebrities.

Then Griff found what he'd been looking for. One year and seventy days into their marriage, Foster and Laura Speakman's lives were irrevocably changed. The story made the front page of *The Dallas Morning News* under a banner headline and a graphic photograph. The news hadn't reached Big Spring. Or if it had, he'd missed it. Or if he had heard about it, he'd forgotten it because it didn't pertain to him and he'd had no interest.

Griff read the story twice. There were links to numerous follow-up stories. He read them all, then, using the back icon, returned to the original story and read it yet again. And when for the third time he reached that telling sentence, which explained so much, he sat back in his chair and said, "Huh."

It was a nice neighborhood. Unlike the one he'd grown up in, there were no loose shutters or curling window screens on these houses. Lawns were mowed, hedges were clipped, and flower beds were weeded. The basketball hoops actually had baskets, and if the driveways were littered with anything, it was shiny bikes and skateboards, not rusted-out cars sitting on blocks.

Although this neighborhood was younger by twenty years, it had the same kind of "family" feel as the one where Coach and Ellie Miller lived. Where *he'd* lived from the day Coach had removed him from his mother's ramshackle place. Coach had contacted Child Protective Services and handled the legalities, which were incomprehensible and uninteresting to Griff as a fifteen-year-old. He supposed Coach got himself appointed his guardian. In any case, he'd stayed with the Millers until he graduated high school and went away to play football for the University of Texas.

He located the address he sought and drove past the house slowly, checking it out. On either side of the front door was a pot of white flowers. Above the backyard fence, Griff could see the top of a swimming pool slide. Two kids were tossing a football back and forth on the front lawn. They were old enough to be cautious of strangers and eyed Griff warily as he slowly rolled past.

He went to the end of the block and turned the corner. He realized his palms were damp with apprehension. And that made him angry at himself. Why the hell should his palms be sweating? He had as much right as anybody to be on these nicely maintained streets. The people who lived here were no better than he was.

But he'd felt the same anxiety that day when Coach Joe Miller had pulled into his driveway and said, "Here it is." Griff had looked at the house with the welcome mat on the threshold and the blooming ivy crawling up a trellis and felt as out of place as a turd in a punch bowl. He didn't belong here. But he'd die before he let on that he felt inferior.

Sullenly, feet shuffling, he'd followed Coach up the steps and through the front door. "Ellie?"

"In here."

Griff had seen Coach's wife at the games. From a distance, she looked okay, he guessed. He'd never really given her a second thought.

She turned to them as they entered the kitchen. Her hair was in curlers, and she had bright yellow rubber gloves on her hands.

"This is Griff," Coach said.

She smiled at him. "Hi, Griff. I'm Ellie."

He kept his like-I-give-a-shit frown in place so they wouldn't guess that his heart was beating harder than it did before a fourth-and-goal play, and in the hope they wouldn't hear his stomach growling. He'd glanced through the open door of the pantry. Besides at the supermarket, he'd never seen so much food stored in one place. On the counter was a pie with a golden crust, oozing cherry juice. The aroma was making Griff's mouth water.

Coach said, "He's going to be staying with us for a while."

If this news came as a shock to Ellie Miller, she hid it. "Oh, well, good," she said. "Welcome. Now, can you give me a hand, Griff? That pie leaked sticky stuff all over this oven. I'm trying to get the racks out so I can clean it while it's still warm, but my gloves will melt if I grab hold. Pot holders are there in the top drawer."

Not knowing what else to do, he'd got the pot holders and removed the hot metal racks from the oven. With no more ceremony than that, he moved into the Millers' house and into their lives.

He always suspected that Coach and Ellie had discussed the possibility of this before Coach came to get him that morning. Because he was shown into a room set up for an adolescent boy. It had a double bed covered by a red-and-white blanket with the image of the high school team mascot on it—a fiercely scowling Viking. Other sports pennants were tacked to the wall.

"That's the closet. Let me know if you need more hangers." Ellie glanced down at the small duffel bag Griff had brought with him but didn't comment on how little it would hold, how little he had. "You can keep your folding clothes in this chest. If anything needs washing, the hamper is in the bathroom. Oh, goodness, I haven't shown you the bathroom." It was so clean, he was afraid to pee in the toilet.

They all went to Sears that afternoon so Ellie could "pick up some things," but what they came home with was new clothes for him. He'd never had food like Ellie cooked, including the pie they ate for dessert that night. He'd never been inside a house that smelled good, that had books on shelves and pictures on the walls.

But he learned from the oven-cleaning experience that such luxuries didn't come free. He was expected to do chores. Never having been required to do a damn thing in his life except stay out of the way when a man was in the bedroom with his mother, Griff found that this aspect of family life took some getting used to.

Ellie's rebukes were gentle and usually included

some reproach to herself. "You forgot to make your bed this morning, Griff. Or did I forget to tell you that sheets aren't changed till Friday?" "You won't be able to wear that favorite T-shirt tomorrow, because I didn't find it under the bed until after I'd done the laundry. Be sure it gets in the hamper next time."

Coach was less subtle. "Have you finished your history paper?"

"No."

"Isn't it due tomorrow?"

He knew it was. One of his assistant coaches was Griff's history teacher. "I'll get it done."

Coach turned off the TV. "Right. You will. Now."

Whenever he was disciplined, Griff muttered rebellious plans to leave. He was sick and tired of their harping. Do this, do that, clean up this, carry out that. Only dorks went to church on Sundays, but had he been given a choice? No. It was just expected. And what did he care if the car was washed and the lawn mowed?

But he never followed through on any of his threats to leave. Besides, his muttering was largely ignored. Ellie chatted over it, and Coach either turned his back or left the room.

Coach didn't go soft on him at practice, either. If anything, he was tougher on him, as though to assure the other players that Griff was nothing special to him just because he was lodged under his roof.

One afternoon, still mad over being denied access to the TV the night before, Griff sloughed off during drills. He didn't connect a single pass to the receivers. Running backs had to come take the ball from him because he didn't scramble to get it to them. He fumbled a snap.

Coach watched him; despite his scowl, he didn't blow the whistle on him, give him a pointer, or chew him out.

But at the end of practice, when everyone else headed for the locker room, Coach ordered him to stay where he was. He placed a blocking dummy thirty yards away and tossed Griff the football. "Hit it."

Griff threw the ball with no more effort than he had put into the rest of the practice and missed the dummy. Coach glared at him. "Try again," he said, tossing him another football. Again he missed.

Coach handed him a third football. "Hit the damn thing."

"I'm having an off day. What's the big deal?"

"The big deal is that you're a chickenshit."

Griff threw the ball then, straight at Coach. The ball bounced off his barrel chest. Griff turned toward the locker room.

When Coach grabbed him by the shoulder and whipped him around, his helmet nearly flew off, taking his head with it. Before Griff could recover, Coach planted his wide, leathery hand in the center of his chest and shoved. He landed hard on his ass. Pain shimmied up from his tailbone, straight along his spine, and directly into his brain. It hurt so bad, he caught his breath and tears came to his eyes. They were more mortifying than his position on the ground.

"I'm not scared of you!" he shouted up at Coach.

"Do I have your attention now?"

"Why don't you pick on somebody else for a change? Phillips missed ten of ten today. I don't see you making him kick till he gets one between the frigging uprights. How many times did Reynolds fumble during the last game? Three? Four? Why aren't you on his ass? Why is it always mine?"

"Because Phillips and Reynolds don't have any talent!" Coach seemed to use up all his breath in that one roar. His voice was much softer when he said, "And you do."

He flicked sweat off his forehead with the back of his thumb. He looked away, then back at Griff, who was still sitting in the dirt because his butt bone hurt too bad to try to stand.

Coach said, "Not another player on this team, not another one in this school, or in any of our rival schools, has talent to match yours, Griff. And you're *pissing* it away, feeling sorry for yourself and carrying a chip on your shoulder because your mother was a whore. You've had a lousy life up till now, no denying that. But if you let it ruin the rest of your life, who's the fool? Who will you be spiting? You, that's who.

"You may not be scared of me, but you're scared shitless of yourself," he said, jabbing the space between them with his finger. "Because in spite of yourself, you're better than the two who made you. You're smart and good looking. You've got more natural athletic ability than I've ever seen in any sport. And because of those gifts, you just might make something of yourself.

"And that scares you, 'cause then you wouldn't be able to wallow in your goddamn self-pity. You wouldn't be able to hate the world and everybody in it for the shitty hand you were dealt. You wouldn't have an excuse for being the self-centered, self-absorbed, complete and total jerk that you are."

Speech over, he stood looking down at Griff a moment longer, then turned away in disgust. "If you've got the guts for it, suit up tomorrow and be ready to apply yourself. If not, stay the hell off my team."

Griff was at practice the following day and for every day after that, and that season he led the team to the state championship, as he did for the three following years. Neither the incident nor Coach's lecture was ever referred to again. But Griff didn't forget it, and he knew Coach didn't.

Their relationship improved. They had ups and downs because Griff constantly pushed him and Ellie to see just how far he could go before they got sick of him and kicked him out.

When he defied his weekend curfew and came in an hour and a half late, they didn't kick him out, but Coach imposed the worst punishment fathomable—making him wait two months beyond his sixteenth birthday to take his driver's test and get his license.

They encouraged him to invite friends over, but he never did. He'd never developed friend-making skills and didn't really have the desire to. Overtures by classmates were rebuffed. Sooner or later people abandoned you, so why bother? In the long run, you were better off keeping to yourself.

Sometimes he caught Ellie looking at him sadly and knew she harbored unspoken worries about him. Maybe she sensed, even then, that the worst was yet to come.

Things rocked along pretty well. Then, early in his junior year, an incident in the locker room got Griff suspended from school for three days. It hadn't been a fair fight—Griff against five other athletes, three football players and two on the basketball team.

When they were pulled apart by assistant coaches, two of the boys were taken to the emergency room, one with a broken nose, the other needing stitches in his lower lip. The other three had bloody noses and bruised torsos but didn't require hospitalization.

Griff, instigator of the seemingly unprovoked fight, suffered no more than a few scrapes and a black eye.

"We have no choice, Coach Miller," the school principal said as he relinquished Griff to him. "Just be glad the parents of the other boys declined to press assault charges. They could have," he added, glaring at Griff.

Coach took him home, marched him past a subdued Ellie, and confined him to his room for the duration of his suspension. On the evening of the second day, Coach walked into his room unannounced. Griff was lying on his back on the bed, idly tossing a football into the air.

Coach pulled up his desk chair and straddled it backward. "I heard something interesting today."

Griff continued tossing the football, keeping his eyes on it and the ceiling beyond. His tongue would rot out before he would ask.

"From Robbie Lancelot."

Griff caught the football against his chest and turned his head toward Coach.

"Robbie asked me to thank you for what you did. And especially for not telling."

Griff remained silent.

"He figured I was in on whatever it is that you're not telling. I'm asking you to tell me now."

Griff pressed the football between his strong fingers, studied the laces, avoided looking at Coach.

"Griff."

He dropped the football. Sighed. "Lancelot weighs what? A hundred twenty-five, maybe? He's a nerd, a geek. A pest, you know? People cheat off him during chemistry tests, but otherwise . . ." He looked over at Coach, who nodded understanding.

"I had finished my workout with weights and went into the locker room. I heard this commotion back by the showers. Those five guys had Robbie backed into a corner. They had his underwear. He was standing there without anything on, and they were making him . . . you know. Work it. Saying stuff like 'Are you really, Lance a lot?' 'Let's see this big lance of yours.' 'Too bad your lance isn't as big as your brain.' Stuff like that."

He glanced at Coach, then away. "He was crying. Snot was running out his nose. His dick was . . . he was yanking on it something fierce, but it wasn't . . . doing anything."

"Okay."

"These guys were giving him hell. So I plowed through them and pulled him away from the wall, walked him to his locker, told him to get his clothes on, wipe his nose for God's sake, and get the hell out of there."

"And then went back and beat the crap out of his tormentors."

"Tried anyhow," Griff mumbled.

Coach watched him for a long moment, then stood up, replaced the chair beneath the desk, and went to the door. "Ellie says dinner's in half an hour. You'd better wash up."

"Coach?" He turned back. "Don't tell anybody, okay? I've only got one more day of suspension, and . . . and I promised Lancelot."

"I won't tell anybody, Griff."

"Thanks."

To this day Griff remembered the expression on Coach's face as he left his room that evening. He was never able to define it, but he knew that something important had happened, that some sort of understanding had passed between them. As far as he knew, Coach had never betrayed his confidence about the incident.

By now he'd made the neighborhood block and for the second time approached the house with the white flowers on either side of the front door and the backyard pool with the slide. He'd wasted enough time. It was do or die.

The two kids with the football were still throwing passes to each other when Griff parked at the curb and got out.

CHAPTER
8

T HE BOYS STOPPED THEIR PLAY, WATCHING as he walked toward them. "Hey," he said.

"Hey." They said it in unison, cautiously.

"Is this Bolly Rich's house?"

"He's inside," replied the taller of the two. "He's my dad."

"What's your name?" Griff asked.

"Jason."

"You play ball?"

Jason nodded.

"What position?"

"Quarterback."

"Yeah?"

"Second string," Jason confessed self-consciously.

"Want to play first string?"

Jason looked at his friend, then back at Griff. "Sure."

"Give me the ball."

Again Jason first consulted his friend with a

look, then passed the football to Griff, keeping himself at arm's length. "I'm throwing ducks."

Griff grinned at his use of the term for a slow and wobbly pass. "That happens to everybody once in a while, but you can avoid it." He took the ball in his right hand, pressed his fingertips against the laces. "See this?" He held the ball for Jason and his friend to observe.

"You've gotta keep the pads of your fingers tight, like you're trying to squeeze the air out of it. So when you let it go . . ." He motioned for Jason's friend to run out for a pass. The kid went willingly. Griff drew back his arm. "You've got control, better aim, and speed."

He threw the ball. It sailed straight and sure. The kid caught it and beamed. Griff gave him a thumbs-up, then turned to Jason. "A bullet instead of a duck."

Jason raised his hand to shade his eyes against the sun. "You're Griff Burkett."

"That's right."

"I had a poster of you in my room, but my dad made me take it down."

Griff snuffled a laugh. "I'm not surprised."

"Griff?"

He turned. A slight man, wearing cargo shorts, a holey T-shirt, and old sneakers, had opened the front door and was standing on the threshold between the flowerpots. He was balder, but his eyeglasses were the same ones Griff remembered from the last time Bolly had interviewed him.

"Hello, Bolly." He looked down at the boy. "Keep practicing, Jason." The youngster nodded respectfully. Then Griff joined Bolly at the door and extended his hand. To the man's credit he shook hands with him—after only a second or two of hesitation. But the eyes behind the wire frames weren't exactly glowing with happiness to see the most hated man in Dallas at his front door.

"I think Jason has the potential of being good one of these days."

Bolly nodded absently, still trying to recover from his shock. "What are you doing here, Griff?"

"Can I have a minute or two of your time?"

"What for?"

He glanced over his shoulder at the two boys, who were watching this exchange with undivided attention. Coming back around, Griff said, "I promise not to abscond with the family silver."

The sportswriter hesitated for several seconds more, then went into the house and motioned for Griff to follow him. Off the entryway, Bolly led him down a short hallway and into a compact, paneled room. Shelving was jam-packed—even overflowing—with sports memorabilia. Framed photographs of Bolly with star athletes took up most of the wall space. There was an untidy desk in the corner dominated by a telephone and a computer. The monitor was on. The screen saver showed fireworks blossoming in multicolored silence.

"Sit down if you can find a spot," Bolly said as he squeezed himself behind the desk.

Griff removed a stack of newspapers from the only other chair in the room and sat down. "I called the sports desk at the *News*. The guy who answered said you were working from home today."

"I do most days now. Go into the office only a couple days a week, if that much. If you've got e-mail, you can conduct just about any business from home."

"I used a computer in the library this morning. Felt like a caveman looking at the control panel of a 747."

"They build in obsolescence. Keep you buying upgrades."

"Yeah."

An uncomfortable silence followed. Bolly picked up a stray tennis ball on his desk and rolled it between his palms. "Listen, Griff, I want you to know I didn't contribute anything to that piece about you that came out during your trial."

"I didn't think you did."

"Well, good. But I wanted you to know. That writer— You know he's in Chicago now."

"Good riddance."

"Amen. Anyway, he pumped me for information on your background. Your folks. Coach Miller. All that. All I told him, the *only* thing I told him, was that you had the best arm and best hustle of any quarterback I'd ever seen. Topping Montana, Staubach, Favre, Marino, Elway, Unitas. You name me one, you were better. I mean that."

"Thanks."

"Which makes me all the more pissed off at you for what you did."

Bolly Rich, a sports columnist for *The Dallas Morning News,* had always been fair to him. Even when he didn't perform well, like one *Monday Night Football* game against Pittsburgh. It was his rookie year, his first time playing the Steelers on their turf. He played the worst game of his career. Bolly's column the next morning had been critical, but he'd placed part of the blame for the humiliating loss on the offensive line, which had done precious little to protect the new quarterback. He hadn't crucified Griff the way other sportswriters had. That wasn't Bolly's style.

Griff was hoping to appeal to Bolly's sense of fair play now. "I fucked up," he said. "Huge."

"How could you do it, Griff? Especially after such an outstanding season. You were one game away from the Super Bowl. All you had to do was win that game against Washington."

"Yep."

"No way Oakland could have defeated the Cowboys that year. Y'all would have waltzed through the Super Bowl game against them."

"I know that, too."

"You only had to get the ball to Whitethorn, who was standing on the two. The two! Nobody near him."

Bolly didn't have to recount the play for him. He'd replayed it in his mind a thousand times since he threw that pass while the final seconds of the game ticked off the clock.

Fourth and goal on the Redskins'—*it would be the goddamn Redskins*—ten-yard line. Cowboys trail by four. A field goal won't do it.

The center snapped the ball into Griff's hands.

Whitethorn shot forward off the line of scrimmage.

A Redskins lineman slipped, missed the tackle. Whitethorn got to the five.

Skins defenders trying to blitz were stopped dead. They couldn't climb or penetrate Dallas's line, collectively named "Stonewall" that season.

A Skins linebacker was charging toward White-thorn, but Whitethorn was now on the two with space around him. The team was only one step shy of the goal, of victory, of the Super Bowl.

All Griff had to do was lob a short screen pass over the line into Whitethorn's hands.

Or miss him, and get paid a cool two million by the Vista boys.

Cowboys lost 14–10.

"It was a crushing loss," Bolly was saying, "but I remember how the fans still cheered you as you left the field that day. They didn't turn against you until later, when it came out that you'd missed Whitethorn on purpose. And who could blame them? Their Super Bowl–bound star turned out to be a cheat, a crook."

Talking about it five years after the fact still made Bolly angry. He dropped the tennis ball, which bounced off his desk onto the floor, ignored. He took off his glasses, rubbed his eyes with agita-tion, and asked brusquely, "What do you want, Griff?"

"A job."

Bolly replaced his glasses and looked at him as though waiting for the punch line. Eventually, real-izing that Griff was serious, he said, "What?"

"You heard right."

"A *job*? Doing what?"

"I thought a paper route might be available. Could you put in a good word for me with someone in that department?" Bolly continued to stare at him; he didn't smile. "That was a joke, Bolly."

"Is it? Because beyond that, I can't imagine why you've come to me asking about a job. You go anywhere near the sports desk at the newspaper and you'll probably be tarred and feathered. If you're lucky."

"I wouldn't have to go near the sports desk. I could work directly for you."

Bolly frowned. "What'd you have in mind? Not that I think there's a chance in hell of this going anywhere. I'm just curious to see how your mind is working."

"You can't be everywhere at once, Bolly. You can't cover more than one game at a time. I know you use people to cover games for you. Provide the color only someone who is actually at the game can get."

"I use some stringers, yeah."

"Let me be one. I majored in English. I have a fair command of the language. As much as anybody in Texas." His quick grin wasn't returned. "I can at least put two sentences together. Most important, I know the game. I *lived* the game. I could give you insightful play-by-plays that nobody else could, add a perspective that would be unique, based on actual experience. Years of it."

He'd rehearsed the pitch, and to his ears it sounded good. "I could describe how great it feels to win. How lousy it feels to lose. How much worse it feels to win when you know you've played like shit and the win was a fluke." He paused, then asked, "What do you think?"

Bolly studied him a moment. "Yeah, I think you could give an accurate account of wins and losses with some original flavoring thrown in. You'd probably be pretty good at it. But even with terrific language skills, you couldn't come close to describing what it's like to be a team player, Griff. Because you don't know."

"What do you mean?" But he didn't have to ask. He knew what Bolly meant.

"You were a one-man show, Griff. You always were. Going all the way back to high school, when you first started gaining notice from college recruiters, it was all about you, never the team. You led your teams to victory after victory with your amazing ability on the field, but you were a piss-poor leader off it.

"Far as I know, you were never voted a team captain, which doesn't surprise me. Because the only thing that made you part of any team was wearing the same color jersey. You made no friends. Teammates admired your game. Those who didn't envy you idolized you. But they didn't like you, and that was okay with you. You didn't give a damn so long as they carried out the plays you called.

"I never saw you encourage another player who'd made a mistake, never saw you congratulate one for making a good play. I never saw you extend your hand in friendship or lend a helping hand to anyone. What I did see was you giving back Dorsey's Christmas present unopened, saying, 'I don't do that crap.'

"I saw you rebuke Chester when he invited you to a men's prayer breakfast for his wife, who was going through horrible chemo and radiation. When Lambert's fiancée was killed in that car wreck, you were the only one on the team who didn't attend the funeral.

"You were an outstanding athlete, Griff, but a sorry excuse for a friend. I guess that's why I'm surprised, and slightly offended, that you would come to me now, like we'd been good buddies, and ask for my help."

It wasn't easy to hear those things about himself, especially since they were true. Quietly, humbly, Griff said, "I need the work, Bolly."

Bolly took off his glasses to rub his eyes again, and Griff knew he was about to turn him down. "I hate what you did, but everybody can make a mistake and deserves a second chance. It's just . . . Hell, Griff, I couldn't get you into any press box in the league."

"I'd cover college ball. High school."

Bolly was shaking his head. "You'd be met with the same animosity there. Maybe even more. You cheated. First you broke the rules by gambling. Then you threw a game. You fucking threw a game," he said with heat. "For money. You robbed your own team of a sure-win Super Bowl. You were in bed with . . . with *gangsters,* for crissake. Do you think anybody would allow you near kids, young players?" He shook his head and stood up. "I'm sorry, Griff. I can't help you."

He had lunch at a Sonic drive-in. Sitting in the borrowed Honda, he gorged on a jalapeño cheeseburger, a Frito pie, two orders of Tater Tots, and a strawberry-lemonade slush. It had been five years since he'd had junk food. Besides, he figured that if he was going to be a despised outcast, he might just as well be a fat one.

On the drive out to Bolly's neighborhood and up till the time Bolly had told him not only *no* but *hell, no,* Griff had congratulated himself for having the character to seek a job when, by two-thirty this afternoon, his immediate money problems would be solved. He'd sought work *before* going to the bank to check the contents of that safe-deposit box. In his opinion, it had taken a lot of integrity to humble himself and appeal for a job, hat in hand, when after today he wouldn't have to do any labor, ever, if he didn't want to. He'd even endured Bolly's sermon, and the sportswriter hadn't gone easy on his personality flaws.

Although he had to admit that Bolly's memory was sound. The man also had a keen insight into his nature. That was why he hadn't asked forgiveness or tried to justify himself. He'd never been the touchy-feely type. He'd never wanted to pat his teammates on the ass after a big play, and he sure as hell hadn't wanted any of them patting his. He'd left all that rah-rah bullshit to the benchwarmers, while he was out there on the field doing the bone-breaking, bloody work, getting creamed by tacklers who got marks on their helmets if they sacked him.

But why was he stewing about Bolly's censure? None of that mattered. Now he had only two teammates, and all he had to do to make them happy was get one of them pregnant. Easy enough.

He had indigestion as he walked inside the bank building. He blamed it on the jalapeños, not nerves. He looked about him, as though expecting to be spotlighted and exposed for the most gullible fool ever to walk the planet.

But it went exactly as Foster Speakman had told him it would. No muss, no fuss. He made an inquiry at the information desk, then was escorted to an elevator that went into a subterranean part of the bank, where a polite, grandmotherly type asked him to sign a card. She compared it with the signature card that Foster Speakman had filed, as promised. Satisfied, the grandmother showed Griff into a cubicle.

His heart was knocking in a beat out of time with the Yanni filtering through the overhead speakers. Grandmother delivered the box, told him to take his time and to press the button on the wall when finished, then withdrew. The key Speakman had given him last night was in the pocket of his jeans. He fished it out and unlocked the box.

From the bank, Griff drove straight to NorthPark for a shopping spree. He liked his jeans old and "worked in," but he bought two new pairs anyway—because he could. His boots were too comfortable to replace, but he had them shined. He found three designer shirts in Neiman's that didn't look too faggy. He changed in the dressing room and wore one of them out of the store.

None of the sports jackets in the Armani boutique were wide enough in the shoulders for him, but he found one that would work with some tailoring. He was told he could pick it up in a few days.

He bought a four-hundred-dollar pair of sunglasses. Odd that styles of sunglasses had changed more than anything in the past five years. He also bought a cell phone. It probably wouldn't have taken as long to buy a house. By the time all the added features had been demonstrated to him, and the calling plan options explained, and his voicemail retrieval set up for one-digit dialing, he was impatient to get out of there and actually use the damn thing to make a call.

Which was to Marcia. He dialed the first number listed on the card she had given him and got an anonymous, innocuous recording asking him to leave a message, which he did. Waiting on her to return his call, he drove around the area, taking in all the commerce, going past his old haunts and favorite restaurants. Some were still in business, others had given way to new.

When, after an hour, Marcia still hadn't called, he dialed a number that belonged to one of her girls. Young, gorgeous, satisfaction guaranteed.

"Hello?"

She had a husky, sexy voice. He liked her already. "Hi. My name is Griff Burkett. I'm a client of Marcia's. She recommended I call you."

At first he thought she'd hiccuped, but then he realized she was crying. "Marcia—" She got choked up and couldn't finish. Then she wailed, "Oh, God! It's just so awful!"

"What's so awful?"

"Marcia's in the hospital."

Presbyterian Hospital was surrounded by a network of roads under repair. By the time he wound his way through the construction zones and the detours they imposed, Griff was swearing as profusely as he was sweating.

He jogged across the seeming miles of parking lot and, after finally reaching the main entrance lobby, had to wait his turn at the information booth. He was raw with impatience by the time the attendant gave him Marcia's room number.

Standing outside her door, leaning against the wall, was the neighbor Griff had seen last night getting off the elevator. When he noticed Griff striding down the corridor toward him, he jumped as if he'd been struck with a cattle prod and positioned himself in front of the hospital room door.

Frantically, he waved his hands in front of his face. "No, no. Go away. She won't want you to see her like this."

"Why is she here?" Griff hadn't got anything out of the hysterical girl on the phone.

The man stopped his protestations and lowered his hands. His sharp, foxy face contorted into a mask of misery. His eyes were already red from crying. They began to leak fresh tears. "I can't believe this happened to her. At first I thought it was you, although you didn't look the type. The savagery of it was—"

"Savagery?"

The man started waving his hands in front of his face again, this time in embarrassment over his emotion. Frustrated, Griff moved him aside, ignored the No Visitors sign, and went into the room. The blinds were drawn against the glare of the afternoon sun, and all the lights were off. But he could see well enough, and what he saw caused him to halt midway between the door and the hospital bed.

"Oh, Jesus."

"I told you it was savage." The neighbor had followed him in. "I'm Dwight, by the way."

"Griff. And I didn't do this to her."

"I realize that. Now."

"What happened?"

"About an hour after I saw you in the lobby, my doorbell rang. I wasn't expecting a guest, and the concierge hadn't announced anyone. I looked at the security monitor and saw Marcia, standing there in the foyer, only sort of . . . doubled over. She was . . . like this."

She'd had the living daylights beat out of her. Griff couldn't see all of her, of course, but there were bruises and swelling on every inch of exposed skin. If the rest of her looked like her face, she was lucky to be alive. Several cuts had been closed with butterfly clips. Blood had matted her hair to her head. Her face was so misshapen with swelling that if he hadn't known who she was, he would never have recognized her.

"Her jaw was broken," Dwight whispered. "They did surgery this morning to wire it together. Last night, no amount of morphine could dull the pain."

Griff lowered his head and took several deep breaths. When he raised his head, he asked with deadly calm, "Who was her next client? After me. Someone was coming at midnight. She hustled me out so she could get ready for him. Do you know his name?" He turned to Dwight suddenly, and his expression caused the man to back away in fear. "Do you know his name?" he repeated angrily.

A moan from the bed drew their attention to Marcia. In two strides Griff was at her side. Being careful of the IV needle taped to her hand, he gently pressed it between his. "Hey there," he said softly.

Both eyes were swollen shut, but she managed to pry one of them open. The lovely green iris was floating in a lake of bright red. Since she couldn't move her jaw to speak, she merely made a whimpering sound in her throat.

"Shh." He bent down and kissed her forehead, barely letting his lips touch for fear of hurting her. "Take advantage of the drugs. Rest." He kissed her forehead again, then straightened up and turned to Dwight, who was standing at the foot of her bed, sniffling softly.

"Did you call the police?"

Dwight shook his head.

"Why the hell not?"

"She couldn't talk because of her jaw, but she became hysterical when I mentioned calling the police. I guess . . ." He glanced over his shoulder to make sure there were no eavesdroppers about. "Because of her profession, she didn't want the police involved."

"But you called 911."

"Immediately. Paramedics were there within minutes."

"How did you explain her condition?"

"I have a circular staircase in my apartment. I told them she'd gone up to use the powder room and had fallen on her way down."

"And they believed that?"

"Probably not. But they left it to the ER staff to summon a policeman. He didn't believe the staircase story either and urged Marcia to identify her attacker by writing down his name. She refused."

With limited strength, Marcia squeezed Griff's hand. He leaned down over her again and gently lifted a strand of hair away from a patch of her scalp that had been shaved to allow for sutures. "Who was it, Marcia? Who were you seeing after me?"

Barely moving, she shook her head. She applied more pressure to his hand, and he realized she wanted him to lean in close enough to hear her speak. He bent low, placing his ear just above her lips.

When he heard the single word she whispered, he jerked his head up and looked down into the single eye she could hold open. She closed it for several seconds, letting him know that he'd heard correctly.

"This was about *me?*"

She nodded.

Rage surged through him. His veins swelled and pulsed with it. But his voice remained remarkably calm. "He's going to die." He said it as a fact, meaning it unequivocally, telling her that she could bank on it. "Stanley Rodarte is going to die."

Now he understood why she had refused to call the police. Rodarte would have made it understood that accusing him would bring on a reprisal even worse than the beating he'd already given her.

Most sickening was knowing that the only reason Rodarte had victimized Marcia was to send a message to Griff. In that, he'd succeeded. Griff read the message loud and clear. Rodarte wasn't finished with him yet.

Well, guess what, cocksucker, Griff thought. *I've only begun with you.*

"I'll make him pay for this," he vowed to Marcia in a whisper. "I swear to you."

She pressed his hand. He bent down to her lips again. The garbled sounds came from the back of her throat, but she managed to make her warning understood. "Be careful of him."

CHAPTER

9

THE CALL CAME EARLY ON A MONDAY morning, just as he was waking up, but before he'd got out of bed. He rolled over, sleepily groped for his new cell phone on the nightstand, and flipped it open. "Hello?"

"Mr. Burkett?"

That woke him up. "Yeah. Here."

She didn't identify herself. She didn't have to. "Would one o'clock today be convenient for you?"

"One o'clock?" Like he had to think about it. Like he might have a conflict. Like he had something else to do. "One o'clock's fine."

"Here's the address." She gave him a number on Windsor Street. "Got it?"

"Got it."

She hung up. Griff snapped his phone shut, then lay there clutching it, clutching the fact that they were really going through with it. Then he sat bolt upright. The hitch in his back protested loudly enough to cause him to catch his breath. He threw off the sheet, got out of bed, and, buck naked, went clambering through his apartment until he found a pen and paper to write down the address. He was certain he'd committed it to memory, but he was taking no chances.

He went into the bathroom. Standing at the toilet, he looked down at himself and muttered, "Don't even think about getting stage fright."

As expected, he'd passed the physical exam with flying colors. The nurse had come through for him in only two days. The report showed his EKG to be normal, his lungs clear. He had low blood pressure, low cholesterol, and a low PSA—he thought that had something to do with his prostate. His sperm count, by contrast, was high. Excellent.

He'd put the report, along with his cell phone number, in the addressed and stamped envelope Speakman had given him for this purpose, and dropped it into the nearest mailbox.

That had been two weeks ago. Since then, he'd moved to another apartment and acquired a tan.

Using his newfound cash, he had abandoned the roach-infested place and moved into a duplex. Living strictly on a cash basis presented the expected problems. Eyebrows were raised when he signed his lease, but the management of the complex took the cash without asking too many questions. His new place wasn't in the ritziest of neighborhoods, which would have required letters of recommendation and closer scrutiny, but it was worlds above where he'd been.

The complex had a security gate, well-kept grounds, a gym, and a pool—which accounted for his tan. After moving in his new furniture and setting up a sound system and plasma-screen, high-definition TV (the best invention ever), he didn't have much else to do except work out—it had been during a moment of pique that he had considered getting fat—and lounge by the pool.

He also went to the hospital nearly every day to visit Marcia, and he always took something with him. He'd taken flowers until the nursing staff complained that the room was becoming a greenhouse. Dwight, who'd proved to be a steadfast and attentive friend to her, chided Griff for not being more creative. So one day he took her a teddy bear. The next day he carried in a goofy hat. "To wear until you can get out of here and have your hair done," he told her as he gently placed it on her head.

She still couldn't speak, but she communicated her gratitude for his visits with her expressive eyes. By now she could take short strolls down the corridor. Dwight had referred a plastic surgeon who, according to Dwight's affluent and well-preserved clientele, was a genius. After examining Marcia, the surgeon promised to do great things but said he couldn't even begin until she had completely healed.

She still sipped her meals through a straw, and every time Griff witnessed that, his fury resurfaced. What he conjectured was that Rodarte had gone up to Marcia's penthouse immediately after their encounter in the garage. Expecting her client, she'd opened the door to him. He'd pumped her for information about Griff, and when she didn't—actually couldn't—divulge any, he'd tried beating it out of her.

From Rodarte's standpoint, it was a failed mission only insofar as he still didn't know what Griff's future plans were. But he'd had the satisfaction of terrorizing and disfiguring a beautiful woman who was an acquaintance of Griff's. Knowing he could get away with it because of her profession was a bonus. Rodarte was a lowlife, a bully who would enjoy inflicting pain just for the hell of it. Gratifying his mean streak was really all the motivation he needed.

Griff couldn't think about it without becoming enraged. On one of his visits to the hospital, he again broached the subject of reporting Rodarte to the police, but the fear and anguish that filled Marcia's eyes dissuaded him.

"He won't get away with it," he told her. "I promise you."

There had been no sign of Rodarte since the assault. Griff knew where to find him, but he didn't dare go looking. Rodarte would love for him to come crashing down doors threatening bloodshed. No doubt that was the kind of reckless reaction he had hoped to provoke.

Griff wouldn't give Rodarte the satisfaction of getting his butt thrown in jail again, nor did he wish to make matters worse for his suffering friend. So for the time being, he honored Marcia's silent pleas and didn't seek retribution.

Today thoughts of Rodarte were obscured by Laura Speakman's call. Having had two weeks to prepare for it mentally, he was surprised by how nervous he was. To distract himself until the appointed time, he went for a five-mile run, then worked out with weights in the gym. His goal wasn't to build himself back up to his football playing size but to maintain the lean, strong form he had now.

He followed the weights session with laps in the pool. But when it occurred to him that too much exertion might be detrimental to his sexual performance, he immediately got out.

He flossed before he brushed. He clipped his fingernails. He put on his new Armani sports jacket. He left his apartment at twelve-thirty. He arrived at the address at twelve thirty-seven. He had twenty-three minutes to kill.

The house was in an established area that had a Neighborhood Crime Watch, where residents were on the alert for people who lurked about and looked suspicious. He decided it would be better not to wait parked on the tree-lined street where he would fit that description to a tee.

Instead, he pulled into the narrow driveway and followed it around to the rear of the house, where there was a sheltered parking area and a neat backyard, made shady by two venerable sycamore trees. A privacy fence separated the property from the houses on either side.

In this older neighborhood, people were buying the houses and either razing them to rebuild on the coveted wooded lots or completely renovating. Griff guessed this was one of the latter, because it appeared as though what had once been the garage had been converted into a room. But it had been done well, and the house had retained its character and charm.

He'd bought the red Honda from Wyatt Turner. It wasn't what he wanted to drive, but it ran okay and he figured that paying cash for a flashy new car—soon after shelling out a deposit on the duplex—would send up all kinds of red flags to his probation officer, the IRS, the FBI. Even his lawyer eyed him suspiciously when Griff asked how much he wanted for the car and then counted out hundred-dollar bills to pay for it. Turner didn't ask how he'd come by the cash. Griff didn't volunteer the information.

Now he kept the Honda's motor running so he could leave the air conditioner on. He drummed his thumbs on the steering wheel and hummed accompaniment to the country song playing on the radio. The artist had sung the national anthem to open one of the Cowboys' home games, then, at the invitation of the owner, had watched all four quarters from the sideline.

After an easy win against Tampa Bay, he'd asked Griff for his autograph. This guy was a hot new star. He'd won several Grammy Awards, but he'd hem-hawed and stammered, tongue-tied and starstruck, as he extended Griff his program and a Bic pen.

Today that singer wouldn't piss on him if he was on fire.

He heard her car over the radio and his own humming. He shut down the Honda, took a deep breath, exhaled, and got out.

He followed the driveway along the west side of the house and came up behind her on the small porch as she was unlocking the front door. Sensing him there, she turned, startled. "Oh."

"Hi."

"I didn't realize you were already here."

"I parked around back."

"Oh," she said again, then hurriedly unlocked the door and went in ahead of him. She closed the door as soon as he'd cleared the threshold. A short entry hall opened into a living area. Louvered shutters were closed over the wide windows, so the room was dim. It was basically square, with a small fireplace in the center of one wall, a hardwood floor, standard pieces of furniture.

She lowered the strap of her handbag from her shoulder but clutched the bag against her chest, as if she was afraid he might grab it from her. "I thought I'd got here ahead of you."

"I don't live far."

"I see."

"Couple of miles. I got here sooner than I expected."

"Have you been waiting long?"

"Not too long. But you're not late. You're right on time."

During this scintillating conversation, she had adjusted the wall thermostat. Cool air began whirring through the ceiling vents. Griff was grateful. He'd begun to perspire. He wanted to take off his sports jacket but thought she might read something suggestive into the removal of a garment, any garment. Since he didn't have a clue how this was supposed to go, he figured he'd follow her lead, even though doing so involved some sweating.

She was dressed for the office. Her suit was black, but the fabric was summer weight. Linen, he thought. The skirt came to the tops of her knees, the jacket was nipped in at the waist. Under it was a pale pink top that draped across her chest and looked soft. Same jewelry as before. Black high-heeled sandals. Her toenails were painted a pearly ivory color.

He'd noticed all this as he came up behind her on the porch. He didn't dare scope her out now, because she was drawn as taut as a piano wire, acting uptight and all business. If she'd had DO NOT TOUCH tattooed on her forehead, it couldn't have been any plainer how she felt about being alone with him.

"There are some magazines in there." She pointed out an armoire in the corner. "And a TV with . . . with videos." Simultaneously they looked at the closed doors of the armoire, then back at each other.

"Okay," he said.

"Give me a few minutes. Then, whenever you're ready, I'll be in the bedroom."

And with that, she walked across the living room, down a hallway, turned in to a room at the end of it, and closed the door.

Well, at least now he knew how it was going to be. They'd do it like porcupines.

He shrugged off his sports jacket and folded it over the back of a chair. He went to the armoire and opened the double doors. It contained a treasure trove of pornography. He sorted through the stack of magazines. A panoply of possibilities. Something for everybody. Same with the collection of videos.

Who had stocked this stuff? he wondered. Foster? Her? Somehow he couldn't see them visiting a triple-X video store, browsing among the titles for something that would turn him on. "What do you think he'd like, honey? *Twixt Twins* or *Euro Snatch*?

Maybe they'd sent Manuelo on that errand; one of the magazines was in Spanish. Maybe Manuelo was into porno. Maybe that accounted for his vacuous smile.

Griff recognized his musing for what it was: stalling.

He wandered into the kitchen at the back of the house. There was bottled water and a six-pack of Diet Coke in the fridge. He took a bottle of water, twisted off the cap, drank some as he went into the former garage, which was now a sunroom, although not that much sunlight was coming in through the drawn blinds. The house was as sealed off as Mrs. Speakman.

He returned to the living room and sat down on the sofa that faced the armoire. He tugged off his boots, wiggled his toes, and tried telling himself he was comfortable and relaxed. He sorted through the magazines again, and the glossy photos on the covers got things started. But, deciding he preferred his own imagination, he set the magazines aside, pulled his shirttail out, and unbuttoned his jeans.

He leaned back against the sofa cushions, closed his eyes, and recalled the night he'd been with Marcia. But erotic images of her were instantly obliterated by those of her lying in her hospital bed looking like something out of a war zone.

Shit!

Before he lost what he had, he searched his mind for something to think about that would keep it up. What had recently tickled his fancy or even sparked his curiosity? That mind search took only a few seconds, but it was the real deal, all right. He became instantly aroused.

And once he really focused on it . . .

He tapped on the closed door.

"You can come in."

He opened the door and stepped into the bedroom. It was completely furnished, although later he couldn't remember a damn thing about it except the pastel sheet that covered her to her waist. She was lying on her back, a pillow beneath her head, her hands clasped over her stomach. She still had on the pink top, and he could see a sliver of bra strap at her shoulder.

And under the sheet?

Her jacket and skirt were folded on a chair. Shoes were beside the bed.

Panties? He didn't see them. On or off?

In any case, he was glad he'd followed a hunch and kept his clothes on. Obviously getting naked wasn't part of the program.

But out of necessity his jeans were unbuttoned. Her glance in that vicinity was so fleeting he wondered if what she saw even registered before she looked up toward the ceiling and kept her eyes trained on a spot there.

He walked to the side of the bed and faced away from it. She didn't say anything, so neither did he. He took off his jeans but left his boxers on. For good measure—literally—he discreetly squeezed himself through his shorts and felt a reassuring bead of moisture dampen the cloth. Then keeping his back to her, he lifted the sheet and lay down. He felt ridiculous modestly pulling the sheet over his legs, but he did.

He lay there on his back, also staring at the ceiling, for thirty seconds or so. But this was a real mood killer, not to mention the jeopardy in which it was placing his ability to make a kid.

He turned onto his side to face her. She didn't speak, or even blink. But she opened her legs. The one nearest him made contact. The outside of her thigh glanced the top of his. Just that much skin-to-skin contact gave him the needed staying power.

He moved onto her, situated himself between her legs, and pushed his boxers past his hips. She raised her knees, not in a way that was particularly inviting, but at least they were anatomically positioned to have sexual intercourse. He probed where he was supposed to probe.

His heart bumped. No panties. Just . . . her.

She turned her head aside and closed her eyes.

Which made him angry. It was a given that this was going to be awkward. Difficult even. But she'd done nothing so far to make it any easier. While he'd been out there thinking dirty thoughts to get himself aroused, what had she been doing? Obviously nothing. Masturbation probably wasn't in her vocabulary, but couldn't she have done something to make herself more receptive? If not for his sake, then for her own? Couldn't she tilt her hips up just a little? Shift forward, shift back? Take him in her hand and guide him home? *Something?*

The only thing she did was to turn her face away.

The more he thought about it, the angrier he

became. This was her idea, not his. She was orchestrating this, not him. She didn't want conversation beforehand? All right. He didn't have anything to say to her anyway.

She wanted to do it with their clothes on? Okay by him.

No foreplay? Who needed it? Not him.

She wanted to turn her head away like she was about to be sacrificed or something? Let her cope any ol' way she liked.

She wanted to lie as stiff and unyielding as a board? Fine.

But it wasn't fine, because it soon became apparent that he couldn't penetrate her without hurting her, and the thought of hurting her—

"Just do it," she said.

So he did it.

After that, biology and primal instinct took over. The tight resistance only compelled him to push harder, deeper. He closed his eyes, but only because he couldn't stand to watch her grimace. That was what he told himself anyway. He tried to empty his mind of all thought except the money he was going to have.

That's it, think about the money. Don't think about her. Don't think about how this feels or how snug . . . Shit! Don't think snug. Don't think . . . ah, hell . . .

With a long groan, he emptied himself, then forgot the rules and collapsed on top of her. His face remained pressed into the pillow, near her head, strands of her hair curling against his nose, until he could catch his breath.

She didn't move when he levered himself up and

withdrew. She just lay there with her face still turned to the wall, eyes closed, a vertical frown between her eyebrows. He got out of bed, pulled up his boxers, and stepped into his jeans. When he finished buttoning up and buckling his belt, he looked over his shoulder. She had lowered her knees. The sheet had been pulled up to her waist again. She lay with one forearm across her eyes.

"Are you all right?"

She only nodded.

He stood there, feeling guilty, although he didn't know why. He felt like the time Ellie had caught him stealing a ten-dollar bill from her wallet and then had insisted that he keep it. He opened his mouth to say something, called it back, then finally said, "Look, you told me to—"

"I'm fine, Mr. Burkett." She lowered her arm and opened her eyes, but she didn't look in his direction. "It betters my chances to conceive if I lie here for a half hour or so. That's all."

"Oh. So, you're okay?"

"Yes."

She didn't thank him. It sure as hell seemed inappropriate to thank her.

She was pulling on her suit jacket when she walked into the living room. Seeing him on the sofa, she stopped, shocked to find him still there. Gauging by her expression, she wasn't at all happy about it, either. She shoved her arm into the sleeve and wrestled the jacket into place. "Why didn't you leave?"

He stood up. "I—"

"You should be gone by now."

"I—"

"You shouldn't have waited, Mr. Burkett." Her voice sounded like tearing cloth. She was either mad as hell or on the edge of hysteria. He couldn't be sure which, but this was the most emotion he'd ever seen from her. Her cheeks were red. The calm, cool, and collected lady of the manor was about to lose it. "Why didn't you just *go*?"

Quietly he said, "Your car has mine blocked in."

In an instant, her posture went from rigid to limp. She released her breath slowly, touched her forehead with the tips of her fingers, then her flaming cheek with the backs of them, looked embarrassed. "Oh."

"I would have moved it myself, but you had the keys."

He gestured toward her handbag. She looked down where it hung at her side. "Right." Then, changing back into the got-it-together businesswoman persona, she said, "I apologize for holding you up."

"No problem."

"You should have come and told me."

"If it helps to keep lying down after . . . you know . . . I didn't mind waiting awhile. The whole point of this is to get you pregnant."

She nodded, then consulted her wristwatch. "I must go or I'm going to be late for a meeting. Will you reset the thermostat, please?"

"Sure."

"Just pull the door closed after you. It will lock. I'll be in touch, one way or the other."

She couldn't get out of there fast enough, and her haste to leave made him feel ornery. He had decided he wasn't going to say anything. If he was smart, he wouldn't.

But.

He said, "I wondered why you would go along with this, Mrs. Speakman."

Already halfway through the entry, she halted, turned, looked at him. "You know why, Mr. Burkett. I want a child."

"But *this*?" He tapped his fly, then motioned toward her middle. The gesture caused a frisson in her cool bearing. Some of the high color came back into her cheeks. He went to her, stopping only a few steps away. "After meeting both of you, I could almost understand your husband."

"Your understanding isn't important to us. Or necessary."

"Okay. Say I wanted to understand for my own peace of mind. Your husband is eccentric, maybe even altogether crazy, but looking at this child and heir thing from his point of view, from a rich man's point of view, I could sorta get it. *Sorta*." He shook his head, frowning with perplexity. "But you, I just couldn't figure."

"So don't bother trying."

He took another step closer, crowding her, making her uncomfortable, wanting to because in the bedroom she had made him feel like a vandal ravaging the village virgin. "Why, I asked myself, would you agree to making a baby this way?" His eyes held hers. He lowered his voice. "And now I know."

Coldly, she said, *"Now?"*

"Now that I know why your husband is in that wheelchair."

* * *

I can do this, Laura asserted to herself as she entered the conference room. Everyone else had assembled. She moved to the head of the table. "Sorry I'm late."

"We promise not to tell Foster," one of the department heads quipped.

"Thank you. We all know that punctuality is a religion to him."

"Long lunch?" someone teased.

Her hand faltered just a bit as she reached for the water carafe. "No, just an errand that took longer than I anticipated."

The errand hadn't taken that long. Her recovery from it had. She wondered how women who had extramarital affairs in the middle of the day completed their afternoons with any level of composure. She'd been certain that when she returned to her office, her assistant, Kay, would look at her with accusation and say, "You've just had sex."

But apparently there were no visible signs of how she'd spent her lunch hour. Kay had treated her as she always did, efficiently reminding her of the meeting as she handed her a stack of phone messages in the order of their priority.

To everyone else, this was any ordinary Monday. To Foster, it was a day of monumental importance. For her, one of substantial ambiguity. Foster was spending the day at home. She didn't have that luxury. She had to face this assembly of corporate heads while, less than an hour ago, she'd had sex with a stranger.

Yes, it was strictly for the purpose of procreation, and, yes, she'd done it with her husband's

blessing, and, yes, for the sake of their future together she could do it again until they were successful. She *would* do it.

She sipped from her water glass, then smiled
down the length of the conference table. "Who's up
first?"

"Me," said the man in charge of baggage handling. "Unfortunately, we've had an incident in
Austin. Foster isn't going to like it."

Foster was still very much a presence, but lately
she had been his proxy for some of the executive
meetings. The daily commute to the office, short as
it was and with Manuelo along to facilitate it, had
proved to be too much. So Foster had limited his
days in the office to two per week. On days when it
was mandatory for the department heads to meet,
Laura presided, then in the evening she would give
him a detailed recounting of what had been discussed.

In only a few short years she'd gone from asking
passengers "Coffee or tea?" to serving as the CEO's
understudy. When Foster had hired her as Hazel
Cooper's replacement, her transition into management had gone smoothly. For years, she had been
preparing herself for such a position. It was what
she had aspired to and, having been given the opportunity, she felt confident she could meet the
challenges.

But when her job description suddenly expanded to include dealing with a disabled husband
as well as assuming many of his corporate responsibilities, the transition wasn't quite so seamless.
Up until that point in her life, she'd been resistant
to delegating any responsibility. Now she had no

choice. Minor and routine jobs that she had formerly insisted on doing herself, she began assigning to subordinates.

Even so, the largest share of the workload remained hers. Nor could the tasks she did for Foster be turned over to someone else. Only she could do them because Foster demanded they be done in a particular order and in a particular way, *his* particular way, which was a way far more meticulous than anyone else's. His insistence on perfection put a strain on her time.

But no matter how difficult and demanding her schedule became, she refused to buckle under. Quitting, or even slacking off, wasn't an option. She was doing what must be done, and she would continue to.

However, she had begun to fear the impact motherhood would have on the careful balance she was maintaining. How could she possibly be a full-time mother, which she wanted to be, without detracting from her duties as wife, department head, and stand-in CEO? The prospect of juggling that additional responsibility was daunting. But if—*when*—she was forced to confront it, she would.

At present there were other matters demanding her attention, such as this one involving baggage handling. "What kind of incident?" she asked that department head.

"The worst. Stolen bags."

"You're right. Foster isn't going to like it. Details?"

The explanation was lengthy and involved, and generated discussion around the table. Laura tried to concentrate on what was being said, but her mind wandered. Her ability to focus simply wasn't there. She'd left it behind in that small, tidy house on Windsor Street, along with her dignity.

Why, I asked myself, would you agree to making a baby this way?

"Laura?"

She yanked her mind back to the business at hand. Everyone was looking at her, and she wondered how many times she'd been addressed before she realized it. "I'm sorry. My mind drifted for a moment."

The question was repeated. Laura answered. The meeting continued. While she wasn't wholly attuned, she wasn't caught again being inattentive. But as soon as there was a convenient point to adjourn, she did so. "We'll pick up the rest at the next meeting, okay? I've got a killer schedule this afternoon."

As the others filed out, no one seemed especially curious about her absentmindedness or abrupt adjournment. Joe McDonald did stop on his way to the door. "Hard day?"

"Harder than most."

"Maybe this will cheer you up." From behind his back, he produced a large white envelope and, with a flourish, laid it on the table in front of her. "Ta-da!"

"What's this?"

"Your baby."

"My *what*?"

"Uh . . ." Obviously taken aback by her stunned reaction, he said, "What I mean is, you've been waiting a long time for it. Check it out."

Having recovered from his choice of words, she

opened the envelope and slid the contents onto the table. It was an eleven-by-fourteen artist's rendering of a SunSouth jet with a new and distinctive logo on the fuselage.

"Oh, my God!" Laura exclaimed. "This looks great, Joe! Truly great!"

He hooked his thumbs into his suspenders. "I thought you'd like it."

"Like it?" she said, unable to contain her excitement. "I *love* it." She ran her finger over the artwork as she read the words printed on the airplane. "SunSouth Select."

Joe beamed. "As I said, your baby."

CHAPTER

10

JOE LEFT HER, AND LAURA DECIDED TO TAKE advantage of the solitude in the conference room. She remained seated in the tall leather chair at the head of the table—the one in which Foster had sat the first time she saw him—and looked again at the four-color rendering of the sleek jet.

SunSouth Select was a concept that she'd been working on for more than a year. It was a service-oriented innovation for the business traveler that she hoped to implement before SunSouth's competitors did something similar. She wanted Sun-South to be the initiator, not an imitator.

Joe seemed surprised that Foster hadn't yet seen the syllabus. Laura had worked on it for months, and once it was done, Joe had assumed she would take it straight to Foster. "No," she told him. "I want SunSouth Select to be a surprise. I want to present it to him as a complete package."

"You want to have all your ducks in a row."

"Exactly. And I'm still waiting on some market analyses and cost projections. When they're ready and I've had a chance to study them, I'll lay out the entire plan for him."

This was uncustomary. Always before, she and Foster had worked in tandem. One rarely made a move without the other knowing about it. While it was true that she wanted to surprise him with a kit-and-caboodle proposal, it was also true that, when she did, she wanted his undivided attention. She hadn't had that in months. He'd been preoccupied with finding the right man to sire their child.

He thought of little else, talked of little else. Every conversation included at least one reference to a child and its conception. That was the prevailing issue of their lives now. If she became pregnant, she knew that Foster would become an expert on prenatal care, diet, exercise. He would spend hours researching and committing to memory every aspect of pregnancy. No doubt he would chart their child's development on a daily basis.

He had once been quoted in *Business Week* as saying that his airline's success was in large part due to his OCD—obsessive-compulsive disorder. The interviewer thought he was joking. He wasn't.

He had been diagnosed as an adolescent, although he had exhibited the symptoms in early childhood. His parents had thought his compulsions went hand in glove with his brilliant mind and were nothing to worry about. But when those compulsions began to interfere with normal function and everyday life, his parents had sought psychiatric help.

Foster was put on medication to keep the disorder under control. He wasn't "healed," however, and so in a very real sense his obsessiveness was indeed responsible for his fanatic attention to detail, and therefore for SunSouth's extraordinary success.

Unless the weather was prohibitive, late arrivals and departures were not tolerated at SunSouth Airlines.

Each packet of peanuts contained exactly the same number. One too few, the customer was cheated. One too many cost the airline money.

Flight attendants and pilots did not alter their uniforms, not even by wearing nonregulation cuff links or an unapproved shade of panty hose.

If he'd had less charisma, Foster's obsessiveness would have incited mutiny by subordinates. But he was so personally disarming that it was indulged. Most regarded it with amusement instead of impatience. He was even teased about it. It was looked upon as an idiosyncrasy, an endearing one at that. And no one, not even his sternest critics, could argue with his success.

But Laura had a different perspective on Foster's OCD because she lived with it. She covered for him to keep it less noticeable to colleagues. Only she knew how much it governed his life. Increasingly so, it seemed. His compulsions were an integral part of him. Because she loved him, she accepted and tolerated them. But doing so had once been easier. Before.

Laura got up and walked to the window, rubbing her arms to ward off the chill of the air-conditioning. She twirled the wand on the blinds and looked through the slats at the traffic speeding along the expressway. A SunSouth jet, only minutes into its flight, was banking toward the west. The 3:45 to Denver, she thought automatically.

She watched the jet as it climbed, the sun reflecting off its silver fuselage, hurting her eyes when the shaft of light pierced them. But then she realized that her eyes stung with the need to cry. Resting her head against the window frame, she closed her eyes tightly, squeezing out tears. She whispered, "I want my life back."

Foster had waited one year after Elaine's death before asking Laura out. Initially Laura had misinterpreted the invitation, believing he had invited her to attend a black-tie charity event with him for some business purpose. But when several dozen white roses were delivered to her apartment in advance of his picking her up, she began to think perhaps there was more to it. Undeniably, the thought of that made her feel bubbly on the inside.

By the end of the evening there was no question that it had been a bona fide date. If Foster had asked any other executive—say, the CFO—to accompany him, he wouldn't have taken hold of both his hands and kissed his cheek good night.

Their evenings out became more frequent. There were dinners together after work, sailing on area lakes on Saturday afternoons, and Sunday suppers, which she cooked at her place. She attended his polo matches, and he had no compunction about kissing her in front of his teammates after a victory. She became his regular date to private dinner parties and public events. She stopped accepting other dates, even invitations from her tennis buddy, who began teasing her about her new beau.

She couldn't apply such a frivolous moniker to Foster Speakman, but away from the office he acted like one. The more time they spent alone together, the less chaste their embraces became. She had started devoting a lot of thought to him, his smile, his eyes, his mannerisms. She found herself engaging in gauzy daydreams about him unlike any she'd had about other men, not even in adolescence. She'd always enjoyed an active social life. She'd had a generous number of boyfriends, and enough lovers to be confident of her allure, but not so many that she need be embarrassed by the number.

But among them there were no standouts, no disappointing heartbreaks, or near-miss commitments. Because every romantic relationship she'd ever had, from the first car date to the last man she'd slept with, had been qualified. It could not interfere with her ambition.

Which now placed her in a real conundrum with Foster. Because of the professional implications, neither acknowledged their increasing intimacy and longing for more. Their kissing and groping left them fevered and frustrated, but each was determined to preserve their working relationship.

One evening while they were cuddled on the sofa in her den, watching a movie on TV, he suddenly reached for the remote and turned it off. "Thank you," she said. "I was finding it hard to get into, too."

"I loved Elaine with all my heart, Laura."

Recognizing the seriousness of his tone, she sat up and looked into his face. "Yes, you did. I know that."

"If she had lived, I would have loved her forever."

"I don't doubt that."

"I'll always cherish her memory and the years we had together."

None of this came as a surprise to Laura. She'd seen them together on numerous occasions following that first time at their home. It was obvious how deeply they had loved each other. Since Elaine's death, Foster had honored her by establishing a foundation to raise money for leukemia research. He wasn't just a mouthpiece with a checkbook, either, but a crusading advocate and hands-on fund-raiser. In death, as in life, Elaine was a vital part of him.

He stroked Laura's cheek. "But Elaine is no longer here. You are. And I'm in love with you."

He spent that night with her. Most nights following that, they spent together. In the office, they continued as they always had done, performing their individual jobs, conducting themselves in a professional manner, treating each other no differently than they treated their colleagues. They were confident no one knew about their personal relationship, but Laura learned later that they had fooled only themselves. Everyone knew.

One morning, she walked into his office unannounced and laid an envelope on his desk. "What's that?"

"My resignation."

He struggled to contain his smile. "We're not paying you enough? You've had a better offer?"

She sat down in the chair facing his desk. "Foster, the last four months have been the happiest of my life. Also the most miserable."

"Well, I hope that being with me has been the happy part."

She gave him a soft look. "You know how happy I am to be with you. But the secrecy makes it seem . . ."

"Sordid?"

"Yes. And sleazy. I'm sleeping with my boss. As a career woman, I don't like what that suggests about me. I don't like the connotation co-workers would apply to it. I don't want to give up my job. It's what I've worked so hard to attain. You know how much I love it.

"But I can't possibly give you up," she said, her voice turning husky with emotion. "Between the two, I love you more than I love my job. So . . ." She gestured toward the envelope lying on his desk. "I must leave SunSouth."

He picked up the envelope then and looked at it, turning it this way and that as though contemplating the contents. "Or," he said, "you could marry me."

Elaine Speakman had set a precedent by serving on the board of directors, so no one cried nepotism. No one wanted to anyway. When Foster and Laura announced their plans to the other executives and the board members, the only discussion was the date the nuptials would take place and if they would be taking a SunSouth jet on their honeymoon.

If there was watercooler talk about her marrying Foster for his money, or any other self-serving reason, Laura never knew of it. Even if she had been aware of such scuttlebutt, she would have ignored it. While some may have regarded what had happened as a Cinderella story—in those very words it had been hinted at in a newspaper column—she knew her only reason for marrying him was that she loved him wholly and completely. She couldn't be bothered by the conjectures of mean-spirited people.

Their marriage was covered extensively in the press, although there were no pictures accompanying the stories. They kept the wedding itself private, inviting only their most intimate friends to the chapel service and the dinner following it.

Foster paid lip service to moving from his family estate, but Laura realized what a sacrifice that would be for him. He loved his family home and hugged her tightly when she told him she loved it, too, and that that was where they would stay and make their life together.

She moved in, changing very little of Elaine's decor. Like his wealth, his love for Elaine was only another aspect of him. Laura didn't feel threatened by his late wife's memory, any more than she was intimidated by his fortune.

Foster would have preferred her to be pregnant by the time they returned from their honeymoon in Fiji. When she demurred, he had teased her about her biological clock. "I'm thirty-one!" she exclaimed.

He placed his ear against her lower body. "But I can hear it ticking."

Even so, she had begged for time to be a bride before she became a mother. It was a decision that later seemed terribly selfish, and one she would always regret.

That first year they were kept busy with the burgeoning airline and settling into married life. Although Laura was to learn that "settling" was a foreign concept to her husband. The man never rested. The more he had to do, the more he got done. He was a tireless, incessant generator of energy. He had the work ethic of a Trojan but was also a proponent of la dolce vita. His enthusiasm for life and living was contagious. Laura reveled in the whirlwind of their life.

Foster used the media to his advantage, regularly feeding them tidbits of information about his airline even when there was no actual news to report, so that SunSouth was kept constantly in the minds of the public. His name, along with Laura's, appeared frequently in the business sections of the newspapers.

They received national magazine coverage, once pictured playing doubles tennis with the president and first lady. The television newsmagazine *20/20* did a segment on them, touting them as the team that had, despite industry naysayers, resurrected a failed airline. They appeared on *Good Morning America* to talk about the Elaine Speakman Foundation and the medical research it was funding.

The gossip columnists who had snidely implied that Laura was a gold digger were soon extolling her intelligence, business acumen, impeccable taste, and unaffected charm. The Speakmans became the darlings of the local society pages, and their photographs began appearing regularly as hosts, guests, or sponsors of one event or another.

As they were leaving one such event, a decision was made that would change the course of their lives forever.

It was a Tuesday night. They had attended a retirement dinner for a notable Dallasite. The hotel where the dinner had been held and the Speakman estate were separated by only three miles of city streets.

When the parking valet brought up Foster's car, Laura went around to the driver's side. "You toasted him more times than I did," she said.

"I'm fine to drive."

"Why chance it?"

She got behind the wheel. He sat in the passenger seat. They were talking about the next day's agenda. She had just reminded him of a meeting the following afternoon. "I have a busy day," he remarked. "Any chance we could change that?"

Then everything changed.

The driver of a delivery truck ran a red light, an error that cost him his life. Opposed to wearing a seat belt, he was ejected from his truck through the windshield.

Otherwise he might have had to be cut from the mishmash of metal caused by the collision, as Foster had been. The cab of the truck fused with the passenger side of Foster's sedan. It took rescue workers over four hours to extricate him from the wreckage.

Laura was rendered unconscious by the impact. She came to in the ambulance, and her first thought was of her husband. Her rising hysteria concerned the paramedics treating her. They answered honestly, "We don't know about your husband, ma'am."

It was agonizing hours before she was told that he was alive but that his condition was critical. She learned later that he underwent emergency surgery to repair extensive internal injuries causing life-threatening hemorrhage. Because she had sustained only a concussion, a broken arm, some scrapes and bruising, she was finally permitted into the ICU, where Foster struggled to survive. Specialists came and went. In hushed voices they conferred. None looked optimistic.

Days passed; Foster clung to life. Laura kept vigil at his bedside while monitors telegraphed in blips and beeps his extraordinary will to live.

In all, he had six operations. From the outset, she realized that the orthopedists knew he would never walk again, but they performed the surgeries as though there was hope. They used pins and screws to reattach bones that would never move unless someone moved them for him. Other specialists spliced blood vessels to provide better circulation. He underwent a second abdominal surgery to repair a tear in his colon that had gone undetected during the first.

She couldn't remember what the other surgeries were for.

It wasn't until weeks after the accident that Foster was fully apprised of his condition and prognosis. He took the news with remarkable aplomb, courage, and confidence.

When they were alone, he reached for Laura's hand, pressed it between his, and reassured her that everything would be all right. He looked at her with unqualified love and repeatedly expressed his gratitude to God that she had escaped the accident without serious injury.

He never implied that she was responsible. But as she gazed down at him through her tears that day, she said what she knew must have crossed his mind, as it had hers a thousand times. "I should have let you drive."

Two years later, staring sightlessly through the window in SunSouth's conference room, she was still anguishing over her decision to drive that night. Would Foster have driven a bit faster, a bit slower, preventing them from being in the center of the intersection when the truck failed to stop? Would he have seen it ahead of time and swerved to avoid the collision? Would he have done something she hadn't?

Or, if fate had dictated that they were in that spot at that precise moment, she should have been the one sitting in the passenger seat.

Foster had never suggested she was to blame. He had never even referenced their brief conversation about how much each had had to drink and who should drive. But, although it remained unspoken, the question was always there between them: Would this have happened if he'd been behind the wheel?

Laura acknowledged how pointless it was to ask. Even so, the suppositions tortured her, as she knew they must Foster. They would go to their graves asking, *What if?*

Griff Burkett had somehow learned about the accident. She hadn't stayed to have a conversation with him about it, but if he knew the details of why Foster was in his wheelchair, he surely understood why she would go along with this or any plan Foster devised.

Foster hadn't died, but his previous life had ended the night of the wreck. And Laura was left guilt-ridden.

Having a child, conceiving it in the way Foster wished, demanded very little of her, considering everything he'd had to give up. A child and heir was one of the dreams that had been snatched from him that night. Maybe by granting him that dream, she would relieve her guilt and, by doing so, get back a portion of her former life.

Impatient with her self-pity, she turned away from the window. As she did so, a pinching sensation between her legs caused her to wince, as much from the memory it evoked as from the physical discomfort.

It had been difficult for Griff Burkett to penetrate her. That she was dry and inflexible said much about the status of her private life, and that had been mortifying. But at least he'd had the sensitivity to realize her condition and to hesitate. He'd even seemed reluctant to proceed, knowing it would hurt her. In fact, he had . . .

No. She wouldn't think about it. Wouldn't think about him. Doing so would make it personal. If it became personal, her argument wouldn't hold. The argument she'd used to convince herself to go along with Foster's plan was that *using a surrogate father to conceive was just as clinical as, and no more emotionally involving than, undergoing artificial insemination in the sterile environment of a doctor's office.*

But the tenderness between her thighs was a taunting reminder that she had been with a man. A man moving inside her. Climaxing inside her.

How could she have thought for one foolish moment that it would feel clinical?

CHAPTER
11

THE SPORTS BAR WAS CROWDED AND NOISY, but Griff had thought if he spent one more evening cooped up inside his apartment, he was going to go round the bend.

Without anything constructive to do during the day, the evenings were particularly long. His tan was already too deep to be healthy. Although he kept to a strict exercise regimen, he was bored with working out. He'd seen all the current movies, some more than once. He'd caught up on his reading. Everything he found entertaining anyway.

Marcia was completing her recuperation at home, and via Dwight, she had asked Griff not to visit her there. "She's dealing with a lot just to recover. Then she's facing the plastic surgery," Dwight had told him. "She needs some space. I'm sure she'll contact you when she's back to her glorious self."

The message had been polite enough, but Griff

could read between the lines. He was an additional complication she didn't need. She didn't blame him for what had happened, but distancing herself from him would be safer and healthier, for herself and for her business.

Consequently, he didn't even have his daily trips to the hospital to look forward to. He was bored. And, possibly for the first time in his life, lonely. Being a social outcast was different from choosing to be alone.

One of the things he'd hated most about his incarceration was the lack of privacy. During those five years, he'd yearned for solitude, and swore that when he got out, he was never going to take it for granted again. But at least when he was in the mood to talk, there were other prisoners to shoot the bull with. His meals were eaten in the company of other people.

Now he had nobody with whom to do anything. Days would pass when he didn't exchange a single word with another person.

Not that he was gregarious by nature. As Bolly had so candidly pointed out, he'd always been a loner. No doubt that tendency was a holdover from his childhood. His mother's neglect had taught him to be self-sufficient. He'd relied only on himself for everything—sustenance, pacification, and entertainment.

That mandatory self-reliance developed into a personality trait. It also became a weapon he used to keep other people at arm's length, out of either dislike or mistrust. He didn't see the percentage in letting anyone hold sway over him. Even the most casual friendship required too much. To be a friend, one must give as well as accept. Griff found both equally difficult. Coach and Ellie had finally figured that out and had stopped pressuring him to make friends, resigning themselves to his preference for his own company over anyone else's.

But in his former life he'd at least been around other people even if he didn't mingle with them. At school, with the Cowboys, at Big Spring. Now he was actually lonely. So a few days ago, out of desperation, he'd called one of his former teammates, one with whom he'd been comparatively friendly.

The former tight end, who owned a successful software company now, congratulated him on getting released and lied by saying that it was great to hear from him. But when Griff suggested they get together for a beer, the guy ticked off a dozen excuses in the span of thirty seconds, one being that he'd gotten married.

"She's a great lady, don't get me wrong. But she keeps me on a tight leash. You know how it is."

Actually, he didn't. But what he did know was that this big, tough former NFL player would rather Griff think he was a henpecked husband than drink a beer with him.

Tonight, unwilling to spend another night in the solitary confinement of his apartment, Griff had dressed and gone looking for a crowd. He'd found one at an expensive sports bar in an upscale neighborhood. The place was sleek and snazzy, serving more fruit-flavored martinis than beer. It catered to the young, beautiful, and fit. Griff's was the palest tan among them.

He was ogled by the twenty-somethings in skimpy summertime tops and short skirts. He ogled back, but not ambitiously. Which was somewhat surprising, since he hadn't had sex with anyone since Marcia.

Well, and Laura Speakman.

Don't go there.

That was what he told himself every time his thoughts went there.

People were standing three deep at the circular bar. He had to wait almost half an hour before a barstool became available. He claimed it, ordered a beer and a burger. While he ate, he watched a baseball game on the large-screen TV suspended over the center of the bar.

He'd become aware of a brunette sitting on the far side of the bar, facing him. She flashed him a smile and a glimpse of tit every time her boyfriend—or husband or whatever he was—wasn't looking. Beyond that, Griff let the barroom dramas pulse around him without taking notice.

He stretched his meal out over five innings of the Rangers game. To maintain ownership of his barstool, and to keep from going back to the empty apartment, he ordered a second beer he didn't want.

The Rangers were up by three. They were having a good season. If they made it to the play-offs, he would become interested. Otherwise, he didn't much like baseball. He couldn't make sense of a sport where the perfect game was one in which nothing happened. Baseball aficionados would disagree, saying that plenty happened during a no-hitter, but he couldn't appreciate it.

Of course, it was a hell of a lot more fun to watch when you'd wagered on the outcome.

His gambling had started out as innocently as that. He did it for fun. Even while he was at UT, he would make calls, place bets on NCAA games, although he'd never bet on a Longhorns game. But he'd wanted to. He didn't yield to the temptation of betting on his own games until he was drafted by the Cowboys.

The shrink who'd counseled him at Big Spring had a theory. He said Griff had felt guilty over his good fortune. The Longhorns had won the national championship his senior year. He'd missed being awarded the Heisman by two votes. He was the number one pro draft pick that year and an enviable prize for the Cowboys, whose veteran quarterback had retired. When he signed with the team, his picture was on the cover of *Sports Illustrated*. Fame and fortune at twenty-three. Heady stuff.

The shrink's take on it was that he'd gambled in the subconscious hope of getting caught, being punished, and losing everything, including Coach's and Ellie's affection. The shrink had emphasized that. "Coach Miller is perhaps the one individual in the world you respected and for whom you felt affection. Yet you deliberately did what you knew he couldn't forgive, the one act that would cause an irreparable breach in your relationship."

His summarizing analysis was that, subconsciously, Griff felt he should be penalized for all the good things that had happened to him—beginning with Coach giving him a home and ending with him becoming starting quarterback for the Dallas Cowboys—because in his deepest, darkest self, he'd felt these boons were undeserved. His ruin had become a self-fulfilled prophecy.

Maybe that was right.

Or maybe that was horseshit.

He'd gambled because it was fun and because he could get away with it.

Then, when he got deep in hock, it stopped being fun. And he couldn't get away with it anymore.

As he sat sipping his second beer, trying to make it last, he idly wondered how much money had been gambled on the outcome of this Rangers game. How much would his former business associates in the fancy Las Colinas office make off these nine innings? Plenty, you could be sure. The Vista boys had book-makers all over the country working for them.

One less, now that Bill Bandy was no longer in their employ.

Griff hoped that sniveling little snitch was being slowly turned on a spit over the fieriest fire in hell.

"You got any money on it?"

Having been lost in thought, Griff turned his head to his right, to make sure he was the one being addressed. The man on the next stool was glaring at him, his upper lip raised in a belligerent smirk.

"Pardon?" Griff said.

"Ask him again." A second man was standing behind the first. His truculent expression matched that of his friend, and his eyes were equally blood-shot from too much drink.

Calmly Griff said, "Ask me what?"

"I asked if you put any money on this game." The one on the stool hitched his thumb toward the TV screen.

"No. I didn't." Griff turned away, hoping that would be the end of it.

"You don't gamble anymore?"

Ignoring him, Griff reached for his beer.

The one on the stool jabbed his arm, causing him to slosh beer onto the bar. "Hey, asshole. Didn't you hear me? I asked you a question."

By now, those nearest to them had become aware of the cross words being exchanged. The music continued to blare through the speakers with palpable percussion. Action continued on the TV screen, but conversations were suspended as attention was directed toward them.

"I don't want any trouble," Griff said under his breath. "Why don't you guys just back off, go somewhere and sober up, okay?" But he knew they weren't going to simply walk away. The second one had moved up behind his barstool, crowding in close. Griff's back was to him, but he sensed the man's hostile, challenging stance.

He made eye contact with the bartender and motioned that he wanted his check. The bartender hastened over to a computerized cash register. Griff glanced across at the brunette who'd been flashing him. She was sucking her drink through a straw, watching him over the frosted glass. Her escort was looking at him, too.

The guy standing behind Griff's barstool said, "I guess he only bets on the games he throws."

"Fucking cheater." The first guy jabbed his arm again, hard. "Fucking, fucking cheat—"

Griff's hand shot out with the speed of a striking snake, grabbed the man's wrist, and slammed it down onto the bar like the coup de grâce of an arm-wrestling match.

He howled in pain. The second one landed on Griff's back like a mattress stuffed with lead. Griff came off his barstool and tried to shake the guy off. There was a noisy shuffling of feet as people hastily backed away. Somewhere a glass broke. Two bouncer types appeared and pulled the guy off Griff's back. "Break it up."

One of the bouncers pushed Griff's shoulder, shoving him back several steps. Griff put up no resistance. He raised his hands. "I didn't ask for any trouble. I didn't want it."

The two bouncers took firm hold of his hecklers and escorted them away. They protested drunkenly but were taken outside. But the show wasn't over. All eyes remained on Griff, especially now that he'd been recognized. His whispered name moved through the crowd like a spreading stain.

The bartender presented his check. Before he could count out the bills to pay it, a young man in a fashionable suit materialized beside him. He was obviously the man in charge. "It's on the house," he said to the bartender, who nodded and retrieved the check.

Griff said, "Thanks."

But the young man's expression wasn't hospitable. "I'm asking you to leave and not come back."

Anger and embarrassment caused Griff's face to grow hot. "I didn't do anything."

"I'm asking you to leave and not come back," the young man repeated.

Griff stared at him for several seconds more, then pushed him aside and strode past. The crowd parted to clear a path. When he reached the door, one of the bouncers held it open for him. As Griff walked through, the bouncer muttered, "Cocksucking cheat."

Outside, the air wrapped around Griff like a damp shroud. However, he would have had better luck throwing off the cloying, humid atmosphere than he would his anger. He'd been minding his own business, hurting nobody, and he'd been asked to leave and not come back by a guy wearing one of the shirts he'd passed over at Neiman's because it looked too faggy.

Screw 'em. He'd had better burgers at Dairy Queen for a fraction of the cost, so what the fuck did he care, anyhow?

He cared because he'd been humiliated in front of people who used to cheer him. And going from a superstar of the Dallas Cowboys, surrounded by media photographers and screaming fans, to being escorted out of a glorified burger joint was quite a comedown.

He got to his car and unlocked it. Before he had time to open the door, he was grabbed from behind and flung against the rear quarter panel.

"We're not finished with you." It was the guy from the bar, the one who'd first spoken to him. His buddy was standing right beside him. They weren't drunk. They were stone-cold sober. And, Griff realized with a blast of clarity, they weren't disgruntled fans, either.

"This is for my wrist," the guy snarled. He buried his fist in Griff's stomach.

No, Griff thought as his knees liquefied, *these guys aren't sports fans with too many beers under their belts. They're pros.*

CHAPTER
12

F OSTER?"

"Hmm?"

"Will you come to the office tomorrow?"

He set down the book he'd been reading and looked across at Laura. She'd brought home paperwork from the office. Since dinner, she had been sitting on the sofa in the library, riffling through various reports. "If you want me to."

"Some of this stuff is over my head," she said. "It's technical and requires your input. It's been almost a week since you were there. I think it's important for you to go to the office whenever you can."

"You think the mice are playing?"

She smiled. "No, because they know I would tattle on anyone slacking off." She hesitated, then said, "I think it's important to *you* that you go."

"Oh, so you think that *I'm* slacking off."

She placed her hands on her hips in feigned exasperation. "Are you trying to pick a fight?"

"Okay, no more teasing. But you do understand, don't you, that just because I'm not physically at the office doesn't mean I'm not working."

"I know that your mind is always busy, but there's an energizing quality about actually being in the office."

He considered her for a moment. "You're doing your job as well as covering for me. Have the dual responsibilities become too much for you?"

He'd touched a sensitive spot, and she reacted. "Do *you* think they have?"

"Not at all. I've just noticed that you seem tired."

She let that go for the moment. "I'm concerned for you, not me. You love SunSouth. It's your life-blood. You need that airline as much as it needs you. And when was the last time we went out to dinner?"

His head went back a fraction. "Sorry. I must have missed the segue. When did we switch subjects?"

"We didn't. It's the same subject."

"It is?"

"We rarely see our friends anymore. I can't remember when we last went out or had a couple over for cards or Sunday brunch. You stay here most days. All I do is work. I love it, and I'm not complaining, but . . ." She stopped, dropped her chin, and let the sentence trail off.

"You got your period."

She raised her head, met his gaze, and as her shoulders gradually sank, she nodded. "I'm sorry."

He frowned with regret. "I knew it."

"By my whining?"

"No. This was the first morning that I didn't ask about your period."

"Foster." She'd been mistaken. It wasn't regret behind his expression but self-reproach. He'd been tracking her cycle diligently, asking about it every day, sometimes several times a day.

"I jinxed it this morning by not getting up in time to see you off before you left for your breakfast meeting. I always ask you about your period first thing in the morning. This morning, I didn't ask."

"Foster, believe it or not, my menstrual cycle doesn't depend on your asking about it."

"You were late."

"Only two days."

"Why were you late?"

"I don't know."

"You've never been late before."

"Not usually, no."

"Then why now?"

"I don't know, Foster," she said, trying to contain her impatience. "Stress, maybe."

"Dammit!" He struck the arms of his wheelchair three times. "When you didn't start two days ago, I let myself begin to hope. I should have asked. If I'd have asked—"

"I would have menstruated anyway."

"We'll never know."

"*I* know. My temperature had dropped, indicating I wasn't pregnant. I've felt premenstrual for days. That's why I've been draggy and tired. I hoped I was wrong but . . ." She shook her head wistfully. "I dreaded telling you."

"It's not your fault. Come here."

His soft tone compelled her to set aside the paperwork. When she reached him, he guided her onto his lap. She sat down gingerly. "Don't let me hurt you."

"If only you could." They smiled at each other but left unsaid the many things they always left unsaid about the accident and its residual effect on their lives. He squeezed her shoulder affectionately. "This is a letdown, but it's not a defeat. You did everything you could."

"Which obviously wasn't enough."

"Success has been delayed. That doesn't equate to failure."

She ducked her head, murmuring, "You know me so well."

"I know how your overachiever's mind works. Sometimes to a disadvantage."

Both being type A personalities, they had compared their childhoods and discovered that, despite the sizable financial gap between the two families, they had been reared similarly. Her parents, like his, had expected much from their only child.

Both their fathers had been dominant but not unloving. The pressure to succeed that they had placed on their children was more implied than overt, but that didn't make it any less effective.

Her father had been career Air Force, a bomber pilot who'd served two tours of duty in Vietnam. After the war, he was a test pilot and trainer. A natural daredevil and risk taker, he rode his motorcycle without a helmet, slalomed on both water and snow, went skydiving and bungee jumping.

He died in his sleep. A cerebral aneurysm burst. He never knew what hit him.

Laura had adored him and took his death hard,

not only because of the bizarre unfairness of it but because he hadn't lived to see her achieve all the goals she'd set for herself.

Her mother had considered her dashing husband an unparalleled hero. She worshiped him and never recovered from the shock of finding him lying dead beside her. Grief deteriorated into depression. Laura was helpless to stop its inexorable pull until eventually it claimed her mother's life.

Laura had been a straight-A student, valedictorian, Phi Beta Kappa. She had achieved every goal she'd ever set for herself. Her parents had openly showed their pride. They'd called her their crowning achievement. But their deaths, both tragic and premature, had left her feeling that she had failed them miserably.

Foster knew this. She pointed her finger at him now, saying, "Don't start with that psychobabble about me not wanting to disappoint my parents."

"Okay."

"But that's what you're thinking," she accused. "Just like you're thinking that this is your fault because you didn't ask me about my period this morning."

He laughed. "Who knows whom well?"

She ran her fingers through his hair. "I know that you don't like changing your routine, because if you do, terrible things will happen. Isn't that the principle by which you live, Foster Speakman?"

"And now here's proof of how sound that principle is."

"The laws of nature are also sound." She shrugged. "An egg wasn't fertilized. It's as simple as that."

He shook his head stubbornly. "Nothing's that simple."

"Foster—"

"It's indisputable, Laura. Unwritten laws govern our lives."

"To some extent, possibly, but—"

"No but. There are cosmic patterns in place that one should not violate. If one does, the consequences can be severe."

Lowering her head, she said softly, "Like switching drivers at the last minute."

"Oh, Christ. Now I've made you even more unhappy." He pulled her head down onto his chest and stroked her back.

She couldn't argue this with him. To try to do so would be futile. Shortly after they were married, in an effort to better understand his OCD, she had talked with his psychiatrist. He had explained Foster's conviction that disorder predestined disaster. Patterns could not be broken. Series could not be interrupted. Foster believed this with his heart, mind, and soul, and the doctor had told her that trying to convince him otherwise was a waste of breath. "He copes with it extremely well," he'd told her. "But you would do well to remember that what to you is a hitch, is chaos to him."

Tacitly agreeing to let the matter drop, they sat quietly. After a time, Foster said, "Griff Burkett will be disappointed, too."

"Yes. He'll have to wait at least another month for his half million."

He hadn't asked her anything specific about her first meeting with Burkett. When she came home that evening, she'd given him a detailed account of everything that had taken place in the office, but she'd told him nothing about that until he asked. "How was your appointment with Burkett?"

"Brief. He did what he needed to do and left."

She hadn't elaborated, and he hadn't asked for more information, perhaps sensing that going into detail would make her uncomfortable.

"So you'll be calling him again in a couple of weeks?" he asked now.

She sat up and looked deeply into his eyes. "Do you want me to, Foster?"

"Yes. Unless it was unbearable to you."

She shook her head but looked away. "If you can bear it, I can."

"Isn't this what we agreed?"

"Yes."

"It's what we want."

"I know. I just hope it happens soon."

"It's what we want."

"I love you, Foster."

"And I love you." Then he drew her head to his chest again, saying, "It's what we want."

A week after the beating, Griff began to think he would live. For the previous six days, he hadn't been so sure.

The sons of bitches hadn't even been kind enough to beat him unconscious. And that had been deliberate. They'd wanted him awake to feel every punch, grind, and gouge. They'd wanted him conscious so that when they lifted up his head by his hair and pointed out to him a car parked nearby, he would recognize it as Rodarte's olive drab sedan and see the cute flashing of its head-lights. They didn't want him muzzy or confused. They wanted him to remember the beating and who was behind it.

They'd given him a concussion. He'd suffered a couple in football, so he recognized the symptoms. Even though he didn't experience the amnesia that sometimes accompanies a concussion, the nausea, dizziness, and blurred vision had plagued him for twenty-four hours.

By rights, he shouldn't have moved, except to use his cell phone to call 911, summoning an ambu-lance to the parking lot. But a trip to the emergency room would have involved paperwork, the police. God only knew what else.

Somehow he'd managed to climb into his car and drive himself home before his eyes swelled shut. Since then, he'd been popping ibuprofen tablets every couple hours and trying to find one position in which to lie that didn't cause throbbing pain. He didn't worry about internal injuries. The pros knew how to damage him so he would feel it, but they didn't want a murder on their hands. If they did, he'd be dead. They'd only wanted him praying for death so he'd feel better.

He got up solely to pee, and not until his bladder was full to bursting. When he did leave the bed, he walked like an old man, bent at the waist, shuffling because every time he tried to lift his feet, a knifing pain in his lower back brought tears to his eyes.

Yesterday his mobility had improved a bit. This morning, he'd worked up enough courage to get in the shower. The hot water had actually felt good, easing some of the aches and pains.

The bedroom stank of him because he hadn't been up to the task of changing the sheets. Sick of looking at the same four walls, he left the room for the first time in a week. Coffee sounded good. He realized he was ravenously hungry. Things were looking up.

He was scooping scrambled eggs straight from the skillet into his mouth when his doorbell rang. "Who the hell?" He couldn't think of anyone who would come calling.

He made it to his front door and looked through the peephole. "You gotta be kidding," he muttered. Then, *"Shit!"*

"Griff?"

Griff hung his head, shaking it in wonderment at his fuck-all rotten luck. "Yeah. Just a minute." He fumbled with the locks, which he'd had the where-withal to secure when he returned home the night of the beating, fearing that Rodarte's thugs might show up for round two.

He pulled the door open. "Hi."

His probation officer gaped at him. "Holy shit. What happened to you?"

He'd met Jerry Arnold in his office a week after speaking to him on the telephone. Griff had figured that a person-to-person meeting might win him some favor. When he'd left the ten-minute meeting, he knew he'd earned a few points.

Now Arnold's good opinion of him was in jeopardy. Ordinarily Griff would tower over the short, stocky black man. Today, since Griff was standing at a sixty-degree angle at best, they were roughly eye to eye. "What happened?" Arnold repeated.

This being the longest time Griff had been out of

bed in a week, he'd begun to feel light-headed and shaky. "Come in." Turning his back on his guest, he slowly made his way to the nearest chair and lowered himself into it as carefully as possible. Even so, every ache and pain that had been lulled by his hot shower was jarred awake again. "Take a load off, Jerry," he said, indicating another chair.

Arnold dressed and conducted himself like a bureaucrat and looked like a man with huge responsibilities and a lot on his mind—a wife, a mortgage, a few kids to rear on a government employee's salary. And unreliable ex-cons to babysit. He placed his hands on his hips, reminiscent of Coach. "You gonna tell me, or what?"

"I got thrown into the gorilla cage at the zoo. Those fuckers can get testy."

Arnold wasn't amused.

Griff sighed, in resignation and pain. "I ran into some former fans. Last, hmm, Thursday, I think."

"And you still look this bad?"

"Don't worry. It hurts a lot worse than it looks." He grinned, but the other man's frown stayed in place.

"Did you go to the emergency room? Has a doctor seen you?"

Griff shook his head. "I didn't report it to the police, either. It was just a couple of drunks. They jumped me in the parking lot of a restaurant." He made a gesture that dismissed the incident's importance. "I didn't fight back, so you don't have to worry about them filing assault charges against me."

Finally Arnold sat down. "Is this kind of thing happening a lot?"

"I get dirty looks, but this is the first time the

hostility has turned physical. As I said, they were drunk." He gave a sanitized version of what had happened.

"Do you think Vista was behind it?"

"Vista?" Griff snorted. "If Vista was behind it, I wouldn't be here to tell you about it. It's nothing, Jerry. Swear to God. I'm feeling much better."

Arnold made a point of looking at the cold sweat Griff could feel beading on his forehead, but he didn't comment further. "How are you doing otherwise?"

"Good."

Arnold looked around the apartment, taking in the fancy TV, the new furnishings. "This is a nice place."

"Thanks."

The man's eyes moved back to him. "How'd you pay for it?"

"Cash. Which I came by legally."

"How?"

"It has nothing to do with Vista, none of that. I haven't broken any laws. I haven't placed a bet."

"Do you have a job yet?"

"I'm looking into a couple of things."

"You were going for an interview . . ."

"It didn't pan out."

"What was it?"

"I didn't get the job, so what difference does it make?"

Arnold didn't get visibly ruffled over the attitude behind the question, but he repeated in a no-bullshit tone, "What was it?"

Resigned, Griff said, "I asked a sportswriter if I could do legwork for him. You know Bolly Rich?"

"I read his column."

"I proposed becoming one of his stringers. He turned me down." Actually, Griff was glad Arnold had pressed him about this. He hoped the probation officer would call Bolly for verification. Bolly would confirm that Griff had tried in earnest to secure employment.

"Anything else?"

"Nothing concrete." Griff hoped Arnold would let it go at that, because basically Griff liked the guy. He had a rotten job, but somebody had to do it. Griff had nothing personal against him, and he'd have hated lying to him.

"Let me know soon as you land something. It'll look good on your record."

"Will do. Soon as I land something."

"In the meantime, no bookies, no Vista."

"Hell, I know that."

"No matter how discouraged you become."

"Believe me, Jerry, I want nothing to do with them."

"I do believe you." He said it like he wanted to but didn't. "Try to stay out of places where you might run into football fans."

Griff gave him a look.

Abashed, he said, "Hard to do, I know, but try not to provoke another incident."

"I didn't provoke this one."

"I believe that, too." And this time he sounded sincere. He stood up to leave. Griff tried not to let his relief show. "Stay where you are," Arnold said when Griff made to get up. "I'll see myself out." He turned to go, then came back around. "Have you heard anything from Stanley Rodarte?"

Griff was glad for the concealing effect the swelling and bruising had on his expression. "Actually, he showed up at the prison the day of my release." He admitted it in case this was a trick question. Arnold might have been in contact with Wyatt Turner, who could have mentioned Rodarte's unwelcome appearance.

"Did you talk to him there?"

"No." Again, the truth.

"He'd mean trouble for you. The last person you'd want to see coming."

"You can say that again."

"I'd like to know if he comes around. In fact, I need to know."

"Absolutely."

"You'd be dumb to take him on alone, Griff."

"I won't."

Thoughtfully Arnold threaded his clip-on necktie through his fingers. "His reputation being what it is, I'm a bit surprised he's keeping his distance. Nothing from him since that day at the prison, huh?"

"Nope. Nothing."

So much for not lying to his probation officer.

Griff's physical strength and conditioning served him well, and he mended. During the week following the surprise visit from Jerry Arnold, the swelling around his eyes and mouth subsided and his face began to look familiar.

The bruises faded to an ugly greenish yellow, then the green began to go away, leaving him with only an overall jaundiced look. The gash above his eyebrow was reduced to a faint pink line. It matched the faint pink line across his cheekbone, a lasting gift Rodarte had delivered himself that night in the parking garage.

Rodarte had a shitload of grief to answer for. Despite what he'd told his probation officer, Griff couldn't wait for the opportunity to pay the bastard back.

He hadn't resumed his multi-mile runs yet, but he had swum laps the past two days. His muscles were sore, but in the good way that came from exercise, not from being pounded on by fists that had felt like meat tenderizers.

He wasn't up to full speed, but he no longer moved like a ninety-year-old with arthritis in every joint. He was feeling more like himself. Which was good. Because Laura Speakman called one morning as he was stepping out of the shower.

"One o'clock?"

"That's good for me."

"I'll see you then."

He looked at himself in the full-length mirror on the back of his bathroom door. If she had turned her head away from him before, she might go into a full-fledged cower at the sight of him today. His appearance had improved, but he still looked like he'd taken a sound beating.

He gave himself another critical once-over in the mirror, front and back. *One good thing,* he thought, *she won't be seeing me naked.*

CHAPTER
13

LAURA OPENED THE DOOR FOR HIM, THEN stood aside and motioned him into the house. No sports jacket this time, she noted. He was wearing a white oxford cloth polo shirt tucked into his jeans, and brown cowboy boots, which he'd been wearing the other two times she'd seen him. He was carrying a small white paper sack.

She closed the door and joined him in the living area just as he was taking off his sunglasses. She managed to keep from gasping but just barely. His face, particularly around his eyes and along his jaw, was bruised.

Gauging by the sickly color of the bruises, they were a week or so old. They must have looked much worse when fresh. The cut above his eyebrow was new. The one on his cheekbone was fainter than it had been a month ago.

Either he was accident prone or . . .

She didn't want to speculate on the *or*. None of

the possibilities that came immediately to mind were good.

He noticed her staring, but since he neither acknowledged nor explained his battered appearance, she didn't ask about it. He set his sunglasses and the sack on the coffee table, then stood looking at the closed doors of the armoire for several moments before turning back to her. "It didn't take?"

Because she was still wondering under what circumstances his face had become so bruised, it took a second or two for his question to sink in. Looking away, she shook her head. "If it had, we wouldn't be here."

"Right."

The a/c cycled off. Without its soft whir, the house seemed abnormally quiet.

"Well—"

"I—"

They began at the same time. Laura motioned for him to go ahead.

He reached for the small sack he had carried in with him and passed it to her. "I brought this."

She looked at him curiously, then opened the sack and peered inside. When she saw the box, her heart gave a little jump.

"It's, uh, it's not the kind that has a spermicide," he said. "I double-checked, 'cause some of them do. Have it, I mean."

Not trusting her voice to speak, she nodded.

The cowboy boots shifted slightly. "I just thought since—"

"Yes. Thank you." Before any more could be said, she hurried toward the bedroom.

Once inside, she closed the door and leaned

against it. She had the sack clutched in a death grip. Her palms were actually damp. This was silly, getting so flustered. But what flustered her more than the tube of lubricant was that he had thought to bring it. That he had thought at all about what they would do today.

She set her handbag on the dresser and went into the bathroom. The mirror above the sink reflected an image that looked surprisingly normal. Dark hair. Gray eyes that verged on green, a distinctive black spot in the right one. A triangle-shaped face, the brow slightly wider than the jaw. It was saved from being too prim by her lips, which were full and—she'd been told—sexy.

Her color was a little high. She attributed that to the midday heat.

A month ago, as well as today, she had carefully selected what to wear, dressing in her most structured business suits. Nothing too feminine, certainly nothing provocative. She took off her suit jacket, skirt, and shoes. As before, she left on her top, which today was an unadorned V-necked T-shirt, light blue, not too fitted. She also left on the three strands of silver chain around her neck, which somehow made her feel more dressed than *un*.

She took the box out of the sack, opened it, removed the tube. Just in case he was wrong, she read every word on the label. Twice.

Afraid that she'd taken too long, she hurried from the bathroom, folded back the covers, and got into bed. She removed her panties and tucked them between the mattresses, as she had done last time. She raised the sheet to her waist, then a bit higher.

She closed her eyes and tried to relax and control her hectic breathing. Her heart was beating way too fast. This waiting for him was agonizing.

What was he doing out there?

Well, of course she knew what he was doing. She just wondered *what* he was doing. Was he sitting up? Lying down on the sofa? Did he feel any self-consciousness at all? Was he the least bit anxious about his ability to perform? Had it occurred to him to wonder what she was thinking about while she waited for him?

She hadn't heard any sound coming from the living room either the last time or today, so she imagined he had decided against the videos in favor of the magazines.

Or maybe he didn't need either and was simply fantasizing, conjuring up his own prurient images. Surely he'd been with countless women. When he was a football star, women would have thrown themselves at him. Undoubtedly many still would. He would have had hundreds of erotic experiences from which to draw.

What kind of woman appealed to him? Tall or petite, slender and athletic or curvy and buxom, blond or redhead? Brunette?

His knock was soft, but it still gave her a start. She took a deep breath. "Come in."

He stepped into the room. Although they were the only two in the house, he closed the door. Even without his boots he seemed towering in the confines of the bedroom. Their eyes connected for a nanosecond as he walked toward the bed. He sat down on the edge of it, his back to her.

He hesitated for several beats, then raised his

hips only high enough to push off his jeans. He worked them down his legs and left them lying on the floor. She thought he removed his socks, too, but she couldn't be sure.

He started to get between the sheets, then muttered something she didn't catch. She cut her eyes to him, about to ask what he'd said, when he hooked his thumbs into the waistband of his boxers and pulled them off.

She glimpsed a tan line at his waist. There was a stark contrast between the brown skin above it and the white skin—*dear God*—below. And then his shirttail dropped back into place.

He raised the sheet and slid in beside her. "Did you use it?"

"Yes."

With no more preamble than that, he rolled onto her and separated her knees with his. His first thrust lodged the head of his penis inside her. But just. She closed her eyes and turned her head aside, but she could sense him looking down at her with dismay and anger.

Using one straight arm to support himself, he worked his other hand between their bodies. She tensed. But he didn't touch her, he stroked himself in short, rapid tugs. A few times his knuckles brushed against her.

Soon, she sensed the tightening of his muscles. His breath became uneven and hot against her face. He gave a soft groan a heartbeat before he removed his hand, pushed himself into her fully, and came.

The arm he'd used to bear his weight gave way. He settled on her heavily, all six feet four of him.

Tanned skin and white skin. He pulled in a deep breath and let it out slowly. He rearranged his right leg. It felt muscular and hard against the inside of her thigh, and rough with hair. His shirt was slightly damp with perspiration. The dampness seeped through her T-shirt, into her skin. She could smell his sweat. Soap. Semen.

When he moved, he moved suddenly, as one does when on the verge of sleep and muscles are seized with a violent twitch. He raised his head and levered himself up but was yanked back down on top of her. Laura, not realizing what had happened, tried to push him off.

"Relax!" he growled.

Then she saw the problem. One of her chains had looped itself around a button of his shirt. He fumbled with it, cursing under his breath, until he worked it free.

Less than five minutes after pulling off his boxers, he was pulling them back on. Laura kept her eyes averted, but in her peripheral vision, she followed his motions, which were jerky and abrupt, those of an angry man barely holding on to his temper.

He stuffed his shirttail into his jeans as though he was furious at it. He buttoned up his fly with dispatch, but his belt buckle presented a challenge. When he finally managed it, he slapped it lightly into place and turned to face her.

"Why did you lie to me?"

"I didn't use it because I was afraid it would make a difference."

"You're damn right it would have made a difference. That's why I brought it."

"I mean I was afraid it would prevent conception."

"I told you it wouldn't."

"It might have affected the motility of the sperm. Something. I don't know," she said defensively. "I just didn't want to take a chance."

"Well, I didn't want to hurt you again." His loud vehemence seemed to surprise him as much as it did her. It rendered them both silent. Finally he said, "Look, I know you have a low opinion of me. You think I'm an outlaw. A criminal. A big, dumb football player. Well, fine. Think whatever you want to. I really don't give a rat's ass so long as your money's good."

He paused for breath, and when he spoke again, his voice was gruff. "But I hurt you. Twice now. And I resent you thinking that would be okay with me. Because it isn't."

She sat up but kept the sheet pulled to her waist. "It shouldn't make any difference to you."

"It does."

"Well, it shouldn't!" He was provoking an emotional response from her, and she didn't want to feel any emotion, even anger. "This isn't about how you feel or how I feel."

"I understand that. But if you've gotta do it this way, you could at least make it easier on yourself. Why don't *you* watch the dirty movies?" He raised his hands to stop her from commenting. "Forget it, forget it."

Again, he paused to take several deep breaths, then said, "No touchy-feely. Fine. I'm not into all that, either. No kissing or foreplay because that would . . . Because . . . I get why there's no kissing or foreplay, okay? But couldn't we at least have a conversation first?"

"What for?"

"Because maybe that would stop you from cringing, and I wouldn't feel like I was violating you."

"I don't think of it as a violation."

He snorted in disagreement. "Could have fooled me. You don't even look at me."

She gave him a meaningful look then, but she didn't dare verbalize what she was thinking—that looking at each other would make it harder, not easier.

He seemed to realize that, too, because he turned away and mumbled a string of swearwords. He tilted his face up toward the ceiling, placed his hands on his hips, and blew out a gust of breath. He ran his fingers through his hair. "Christ." After a time, he looked at her again. "I walk in here, we've barely made eye contact. You're lying there, still and silent, resigned to a fate worse than death. How do you think that makes me feel?"

"I don't care how it makes you feel."

She did, but she couldn't let him know that. Actually, his concern touched her, and that was a dangerous sentiment. They couldn't be friends. Or enemies. They could be nothing to each other. Between them there must be nothing except total indifference, or she could never return to this house.

Her features impassive, her tone cool, she said, "This is biology, Mr. Burkett. Nothing more."

"Then why don't you just have me jerk off into a bottle and hand it over? You've made it plain how distasteful it is to have me on you. Admit it, you came unglued when I put my hand down there. Hell, you panicked when your chain got caught on my button. If it's so god-awful, why do you put yourself through it?"

"I thought you had that figured out."

"You were driving the night your husband lost his manhood. Poor you. You've got that cross to bear the rest of your life. This is your penance, I guess. Screwing a lowlife like me. Is that it?"

He'd scoured an open wound, and she lashed back in self-defense. "If I can stand it, surely you can."

His expression changed to match hers. The skin of his face was pulled tight, actually changing the configuration of the bruises. "I didn't sign on to be insulted."

"And I didn't promise to make polite conversation. Stop worrying about how I feel and just—"

"Play stud."

"That's what you agreed to do."

"Well, I'm rethinking our agreement. I don't need this shit."

"No. Just our millions."

He glared at her for several seconds, then turned. He reached the door in two long strides and flung it open so hard it bounced back when it hit the wall. "I'd say 'Fuck you, lady,' but I already did."

He slammed the front door on his way out, thinking he was leaving for the last time. Even if he wanted to come back, which he didn't, his exit line was reason enough for them to fire him.

Fire him? Like this was a normal job. Like the terms of his employment would ever be a matter of record. He could just imagine some time in the future being interviewed by a prospective employer.

What was your last job, Mr. Burkett?

I was paid to fuck this rich wacko's wife.

Uh-huh. And you failed to perform the task?

Oh no, I performed just fine.

Then what was the cause of your dismissal?

I lost my temper and told her off.

I see. And all you had to do was show up, keep your mouth shut, and just fuck her?

That's right.

You're not very bright, are you, Mr. Burkett?

Apparently not.

It sounded like a third-rate joke.

She must have parked around back, where he'd parked the first time, because the red Honda was the only car in the driveway. In the time it took him to reach it, he was already considering going back inside to apologize. He was still mad as hell, but he couldn't afford his anger. The price tag of it was half a million now, and millions more to come. Not worth it. Not by a long shot.

He turned on his heel and had started back toward the house when he spotted something that drew him up short.

CHAPTER
14

RODARTE WAS PARKED HALFWAY DOWN the block. The windshield of his car reflected the leafy trees above it, so Griff couldn't see him. But he stuck his hand out the driver's window and gave a friendly little wave.

Griff forgot about his apology to Laura Speakman. He jogged to the Honda, scrambled in, and cranked the motor. The tires left rubber in the driveway as he backed out. He sped the short distance and came to a squealing stop a half inch from the grille of Rodarte's sedan. He was out of the Honda before inertia settled in.

Rodarte was waiting for him. His car engine was idling, but the driver's window was down. It took all Griff's self-control not to grab him by the neck and haul him out through that window. "You're a goddamn coward, Rodarte."

"Are you trying to hurt my feelings?"

"You hire goons to do your dirty work on men. Women you beat up yourself."

"Speaking of, how is your favorite whore?" Rodarte laughed at Griff's expression of rage. "Okay, so I got a little carried away. Why didn't you report me to the police?"

"That was Marcia's decision."

"But I bet you didn't argue against it, did you? The very thought of police involvement puckers your sphincter, doesn't it? As for the working over you took, I heard you got jumped by a couple of former fans."

"They were pros."

"You know this?"

"You were behind it."

Rodarte wagged his finger at him. "But you didn't file a police report. I'll bet you didn't tell your lawyer, either. Or your probation officer. Jerry Arnold, right?"

"You know who my probation officer is?" Griff regretted the question as soon as he asked it. It revealed how surprised and alarmed he was to learn that Rodarte was so well acquainted with his life.

Rodarte grinned. "I know lots about you, Number Ten."

He must. He must have been tailing him or he wouldn't have known that Griff would be in that particular sports bar the night he sicced the brutes on him. He also wouldn't have known to find him here, on this street, today. Right now.

Jesus.

And before Griff could even fully process the worrisome implications of that, Rodarte said, "One thing I don't know is the name of your new gash there."

Griff turned his head quickly to see Laura Speakman backing her car out of the driveway. Fortunately, she drove away in the opposite direction.

"Real estate agent," Griff said. "She was showing me the house."

Rodarte snickered. "You're looking for a house just after getting settled into your duplex?"

"Turns out I'm not crazy about the neighborhood."

"Where did you get the money to buy all those fancy toys? Sound system. Big-screen TV. All that."

Griff's mind was spinning. He wanted to cram his fist into Rodarte's mouth because every word from it increased his alarm. Rodarte knew where he lived. He knew how he spent his money. And now he knew about this house. Most alarming was that he might learn about Griff's arrangement with the Speakmans.

"See," Rodarte said conversationally, "what I think is, is that before you used your big, strong quarterback's hands to snap Bill Bandy's neck, you dipped those hands into his private till."

"That's crap and you know it. How could I have taken any money? I was arrested at the scene."

"A technicality," Rodarte said with a dismissive gesture. "Before the real heat came down on you, you managed to stash the ill-gotten funds where nobody could find them. They've been sitting somewhere, earning interest, waiting on you to get out. Now they're coming in handy. Just as you planned."

He paused, frowned, and said sadly, "Only thing

is, Griff, the way those Vista boys see it, it's their money, not yours. They would be real grateful to anybody who could recover it and bring it home to them."

"In other words, you."

"I'm just trying to make things easier for you, is all. I'm doing everybody a favor. These guys get their money back, and they just might forget about what you did to poor ol' Bandy. You see where this is going? How nice it would be for everybody?" His ingratiating smile collapsed. "Where's the money?"

"You're delusional. About Bandy. About ill-gotten funds. About every frigging thing. You think if I had money, I'd be driving this piece of shit?" He raised his arm toward the Honda. "A secondhand car I bought from my lawyer?"

Rodarte regarded him for a moment, then said smoothly, "You cut quite a figure in that new Armani jacket."

Griff tried to keep his expression neutral. "Thanks. It would look like shit on you."

Rodarte chuckled. "I'm afraid you're right. I haven't got the figure."

"You haven't got the balls, either. If you did, you'd get out of that butt-ugly car, stop making veiled threats, and fight me like a man."

Rodarte pulled a face as though considering it. "You sure you want me to do that, Griff? Think hard now."

Griff was seething, but he knew he could not give vent to his rage. If he laid into Rodarte, he'd be giving the woman-beating son of a bitch exactly what he wanted. "Marcia didn't have anything to tell you," he said. "You ruined her face for nothing."

Rodarte shrugged. "I guess. She didn't tell me anything useful, and from what I understand she won't be telling anybody anything for a long time. Wonder if she's able to give blow jobs, what with her jaw wired shut and all. And something else . . ." Griff didn't bite, but Rodarte told him anyway. "You'd think a whore wouldn't make such fuss over getting it in the ass."

A tide of red-hot fury washed through Griff.

Rodarte sensed it and grinned. "You ever had her that way?"

Griff had wondered if Rodarte's assault included rape. He hadn't asked Marcia because he hadn't wanted to cause her further distress. And, possibly, he just didn't want to know exactly how badly she'd suffered on his account. Now that he did, he wanted even more badly to kill the man grinning up at him.

Rodarte nodded toward the house midway down the block. "And what about her? Even from this distance, I could tell your new lady friend has a sassy little butt. Just as well tell me her name. I'll find out anyway."

Griff's outrage went from fiercely hot to icy cold in seconds. The degree of his rage frightened him, and it should have frightened Rodarte. "One of these days," he said softly, with conviction, with promise, "I'm gonna have to kill you."

Rodarte dropped the gearshift into reverse and smiled as he backed the car away. "I have wet dreams about the day you try."

* * *

Reluctantly, the concierge rang Marcia's penthouse. With his back turned to Griff, he spoke in whispers into the telephone until Griff reached across the counter and tapped him on the shoulder.

"Give me the phone. Please," he added but with impatience. Reluctantly, the man passed Griff the receiver. "Marcia?"

"Actually, it's Dwight."

"Hey, Dwight. Griff Burkett. I want to come up."

"I'm sorry, you can't."

"Who says?"

"She doesn't want company."

"I need to see her."

"She's resting."

"I'll wait."

There was a dramatic sigh, followed by "She'll probably kill me, but okay."

Dwight answered the door to the penthouse and stood aside to admit Griff. "This isn't one of her good days."

"Mine, either," Griff returned grimly as he followed Marcia's neighbor into the spacious living room, where Marcia was reclined on her sofa. She appeared to be sleeping, although it was hard to tell because her head was swathed in bandages.

"She had surgery?"

"The first of many. Three days ago. Her nose had to be rebroken. She's still got a lot of pain, but they said she was well enough to come home."

"Generally, how's she doing?"

"Not very well. She—"

"I can hear you, you know." Her voice was

muffled by the bandages and her jaw still had limited range of motion, but she was her droll self, and Griff took heart in that.

Injecting some levity into his voice, he said, "Hark! The mummy speaks!"

"I've got lobster bisque simmering on the stove," Dwight said. "She's cranky as a mama bear, but be sweet to her." He patted Griff on the arm as he passed on his way into the kitchen.

Griff pulled an armchair closer to the sofa and placed it where Marcia could see him without having to turn her head. She said, "If you think I look bad now, just wait till the bandages come off. I'll be a real freak show."

She was wrapped neck to ankles in a bathrobe, but he could tell that her lush curves had been diminished. He wondered how much weight she'd lost just since he'd last seen her. He reached for her hand and pressed a kiss onto the back of it. "You couldn't be a freak show no matter how hard you tried."

"I'd hate for my own mother to see me like this. Not that she will, since she disowned me years ago."

"So much for how you look, how do you feel?"

"Stoned."

He laughed. "Good drugs?"

"I could make a fortune selling this stuff. If only it weren't against the law. But then so is prostitution."

"Speaking of breaking the law . . ." He looked directly into her eyes, which peered at him through a slit in the bandage. "I'm going to the police about Rodarte."

Her reaction was immediate. "No!"

"Listen to me, Marcia. I know what he did to you. He bragged to me about it not an hour ago."

She stared up at him for a long moment, then closed her eyes as though to shut out him, her memory, everything. Griff felt the shudder that went through her.

"Why didn't you tell me?"

"I didn't want to talk about it."

"He hurt you."

"Yes."

"Bad."

She opened her eyes then. "I'm a whore. I've done everything. But always when I was in control. Having it forced on you is different." She closed her eyes again. "Believe me." When she reopened her eyes, she said, "Try explaining that to a cop."

"I will. You were raped."

"And he'll say it doesn't matter."

"It matters to me!" He shot up from his chair, sending it over backward. Dwight came running, wearing an apron, a dripping spoon in his hand. "Get back to your bisque," Griff ordered. Dwight hesitated, then cupped the spoon with his free hand and, walking backward, retreated into the kitchen. The decorator's almost comical rush to her rescue had defused Griff's temper. He righted the chair and sat down, taking Marcia's hand again.

"Rodarte's not going to give up. The son of a bitch has been stalking me. He knows everything going on in my life. But all that's nothing compared to sodomy. I'd like to kill him for that. But I can't, and he knows it. I can't do anything without violating my probation. He's going to stay after me,

Marcia. Pushing. He'll continue hurting people close to me. The only option left is to take it to the police."

"I'm begging you, Griff, don't."

"But—"

"Look at me!" Tears filled her eyes. "If you do this, I'll have a huge spotlight focused on me and my business. Every Bible-thumping Holy Roller— some of whom are clients, by the way—will come out of the woodwork, condemning me and my occupation. It wouldn't matter to my self-righteous critics that I went to the emergency room, torn and bleeding. They'd say it was punishment befitting my sins.

"If Rodarte is made to answer for himself at all, which is doubtful, he'll deny the beating and blame it on a customer or boyfriend who was there after him. Probably you. There's no DNA. He used a condom." Sourly, she added, "I'm glad of that at least."

"Christ," Griff swore, knowing that what she said was probably right. "So you expect me to do nothing?"

"I'm *asking* you to do nothing. I avoided public scrutiny when I was my gorgeous, voluptuous self. Do you think I could endure it looking like *this*? I couldn't, Griff. I'd jump off the roof first." She said it in such a way that he believed she would. "The threat of exposure would frighten my clientele away for good. I'd lose everything. If you have any regard or feeling for me at all, let it go. Let it go." She withdrew her hand from his and closed her eyes.

"I think you should leave now. She needs to

sleep." Dwight had slipped back into the room. His tone wasn't unkind, but unquestionably he was Marcia's self-appointed advocate and protector.

Griff nodded and came to his feet. Before turning away, he bent down and kissed Marcia's closed eyes.

Dwight saw him to the door. "I suggest you call before you come here again." Griff gave his silent consent with a nod.

In the foyer, he punched the button for the elevator but was so lost in thought, he stood looking into the empty cubicle for several moments before it registered with him that it had arrived.

On the descent, he realized that further argument wasn't going to change Marcia's mind. Pressuring her would only add to her mental anguish. He had already inflicted enough suffering on her, and when all was said and done, she was right. Taking this matter to the police would fix a spotlight not only on Marcia but on him. He didn't want that any more than she did.

No, he would have to solve his Rodarte problem alone, one-on-one with the son of a bitch.

He stopped at the florist's in the lobby and ordered an orchid plant to be delivered to Marcia's penthouse. On the enclosure card, he wrote, "Okay. It stays our secret. But he *will* pay."

He didn't sign it.

CHAPTER
15

GRIFF HEARD THE DOORBELL CHIME IN-
side the house and then approaching footsteps. His gut tightened with apprehension
over how he would be greeted. Maybe with the door
slammed in his face.

Was coming here a bad idea?

Too late to change his mind now. Because the
door was pulled open and he was looking into Ellie
Miller's smiling face.

He waited in dread to see her smile dissolve. Instead, it brightened. "Griff!"

She looked ready to launch herself against him
and give him a big hug but checked the impulse and
instead reached across the threshold and grabbed
his hand with a strength surprising for a woman so
petite. She looked him over from head to toe.
"You're thinner."

"I've been doing a lot of swimming, less
weights."

She hadn't stopped smiling yet. "Come in, come in, we're standing here letting cold air out, and our electric bill is sky-high as it is."

He stepped into the house and was instantly enveloped in its familiar scents and sights and textures. He paused to take a look around. The hall tree was where it had always been. The wallpaper hadn't changed. The framed mirror, which to him had always seemed a little too small for that particular spot, was still there.

"I replaced the living room carpet last year."

"It's nice."

Beyond the carpet, everything was exactly as it had been the last time he was here. Except that the picture of the three of them was no longer on the end table. The photo had been taken minutes after the NCAA national championship victory, he still in his grass- and bloodstained jersey, hair matted down by sweat and the weight of his helmet, standing between Ellie and Coach. Three beaming smiles. Ellie had had the picture framed and prominently displayed within days of the game.

The Millers had never been happier or more proud of him than after that Orange Bowl victory, except maybe the day he signed his letter of intent with the University of Texas. That day this house had been filled to capacity with sportswriters from all over the state. Ellie had fussed over the mess they were making, dropping cookie crumbs and spilling punch. Coach had complained when the TV lights blew out a fuse.

But their grumbling wasn't taken seriously. It was obvious to everyone there that the couple was bursting with pride over Griff. Not only had he been offered a full scholarship to play football for the university but he was graduating cum laude from high school. Coach's decision to take him in had been validated. His investment in that recalcitrant fifteen-year-old had paid off, and in ways beyond Griff's athletic ability.

The four years Griff had played for UT, he was coached by some of the most respected and knowledgeable men in the game. But he still had relied on Coach Miller's advice. He took everything he'd learned from Coach into that Orange Bowl game with him. It was Coach's triumph as much as his.

It was later, after signing on with the Cowboys, that Griff stopped listening to his mentor's advice and started thinking of Coach as a nuisance rather than a sensible guiding hand. The absence of that framed photo on the living room end table spoke volumes about Coach's feelings toward him now.

"Come on back," Ellie said, shooing him into the kitchen. "I'm shelling peas. You can buy them already shelled, but they don't taste as good to me. Want some iced tea?"

"Please."

"Pound cake?"

"If you've got it."

She frowned at him as though her not having pound cake on hand would happen the day hell froze over. She cleared her pea-shelling project off the kitchen table. He sat down in the chair that had been designated his after his first dinner here and was embarrassed by the unmanly nostalgia that made his throat seize up. This was the only real home he'd ever known. And he'd brought disgrace to it.

"Coach isn't here?"

"He's playing golf," Ellie said with vexation. "I told him it was too blamed hot to play at this time of day, but he hasn't grown any less hardheaded. In fact, he just gets worse."

She served the tea and pound cake, and sat down across from him, clasping her hands on the table. He looked at those tiny hands, remembering the bright yellow rubber gloves she'd had on the day he moved in and recalling one of the rare times he hadn't avoided her touch. He'd had the flu. Sitting on the edge of his bed, she'd laid her palm against his forehead, testing it for fever. Her hand had been soft and cool, and to this day he remembered how good it had felt against his burning skin. To her it had been an instinctual thing to do, but until then, Griff hadn't known that was what moms did when children complained of feeling sick.

Ellie and Coach had never had children. The reason for that was never explained to him, and even as a teenager he'd had the sensitivity not to ask. Maybe her childlessness had factored into her welcoming that surly and sarcastic boy into her home.

She hadn't smothered him with motherly affection, which she'd sensed, correctly, that he would have rejected. But with the merest signal from him, she made herself available. She would lend an ear if he wanted to talk through a problem. In a thousand small and subtle ways she had demonstrated the maternal tenderness she obviously felt for him. He could see it in her eyes now.

"It's good to see you, Ellie. Good to be here."

"I'm so glad you came. Did you get my letters?"

"Yes, and I appreciated them. More than you know."

"Why didn't you write back?"

"I couldn't find the words. I—" He shrugged helplessly. "I just couldn't, Ellie. And I didn't want to cause a rift between Coach and you. He didn't know you wrote to me, did he?"

She sat up straighter and said smartly, "It's not up to him what I do or don't do. I make up my own mind about things."

Griff smiled. "I know you do, but I also know you support Coach. The two of you are a team."

She had the grace not to argue that.

"I knew how pissed he was," Griff said. "He tried to warn me against setting myself up for a big fall. I didn't listen."

He distinctly remembered the day that their steadily declining relationship was finally severed. Coach had been waiting for him at his car after practice. The Cowboys' coaching staff knew Coach Miller well, knew how influential he'd been on their starting quarterback, and always welcomed seeing him.

Griff didn't. Their conversations had grown increasingly contentious. Coach had no quarrel with his performance on the football field, but he didn't approve of much else, such as the rate at which Griff went through money.

Griff wanted to know the point of having it if you couldn't spend it. "You'd be wise to put aside some for a rainy day," Coach told him. Griff ignored the advice.

Coach also disapproved of the pace of his life.

He cautioned Griff against burning the candle at both ends, particularly during the off-season, when he got sloppy with his workouts and kept late hours in the glossy nightclubs of Dallas and Miami, where he'd bought a beachfront condo.

"Discipline got you where you are," Coach said. "You'll sink fast if you don't maintain that discipline. In fact, it should be more rigid now than before."

Yeah, yeah, Griff thought. He figured Coach's dissatisfaction was based on jealousy. He no longer had control over the decisions Griff made or the way he lived his life, and that rankled the older man. While Griff appreciated everything Coach had done for him, he was old school in his thinking. His strict lessons no longer applied. Coach had got him where he was, but now that he was here, it was time to cut the apron strings.

Griff began distancing himself. Their visits became less frequent. He rarely returned his mentor's phone calls. So he wasn't happy to see Coach that day he ambushed Griff at his car. With his typical tactlessness, Coach came straight to the point. "I'm worried about your new associates."

"'New associates'?"

"Don't play dumb with me, Griff."

He could only have been talking about the Vista boys, and Griff wondered how Coach knew about them. But then, he'd rarely been able to sneak something past the man. Coach's vigilance had been a pain in the butt when Griff was a teenager. It was a bigger pain now that he was a grown-up. "You're the one always harping on me to make friends. I've made some friends. Now you don't like them."

"I don't like you getting too friendly with these guys."

"Why? What's wrong with them?"

"In my view, they're a little too shiny."

Griff guffawed. " 'Shiny'?"

"Slick. Slippery. I don't trust them. You should check them out."

"I don't snoop on my friends." Looking Coach straight in the eye, he said what he hoped would end the discussion. "I don't go poking my nose into other people's business."

Coach didn't take the hint. "Make an exception. Do some snooping."

"What for?"

"See what they're really about. How do they pay for those fancy limos and chauffeurs?"

"They're businessmen."

"What's their business?"

"A tin mine in South America."

"Tin mine, my ass. No miner I ever knew needed a bodyguard."

Griff had heard enough. "Look, I don't care how they pay for the limos. I like the limos and the chauffeurs, not to mention the private jets and the pussy they get me free for the asking. So why don't you go away and leave me the hell alone? Okay?"

Coach did just that. It was the last conversation they'd had.

Griff looked at Ellie now and shook his head sadly. "I thought I was smarter than him. Smarter than everybody. When I got caught, Coach denounced me. I didn't blame him. I understood why he washed his hands of me."

"You broke his heart."

He gave her a sharp look. She nodded and repeated solemnly, "You broke his heart, Griff." Then
she laughed lightly. "Of course, he was pissed, too."

"Yeah, well, it's probably just as well he's not
here. If he was, I doubt I'd have been invited in for
cake."

"Honestly, I doubt it, too."

"I knew I took a chance by coming."

"Why did you? I'm delighted. But why did you
come?"

He left the table and moved to the counter. He
took a black-eyed pea from the brown paper sack,
held the pod between his thumbs and split it open,
then shook the peas into the stainless steel bowl. He
tossed the empty pod back into the sack.

"I keep hurting people, and I don't want to."

"Then stop doing it."

"I don't mean to. I just do."

"How?"

"Just by being me, Ellie. Just by being me." He
turned and rested his hips against the counter,
crossed his ankles, folded his arms over his chest,
and studied the toes of his boots. They needed another shine. "I'm destructive. It seems to be the
curse of my life."

"Stop feeling sorry for yourself."

His head came up, and he looked across at her.

"Stop crying in your beer and tell me what's
going on. Who's been hurt?"

"An acquaintance. She was hurt bad on account
of me. No other reason, just because of her association with me."

"I'm sorry for that, but it doesn't sound like it
was your fault."

"Feels like it was. It goes back to . . ." He gestured as though saying, *back then.* "There's this guy. Ever since my release, he's been right here," he said, holding his palm inches from his nose. "He's got it in for me, and he's not going to go away until I'm dust under his heel."

Griff had kept one eye on his rearview mirror the whole time he'd been driving here. He'd taken a circuitous route, too, doubling back several times, to make certain he wasn't being tailed by either Rodarte or somebody Rodarte had hired to follow him.

Of course Rodarte would know where the Millers lived. If he'd wanted to get to Griff by harming them, he would have done so. Griff supposed Rodarte didn't consider Coach as vulnerable as Marcia. The idea of coming up against Coach might even scare him. And it should.

"Are you in trouble, Griff?"

He knew she was asking if he was involved in something illegal again. "No. I swear it."

"I believe you. So go to the authorities and tell them about this person who's hounding you and—"

"I can't, Ellie."

"Why not?"

"Because he's not acting strictly on his own."

"You mean—"

"Vista. The same men Coach called slippery, and he didn't know the half of it."

"Then you certainly need to talk to the authorities."

He shook his head, thinking back to what he'd resolved yesterday as he left Marcia's penthouse. "I've been up to my eyebrows in the 'authorities' for the past five years. I don't want anything to do with the authorities."

He couldn't report Rodarte's crime without bringing a lot of shit down on himself and Marcia. The hell of it was, their silence gave Rodarte protection and room to maneuver. Rodarte could make a real menace of himself, and Griff was hamstrung.

"But the police or the FBI need to know if—"

"I no longer trust the system, Ellie. I'm doing what I'm supposed to do. I've formed a good relationship with my probation officer. I think he's on my side. I want to stay under the radar, do nothing that would call attention to me."

"And to that murder."

"And to that murder," he admitted.

"They never caught the person who killed that Bandy character, did they?"

"No, they never did."

The silence became dense, stretched out. She didn't come right out and ask. She didn't want to insult him by asking. Or maybe she didn't want to hear the answer. She took a sip of tea, returning the glass to the table with more care than necessary.

"You can't live your life dodging the bad guys, Griff. You'll just have to ignore them."

"I've tried. It's not that easy. In fact, it's impossible. Ignoring them only makes them more determined to get my attention. And they'll use other people to do it, to bend me to their way of thinking. I won't play with them, Ellie. I won't break the law again. But I don't want other people getting hurt."

Specifically, the Speakmans. If Rodarte found out about Griff's deal with them, he could ruin it, and it was the only thing Griff had going. Beyond that, Rodarte could do irreparable damage to the couple's reputation. Speakman might be as crazy as a loon, but he seemed like a decent enough guy. He was respected for his community service and for giving away barrels of money to charity.

And it made Griff queasy to think of Laura Speakman being subjected to Rodarte's violence as Marcia had been. Given half a chance, Rodarte would hurt her and not think twice about it. He'd already noticed her, spoken of her in terms that enraged Griff.

Noticing Ellie's look of concern, Griff relaxed his stance and smiled. "I didn't come here to worry you. I just needed a sounding board, and you've always been a good one."

She got up and took his hand again. "More than anything, I want you to be happy, Griff."

"Happy?" He repeated the word as though it was of another language. Happy seemed an unattainable goal.

"Have you got a job yet?"

"I'm looking into some things. One will open up soon."

"In the meantime, what are you doing for money?"

"My lawyer sold all my stuff. There was a little left after he paid the fines and such. What wasn't sold he put in a warehouse. I cleared it out a few weeks ago. Sold a few things on eBay. I'm doing okay."

She pulled her handbag off the peg near the back door and took a fifty-dollar bill from her wallet. "Here."

He staved her off. "Ellie, I can't take that."

"Yes you can. I insist. It's part of my Hawaii money."

"Hawaii money?"

"After years of my pestering him about it, Joe's finally consented to take me to Hawaii later this summer. I've saved some spending money. If you don't take this, I'll buy fifty dollars' worth of tacky souvenirs I don't need and will never want to look at again. Take it."

He took it. Not because he wanted to or needed it but because she wanted to give it to him, and she needed him to accept it. "I'll pay you back."

They heard the car at the same time. She looked up at him, gave him a very weak smile of reassurance, and turned to face the back door as Coach came in. "Whose car—"

That was as far as he got. Seeing Griff in his kitchen stopped him in his tracks. His sparse hair had gone grayer. He'd put on maybe ten pounds, but he was still as solid as a brick wall, not fat. There were more squint lines extending from the corners of his eyes, showing up white against his perpetually sunburned face. Otherwise he looked much the same as he had the day he'd brought Griff to this house almost twenty years ago.

Griff registered all this within the span of a second, which was only as long as Coach stood still before continuing on his lumbering way through the kitchen, past the living room, and down the hall. The slamming bedroom door echoed loudly through the house.

It was a while before Ellie spoke. "I'm sorry, Griff."

"I didn't expect him to be glad to see me."

"He is. He just can't show it."

Griff didn't have the heart to disabuse her. "I've gotta go."

She didn't argue. At the door, she looked at him with concern. "Take care of yourself."

"I will."

"You promise?"

"I promise."

"I never got an opportunity to tell you this, but when all that happened five years ago, I hurt for you. What you did was wrong, Griff. Very wrong, and you have no excuse for doing it. But I couldn't have hurt more for you if you'd been my own flesh and blood."

"I know that." His voice was dangerously rough.

"Don't get discouraged." She patted the back of his hand. "The best for you is yet to be. I'm certain of it."

He didn't disabuse her of that, either.

"Need help with that, ma'am?"

Laura turned, ready to accept the kind offer of assistance. But when she saw Griff Burkett, her smile froze in place as her eyes filled with alarm. "What are you doing here?"

He lifted the large box she was carrying out of her arms, which seemed to have gone boneless at the sight of him. "Where were you taking this?"

She continued to gape at him.

"You keep looking at me like that, you're going to attract attention," he said. "Where were you taking the box?"

"To my car." She nodded in the direction of the

reserved spaces in the executive parking lot, not too far from the employee entrance from which she had emerged. She glanced around nervously. Rows of cars baked beneath the blazing sun, but there was no one else around, which was why she'd been carrying the box in the first place.

The building that housed the corporate offices of SunSouth Airlines was one of Dallas's famed contemporary structures, built basically of glass held together by a framework of steel. So anyone looking out from this side of the building had an unrestricted view of the parking lot and could see her with him, possibly even recognize him.

However, if he hadn't been this close, she probably couldn't have identified him herself. He'd altered his appearance with a baseball cap and sunglasses. He had on a faded T-shirt that was nearly threadbare, knee-length shorts with a ragged hem, and sneakers instead of cowboy boots. But his height and the width of his shoulders were impossible to disguise, although he attempted to by walking in a slouch.

"What are you doing here?" she repeated.

"I know it's against the rules."

"Foster would—"

"Go apeshit, I know. But it was important that I see you."

"You could have called."

"Would you have taken the call?"

Probably not, she thought. "Okay, you're here. What's so urgent? Are you backing out?"

He stopped, turned to her. "Do you want me to?"

"You left saying you didn't need this shit, remember?"

"And you reminded me how much I do."

They looked at each other for several seconds, then simultaneously remembered how vulnerable they were to being seen together and resumed walking in the direction of the reserved spaces.

"Which one's yours?"

"The black BMW."

"Hit the trunk button."

She juggled her keys, depressed the button, and the lid of her trunk automatically opened. He lowered the cumbersome box and placed it inside. "What's in here? For being so bulky, it's light."

"An airplane model. I'm taking it home."

"To Speakman? I notice he didn't come to work today."

He was still bent at the waist, fiddling with the box. To a casual observer it would have looked as though he was situating it in the trunk to prevent damage during transport.

"How do you know that?"

"Because that first parking slot has his name stenciled on it, and it's empty. I know he wasn't here earlier because I've been staked out across the street—"

"Staked out?"

"At that pizza place. For hours. Watching this door, waiting for an opportunity to talk to you."

"What's so important that it couldn't wait until the next time we meet?"

"Will there be a next time?" He straightened up and turned to face her.

She gave a small bob of her head.

"You, uh—"

"Yes. Day before yesterday."

"Oh."

He just stood there.

She examined her keys.

Forever.

Then he said, "You must've been disappointed."

"Of course I was. *We* were. Foster and I." Drawing a quick breath, she said, "So, you and I must meet again." Having avoided looking at him except peripherally, she tilted her head back and looked directly into the opaque lenses of his sunglasses. "Unless you resign."

"We've been over that."

"Then what's so important that you came here?"

"I came to warn you."

She had expected a demand for more advance money. Maybe even an apology for what he'd said to her before he left last time. But a warning? "Warn me about what?"

"A couple weeks ago. When we were together. You saw the bruises on my face?"

"And your hip."

He tilted his head, and she knew that if she could see into his eyes they would be looking at her curiously. There was only one way she would have known about the bruises on his butt, and she'd given herself away. But to try to maneuver herself out of the blunder would only make it more awkward.

"What about the bruises?" she asked impatiently.

"I wish I could say the other guys looked worse."

"Guys? More than one?"

"Two. I was jumped in a restaurant parking lot

and beaten up. A few weeks before that, a friend of mine got it even worse." His lips formed a hard, thin line. "Much worse. And hasn't recovered yet."

Laura couldn't believe what she was hearing. "What are you into?"

"Nothing!"

"You and your friend got beaten up over *nothing*?"

"Listen to me," he said, bending nearer, talking quickly and softly. "It goes back to five years ago, but it has nothing to do with me now. Except that there's this asshole who's made it his life's mission to ruin my life. His name is Stanley Rodarte. He drives an ugly, olive green car. If you see him, stay out of his way. Under no circumstances let him get near you while you're alone. Are you hearing me?"

"I'm rarely alone."

"You were just now. Look how easy it was for me to get close to you." As though to emphasize that, he looked down at the space between them, which was less than a foot.

"I appreciate the warning," Laura said, distancing herself, and more than just physically. "But your extracurricular activities have nothing to do with Foster and me. This Stanley whatever poses no threat to us."

"Rodarte, and the hell he doesn't," he said, pushing the words out. "Listen to me. He's dangerous. Given a chance, he would hurt you, in ways you probably can't even imagine. This is no bullshit. He—"

"Laura?"

They jumped guiltily at the sound of another voice. She turned and spotted Joe McDonald approaching them from the next row over. "Hi, Joe," she called, trying to sound normal and glad to see him.

"Remember what I told you," Griff said in an undertone, then he walked quickly away.

Forcing herself to move, Laura headed off the marketing head, who was looking curiously after Griff's tall figure as he wove between the rows of cars. "Who was that?"

"Someone cutting across our parking lot. Lucky for me. He saw me lugging the box with the Select model in it and offered to carry it for me."

"Where was the guard at the door?"

"He wasn't there when I came through, and I didn't want to wait." Without it being obvious, she steered Joe toward the entrance. "I'm eager to get the model home and show Foster."

"So tonight's the big night?"

"It is. Wish me luck."

As they approached the entrance, she glanced casually over her shoulder. Griff Burkett had disappeared.

CHAPTER
16

LAURA DIDN'T TELL FOSTER ABOUT GRIFF Burkett's unexpected appearance.

Ordinarily she didn't keep anything from her husband. But she was reluctant to share Burkett's warning about a man in a green car because even a hint of her being in danger would send Foster into a tailspin. He would respond in typical Foster fashion; she would have armed guards within an hour.

Furthermore, she wanted nothing else competing for Foster's attention tonight.

She changed clothes before coming down to dinner, putting on a simple black dress that was one of his favorites. She took extra time with her hair and makeup. She applied fragrance.

Descending the staircase, she realized she had butterflies, and that nervousness surprised her. But then, she reminded herself, she'd been preparing for this night for months. A little stage fright was understandable.

She barely touched her meal, but Foster didn't notice because he was enthusiastically telling her about a new exercise Manuelo had incorporated into his physical therapy sessions.

"It's helping to strengthen my back and arms. I've noticed a big improvement already."

"Did he learn the technique at that seminar you enrolled him in last month?"

"Yes. Obviously he's a quick study."

"He would be even quicker if he knew English."

"He's a very proud man."

"How would learning English damage his pride?"

"He would regard it as a betrayal of his heritage."

Before she could comment further, he asked about her day at the office. "I'm glad you mentioned it," she said, giving him a mischievous smile. "I have a surprise for you after dinner."

When they were done with the meal, she asked him to follow her from the dining room. He rolled the wheels of his chair forward and backward three times before moving ahead. He'd adopted that habit a few weeks ago.

Also, plastic containers of hand sanitizer had begun showing up everywhere. Initially he'd used them when he thought she wasn't looking. Now dozens of them were scattered throughout the house so that one was always within Foster's reach. Cleanliness and germ killing had always been obsessions, but these recent signs of his OCD disturbed her. She would insist he speak with his psychiatrist about these manifestations.

But tonight they would not address his disorder or anything else negative. Besides, once Foster was focused on the project she was about to introduce, his symptoms would probably recede again.

She'd set up everything in the den beforehand. Leading him to the closed door, she pushed it open and dramatically intoned, "Introducing SunSouth Select." She stepped aside so he could see the prominently displayed artist's rendering, the banner she'd had made bearing the new logo, the graphs and charts standing on easels for quick reference, and the model.

Looking a bit overwhelmed by the visuals, Foster did the three-times back-and-forth routine, then slowly rolled his chair into the room. "What's all this?"

"An innovation in airline service, conceived with frequent fliers and business travelers in mind," she said, as though addressing a room full of people from a podium. "Allow me?"

"By all means."

She stood before him as though assuming center stage. "SunSouth Select will offer red-carpet treatment on a limited number of flights from Dallas to high-density destinations. Houston, Atlanta, Denver, Los Angeles, Washington, D.C., New York. One early morning flight. One late evening.

"Select will be for members only. Fliers will be prescreened and registered. They will have passes enabling them to avoid the normal airport security checks. Select will provide white-glove baggage handling. Car service to and from the airport would be optional but recommended to guarantee even better service and fewer of the hassles normally associated with business travel.

"Airplanes designed for one hundred thirty passengers would be reconfigured to accommodate fifty. Even the overseas carriers who cater to their first-class passengers would pale in comparison to the pampering given the subscribers to SunSouth Select.

"Expensive? Definitely. But less expensive than owning even a fractional share of a private jet, and much more leg- and headroom," she added with a smile. "For what a business executive would spend chartering a private jet to these destinations, he could fly in much more comfort with specially trained flight attendants waiting on him. Or her."

So far Foster had said nothing, but he was listening.

She continued. "Because it would operate under the auspices of SunSouth Airlines, the traveler would be assured of Select's dependability, stringent safety standards, and incomparable efficiency.

"That efficiency is SunSouth's trademark, but it hasn't come without a price. The one criticism often heard, especially from the frequent business passenger, is that SunSouth is equivalent to traveling in a Greyhound bus. Ten months ago, the airline began offering a reserved seat as opposed to first-come-first-served. That's proven to be a hugely successful option.

"Eighteen point three percent of our passengers are willing to pay the additional twenty dollars per ticket to guarantee a reserved seat and have the convenience of boarding first. Extrapolating, if even one half of one percent of those eighteen point three percent buy a membership in SunSouth Select, the airplanes will fly full.

"In recent years, private jet ownership has become extremely competitive, but this mode of transportation is still affordable to only a minuscule percentage of travelers. On the one hand, you have no-frills airlines, like SunSouth and Southwest. On the other, private jets.

"SunSouth Select would fill the gap in between. That gap is projected to widen as carriers decrease first-class service in favor of economy travel. Granted, it's a narrow margin of the marketplace, but a vital one because it caters to those who *must* and *do* fly tens of thousands of miles each year. Fortunately, those fliers are also the ones who have the funds to spend on air travel. If SunSouth doesn't claim that niche in the marketplace, a competing airline will. Select will ensure that SunSouth maintains its position as a leader in the airline industry."

It was the planned wrap-up to her pitch. When Foster was certain she had concluded, he rolled his chair forward and back three times, then moved to the table where she had placed the model. One side of the fuselage had been made of clear plastic so that the interior, which far surpassed even the most luxurious and roomy first-class cabins, was visible. He studied it for what to Laura seemed an interminably long time.

Finally he spoke. "It's been tried before. Rolls-Royce service for Rolls-Royce prices. Those airlines didn't last long."

She had an answer for that argument. "They

didn't sell memberships. They relied on single book-ings, so they ran into cash-flow problems. We would sell memberships, renewable annually. Before the first plane ever took off, we'd have operating capital to sustain the service for at least a year. And earning interest at the same time."

"The membership would entitle the passenger to fly a given number of segments?"

"Miles, actually, since some of the segments are longer than others. We're thinking in the neighbor-hood of seventy-five thousand miles. If the member doesn't fly them all, he forfeits them. If he flies above that number, for each additional flight, he pays a fee equivalent to the price of a first-class ticket on another airline."

"And those numbers work?"

"It's in the syllabus." She passed him a three-ring binder with the SunSouth Select logo embossed on the leather cover. He studied the logo but returned the binder to the table unopened.

"How much would we have to charge for the memberships?"

"As I said, the syllabus contains several financial projections. If we charge this much, our margin of profit would be larger than if we charged that much."

"I know what a financial projection is, Laura."

Taken aback by his tone, she murmured, "Of course you do. I just wanted you to understand that this is all preliminary."

"Really? It seems so well thought out."

"I've worked on it long and hard, Foster. I've tried to think through every aspect and contin-gency."

"Who else has been in on it?"

She laughed. "That makes it sound like a conspiracy."

"It sort of looks like a conspiracy. A few weeks ago when I asked you if the mice were playing while the cat was away, I meant it as a joke."

"Are you angry?"

Forward, back, forward, back, forward, back, then over to the bar, where he poured himself a shot of scotch. He didn't offer to pour her one. "What does the TSA say about these special passes issued to members?"

"It isn't a new idea. Passes for frequent fliers is a topic already on the table. Some are already in use at selected airports."

"Where would the planes come from?"

"With so many airlines reducing flights for economic reasons, we could buy the grounded planes for pennies on the dollar."

"It would still cost millions. Millions more to convert them to that," he said, gesturing toward the model.

"SunSouth has an extensive line of credit. We borrow the money—"

"And if this concept fails, we're stuck with a huge debt and no way to pay it back."

"We would incorporate those newly purchased planes into our normal operation. Our planes always fly full, usually they're oversold, and we were planning to expand the fleet next year anyway."

He finished his scotch in one swallow, then went back to the bar, took a cocktail napkin, and wiped the rim of his empty glass, circling it three times, before placing it in the rack beneath the sink. He replaced the stopper in the crystal decanter and put it back exactly where it had been. He used one of the bottles of hand sanitizer.

Finally he said, "It's all very speculative, Laura."

"And preliminary. I said as much. It needs a lot of fine tuning. I'm relying on you for that."

He didn't address that. "The likelihood of it succeeding is slim."

"So was the likelihood of SunSouth's making it when you took over. Everyone told you there wasn't room for another commercial airline based in Dallas. Economists said you were crazy. Business analysts laughed in your face. You didn't listen. You steamrolled over the skeptics. You didn't let anything keep you from realizing your dream."

"I wasn't a cripple then."

If he'd slapped her, she couldn't have been more shocked. Indeed, he had struck her where he knew it would hurt the most. She stared at him, then, recovering from her initial astonishment, turned and headed for the door.

"Laura. Laura, wait! I'm sorry." She paused, her hand on the doorknob. He came up behind her and reached for her hand. "God, I'm so sorry. Forgive me."

He pulled her down onto his lap, took her head between his hands, forcing it around so she would have to look at him. "I'm sorry." He kissed her cheek, then her lips. "I'm sorry. Forgive me."

Hearing genuine regret in his voice, she relaxed her posture. "Why would you say something like that, Foster?"

"It was uncalled for. Completely."

She looked over his shoulder at the display,

which represented so many hours of labor for her and many others. "I thought this would excite and invigorate you."

He stroked her hair. "I ruined your surprise with my negativity. I apologize for that. Especially since you've already had one letdown this week."

He was talking about her period. True, that was a letdown, but she wouldn't be distracted from this subject by talking about that. "Do you hate the idea of SunSouth Select?"

"It's a lot to absorb in fifteen minutes." His gentle smile was an attempt to soften the blow, as were his carefully chosen words. "You've had months to fuel your enthusiasm. I was blindsided. Give me some time to mull it over."

"But your initial reaction is thumbs down."

"Not at all. It's cautiously favorable to an idea that needs further study."

Which translated to thumbs down.

He guided her head to his shoulder. "In the meantime, congratulations on a job well done. It's one of the best presentations I've ever heard."

He was rejecting the idea but giving her an A for effort. She hated being patronized but was too downcast to take issue with it tonight. She'd poured all her energy into the presentation. Now that it was over, and hadn't yielded the result she'd wished for, she felt hollow and depleted.

"Now," he said, as though a minor matter had been dealt with and dismissed, "tell me what else happened today."

CHAPTER
17

BOLLY RICH CLIMBED THE BLEACHERS AND sat down beside Griff. For a full sixty seconds they sat there in identical poses—forearms braced on their thighs, hands clasped between their knees—staring at the players on the field.

Bolly was the first to break the silence. "What the hell are you doing, Griff?"

"I'm watching practice."

"This is the third day in a row you've been here."

"You're counting?"

"Yeah, I'm counting. What's the deal?"

"Well, in my learned opinion, Jason is as good as any other player on this team. They don't have a strong running back. Their safety's for shit. Jason's scrambling, but he's—"

"Cut the crap, Griff," Bolly said, even angrier than before. "What are you doing watching a middle school's football practice?"

Griff turned his head then and looked at him. "Killing time, Bolly. 'Cause I've got nothing else to do. Last time I checked, this was public property, giving me as much right to be here as you. You don't like it, you don't have to speak to me. I didn't invite you up here. So why don't you go back down there and rejoin the decent folk before I rub off on you and you get ousted from the Booster Club?"

Down on the field, the coaches had the boys huddled, letting them drink from their water bottles while talking them through plays. The boys looked too small for their wide shoulder pads. From this distance they looked like bobble-head dolls, all out of proportion. Griff had started playing football at about Jason's age. He supposed he had looked small then, too.

Bolly stayed where he was. He said, "My kid idolizes you."

"I make a sorry hero."

"I told him as much."

They watched as the coaches divided the offensive players from the defensive and herded the two groups to opposite ends of the field to run practice drills. Five minutes passed. Ten.

Then Bolly cleared his throat. "That night in Buffalo?"

Griff didn't acknowledge that he'd heard him, although he knew immediately the particular night he was referring to.

"Never been so cold in my life."

"Ten below at game time," Griff said. "Or so they told me later. They didn't have the heart to tell us in the locker room before the game. Sixty minutes of football played in blowing snow, and at the final whistle, all we had to show for it was a freaking field goal. The kicker, wrapped in Mylar and sipping hot drinks on the bench the whole game, trots his skinny ass out there and makes the only three points of the game. My fingers are bleeding from some Bills lineman digging his cleats in. They're so cold I can't even bend them. That runty kicker gets all the glory."

Bolly snuffled a laugh. "He was a cocky bastard to start with."

"Tell me. Where was he from anyway? There were no vowels in his last name."

"One of those eastern European countries. Switched from soccer to football so he could come to the States and make more money. Cowboys are well rid of him."

It had been an inglorious win to a game that came late in the season, its outcome irrelevant to the play-offs. The airport was closed because of the blizzard, so the team couldn't fly home. No one was in a party mood as they returned to the hotel for another night. Most went straight to their rooms.

"You and I wound up the last ones in the bar," Bolly said, as though following Griff's thoughts. "I got wasted."

"Bolly—"

"No, no, this needs to be said, Griff. I got drunk on my ass and blubbered like a baby about my marital problems."

Best Griff could recall, Bolly's wife had packed up and moved out on him, saying she was sick of staying at home with their young son while he was away having fun with the guys, covering one sporting event or another.

"It worked out okay, apparently," Griff said.

"Lucky for me."

As drunk as Bolly had been that night, Griff was surprised that he even remembered his emotional meltdown. Maybe he'd needed that catharsis to make things right at home. He and his wife were still together. He had a nice house, a kid with a reasonable haircut and no visible body piercings. Why bring it up now?

"I never thanked you for keeping my confidence," Bolly said quietly.

Griff looked over at him.

Shrugging self-consciously, Bolly removed his tinted eyeglasses and twirled them by the stem. "A lot of my colleagues cheat on their wives when they're on the road. They sure as hell don't cry over them. I'd given you plenty to talk about in the locker room. But you never breathed a word of it to anybody."

"I didn't have any friends, remember? Nobody to tell."

Bolly gave him a wry look. "But you never brought it up to me, either. Held it over me. You know. In fact, you pretended it hadn't happened." He ducked his head and squinted down at his sneakers. "And you never called in the favor, not even when you came asking me for a job. That's been eating at me ever since."

Bolly replaced his glasses. Several minutes passed while they watched as Jason's coach gave him some pointers on taking the snap. Finally Bolly said, "This guy's okay for a middle school coach, but Jason could use some extra help. I realize it's not much of a job. In fact, Griff, it's not—"

"I accept."

"Hold on. Any offer of payment I make will be insulting."

"You don't have to pay me. I need something constructive to do. Buy a dozen footballs for me to use, and we'll call it square."

Bolly considered him a moment, then seemed to reach a decision. "How about here, an hour before practice each day?"

"Suits me." They shook hands. "Tell Jason to come prepared to work his butt off."

"He'll be thrilled. Start tomorrow?"

"I'll be here."

Bolly stood and clumped down several of the bleachers, then stopped and turned back. "This doesn't mean I excuse what you did, Griff. You're still on probation, with me as well as with the court. The least hint of trouble, you're outta here."

"There won't be any trouble. I swear."

Bolly nodded, then continued down the bleachers to join the other dads who were standing on the sideline watching practice.

Griff wasn't invited to join them, and wouldn't be, but that was all right. He felt better than he had in a long while. He had a project now, something to look forward to, a reason for getting out of bed in the morning. And for coaching an aspiring quarterback, no one was better qualified. Knowing that made him feel good.

He was smiling when his cell phone rang.

He arrived ahead of her and parked in back. A few minutes later, she pulled her car in behind his.

"A meeting ran long," she said as she got out.

"I just got here myself."

Together they walked toward the front of the house. While she was unlocking the door, he looked in both directions along the street. No olive sedan. He'd come straight from the middle school practice field and knew he hadn't been followed there. In fact, he hadn't seen Rodarte or anyone suspicious since their last confrontation—a month ago, he realized.

But he didn't think for a moment that Rodarte had been scared off. In fact, his noticeable absence was unnerving. Griff would prefer him to stay visible, at least occasionally. With that in mind, as soon as they got inside, he asked Laura if she'd seen the guy he'd warned her about.

"In the ugly green car?" One of her eyebrows arched slightly.

"Why are you looking at me like that? Do you think I made him up?"

"What I think is that you took an unnecessary risk of being seen with me."

"I know the rules, but you needed to know about Rodarte."

"I doubt it."

"Look—"

"I don't want to argue about it," she snapped. Then she rubbed her forehead and sighed wearily. "I haven't seen a man in a green car lurking about."

"Good. Thank you. That's all I wanted to know. Why didn't you just say that and save us the argument?"

She looked ready to take issue, then changed her mind and started toward the bedroom.

"What was the model?"

"What?"

"The model. In the box I carried to your car."

"It was an airplane model."

"I figured that much. You were taking it home to show your husband. What for?"

"For a presentation."

"Yeah? How'd it go?"

Avoiding eye contact, she combed her fingers through her hair. "It doesn't matter now." Before giving him an opportunity to say more about it, she walked down the hallway and disappeared into the bedroom.

Griff stood looking after her, wondering what had caused her to be in such a snit. A quarrel at home? Bad day at the office? Or just put out that she had to endure him again.

Screw it. Let her be snippy. Let her sulk. Whatever. He didn't care. He only hoped to God it worked this time. He was ready to cash in and blow.

He tugged his shirttail from his waistband and pulled off his boots. He checked the wall thermostat and lowered it several degrees. He went into the kitchen and checked the fridge. Same bottled water, same six-pack of Diet Coke. He didn't want either, but he unbuttoned his shirt and stood in the open door of the fridge, fanning the cold air onto his chest.

Back in the living room, he opened the armoire and scanned the titles of the videos. Maybe he should check one out, just for variety. Let's see. Men with women. Women with women. *A Tail of Two Cities.* Hmm. *Which two cities?* he wondered. On one cover a chick wearing nothing but strips of black leather was straddling a motorcycle. Her snarl and sharp red fingernails turned him off, not on.

He closed the armoire doors, once again rejecting the videos and magazines in favor of his own imagination.

"Come in."

He went into the bedroom and closed the door. Midway across the room, he stopped. She was lying as before, staring at the ceiling, covered to her waist by the sheet. Above it, she was fully dressed.

But this time there were tear tracks on her cheeks.

When he didn't immediately move to the bed, she glanced at him, then back at the ceiling.

He walked to the foot of the bed. "What's the matter?"

"Nothing."

"You've been crying."

"I'm just tired."

"You cry when you're tired?"

She looked at him and said testily, "Sometimes. Now, can we please just get this over with?"

Pissed off by her tone and the condescension behind it, he muttered, "At your service, ma'am," and shoved down his jeans, actually hoping the sight of his tented boxers would offend her. It did. She turned her head aside.

He kicked off his jeans, peeled off his shorts, and crawled onto the bed, stretching out on top of her. He wrestled with the sheet, cursing its tenacity, before he got it out of the way. Her legs parted. He moved into position, thrust, missed, thrust again.

It was easier than the first two times. Faster, too. Quickly over. If you looked up *slam-bam-thank-you-ma'am* in the dictionary . . .

He didn't even give himself time to catch his breath before levering himself up. As he did, he glanced at her averted face. And froze. Fresh tears were rolling down her cheeks like silent admonitions. Her lower lip was clamped between her teeth as though to keep it from trembling.

Well, shit. How bad could it have been?

Apparently pretty bad, because her chest hitched on a sob.

"Hell, did I hurt you?"

She shook her head.

"You said you wanted it over with."

She tried to say something, but the words got lodged in her throat. She swallowed convulsively.

Griff, at a loss, didn't say anything. Instead, he laid his hand against her wet cheek. At his touch, she tensed beneath him. When she raised her hand, he expected her to remove his from her face. Instead, she covered his hand with hers, then turned her face into his palm so that the heel of his hand was under her chin and the tips of his fingers were curved up over her hairline.

Her breath struck with hot gusts of emotion. Tears were captured in his palm. He watched her throat as she struggled to contain the choppy sounds of weeping. And then, when she couldn't hold them back anymore, she clamped her teeth again. Except this time it wasn't her lip that was caught between them. It was the meaty pad at the base of his thumb. She sank her teeth into it.

The effect on Griff was instantaneous. He sucked in a quick, audible breath.

Her teeth let go immediately. He lifted his hand off her face. Their eyes connected with an impact as startling as the bite. Her eyes, swimming in tears, widened fractionally when she felt what he couldn't control. Didn't want to control. He swelled inside her with an infusion of blood so hot and insistent, he had neither the time, the willpower, nor the desire to withdraw.

He filled her completely. Or was she shrinking around him? It was difficult to tell. And it didn't matter. Because, God, it was a rush, the most erotic damn thing ever to happen to him.

He pressed his hips forward, tentatively, testing her reaction. Her eyes closed briefly, then reopened. Her eyelashes were wet, forming spiky clumps, very pretty. There was a black speck in the iris of her right eye that he'd never noticed before, but he'd never been this close to her before. He had never really looked into her eyes. He hadn't allowed himself to look into them.

Still tentative, he angled his hips forward and up. Her breath made a soft hissing sound as she inhaled through her teeth. Her eyes closed. Encouraged, he slid his arm beneath her, scooped her ass into his hand, and tilted her up at the same time he pressed deep. A hungry sound vibrated in her throat, because by now her lips were rolled inward, tightly compressed. She was breathing rapidly through her nose.

He pulled back, almost out, then sank into her again. She groaned. He did it again. His strokes were long, slow, and deep, and she responded with corresponding movements that soon had him calling on deities in mindless gasps.

Her hands, which before had always stayed motionless at her sides, were moving restlessly. She took fistfuls of the sheet, twisted it, then released it and reached for more, for something, and found the front panels of his shirt, still unbuttoned. She clutched the fabric, tugging until he could feel it pull taut across his back. Her throat arched as her head dug into the pillow. Her hips lifted to meet his thrusts, more shallow now, and faster.

Then holding her tightly to him, grinding against her, he came hard, and so did she. Even when he was spent, lying on her like a dead man, her tiny orgasmic aftershocks nipped at him. It was like being kissed right on the tip of his cock. He was too whipped even to smile, but in his mind he did.

Eventually they were still.

He cupped the back of her head in his hand and rolled onto his side, carrying her with him. And he held her like that, one hand securing her head beneath his chin, the other still firmly on her ass, holding her in place, keeping him inside her. The sensations were indescribable. He was torn between wanting to stay there like that until they petrified, and looking at her.

He wished there was a way to get out of their clothes without moving. He was suddenly desperate to be skin to skin. He wanted to look at her breasts. At all of her. To touch, explore, nuzzle, and pet all those tantalizing spots he hadn't let himself even think about.

Later. Right now, her lethargy was so absolute, she appeared to be asleep. He angled his head back so he could look into her face. Her lips were slightly parted, damp and soft looking, swollen and red from her biting them. Where the fuller lower lip met the upper one, there was a shallow dimple. Jesus, that was a sexy spot, begging to be caressed by the tip of his tongue.

He was lowering his head to do just that when her body went rigid. Her eyes sprang open, and in a flurry of thrashing limbs she separated them and sat up. "Oh, God." She buried her face in her hands. "Ohgodohgodohgod."

"Laura—"

"Don't say anything! Just please don't . . . don't . . . Oh, God." She was groping for something at the side of the bed, and he saw it was her underwear. She wrestled the panties on and left the bed, disappearing into the bathroom and soundly closing the door behind her.

He got up and clumsily pulled on his boxers, went to the bathroom door, and knocked. "Laura." Without waiting for permission, he opened the door.

She was working her skirt up over her hips and shoving her feet into her shoes at the same time. Once she had the skirt fastened, she grabbed her jacket off a hook on the back of the door. In perpetual motion, she pushed him aside and went past, snatched her handbag from the top of the bureau, and flung open the bedroom door.

"Laura, wait!" He trailed her down the hall. Halfway across the living room, he hooked her elbow with his hand to bring her around. "Will you wait a damn minute? Talk to me."

She yanked her arm free, wouldn't look at him. "There's nothing to talk about."

"Only everything."

"That didn't happen." She patted the air with both hands, emphasizing each word. "It did not happen."

"It happened."

Squeezing her eyes shut, she shook her head furiously. "No, it didn't. I—" She covered her mouth with her hand to catch a sob. "Oh, my God." Spinning away from him, she walked quickly to the door.

He lunged after her, but she was out like a flash.

"Laura!" he shouted.

She didn't look back.

CHAPTER
18

FOSTER WAS ON THE TELEPHONE WHEN Laura came into his office. She hesitated on the threshold, but he waved her in. Her arrival gave him a welcome excuse to conclude his conversation with one of the board members. It had begun to bore him.

Running the airline wasn't as much fun as it used to be. Key personnel were so good at their jobs, they could do them without his supervision. From a management standpoint, it was gratifying to know he'd made wise choices in hiring them. But their reliability made him superfluous.

These days he often felt like the token handicapped employee.

He wrapped up his phone conversation with a promise to continue it soon. Laura was standing with her back to him, staring out the window. "To what do I owe this honor?" he asked. "You're usually too busy to pay me a call during business hours.

Or *is* this business? Are you here as department head or wife?"

"Wife. Do you have time for me now?"

"Always."

She'd taken his rejection of SunSouth Select hard, harder than he would have guessed. Since joining the executive ranks of the airline, she had been overruled and outvoted on numerous issues, but she took those small defeats in stride and ultimately gave wholehearted support to the majority rule.

Not this time, and with reason. Although she'd given others credit for creative and informative input, Select had been her vision, and he had essentially squelched it. Judging from her mood over the past couple of weeks, she had regarded it as a personal rejection.

The subject had come up only once in the meantime. Last week during an executive meeting, Joe McDonald had mentioned Select in passing. Laura had shot him a warning look that said: *Don't talk about that.* It hadn't been spoken of again, at least not in Foster's presence, and he didn't think it was being whispered about behind his back. Nowhere in the building had he seen any of the materials Laura had used for her presentation. He got a sense that, since he hadn't taken up the baton, everyone considered it a dead issue.

He had snuffed SunSouth Select while, actually, the prospect of offering alternative carrier service was exciting. Unbeknownst to Laura, he had been thinking about it himself and doing his own research into that growing market, assessing how he might claim a large segment of it.

He'd studied the new superlight jets and considered ordering a fleet of them with which to begin a top-notch charter service. He'd even given thought to doing as Laura suggested and starting an offshoot of SunSouth.

But whatever form the innovation took, it would be his conception and his design. Not hers or anyone else's. He would be the leader, not the crippled has-been.

He'd given her space and time to nurse her wounded pride, basically by pretending not to notice her dejection. Was this unscheduled visit to his office a sign that she was finally climbing out of her funk? One could hope.

He said, "You didn't bring wine this time."

She turned around and looked at him quizzically.

"Has it been so long ago that you've forgotten? You surprised me with lunch here in this office. To celebrate our three-month anniversary."

"Four-month. And it was champagne."

"Was it? What we drank isn't the part I remember. However, I vividly recall dessert."

She smiled and modestly ducked her head. "Fun times."

"I miss them."

After several beats, she raised her head and looked at him, all seriousness now. "We could still have fun times, Foster."

"Not like that."

"Not *exactly* like that. Different. But just as good."

He gave a mirthless laugh. "Not from my standpoint."

She held his gaze for a moment, then declared, "I'm not going back."

"Back?"

"To the house. To Griff Burkett. I'm not doing it again."

So. This was how she was going to pay him back for hurting her feelings. Keeping his expression impassive, he folded his hands in his lap, clasping them loosely. "Oh?"

"No."

"Why this sudden—"

"It's not sudden. I've thought about little else since . . . since the last time. I'm not going back."

"You said that. I think I deserve to know why."

"Because it's wrong."

"Wrong by what standard? How can it be wrong if I sanction it?"

"*I* don't. It's wrong by *my* standard."

"I see. When did you decide it was wrong?"

She looked away, saying in an undertone, "When you first proposed it." Then, more staunchly, she said, "I was against it from the beginning. I consented to it only because I love you and wanted to give you anything you asked of me. But I can't do this. I won't."

"I thought you wanted a child as much as I do."

"That hasn't changed," she exclaimed. "I *do* want a baby. I want that for us. Very much. But we have options. I can be artificially inseminated using an anonymous sperm donor."

"You know how I feel about that."

She hesitated, then said, "All right. I'll make that concession. Since Griff Burkett is already in our confidence, we can use his semen. He suggested that at our first meeting with him, remember? That way he wouldn't lose out on his money. We'd take his specimens to the doctor's office and claim they were yours. No one would know the difference."

"I'd rather not resort to that method."

"I don't see it as resorting."

"I do. And, anyway, isn't it too soon to go to plan B? It's only been three cycles."

"I know how many it's been," she said curtly. "But even if it was only one, I'm not doing it again."

"Is it Burkett you find objectionable? Does he treat you badly?"

"No."

"Rudely, roughly?"

"No."

"Because if he does—"

"He *doesn't.*"

"Okay." He let that lie without further comment, giving her time to collect herself.

She took a deep breath and let it out slowly. "My decision has nothing to do with him. This is about me. And the whole idea of it."

"We discussed the idea for months, Laura. We went over every aspect of it, time and again."

"I'm aware of that."

"And you agreed."

"Yes. But talking about it in the abstract and actually . . ." Suddenly she drew herself up to her full height. "I shouldn't have to justify the way I feel. Or try to explain it. I don't want to do it," she said with emphasis. "That should be the end of it."

He let several moments elapse, then said, "This surprises me. It's not like you to leave a job unfinished."

"True."

"You've never walked away from a commitment."

"No, and I didn't plan to break this one. I thought I could approach it like any other challenge. But I can't."

"I didn't think it would cause you this much emotional distress."

"Well, it does."

"Perhaps you're taking it too personally."

She looked at him aghast. "I'm your *wife*. I'm having sexual intercourse with another man. How in God's name can it not be personal?"

"You're becoming hysterical, Laura." He cast a cautious glance toward his office door.

She hugged her elbows and turned her back on him. He rolled forward and back three times, then wheeled his chair away from his desk and moved up behind her. He reached out and placed his hands on either side of her waist. She flinched and tried to move away, but he held her firmly. "I miscalculated. I didn't think it would offend your sense of right and wrong."

"I hate disappointing you, Foster. I know how much this means to you. But there's a moral ambiguity that I cannot get past."

"I honor your feelings, of course. As well as your decision."

She expelled a soft breath. "Thank you."

He applied enough pressure to turn her around to face him. "You've been morose for weeks. I haven't remarked on it, but I've noticed."

"I admit I haven't been myself. This has been weighing heavily on my mind. It was distracting me from work. Worse, it was creating a barrier between us. Knowing it would be a disappointment, I put off telling you, but had to before it was time to meet Burkett again. The dread of telling you has been nerve-racking. I'm glad to have this conversation behind us." She gave him a tremulous smile, then leaned down and kissed his lips.

When she pulled away, he said, "It's been fifteen days since you were last with Burkett, correct?"

She nodded.

"Then this discussion may have been for nothing," he said with a bright smile. "You may be pregnant already."

What if she's pregnant?

It was the big what-if in Griff's life now. Each morning he woke up wondering if this would be the day he'd get the congratulatory call.

Of course, that was their goal, wasn't it? A fertilized egg would be the answer to all their troubles. It would make the childless couple happy, and make him a millionaire for the rest of his life.

But if Laura had conceived, he would never see her again.

Which was no cause for celebration.

"Griff?"

He was startled to find Bolly standing elbow to elbow with him on the practice field sideline. The sportswriter was looking at him strangely.

"Sorry. I was—"

"A million miles away. I had to say your name three times. Were you asleep?"

Griff removed his sunglasses and blinked against the blistering sun. "In this heat? Hardly. I was concentrating on Jason. He's showing some good hustle out there today."

"Thanks to you."

"No, he's applying himself. Credit belongs to him."

"The boy is obsessed with football. Worries his mom."

"How come?"

"She's afraid he'll go whole hog and get hurt."

"Moms are like that." He supposed.

"She'd rather he play badminton."

Griff winced and Bolly laughed. "My sentiments exactly. Say, listen, I just got a call. I've been granted an interview with that new goalie the Stars signed yesterday, but it's a narrow window of opportunity before he flies home to Detroit. If I rush, I can catch him at DFW before his flight. I hate to pull Jason out of practice. Would you mind driving him home?"

"Of course not."

"I wouldn't ask, but my mother-in-law had to go to the podiatrist, and my wife volunteered to drive her, so—"

"Bolly, go. Should I stay with Jason till you get home?"

"No, just see him into the house, make sure he locks the door. He knows the rules of staying by himself."

"Okay. No problem."

Bolly looked toward the field and picked out his son, who barely had time to hand the ball off to a halfback before being slammed to the ground by a tackle. But he wasn't down for long. He was back on his feet in time to see the halfback make a first down. He jumped straight up into the air, raised his fist, and whooped with joy.

Bolly, still watching, smiled, but then a worry line formed between his brows. "Griff, on second thought, maybe—"

"You can trust him with me, Bolly."

Bolly turned back to him and held his gaze for several seconds while silently debating the advisability of asking for this favor. Then he nodded. "I appreciate it, Griff. Thanks."

When practice was over, Jason jogged off the field toward Griff, who gave him a high five. "Great practice, QB. Especially that last offensive series."

"Thanks." The boy was red in the face, and sweat had plastered his hair to his head beneath his helmet, but he was basking in the praise.

Griff told him about Bolly's unexpected errand. "Which leaves me your ride home today."

"You mean it?"

"Don't get excited. My car's crap."

On the way, Griff pulled into a Braum's. "I could use a milk shake. How 'bout you?"

As long as they were there, they decided they might just as well have burgers and fries to go with their shakes. They were seated in a booth, talking amiably about Jason's team and the strengths and weaknesses of various players, when Griff became aware of a trio of construction workers. He'd noticed them when they came in but had given them only a passing glance before returning his attention to Jason.

Now he realized that he'd been spotted and recognized. The workmen kept their voices low, but the looks they directed at him sizzled with hostility.

Others began to notice. Griff could feel a dozen pairs of eyes fixed on him.

Jason, who'd been chatting nonstop, barely pausing long enough to fill his mouth with food, became aware of the charged atmosphere. His chatter slowed down and then stopped altogether. He looked toward the three men, then across at Griff, his eyes clouded with concern.

"It's okay, Jason."

But it wasn't. Because when the men got their carryout orders and were on their way to the exit, they had to pass the booth in which Griff and Jason sat. As the last one filed past, he said, "You suck, Burkett." Then he hawked up a gob of phlegm and spat it at Griff. It missed, smacking into the vinyl upholstery inches from Griff's shoulder.

Their departure left a vacuum. No one moved. Griff figured everyone was waiting to see what he would do. What he wanted to do was follow the guy out and kick his ass up into his hard hat. Had he been alone, he would have.

But with Jason there, he couldn't. He didn't mind the embarrassing scene for himself nearly as much as he minded it for the boy, who was sitting with his head down, his hands in his lap beneath the table.

Soon the clerks and other customers resumed their business. Everyone but Jason. "You finished?" Griff asked.

The boy raised his head. "It's not fair!"

Griff was surprised to see that he wasn't embarrassed but angry. "What's not fair?"

"What that man did just now. What people say about you."

Griff pushed aside his plate and propped his forearms on the edge of the table. "Listen to me, Jason. Spitting like that was disgusting. It only made him look like an asshole, but what I did five years ago was much, much worse." He looked through the window at the three, who were climbing back into their utility truck. "How much do you think that guy earns in a year?"

Jason raised his shoulder in a disinterested shrug.

"A fraction of what I made when I was playing football. A tiny fraction. That guy works hard and doesn't earn as much as I spent on having my tailored shirts laundered. He doesn't hate me for making more money than him. What he hates is that I was living the life every guy dreams of, and I threw it away. I took money for cheating. I was stupid and selfish, and I broke the law. There's no getting around that."

"But you're not bad now."

He was screwing a paraplegic's wife for money. That was pretty damn bad. The only thing worse would be to want to screw her whether he was being paid to or not.

He'd tried not to think at all about what had happened. When he did, he tried passing it off as physiological cause and effect, sexual mechanics that, with all the gears oiled and working, had produced a predictable result.

Or as caprice. A fluke. Stars had collided, but it wouldn't happen again for another million years.

But in whatever terms he tried to explain it, it stayed on his mind. Constantly. Every time he thought about her teeth sinking into the bottom of his thumb, he got hard, his gut tightened with long-ing, and all he wanted was to be inside her again.

"I'm nobody's hero, Jason. Don't make me into one. You want a hero, look at your dad."

"My dad?" Jason scoffed. "What's he do that's heroic?"

"He loves your mom. He loves you. He takes care of you, worries about you."

Jason, still sullen, said, "That's nothing."

"That's huge." Then, to keep from sounding too preachy, he added, "But he can't throw a football for shit. And don't tell him I said *shit* in front of you."

"He says it all the time."

Griff laughed. "Then he's *my* hero."

Jason started smiling again.

The following day started out like every other. Griff got out of bed and went into the bathroom. As soon as he'd peed, he consulted the calendar he'd tacked to the wall. This was his routine now. He was marking off the days, for crissake.

He'd bought a computer and taught himself to use it. After extensive Internet research, he thought he had a fairly comprehensive overview of the female reproductive system and how it worked, more than he had learned from basic biology in school.

Some of the message boards he'd logged on to gave him more information than he wanted—did he really need to know about mucus plugs and yolk sacs?—but he'd learned a lot about timing and what happened within that twenty-eight-day cycle. He'd learned what an LH surge was.

If he'd been with Laura on the day she ovulated, he approximated when she would have menstruated—if she was going to. Those five days had come and gone. If she'd had a period, and if his calculations were correct, he should have heard from her three days ago, when she should have been ovulating again.

But she hadn't summoned him back to the house on Windsor Street. So did that mean she hadn't had a period and therefore had conceived? Maybe she was holding off breaking the glad news until she'd had her pregnancy confirmed by a doctor. Or maybe, because of what had happened the last time, she didn't intend to call him, ever again. But wouldn't he have been notified that the deal was off?

Not knowing was making him crazy, but all he could do was wait.

As he did every morning, he made a notation on the calendar, then showered. When he stepped out of the tub, he heard his newspaper being thunked against his front door. Disinclined to dress yet, he wrapped a towel around his waist. He retrieved the paper from his small porch, went into the kitchen, and started a pot of coffee.

While waiting for it to brew, he perused the front page and drank orange juice from the carton. He flipped the paper over, read the headlines beneath the fold, and finding them relating to the same world crises that they'd related to yesterday, he pulled out the sports section.

The headline caused his heart to stutter. Blood rushed to his head and made him momentarily dizzy. "The fuck is this?"

BURKETT QUESTIONED IN DEATH OF BOOK-MAKER, the headline read.

FURTHER WOES FOR FORMER COWBOY?

VETERAN COACH DENOUNCES FALLEN STAR.

Recognizing the stories, he looked at the dateline. Not this morning's issue. It was five years old, and though it was well preserved, he saw now that the paper on which the sports section was printed didn't match the rest of the newspaper. It had yellowed some with age.

Rodarte.

He knocked over a kitchen chair in his rush. In seconds, he was out of the kitchen, through the living area, and flinging open his front door. He charged out onto his narrow patch of yard and scanned the street. He didn't really expect to see the green sedan, and he didn't. Rodarte had given himself time to get away.

"Son of a bitch!" Griff grabbed the towel, which was slipping off his waist, and stormed back inside, slamming the door behind him. Rodarte hadn't reappeared in almost two months. Now, just when Griff had begun to think—hope—the bastard had given up and gone away, this.

Clever of him, planting this old sports section in today's newspaper where Griff was certain to find it. Rodarte was rubbing his nose in the shit he'd made of his life five years ago.

When he felt composed enough to confront the fine print, he righted the chair and poured himself a cup of coffee, then sat down at the kitchen table and began to read. Every word was like a blow, hurtful because it was true.

Not since Pete Rose's gambling and Jose Canseco's admission to using steroids had a professional athlete scandalized himself as much as the record-breaking, all-star quarterback Griff Burkett had. Media coverage had been extensive and pervasive. The story had made headlines internationally. ESPN had dedicated hours of programming to it.

But Rodarte had done well to choose this particular issue of *The Dallas Morning News,* because these stories were summarizing chronicles of his long, inexorable fall.

The gambling had started small, but it grew like a creeping vine he couldn't kill or control, until it dominated, becoming more exciting for him than the Sunday games. Winning big on a wager was more thrilling than winning big on the gridiron.

It had evolved into an addiction. Before it had got out of hand, he should have been smart enough to recognize the danger signs. Maybe he had. Maybe he had just ignored them.

He got caught up in a dangerous but exhilarating spiral. If he won, he raised the stakes of the next bet in order to win more. If he lost, he raised the stakes to recover the loss. The spiral became a maelstrom that eventually sucked him under.

Bill Bandy looked more like a tax accountant than one's idea of a bookie. He was a slightly built man who probably had weighed no more on the day he died than on the day he graduated high school. He had thinning brown hair, a small face with a pointed chin, and a sharp nose. His pinched nostrils and pale blue eyes waged a constant war with airborne allergens. His hands were as soft and white as a woman's, and one got the sense they would feel moist if touched.

No one would have pegged him for a mobster. Yet that was exactly what he was. It was rumored that, back in St. Louis, before he'd been relocated to Dallas, he had poisoned an uncle who had double-crossed him. Griff never knew if that was fact or fiction.

Bandy worked for Vista, the syndicate's dummy corporation that ostensibly ran a tin-mining operation somewhere in South America. The actual location and other details were vague. Vista's real enterprises were high-stakes gambling, money laundering, and, Griff suspected, drug trafficking.

Vista's *miners* in the Las Colinas high-rise wore designer suits and diamond-studded Rolexes. They packed heat even when they went to the men's room. They had bodyguards with automatic pistols and cars with bulletproof windows.

You did not fuck with them.

That was what Bill Bandy had told Griff over a plate of chicken enchiladas one night at his favorite Mexican restaurant. Griff was midway into his fourth season with the Cowboys. Bandy had invited him to dinner to discuss business, specifically the repayment of his gambling debt, which was now three hundred thousand and change.

"You don't fuck with these guys, Griff. If it was me, I'd extend you some more credit. Hell, you make millions. I know you'll be good for the money in a few months. But these guys?" He blotted his dripping nose with a damp white handkerchief. "There's no charity in their hearts. Believe me."

Griff dunked a tortilla chip into the salsa and munched it noisily. He took a sip of frozen margarita and winked at the starstruck teenage girls staring at him from the next table. "What are they going to do? Send some guy with hairy knuckles to break both my legs?"

"You think this is funny?"

"I think you're about to panic when panic isn't called for. They compound the interest every week, making me a profit center for them. So what's their problem?"

"They want their money."

Finally Bandy's funereal tone captured Griff's attention. No longer nervous or fidgety, Bandy's pale gaze was rock steady. Even his nose had dried up temporarily. Griff thought maybe the fable of his poisoning an elderly uncle was true.

Maintaining that cold expression, he continued. "Be glad they sent me as the messenger, or you might not be starting on Sunday, or any Sunday for the remainder of the season. Make no mistake, they can inflict serious injury on you, Griff. They *will*."

"It wouldn't make sense for them to injure me. If I can't play, they'll never get their money."

The argument didn't make a dent in Bandy's resolute expression. Griff pushed aside his plate and sighed with disgust that he had to deal with this now. The team was facing the Falcons on Sunday in Atlanta. The Cowboys were favored, but not by much. It wasn't going to be a cakewalk by any stretch. He should have been psyching himself up for a tough game, studying the playbook, not pandering to gangsters.

"Okay. Give me a few days," he told Bandy. "I'll

liquidate something. A car. My condo in Florida. Something. What's the minimum amount that would temporarily satisfy them? Two hundred thousand? That's more than half what I owe them. Would that buy me some grace?"

Bandy dabbed his leaking eyes with a corner of his handkerchief. "There may be another way."

"To buy me time?"

"To cancel the debt."

Griff gaped at him as if he'd said that he could have a week on a desert island with every Playmate of the Month for the past year, that they were all nymphomaniacs with the hots for him, and that no clothes were allowed.

Bandy asked, "Are you willing to meet with them? Discuss options?"

"Where and what time?"

The "them" Bandy had referred to were three men, who welcomed Griff into Vista's opulent offices with hearty handshakes and unlimited hospitality. *What would you like to drink? Help yourself to the tray of sandwiches there. I highly recommend the beef tenderloin with the horseradish sauce. How about a massage after the meeting? We've got a girl on staff who'll give you a massage with a happy ending.* Wink, wink. *If you get my meaning.* Which Griff did.

You'd never know by the reception they gave him that he owed them over a quarter million dollars and that they were making threats against his person if he didn't pay this debt immediately.

The only native Texan was tall, trim, darkly tanned, with large and very white teeth. He was an avid golfer who talked loudly, lewdly, and nonstop. It was he who placed his arm across Griff's shoulders and told him about the masseuse with the magic hands and mouth. Larry was the guy's name.

Martin had a swarthy, Mediterranean look. He was obese. He didn't breathe, he wheezed like an off-key bagpipe, and looked like he could go into cardiac arrest at any moment if only his heart could work up the energy.

The third, Bennett, was quiet and unobtrusive. Balding and fair skinned, he sat apart, contributing little but studying Griff with the unblinking, lashless stare of something scaly and venomous.

After the initial greetings, they got down to business. The terms of their proposal were simple: Throw the Atlanta game on Sunday, and his debt would disappear. That was not how they put it, but that was the bottom line.

Martin told him they didn't expect him to try to lose. "Just don't play up to your full potential."

Larry winked again. "Give the fucking Falcons a fucking chance. That's all."

"And who knows," Martin wheezed, "if the Falcons pull out a win, we could throw a little extra bonus your way, in addition to clearing your debt." Gasp. "Right, Bennett?"

Bennett the Silent nodded his stiff comb-over.

Griff told them he'd think about it.

Fine, they said. He had till Sunday to make up his mind. And just to show their goodwill, they insisted that he avail himself of the massage with the girl, who capped off the fifty-minute rubdown with a blow job. Not that he couldn't get head whenever he wanted it. There were always girls just dying to notch their bedposts with the Lone Star logo of the Dallas Cowboys. But this girl was exceptional.

On Sunday, while he was suiting up, during the singing of the national anthem, even as he took the field following the opening kickoff, he was still wrestling with his decision. He didn't know what he would do until late in the fourth quarter, with a 10–10 score, when Dallas was deep in their own territory and it was third and twelve.

He took the snap. Dallas linemen went down like bowling pins under a Falcons blitz. His fastest, strongest running back got blocked by two linebackers. The third one was chugging toward Griff, smelling blood. Scrambling, looking for an open receiver, Griff realized how easy—and convincing—it would be to throw an interception.

Atlanta won 17 to 10.

The partnership was forged.

CHAPTER
19

I F YOU WANT TO PUT SPIN ON IT, YOU GOTTA get your thumb under it." Griff demonstrated the rotating hand motion to Jason Rich. "See? You gotta whip your thumb under just as you release the ball. Now try again."

He handed over the football. Jason's face was tense with concentration as he gripped the ball the way Griff had demonstrated and threw a pass. "Much better."

"One more time, Griff? I think I let go a little too late."

"Okay, but only one. Practice is about to start."

Griff saw improvement in the second pass. "Good work, Jason. You're getting the hang of it. Throw a few thousand more and you'll have it down pat. You'll be breaking records."

Behind his mask, Jason's sweaty face broke into a grin. "Yesterday was fun. Except for . . . you know."

"Yeah, I'm sorry you had to see that."

"I told my dad. He said you handled it the only way you could. If you had fought them, it would've made it worse."

"I'll say. Did you see the size of those guys?"

Jason laughed, then said tentatively, "Maybe we could go for milk shakes again sometime."

"I'd like that."

"Me, too. See you tomorrow."

Griff knocked on the top of the boy's helmet, two taps. "I'll be here."

Jason trotted off to join his teammates, who were assembling on the sideline of the practice field. Bolly was among the other dads. Griff raised his hand in greeting, and Bolly waved back.

Griff jogged across the field to retrieve the footballs Jason had thrown and stuffed them into the cloth bag he kept in the trunk of his car. He pulled the drawstring to close the bag and slung it over his shoulder.

That was when he saw Rodarte, standing outside the chain-link fence, watching him.

Griff was already hot from being in the sun for the hour with Jason. When he saw Rodarte, it seemed his blood reached the boiling point in seconds. He had to force himself not to charge the fence.

Unhurried, he went through the gate and joined Rodarte on the other side. The son of a bitch didn't even deign to look at him. Instead, he stared across the field to the far sideline, where the middle school head coach was cautioning his young team not to let themselves become overheated or dehydrated during practice.

"You're pathetic, Rodarte," Griff said. "Collecting old newspapers like a bag lady."

Rodarte chuckled but still didn't turn to face him. "Fun reading. I hated keeping it to myself."

Griff started to grab him by the shoulder and force him around, but he didn't dare lay a hand on the man. Rodarte would fight back. And if it got ugly, which it inevitably would, there were too many witnesses. In particular Bolly. Griff had promised him there wouldn't be any trouble. Yesterday the sportswriter had entrusted his son to him. Griff would have hated like hell to betray that trust now.

He could tell Rodarte to go to hell and simply walk away. Let him stand there and dissolve from the heat till he was nothing but a puddle of sweat being absorbed by the hard, baked ground.

But ignoring him wouldn't be smart. Rodarte's being there wasn't coincidence, any more than this morning's incident with the newspaper was a harmless prank. After staying invisible for weeks, Rodarte had resurfaced. Until Griff knew why, he wouldn't turn his back on him.

Rodarte reached into his pocket and took out a pack of gum. "I'm trying to quit smoking."

"Good luck with that. It would be just awful if you got sick and died."

Rodarte gave him a sly grin as he unwrapped a stick of gum and put it in his mouth. "You still banging that broad?"

Griff's jaw tensed.

"I suppose since your favorite whore is still out of commission, you gotta get it somewhere." His grin got slier. "You could do a lot worse. Not only has Mrs. Speakman got a sweet ass but she's loaded. But I'm sure you know that. Nobody ever called you stupid, Number Ten. A lot of other ugly names, but never stupid."

Griff didn't rise to the bait.

"Is she footing your bills these days? Buying you all that neat new stuff?" Rodarte laughed that nasty laugh again and noisily smacked his chewing gum. "Sure she is. And glad to do it. Stuck with a husband who's only half a man, I'll bet she's willing to pay any price to ride a big, strong football hero like you."

Griff didn't move, even though he craved to see Rodarte bleed.

Lowering his voice to a suggestive whisper, Rodarte said, "I'll bet she's one of those no-nonsense businesswoman types who goes absolutely wild in the sack. Am I right? She works out all her career insecurities on your dick, and she likes to be on top. Come on, Burkett, share. Is she one of those?"

"You're maggot shit."

Rodarte barked a laugh. "You're fucking a paraplegic's wife and *I'm* maggot shit?"

"What do you want?"

"Want? Nothing," Rodarte said innocently. "Just thought I'd drop by, say hi. Didn't want you to think I'd forgotten you. I wanted to reassure you that when you self-destruct—and you will, you know— I'm gonna be there to see it, and hopefully to help bring it about. I'm so far up your ass, Burkett. You have no idea."

Griff feared if he stayed any longer he was going to take the first step toward the predicted self-destruction. Which was precisely what Rodarte wanted. Despite his resolve not to turn his back on the man, he did so and began walking away.

"Jason's showing progress."

Griff whipped back around. Rodarte, laughing softly, spat his wad of gum into the dirt. "The boy hasn't got much natural talent, but he works hard. Plain to see he worships the ground you walk on. Probably wants to follow in your footsteps. Well, not the cheating and murdering path you took, but your football glory days."

Squinting at Griff across the space separating them, Rodarte let his evil grin spread across his acne-cratered face. "Be a shame if something were to happen to the boy. A crippling accident or something that would prevent him from following his dream. He might even die."

Griff took the steps necessary to close the distance between them. "You lay one hand on that kid and—"

"Calm down," Rodarte said in a cajoling voice. "I was just speculating on the fickle finger of fate. Jesus, you're a hothead. I try to have a friendly little chat here at the middle school athletic field and you—"

"What do you want, Rodarte?"

He dropped his saccharine pretense, and his eyes turned flinty. "You know what I want."

"I don't have any of Vista's money."

"They're not convinced. I'm sure as hell not. And I'm not going to stop with you till I break you and you give it up. I'm as permanent as a birthmark."

Griff aimed his index finger at him and began

backing away. "You stay away from me. You stay away from everyone around me."

Rodarte laughed. "Or what, Number Ten? Or what?"

Griff violated a condition of his probation, the primo one that Jerry Arnold continually reminded him of: *Don't go near your former associates.*

The way Griff saw it, he had no choice. Rodarte had threatened Jason. And the way he'd talked about Laura . . . The implied threat, which went beyond the nasty stuff, had raised the hair on the back of Griff's neck. Rodarte wouldn't have a qualm against harming either of them. Even Laura's money couldn't protect her. He would hurt her and Jason without a blink, and would enjoy the hell out of doing it.

To prevent that, Griff must confront this issue head-on, now. He wasn't willing to live with the constant threat of Rodarte. He certainly didn't want to inflict it on two people who were entirely innocent. He couldn't bear the guilt of someone else falling victim to Rodarte's brutality the way Marcia had.

Griff drove straight home from the practice field, rushed through a shower, and dressed. He left behind his new Armani jacket in favor of one he'd had before his incarceration, not wanting to look too well heeled.

It was nervy to arrive at Vista's offices unannounced, but he was betting that the triumvirate would agree to see him, out of curiosity if for no other reason. He was right. After waiting in a reception area for almost half an hour, he was summoned into the inner sanctum where he'd met with them the first time.

Same paneled walls, indirect lighting, and sound-absorbing rugs, but the hospitality was noticeably lacking. No sandwich tray, no open bar. Larry's tan was just as bronze, but it appeared that more time may have been spent in the club bar than on the links. He'd gone a little soft around the middle.

Griff was surprised to see that Martin could still breathe without some form of respiratory appara-tus. But he was now relying heavily on a cane to help support his immense body.

Bennett had given up on the comb-over and shaved his head. It was perfectly white and round, and from the back looked like an overgrown bil-liard ball sitting on his shoulders. With even fewer lashes now, his eyes were more reptilian than be-fore.

Larry had one hip propped on the corner of a desk. Bennett was in an armchair, legs crossed. As Griff walked in, Martin collapsed onto a short leather sofa that was barely wide enough to accom-modate him. Both his lungs and the seat cushions emitted a whoosh of air as he settled.

Griff wasn't invited to sit.

Martin began. "What do you want?"

Griff responded just as bluntly. "Call off Ro-darte."

No one said anything for a full thirty seconds. Finally Larry broke the taut silence. "Would that be Stanley Rodarte you're talking about?"

Griff didn't buy the dumb act. "You'll be glad to know your watchdog is persistent. He was in Big

Spring the day I got out, and he's been making a nuisance of himself ever since. He assaulted a friend of mine. A woman. Sodomized her and ruined her face. When that failed to win me over, he set two guys on me. For a week after, I could barely walk and my pee ran red."

"Gee, Griff, we're sorry to hear that," Larry said, his voice dripping sarcasm. "And this would be our problem . . . why?"

Griff resented their playing innocent. He wasn't telling them anything they didn't already know, so he'd rather they just own up to it and tell him that he and Marcia had it coming.

"Look, it sucks for you if Bill Bandy hid money where you can't find it. But get off my back about it. I didn't take anything from him. And you know damn well I didn't kill him."

"You had motive."

"So did you."

The FBI had arrested Bandy on charges of illegal gambling. Facing several years in federal prison, Bandy had played his bargaining chip—Griff Burkett. He told the feds about Griff's association with Vista, specifically about the upcoming play-off game against Washington. No one in Dallas was happy about the loss that day, except the federal agents who were building a strong racketeering case against the Cowboys' QB.

The deal Bandy had struck worked out great for him. Griff got caught; all charges against Bandy were dropped. But this exchange had made the Vista men nervous. What if the FBI wanted more from Bill Bandy than a cheating football player?

The bookie might have been tempted to use them as another free pass at some point in the future.

The Vista trio had removed the temptation from Bandy by killing him.

At least that was what Griff had surmised and now had essentially accused them of. Unfazed, their stares remained unblinking.

"Maybe there was some secret stash," he continued, "but I haven't spent the last five years on a treasure hunt. I don't want back in your operation, and I'm not working for a competing outfit. You can threaten me till doomsday, and you'll still come up empty. So whatever you're paying Rodarte to put pressure on me is money wasted. Call him off."

Several moments passed. They sat like statues. Eventually Martin looked over at Larry, Larry looked over at Bennett, and Bennett continued to stare at Griff.

If Griff had still been a wagering man, he'd have put his money on Bennett as the enforcer of the group. Larry was the windbag, the people person, the public relations guy. Martin was the brains and the puppet master. Bennett, silent and stationary Bennett, who seemed to have ice water in his veins, was responsible for damage control.

It was Martin who finally spoke. "What makes you think . . ." Wheeze. ". . . that we'd have dealings . . ." Gasp. ". . . with a scumbag like Rodarte?"

"He told me himself. He said he'd talked to you. He passed along your message that there might be a way for me to make amends. That you might be willing to forgive and forget."

"Forgive and forget?"

This was the first and only time Griff had actually seen Martin smile, and it made his balls contract.

"Is Rodarte delusional, or are you?" Larry asked. "After you gave the grand jury the juice on us, you think we'd ever welcome you back?" He snorted his opinion on the chances of that. "First of all, asshole, we're not forgiving or forgetful. Number two, you're the last person we want in our operation. We're not slow learners. Once you screw us over, *you're* screwed. Third, if one of our competitors—not that we have any that matter—takes you in, that's good news to us. It only shows that they're fucking ignoramuses.

"Lastly, you're actually right about one thing. Rodarte did come sniffing around just before your release. He's always had the mistaken idea that he's a hotshot and that we're impressed by him. We're not. He's a lowlife thug, is all.

"But, hey, we don't want to appear unfriendly, especially to someone so inferior. So we dazzled him with bullshit and a couple shots of eighteen-year-old scotch, then sent him on his way. If he's squeezing you, he's doing it on his own time and for his own reasons."

"And more power to him," Martin wheezed.

"Amen to that," Larry said. "More power to him. We won't be brokenhearted the day you die, Burkett. The only reason you're still breathing is because you deserve no better than Rodarte. We'd rather somebody of his caliber handle an asswipe like you, save us having to get our hands dirty. Now get the fuck out of here before we remember just how pissed off we really are."

* * *

On his drive back from Las Colinas, Griff got stuck in a traffic jam behind a freeway accident that had two lanes closed. Staring into the brake lights of the car ahead of him, he ruminated over what Larry had told him. It felt like the truth. They wouldn't mourn his passing, but if they'd wanted him dead, he'd be dead.

The Vista boys were scary, but Rodarte, acting on his own behalf, was even scarier. Griff wasn't comforted by the knowledge that Rodarte was working independently.

That thought was interrupted by his cell phone's chirp. He flipped it open. "Hello?"

"Are you free?"

CHAPTER
20

HIS HEART SKIPPED. "WHEN?"

"Now."

"I'm fifteen minutes out." Thirty at least, but he didn't want her to change her mind.

"I'll see you then."

It took five minutes for him to get past the accident; then he herded the Honda as though driving in the Le Mans and reached the house twenty-two minutes after getting her call. He went in through the unlocked front door and found her standing in the center of the living room.

She was wearing a snug white skirt and a sleeveless red top with white buttons down the front and wide straps over her shoulders. She looked great.

"Hi," he said.

"Hi."

"I was on 114 when you called. There was an accident."

"I didn't give you much notice."

He shrugged off his jacket and laid it over the back of the nearest chair. "How have you been?"

"Fine. What about you?"

"I've been okay. Airline keeping you busy?"

"Always."

"This heat sucks."

"I can't remember when it last rained."

"That time of year, I guess."

Up to that point, they hadn't broken eye contact. Now she did. She looked toward the window, where the louvered shutters let in only slivers of sunlight. "I asked you to meet me today so I could tell you in person."

His stomach dropped. "You're pregnant."

She shook her head.

"No?" he asked, making sure.

"No."

"I thought maybe you would be. We doubled the chances last time."

Her eyes flicked back to him briefly, then away. "I'm not pregnant. But I . . . we, Foster and I, have decided to try A.I."

His encounter with Rodarte, his meeting with the Vista boys, her call, the wild drive here, seeing her, all had combined to jumble his brain. Her words didn't compute. He shook his head slightly. "Sorry?"

"Artificial insemination."

"Oh. Right." Again his stomach took a dive. "Instead of us—"

"Yes."

"Huh."

There was a significantly long pause before she

continued. "We realize the financial implications that our decision will have on you."

"Uh-huh."

"So we'd like for you to remain the donor." Nervously she wet her lips. "If you're willing, that is. And if you are, and the insemination is successful, the terms of the payout will stay the same."

He searched her face, but she avoided looking directly at him. After a moment, he went over to the sofa, sat down on the edge of it, and stared into near space, thinking what a bitch of a day this was turning out to be.

She must have taken his silence for either reluctance or indecision. She said, "You don't have to give me your answer today. You have time to think about it. I have to set up appointments with a specialist. I'm sure there will be tests. I think I have to go on supplemental hormones. So it could be a while before we needed you. Weeks, I would guess."

He looked over at her.

"Once the procedure is scheduled," she went on, sounding rushed, "I'll contact you and we'll work out a time and place for me to pick up the specimen. It'll have to be retrieved on the actual day. I'll give you as much notice as I can. A day, possibly two."

"All right."

"Between now and then, if you decide you don't want to . . . to participate, we'll pay you five hundred thousand anyway. For the times you've . . . for your trouble."

"Generous of you."

"Naturally, whether you opt to continue or cancel the arrangement here and now, it goes without saying that I expect the absolute confidentiality you agreed to."

Finally, something he wanted to address. "You don't want anybody to know about . . ." He tilted his head in the direction of the bedroom. "What happened in there last time."

"About any of it, Mr. Burkett."

"No, I'm sure you don't, Mrs. Speakman."

She drew herself up straight and retrieved her handbag from an armchair. "Well, I think that covers everything. Thank you for coming on such short notice."

"There's a double entendre if I ever heard one." He'd spoken in a mutter, but intentionally loud enough for her to hear.

Ignoring the remark, she moved toward the door. "I have to go. I have a meeting in half an hour."

"Liar."

She came around quickly.

"You don't have a meeting. You're running off." He left the sofa and started walking toward her. "You're scared. You don't trust yourself to be here. Did you confess to your husband that you really got into it last time?"

"What Foster and I talk about—"

"Is that why he changed his mind about our little arrangement?"

"*He* didn't. I did."

Up till then, he'd been growing steadily angrier. But that stopped it. This was her decision, not Speakman's, and not one they'd reached as a couple. He said the first thing that popped into his mind, the first thing he wanted to know. "Why?"

"I can't . . ." She faltered, then started again. "I

can't continue with you like this, that's all. I agreed to it only because it was what Foster wanted. And I love him. I do. I love my husband."

"All right."

"That's the only reason I consented to this."

"So you said."

"But I can't be with you anymore."

"I got that, too. And when it comes right down to it, that's all you had to say. You don't owe me an explanation."

She looked at him strangely, then lowered her head. Neither of them moved. Seconds ticked by while he stared at the way her hair grew in a swirling pattern around the crown of her head. Finally he said, "When did you decide?"

"I knew when I left here last time that I wouldn't come back. But I fretted over it, and didn't tell Foster of my decision until two weeks ago."

"Why didn't you call to tell me then?"

"We decided to wait and see if I was pregnant before we told you. If I was, it would be a moot point. I thought the matter was settled." The red top expanded with the deep breath she took, straining the white buttons. "But Foster has spent the past two weeks trying to change my mind."

"He still wants his baby conceived the natural way."

"Yes. He hasn't really applied pressure, but he's made his wishes known. He's made it clear how disappointed he'll be if we change course now. He's used every tactic he knows to try to persuade me that we should continue as planned, at least through several more cycles."

"Only he didn't persuade you."

"No."

"Then why didn't you call and tell me the deal was off? Why are you here?"

"Because I let Foster think he finally wore me down." Her gaze moved around the room, then came to rest for several seconds on the third button of his shirt before moving up to meet his eyes. "He kept after me until I agreed to meet you one last time. If I don't conceive today, he said, he *promised,* he would never ask me to come here again and will agree to switching to a clinical method."

Griff assimilated that. "One last time."

"Yes."

"Today."

"Yes."

"So he thinks we're—"

"Yes."

"But we're not."

"He'll never know, will he? He'll think this time had the same result as the previous three."

"Only the two of us will know different."

"Unless you tell him."

"Your secret is safe with me."

"I hate that word," she said with obvious anguish. "I don't like keeping secrets from my husband."

She looked beyond him toward the hallway that led to the bedroom, and her gaze stayed fixed on it so long that Griff looked over his shoulder to see what could possibly be holding her attention. The hallway was empty. He thought she might be seeing into the bedroom, seeing them moving together, seeing herself coming. That would be a secret she would want to keep from her husband.

He came back around just as she looked up at him. Their gazes held for several long moments, then she gestured at the front door. "Well . . ."

"Your meeting."

She gave a wan smile. "There's no meeting."

"I know." He returned her smile, but he didn't feel it.

She reached behind her back for the doorknob. "Don't forget your jacket."

"Right."

"Be sure the door is securely closed so it will lock."

"Of course."

She pulled open the door, and they were struck with a blast of hot air. She said, "Depending on circumstances, this could be the last time I'll see you."

"Could be."

She paused, then gave a self-conscious shrug. "I can't think of anything to say that seems appropriate."

"Small talk seems smaller."

She smiled faintly at the reminder of her words to him the night they'd met.

"You don't have to say anything, Laura."

"Then . . ." She stuck out her right hand. "Goodbye."

He took her hand. They looked down at their clasped hands, then at each other. She released his hand and his gaze simultaneously, and turned toward the open door.

But she did only that. Turned and stopped.

Griff hesitated only heartbeats before acting. He moved in close behind her, reached over her shoulder, put his hand flat against the door, and slowly pushed it shut.

Laura stared at herself in the vanity mirror. The reflection looking back seemed to be of someone else. The woman in the mirror was disheveled, not as meticulously turned out as usual. Most disturbing, her eyes were filled with uncertainty. Where was the characteristic self-confidence? What had happened to the surety that she had a grip on the situation? Who was this tremulous stranger?

She ran her fingertips across her lips and dabbed at the smudge of mascara at the corner of her eye. No question, the image in the mirror was hers.

"Laura?"

She spun around, flattening her hand against her chest. "Foster. I didn't hear you."

"Obviously not. You nearly jumped out of your skin." His wheelchair was straddling the threshold between bedroom and bath. "Manuelo told me you were home."

She had parked in the detached garage, entered the house through the mudroom, and used the back staircase. "He said you were on the telephone." She forced a light laugh. "At least I think that's what he said. I didn't want to interrupt your call. I'm glad you chose to stay at home today. The heat is unbearable. It's making everyone cranky. People were driving like maniacs, so rush hour was more hazardous than usual."

Realizing that she was talking too much and too fast, she forced herself to slow down. "All this to say, I'm a mess and wanted to take a quick shower before seeing you. How was your day?"

"Uneventful. Besides the weather and the traffic, how was yours?"

"I had back-to-back appointments this morning, including the one with the reps from the FAA to discuss Southwest's and American's complaints."

"You'll have to be more specific. Southwest and American are always filing complaints against us."

"Highest form of flattery."

He grinned. "If we were failing, we'd never hear a peep out of them. How did your appointment with Griff Burkett go?"

The question came so suddenly and out of context, it took her off guard. "The same as before. Briefly. Efficiently."

"I thought he might be the reason you're so late getting home."

"Why would you think that?"

"No reason."

She let it drop. "I hope you didn't wait dinner on me."

"Mrs. Dobbins made a sandwich to tide me over."

"Good."

"So why are you late?"

"I was almost home when I remembered something I'd left at the office and had to go all the way back for it. Myrna was still there."

"My assistant is usually the last to leave. Unless it's you."

"She was finishing up some business letters and asked if I would wait on them so I could bring them home for you to sign. I have them right here."

She tried to squeeze past his chair into the bedroom, but he caught her hand. "The letters can wait. I want to know Burkett's reaction when you told him this was the last time you'd be meeting him. Or did you tell him?"

"I told him as soon as he arrived."

"And?"

"And nothing, really. Once I assured him that we would adhere to the original terms if he remained the donor, he said it was all the same to him. Something like that."

"He's not backing out then?"

"I didn't get that impression, no."

"I didn't think he would. Did you discuss how we would retrieve the semen?"

"Only in the most general terms. I told him I had to consult a specialist first. Then when he's needed, he'd be notified."

"Maybe the A.I. won't be necessary. Let's hope."

"That's what we all hope, Foster."

He surprised her by pressing his hand against her lower abdomen. "I feel good about this time. Karma. Something. It just feels different, like something significant happened."

She smiled, hoping it didn't look shaky. "Hold that thought." Stepping away, she said, "I really would like to get out of these clothes. You're welcome to stay."

"No, I'll leave you to your shower. I'd only stay if I could offer to wash your back."

"You can pour me a glass of wine instead. I won't be long."

"How about club soda? Just in case."

"Okay."

He kissed the air, then maneuvered his wheelchair across the adjacent bedroom and through the door, each of his motions done in a sequence of three.

Laura waited until she was alone, then closed the door to her bathroom and hastily removed her clothes. Before stepping into the shower, she worked up enough courage to examine herself in the full-length mirror. Her eyes were still glassy and dazed looking, her lips slightly abraded. She touched her nipples, navel, pubic hair.

Holding back a guilty whimper, she placed her fingers vertically against her lips and whispered, "Oh, God." But she wasn't certain for what, specifically, she prayed.

CHAPTER
21

THE MONTH WAS LONGER EVEN THAN ANY he'd spent in prison. Compared with this, those months had whizzed past like comets.

He'd held out for three days before doing the forbidden. He'd called the SunSouth offices. After listening to a seemingly endless menu of confusing options that required pushing a series of digits, he finally reached a human being who told him in a polite but busy-sounding voice that he had reached Ms. Speakman's office. "Kay Stafford speaking, how can I help you?"

"I need to talk to Ms. Speakman."

"In regard to what?"

He wondered what the cool, well-trained Kay Stafford would say if he told her the unmitigated truth. Instead, he replied, "Foster is a former college buddy of mine. I met with the two of them a few months back."

"Your name?"

"Ms. Speakman will remember."

She put him on hold and was gone for an interminable time. When she finally came back on the line, she said, "I'm sorry, Ms. Speakman isn't available to take your call. Would you care to leave a message?"

She asked by rote. If Laura had refused his call, chances were good that her assistant would deep-six any message he left. Besides, what could he say?

Leave your rich husband and be with me.

Or don't leave him and be with me.

I don't care what the hell you do, just be with me.

"No message," he said brusquely and hung up.

He charted her menstrual cycle even more diligently than before, marking the days off on his calendar.

He got hooked on a soap opera.

He watched senior tour golf tournaments and chess matches on the sports networks, and they moved even more slowly than his days.

He perused the classified ads daily, but unless he wanted to be a telemarketer, he found nothing he could do anonymously, and he knew before trying that no one would hire the infamous Griff Burkett.

Desperately lonely one afternoon, he called Marcia and invited himself for dinner. "I'll bring the dinner and the wine. How can you pass up a deal like that?"

"I appreciate the offer. But give me a bit more time, Griff."

Time. It had become his enemy.

By way of consolation, Marcia offered to set him up with one of her girls. He declined, which brought on her husky, sexy laugh. It was good to hear her laughing again, a sign that the old Marcia was emerging from the bandages and the trauma. "You don't want a date with one of my talented girls? That's interesting. Are you seeing someone?"

He experienced a vivid flashback to Laura, moving beneath him, purring that low, sexy sound that he now heard in his dreams. "Yeah. I'm seeing someone."

He spent most of his time restlessly pacing the rooms of his condo, wondering when he would hear from her, *if* he would hear from her, *what* he would hear.

Rodarte didn't reappear. Griff could only hope the Vista boys had strongly advised him against hassling Griff further. But that was naïvely optimistic. Contrary to what Rodarte had implied, he wasn't in league with Vista or answerable to them. And even if he had been, they would have supported any bad ending he had planned for Griff Burkett.

He considered warning Bolly and Jason of an ugly man in an ugly car, but he was afraid that would spook Bolly and he would scotch the coaching sessions, and that one hour each day was the only hour during which Griff was marginally distracted.

He called Laura twice more at her office, without success. After the second time, he brazenly called her cell phone. Knowing that she would recognize his number on caller ID, he was surprised but elated when she answered. But all she said before hanging up was "Stop calling me. You can't call me."

He tried to exhaust himself by swimming laps. On the days he didn't swim, he ran miles. He worked out in the gym as though he were still in training. He went to multiscreen cinemas and saw every movie on the marquee.

He killed time.

Finally, while waiting inside a fruit smoothie store for his yogurt-and-berry blend, the call came. He almost dropped his cell phone as he snapped it off his belt and flipped up the cover. "Hello?"

"Griff, Foster Speakman. Congratulations."

His field of vision shrank to a pinpoint, consumed by onrushing blackness. The clerk behind the counter signaled to him that his drink was ready. Griff looked at him with misapprehension. He turned and left the store. Out on the sidewalk, he stood in the shade, but heat had been trapped beneath the canvas awning. It was like being inside an oven. He was suffocating.

"Griff? Did you hear me?"

"Uh, yeah, I'm just . . ." His hand had grown slippery with sweat. He switched his phone to the other. "I guess 'congratulations' means you've got good news for me."

"We've been successful." The millionaire didn't even try to contain his jubilation. "Laura's pregnant."

The disgruntled clerk came out of the store, bringing Griff's smoothie with him. He had a silver bar piercing his eyebrow and yellow teeth that needed orthodontia. "You can't just order something and then walk out."

Ignoring him, Griff asked, "Are you sure?"

"Three home pregnancy tests this morning were all positive. That's pretty much indisputable."

"Hey, I'm talking to you," the clerk said. "You're gonna pay for this." He thrust the drink at Griff.

"Hold on a minute," he said to Speakman. Covering the phone, he grabbed the drink, which looked nauseatingly frothy and rich, and hurled it into the nearby trash can. He stuffed a five-dollar bill into the pocket of the clerk's shirt. "Now get the fuck out of my face before I rip that thing out of your eyebrow."

"They should've left you in prison to rot." Sneering, the clerk shot Griff the finger and went back inside the store.

Griff took several deep breaths, and all that did was inflate his lungs with scorching air.

"Apparently I caught you at a bad time," Speakman said.

"Not really. I was paying out at a store. I apologize. How reliable are those home pregnancy tests?"

"I shared your skepticism. Laura, too. She was reluctant to take the tests in the first place, afraid that doing so might jinx it." He laughed. "But once the third one came out positive, she began to believe it was true. A test at the doctor's office confirmed it."

"She's already gone to a doctor?"

"This morning. She pleaded with her gynecologist's office to work her in. They did a blood test. They just called her with the happy news that her hormone level indicates that she's pregnant."

"Is she there with you?" Griff imagined them hugging each other, laughing, crying with joy.

"She was at the office, but she's on her way home now. I've iced down the champagne. Well, *I'll* have champagne. Laura, of course, can no longer drink, so I've got club soda on ice for her." Speakman laughed. Griff forced himself to join in. "I wanted to share the news with you immediately. You've just become a very rich man."

"Yeah. It's kinda hard to take in."

"Would it be convenient for you to come to the house tomorrow evening? I've worked out the details of that hitch."

"Hitch?"

"How you would continue to be paid in the event that neither Laura nor I outlived you."

"Oh, that."

It seemed like a long time ago since he had been in the library of the mansion, sipping Coke from cut crystal, talking about deal points, hammering out the details of this bizarre arrangement. Now that he thought back on it, it seemed like a dream. And only now did he realize that he'd never thought it would actually work out as planned. He hadn't counted on it ending to everyone's satisfaction. But it had. The Speakmans were going to have the child they wanted. He was going to be a millionaire again. He was set for life.

He felt like he'd been hit with a sack of shit.

"It's an unlikely scenario," Speakman was saying, "but I've worked out a contingency for it. Also, we'd like to pay you your half million in person."

"I thought we weren't supposed to ever see each other again."

"Just this once. This is a special occasion, and I want to give it the ceremony it deserves. A gesture of our eternal gratitude. Will you come?"

"Sure," Griff heard himself say. "What time?"

He arrived at eight-thirty on the dot. He dialed the house from the gate, identified himself to Manuelo, and the gate swung open. The aide opened the door even before Griff rang the bell. He was wearing his customary black, his smile as vacuous as before. He didn't say a word before ushering Griff through the vaulted entry and into the familiar library, where Foster was waiting. Alone.

"Griff!" he exclaimed happily. He did a funny thing with his chair before wheeling it forward. Smiling ear to ear, he clasped Griff's right hand between both of his and pumped it enthusiastically. "I'm so glad you could come."

"Wouldn't have missed it."

"Worth the errand, huh? Five hundred thousand in cash. Do you have an armored truck to go home in?"

Griff laughed as expected.

"What would you like to drink?"

He nodded at the highball glass sitting on the end table at Speakman's elbow. "One of those will be fine."

"*Uno más,*" Speakman told Manuelo, who went immediately to the bar and poured Griff a drink from a decanter. As soon as he delivered it, Speakman motioned that the aide could leave. Manuelo pulled the double doors closed behind him.

Speakman retrieved his drink from the table. "I drank an entire bottle of champagne last night and woke up with a terrible headache this morning. But you can toast with good bourbon, too, can't you?" He raised his glass. "To our success."

"To our success," Griff echoed. He took a hefty swig of the whiskey, which burned all the way down. "Mrs. Speakman isn't joining us?"

"Unfortunately, no. A matter has been brewing in Austin for several months. A baggage handling problem that needed her attention. Or so she thought. I tried to talk her out of going, but she insisted that one of us needed to see to the resolution, and she thought the quick round-trip would be too much for me."

Griff figured that was the excuse she'd given her husband. The truth of it was that she had high-tailed it to Austin because she didn't want to see *him*. Her absence sent a clear message that caused him to waver somewhere between longing to lay eyes on her again and anger over her cowardice about meeting him face-to-face after that last afternoon together.

"I won't let her take on that extra work for much longer," Speakman said. "From now until the baby is born, my hardest job will be getting her to delegate responsibility. She's stubborn when it comes to turning a chore over to someone else." He chuckled with self-deprecation. "Of course, so am I. But we both want to be full-time parents. When the baby arrives, I have no doubt she'll devote herself to mothering."

Of course, that was what this had been about, wasn't it? Laura wanted a baby. She wanted to give

her husband a baby. A few orgasms had been a
bonus, but they sure as hell hadn't changed her
agenda, and he'd been a damn fool to think they
might.

He was no different than a sperm bank, except
that he had party favors—a hard dick, fingers, a
tongue. He'd got her off a few times. So? So, nothing. She belonged to Foster Speakman, and so did
the baby she would have. Bingo. Mission accomplished. Time to pop corks.

So long, Griff Burkett. It was nice knowing you.
Nice fucking you. Nice fucking you over.

And if he had any doubt of that, he had only to
listen to her husband's gushing monologue. "You
should have seen her this morning when that third
test was positive." He placed his fist over his
mouth to contain his rising emotion. "Her
face . . . I've never seen her look more beautiful
than when she smiled at me and said, 'We have a
baby.' We. That two-letter word was extremely
meaningful to a man in my condition."

"I'll bet."

Speakman didn't seem to pick up on Griff's
snideness. He was too caught up in his euphoria.
"Even before she took the test, I knew she was pregnant. Her breasts are already fuller. So tender she
won't let me touch them." He laughed. "It would
embarrass her, my telling you this. Forgive me for
going on and on. I can't help it. My heart is full to
overflowing. And I'm still a bit drunk, I think."

That reminded him to offer Griff another drink.
Griff declined with a shake of his head. At the
mention of Laura's breasts, he'd shot the remainder of his whiskey. It had made his ears ring and

his heart beat fast. He felt clammy and a little nauseated.

"Do you have any inclinations toward what it is?" Foster asked.

"What what is?"

"The baby. Did you feel particularly abundant in X's or Y's the day it was conceived?"

On the day it was conceived, what he'd felt was Laura. Her skin. Her heat. Her passion. The whiskey had caused his throat to sting, but he managed to say, "No. I never thought about it one way or the other."

"I think about it constantly," Speakman admitted sheepishly. "Our child's sex—in fact, all its characteristics—were determined the instant the egg was fertilized. Isn't that amazing?"

"Amazing." *Amazing how many times I came inside her.*

"I can't wait to know whether it's a boy or a girl, but we can't find out till the fifth month."

Amazing how many times we came together.

Speakman chuckled. "Five months from now you'll probably be lying on the beach of some Caribbean island with a cold drink in one hand and a hot chick in the other."

Griff forced a smile. "Sounds good."

"I guess you'll eventually know about the baby. What it is. What we named it. You'll probably read the announcement in the newspaper."

"If that Caribbean island gets newspapers."

Speakman grinned. "You're sure you won't have another drink?"

"No thanks."

Speakman reached for Griff's glass and carried it

with him to the bar. As before, he went through a ritual of placing their glasses in the rack beneath the sink, wiping the spotless countertop, and folding the towel until all the edges were even. After he'd hung it in the towel ring, he adjusted the hem again. When it finally met with his satisfaction, he washed his hands with sanitizer.

Then he lightly slapped the arms of his wheelchair three times. "Now, down to business." He did that weird back-and-forth thing with his chair, then rolled over to the desk. On top was what appeared to be a box of stationery. Indicating it, he said, "Your money."

Griff made no move toward it.

Speakman, misreading his hesitancy, laughed. "Go ahead. It's yours. Look in the box."

Griff approached the desk and indifferently lifted the lid off the box. Inside it were stacks of hundred-dollar bills, neatly banded with paper strips.

"Pretty, isn't it?"

Griff gnawed the inside of his cheek, saying nothing. He was afraid of what he would say if he spoke, afraid he would tell Speakman the low opinion he had of a man who would pay another to have sex with his wife, no matter how lofty the reason.

Out of curiosity, he'd looked up that Bible story. It was the wife, Sarah, who had sent another woman to her husband, but basically the situation was the same. It hadn't worked out too well in Genesis. In fact, things had got real mucked up. And all because this Sarah had wanted a baby, and wanted it her way.

You could tell yourself it was only biology, but it was still sex. It was still a man and woman lying down together and using equipment that was functional but also pleasure giving. Nobody had yet invented anything more intimate.

What he wanted to know was: How could any man ask that of his *wife*? Contempt for Foster Speakman roiled inside his gut along with the whiskey, along with his jealousy.

Of course, he was no prince of virtue. He was taking the man's cash. He would deal with his disgust for himself later. But right now, he was revolted by Speakman, who was smiling at him like he'd won a jackpot, smiling without giving a thought to the emotional turmoil Griff and Laura had suffered for the sake of his foolish, selfish, stubborn demand.

"I won't be insulted if you want to count it."

Griff shook his head.

Speakman looked at him curiously. "Frankly, I'm surprised."

"By?"

"Your reserve. Have you gone shy on me?"

"What did you expect?"

"More . . ." He made a rolling motion with his hands. "Reaction. Exuberance. You act almost reluctant to take your pay, like you're sorry—" He broke off and studied Griff for a moment, then began to laugh. "Oh, dear."

"What?"

"You don't want it to end, do you? That's it, isn't it? You're sorry those afternoon interludes with Laura are at an end."

"That's nuts."

Speakman shook his index finger at him. "I don't think so."

"Let's just settle our business so I can get outta here." Even to his own pounding ears, his voice sounded like a growl.

"Ah, Griff, don't be embarrassed. Making love to my wife is no hardship duty. Well I know. How could you help but get a crush on her? Like your gambling, you developed a taste for her, didn't you? The more you had, the more you wanted. Now it's hard to give her up. I understand. Truly I do."

Griff clenched his fists.

Speakman chuckled again, then held up both hands, palms out. "I'm sorry, I'm sorry, I'm sorry. I apologize for laughing at you, but it's just so damn amusing. Your job is over and you've earned your money, but you're heartbroken about it. Can't you appreciate the irony?" Speakman winked up at him. "You're so downcast, I think you must have *really* enjoyed doing her."

That clipped the last tenuous thread of Griff's restraint. He gave vent to his disgust. "You sick fuck."

"Possibly," Speakman said affably. "But at least I'm not horny for another man's wife, for a woman I can never, ever have again. Poor Griff, poor Griff, poor Griff."

Griff glared down at him through a red mist of rage, then turned his head away and searched the desktop, looking for something, anything, that would silence that maddening, taunting chant.

"Mrs. Speakman?"

Laura had been staring through the airplane window as the jet made its final approach into

Dallas. She'd been addressed by a flight attendant leaning across the empty aisle seat.

"When we get to the gate, I'll be escorting you off ahead of the other passengers."

"Oh, no, please don't." She disliked being given any special treatment when on a SunSouth flight.

The young woman smiled. "Sorry, orders from the cockpit."

"Why?"

"The tower informed the pilot that you were being met immediately upon arrival."

"Met? By whom?"

The attendant lowered her voice to a whisper. "Maybe by that handsome husband of yours. I remember that time on your birthday when he set up a string orchestra in baggage claim. Such a romantic surprise. Anyway, you're to obey captain's orders and disembark first."

She hoped that Foster didn't have an elaborate homecoming planned for her tonight. It had been an exhausting day, starting early and ending much later than it should have. All she wanted to do was go home, take a quick shower, and then have a long night's sleep.

The pilots made a perfect landing, right on time. She made a mental note to report that to Foster.

After a short taxi to the gate, a flight attendant got on the PA and asked the other passengers to remain seated. Laura felt self-conscious as she was ushered up the aisle. She smiled an apology to passengers with whom she made eye contact.

When she reached the cockpit door, the captain was standing there. He doffed the bill of his hat. "Mrs. Speakman."

"Flawless flight, Captain Morris," she said, reading his name tag with peripheral vision, a knack she'd developed over the years.

"Thank you."

But his expression was grave, and because he didn't engage her in conversation, she felt a prickle of apprehension. "Is something the matter?"

"Please." He gestured toward the open aircraft door. She stepped into the Jetway and was surprised that the pilot accompanied her. Even more surprising, he placed his hand beneath her elbow. Before she could react to that, she noticed two men coming toward them.

They were wearing the dress uniforms of senior police officers. Upon seeing her, they respectfully removed their hats.

Her footsteps faltered. The pilot's hand tightened around her elbow.

"What's happened?" The words came out drily, scratchily, barely audible. Then she cried out, *"What's happened?"*

The homicide detective stared down at the corpse and blew out a gust of air. "Jesus Christ."

His partner, a man of few words, grunted assent.

A member of the Crime Scene Response team, who for the past hour had been collecting evidence, agreed with a sad shake of his head. "Bad, huh? Bad as I've ever seen. Maybe not as gruesome as some murders, but . . . well, only a real cold-blooded bastard could do this."

"Or a real *hot*-blooded one," the first detective remarked.

"Crime of passion, you think?"

"Maybe. Whatever, the son of a bitch deserves to get the needle."

His partner harrumphed again.

"Excuse me, Detectives?" A uniformed officer appeared in the open double doors of the library. "You said to let you know as soon as Mrs. Speakman got here. They're taking her into the living room now. That way." He motioned in the general direction.

When the pair of investigators entered the room, Laura Speakman was standing between two police chaplains. One gave them a surreptitious nod, letting them know that she'd been told, but that was obvious. She was as pale as the dead body.

The taciturn detective took up a position against the wall. The other advanced into the room. "Mrs. Speakman?"

"My husband's dead? There's no mistake?"

"No mistake. I'm sorry."

Her knees buckled. The chaplains guided her down onto a sofa. One sat near her, placing his arm protectively along the back of the seat. The other asked a uniformed officer to get her a glass of water.

As the detective approached, he withdrew his card from the breast pocket of his jacket and extended it to her. "Stanley Rodarte, ma'am. Homicide detective, Dallas PD."

CHAPTER
22

"LAURA, HE'S HERE."

Kay Stafford had appeared in the doorway of Laura's bedroom, where she was reclined on a chaise. The draperies were drawn. The room was cool and dim. Her assistant spoke quietly and slowly, the way everyone was addressing her today, as though fearing a sudden noise might cause her to shatter like crystal. They could have been right.

"I put him in the den," Kay said. "Take your time coming down. He said he would wait."

Laura sat up and slipped her feet into her shoes. "I might just as well talk to him now, although I don't know what I can tell him today that I couldn't tell him last night."

Detective Rodarte had stayed until almost midnight. He'd spent some of that time questioning her. The rest of the time he, his silent partner, and other police personnel had moved in and out of the library, doing whatever it was they did at the scene of an apparent murder.

They consulted in hushed voices, casting looks in her direction, occasionally asking her for information. She was asked by a solicitous policewoman if there was someone she should call. "Someone to stay with you tonight."

Neither she nor Foster had family. Since the accident, they hadn't kept close contact with friends. "My assistant," she replied.

She'd given the policewoman Kay's home number. Kay had arrived within a half hour, sharing Laura's shock but somehow managing to perform the simple tasks that Laura seemed incapable of doing. She gave directions, supplied answers to practical questions, and dealt with the telephone, which had begun to ring with irritating frequency.

Kay had a notepad in her hand as they walked downstairs together. "I hate to bother you with all this now, Laura."

"Go ahead. I don't have the luxury of collapsing. That will come later, when . . . when everything's settled. What do you need?"

A proviso of Foster's will, which he'd altered when they married, was that, in the event of his death, Laura would serve as head of SunSouth until the board could elect another. She'd been granted power of attorney to make decisions and conduct business. So, in addition to becoming a widow last night, she'd stepped into the role of CEO.

Kay said, "The media are camped outside the entrance of our building, awaiting a statement."

"Ask Joe to write something generic. 'Everyone

at SunSouth is stunned by this tragic event, et cetera.' But ask him not to release it before faxing it here for my approval." She trusted her marketing head to write an appropriate press release, but it was her practice, as well as Foster's, to sign off on everything. "Tell him not to conduct a formal press conference or respond to any questions about the . . . the crime. We'll leave that to the police."

Kay checked that item off her list. "Operations has asked if they should coordinate a minute of silence in memory of Foster. Anything like that?"

Laura smiled wanly and shook her head. "Foster wouldn't allow the schedule to be interrupted even by one minute. But the thought is appreciated. Make sure everyone knows that."

"Have you given any thought to funeral arrangements?"

Laura, having reached the bottom of the staircase, stopped and turned to her. "I can't schedule the funeral until the body has been released."

Unexpectedly, tears filled her eyes. Two years ago, following the car accident, Foster had lain in an ICU clinging to life. She'd feared that each breath would be his last and that soon she would be organizing his funeral. But she hadn't had time to prepare for talking in those terms now. This time it was a sudden reality. There would be a funeral. When it would be she didn't yet know.

Last night she had been advised not to go into the library. She had taken that advice. What had been described to her was grotesque, and she hadn't wanted that to be her last image of Foster. It had been jolting enough to see the zippered body bag as it was wheeled out on a gurney. Inside the bag was her husband's body, but to the police, it was evidence.

Sensing her employer's distress, Kay said, "I apologize for having to mention it. But people are keeping the phone lines hot, here at the house and at our offices, asking when the service will be and where. The lobby is already full to overflowing with flowers."

Laura touched her assistant's hand. "I'll let you know as soon as I know something. In the meantime, ask Joe to include in the press release that in lieu of flowers, people could make donations to Elaine's foundation. Foster would prefer that."

"Of course. One last thing. The governor issued a statement this morning, extolling Foster as an entrepreneur, model Texan, and human being. Then she called to ask if there was anything she could do on a personal level, as a friend to you both."

"I'll respond personally as soon as I can. In the meantime, tell her how much I appreciate her thoughtfulness."

Kay accompanied her as far as the den, where Detective Stanley Rodarte was waiting. *Rodarte.* Laura had recognized the name instantly from Griff Burkett's warning. He'd been sure to include mention of an olive drab sedan but had failed to tell her that Rodarte was a homicide detective with the Dallas Police Department.

Rodarte was studying a painting of an English hunting scene. He turned when she walked in. "Is this an original?"

"I believe so."

"Hmm," he said, sounding impressed. "Must have cost a bundle."

She didn't honor that with a response.

"Sure is a beautiful home, Mrs. Speakman."

"Thank you."

"Did you redecorate when you moved in after marrying Mr. Speakman?"

"Elaine Speakman had done such an excellent job with the decor, I saw no need to change it."

Oddly, his smile didn't improve his looks. It made him uglier. "Most second wives want to rub out all traces of the first."

The statement was inappropriate and irrelevant. She thought he'd said it only to see how she would react. She hadn't warmed to him last night, sensing immediately that he was crass and sly. Now she decided she disliked him intensely.

"I'm being asked about funeral arrangements," she said.

"The ME is performing the autopsy this afternoon. Depending on what it shows, we should be able to release the body to you either tomorrow or the next day. But I advise against making any definite plans without clearing them with me."

"I understand."

Turning her back on him, she moved to one of the leather sofas and was about to sit down when he stopped her. "If you wouldn't mind, I'd like you to look at the library now. See if you notice anything out of kilter. Beyond the obvious, that is."

She'd known that sooner or later she would be required to go in. She was torn, one part of her needing to see the spot where Foster had died, another resistant to ever entering the room again. Given a choice, she might have postponed it for as long as possible, making the dread of it torturous.

In a way, she was glad Rodarte had relieved her of having to make the decision on her own.

Woodenly, she left the den and led the way across the vestibule to the double doors of the library. The hardware on them had been dusted for fingerprints. Seeing that she noticed the smudged dark powder, Rodarte said, "Murder is messy business."

He pushed the doors open, and she stepped into the room. "You remember Carter," Rodarte said.

His partner detective, whom she recognized from the night before, was standing in front of a wall of bookshelves, silent and grim as a sentinel. Neither his stance nor his expression changed when she came in.

Except for him, most of the room looked surprisingly normal. Only one area near the desk was in disarray. The desk itself and everything on it had been dusted for fingerprints. An end table lay on its side. The lamp and everything else that had been on the table were scattered across the rug, most broken. The rug itself was buckled. Foster had never allowed even the fringe of it to be mussed, insisting that it be raked several times a day.

She made an involuntary hiccuping sound when she saw his wheelchair.

And there was blood. On the wheelchair. On the rug. On the desk.

Rodarte touched her elbow. "Would you like to do this later?"

What she would have liked was for him not to touch her. She removed her elbow from his hand. "Other than what is obvious, it doesn't appear that anything has been disturbed."

"Good." He pointed her toward a seating group. "Let's sit down."

"In here?"

He shrugged and made a face that asked, *Why not?*

Either he was stupid and insensitive, a jerk, or just plain cruel. Laura suspected the latter, but she didn't want to take issue with him over where he would conduct this interview. "I've been sitting or lying down all day. I'd rather stand." She went over to the wall of windows, keeping her back to the room.

Forgoing a graceful lead-in, Rodarte asked, "Why did you go to Austin yesterday?"

Out of the corner of her eye, she noted that Carter had finally moved. He took a small notebook and pen from his breast pocket. But it was apparent that he was merely reinforcement. Rodarte was the lead investigator.

"At my husband's request, I went to handle a problem. There had been reports of luggage theft. Our handlers had been accused. One, as it turned out, was guilty. The Austin police have the reports if you care to check."

"You took a SunSouth flight back?"

"The nine o'clock, last of the evening. On final approach for landing, the flight attendant notified me that I would be escorted off the aircraft. Your chaplains met me in the Jetway. They took me to a private lounge in the airport and told me that my husband had died. I didn't learn that he'd been murdered until you told me."

"Up to the point when you were escorted off the plane, you didn't know that anything was amiss here at home?"

"How could I?"

"Phone call? Text message?"

"I didn't know anything was amiss."

"You'd been gone all day. Did you talk to your husband yesterday at any time?"

"Around noon, he called my cell to ask how things were going. Then I called him around six to tell him that the matter had been settled and that I would be on the nine o'clock flight back and not to wait dinner on me."

"Just those two calls?"

"Yes."

"Did Mr. Speakman have any appointments scheduled last night?"

"None I was aware of."

"Well, apparently he did meet with someone here."

She turned and looked at him.

"There was no sign of a break-in," he said by way of explanation. "Whoever killed your husband was let into the house."

"Manuelo would have answered the door."

He frowned. "We still can't find him, Mrs. Speakman."

Last night when Rodarte had asked her help in reconstructing the crime scene, she had mentioned the aide. Rodarte had written down his full name. When she explained what Manuelo's duties encompassed, the detective had ordered that the entire estate be searched. There had been no sign of the man.

"His room over the garage is still empty," he told her now. "Bed is made, no dishes in the sink. Clothes in the closet. He doesn't own a car, right?"

"Not to my knowledge."

"And none of the vehicles belonging to you and Mr. Speakman are missing. So how did Mr. Ruiz leave and where did he go?"

"I have no idea. The only thing I know with certainty is that he wouldn't have left Foster alone."

"Does he have relatives?"

"I don't believe so. At least none I know of."

"You're sure he was on duty last night?"

"He's always on duty, Mr. Rodarte."

"Twenty-four/seven?"

"Yes."

"Your housekeeper-cook, Mrs. uh—"

"Dobbins."

"Right. She said she leaves at six o'clock."

"As soon as dinner is prepared. I can't imagine why there would have been a change in that schedule. Have you questioned Mrs. Dobbins about last night?"

"She put a roasted chicken in the warming tray and left at six. She said Manuelo Ruiz was here when she left. She's sure of that because she told him she was leaving. So it's assumed he was here."

"I'm certain he was. He wouldn't have left Foster alone," she repeated. "Never."

Rodarte walked over to the area in front of the desk where the rug was bunched up. He squatted down as though to study the dark stains on it. "Much as I hate to, we need to talk about the actual slaying."

"Must we? You were so descriptive last night. It sounded very . . . horrible."

"It was. That's why I advised you against looking at your husband's body. It was nothing you wanted to see, believe me. He was still in his wheelchair with a letter opener sticking out the side of his neck."

She hugged her elbows tightly against her torso. "I'm certain by your description that it was Foster's letter opener. It was a replica of Excalibur. I gave it to him for Christmas because he loved the Arthurian legend. It stayed on his desk there."

"Mrs. Dobbins confirmed that. But once I get it from the ME, I'll have you identify it so there'll be absolutely no doubt."

Something else to dread, she thought.

Rodarte said, "What it looks like is, the killer pushed it in to the hilt, then tried to pull it out. But the blade had severed the artery, so when he tried to remove the weapon from your husband's neck, the wound started gushing blood. I guess he panicked and decided to leave it."

"And my husband bled to death."

"Right." Rodarte stood up. "We found two blood types on the rug. One was your husband's."

"Two?" She looked at the bloodstains, then at Carter, finally back at Rodarte.

He shrugged. "We don't know who the second type belongs to. Could be Manuelo Ruiz's, but we have nothing to match it with. Except for the DMV, Ruiz isn't in any database we've run him through. He has a current Texas driver's license. That's it."

"He drove Foster in a customized van."

"Did Ruiz have papers?"

"Immigration papers? I assume so."

"He didn't."

Her temper sparked. "If you knew that, why did you ask?"

He gave her what he probably mistook for a disarming grin. "Habit. Always trying to trap somebody in a lie. Hazard of my job."

"I'll tell you the truth, Detective."

His face brightened. "Will you?"

"Yes."

"Good. Tell me about you and Griff Burkett."

She hadn't seen that coming. A wave of dizziness assailed her.

Noticing her instability, Rodarte motioned her toward a sofa. "This may take a while. Want to re-think sitting down?"

She hated conceding that she needed to, but she did. She sat down in an armchair. Rodarte offered to get her a glass of water. She declined with a shake of her head. He sat in the chair facing hers and, leaning toward her, clasped his hands between his widespread knees. She noticed that his fingernails needed trimming.

"I'll save us both some time here, Mrs. Speak-man. Griff Burkett's fingerprints were all over the letter opener that killed your husband."

CHAPTER
23

LAURA COVERED HER MOUTH WITH HER hand, afraid she would be ill in front of the two detectives.

"Are you okay?" Rodarte asked.

She shook her head, surged to her feet, and ran from the room. She barely made it into the powder room in time to retch into the toilet. Because she hadn't eaten anything since dinner the evening before, there wasn't much to empty. But the bile was bitter and continued to make her gag for several minutes. When the spasms finally ceased, her clothing was drenched with sweat. Her ears buzzed, her extremities tingled, and she was trembling uncontrollably.

She covered her face with her hands. From the moment she saw the police chaplains in the Jetway, she'd known that what they were about to tell her was catastrophic and that, whatever it was, Griff Burkett was involved. That overwhelming intuition had now been confirmed, and she wasn't sure she could survive it. Knowing that he'd killed Foster might very well be the death of her, the death of the child she carried.

But she couldn't think of the baby now or she truly would go mad.

"Laura?" Kay was knocking on the door. "Laura?"

"Just a moment." She rinsed her mouth out and splashed cold water over her face, which was as pale as chalk. She ran her fingers through her hair, then, forcibly composing herself, opened the powder room door.

Kay was there, Rodarte just behind her. His expression was more inquisitive than concerned. Kay said, "I'm taking you upstairs and putting you to bed."

"No. I'm better now. But could you please bring me a glass of Coke, Sprite, something fizzy?"

Kay was reluctant to leave her, but she went to fix the drink. Laura brushed past Rodarte and led him back into the library. Her knees were rubbery. Her damp clothes made her chilled in the air-conditioning. She wrapped herself in a throw before returning to the chair she had so quickly vacated.

The other detective hadn't left his post, or even moved as far as Laura could tell. The three remained in silence until Kay delivered her the requested drink. "Call me if you need me," she said, shot Rodarte a baleful look, and gave Laura's arm a reassuring squeeze.

"Thank you, Kay. Please close the doors as you leave."

Laura sipped her glass of soda, hoping it would

settle her stomach and not come right back up.

Again Rodarte began without preamble. "Did you know him before he went to prison?"

She shook her head.

"Only since he got out?"

She nodded.

"How did you meet? Where?"

"In this room." She could tell that surprised him. "Foster was interested in him. He'd heard on the news that he was being released. He wrote to him, asked him to meet with him here."

"Interested in him, how? What was it about a criminal football player that interested your husband?"

Looking him right in the eye, she lied. "I don't know." Telling the truth wasn't an option. She had to protect her child's future. She also had to protect the secrecy that Foster had insisted upon. "Mr. Burkett was only here that one time. By the time I was asked to join them for an introduction, they had concluded the business part of their meeting and were having a drink together."

"It was friendly?"

"Very. At least it seemed so."

He studied her a moment. She wasn't sure he believed her. In fact, she was almost certain he didn't. But there was no one to dispute her. "Was it during this friendly get-together that sparks ignited between you and Burkett?"

"Excuse me?"

"How soon after that did you two start hooking up at that house on Windsor?"

The glass of soda almost slipped from her unsteady hand.

He grinned. "I bet you're wondering how I know about your romance. Well, see, I've had my eye on Burkett ever since the day he got out of Big Spring."

"Why?"

"I investigated the murder of Bill Bandy. Does that name mean anything to you?"

"Griff Burkett was implicated in his murder."

"He *committed* the murder, Mrs. Speakman. No question in my mind. But he was clever, didn't leave any hard evidence, not enough for me to get an indictment from the grand jury. But there's no statute of limitations on homicide. If it's the last thing I do, I'll see justice done for the late Bill Bandy."

Griff had known the detective was following him. It was clear now why he hadn't wanted her talking to Rodarte, why he had used scare tactics to warn her against being alone with him. He hadn't wanted her to hear the conviction in Rodarte's voice when he said, *He committed the murder.*

"He was more careless this time," Rodarte was saying. "Or more arrogant. Leaving behind the murder weapon. Fingerprints."

"Why do you think he did that?"

"First thing I intend to ask him when we find him."

She raised her head and looked over at him. He read the question in her eyes.

"No, we haven't located him yet. He's gone underground. We've got cops staking out his apartment, but there's been no sign of him. That old Honda he's been driving? We found it in a strip center parking lot up in Addison. Lab guys are going over it now. I've got men watching the house on Windsor, too, but he hasn't been there. By the way, the yard service came this morning and mowed the grass, edged the sidewalk. Who pays for the upkeep on that house?"

"I do. I lease it."

He glanced around the luxurious surroundings, making a silent comparison between the two houses. When he came back to her, he said bluntly, "What for?"

She gave him a look full of meaning.

He studied her for a moment, then flashed that revolting grin. "I already knew you rented the house."

"I know," she said coldly.

He spread his hands wide. "Sorry. It was my duty to check it out, Mrs. Speakman. The lease isn't in your name, but I traced it back through that corporate name to you."

"It wouldn't have been that difficult to do." It was a subtle insult to his investigative skills, but if he caught the slight, he didn't take issue with it.

"When's the last time you saw Burkett?"

She dropped her gaze to her hands, moistly clenched in her lap. She knew the cagey detective would pick up on the body language, but she couldn't help herself. "Almost six weeks ago."

"Six weeks? That long?"

"Yes."

"You're sure?"

She gave him the exact date and saw that Carter wrote it down in his small spiral notebook.

"What made the date memorable?" Rodarte asked.

"I told him that I wouldn't be coming back."

He whistled softly. "How'd he take it?"

"He understood and accepted my decision."

"Really?" he asked skeptically.

"Really."

"Why did you end the affair?"

"I don't see the relevance of that."

"There may be none. Or it could be extremely relevant."

She lost the staring contest. "What we were doing was wrong. I couldn't do it anymore. I told him we couldn't see each other again."

"Before him, had you had other affairs?"

"No."

"No one would blame you. In light of Mr. Speakman's . . ."

"Mr. Speakman's what?" she demanded frostily.

He backed down. "Burkett was your first and only affair since you married Speakman?"

"That's what I said."

"And when you broke it off, Burkett didn't argue, put up a fuss, beg you to reconsider?"

"No."

"Huh." Thoughtfully, he scratched his acne-scarred cheek. "That doesn't sound like the Griff Burkett I know."

Coolly she said, "Then perhaps you don't know him very well."

"Apparently you don't, either, Mrs. Speakman. Because when you called off your affair, Burkett didn't take it lying down. Not at all. He's been simmering over it. Last night he came here, overpowered Manuelo Ruiz, then drove a letter opener into your husband's neck. Classic crime of a jilted lover."

She forced herself not to look away from him. She deserved his implied scorn, she supposed, although in light of her grief, and guilt, it seemed unusually cruel punishment. It was one thing to endure the censure of people you respected. It was quite another to bear the scorn of someone you held in low esteem.

He got up and walked to the desk. "You're sure nothing is missing from this room?"

"I don't believe so. I can't be sure until I've looked more thoroughly."

"When you feel like it, please do."

"Certainly."

"Does this mean anything to you?"

He'd pulled on a pair of latex gloves to pick a single sheet of paper up off the desk. He carried it over to her. "I wanted you to see this before I bagged it as evidence."

He held the sheet so she could read the type-written paragraphs. There were three of them. After several tries to get through the first sentence with any degree of comprehension, she looked up at him with puzzlement. "It's nonsense."

He laughed shortly. "I'm glad you said that. I thought I was losing it. It made no sense to me, either. It's just a bunch of big words strung together, right?"

"Just a bunch of big words."

"Any explanation?"

"No."

"Do you think your husband typed these paragraphs?"

"Why would he?"

"Beats me. I wondered if maybe he'd lost some of his mental faculties, too."

She was affronted by the question, and she let it show. " 'Too'?"

"If I seem insensitive, I'm sorry. Your husband's physical condition was obvious. How was he mentally? A lot of people depended on him being Foster Speakman, CEO. Employees. Stockholders. Even passengers who fly SunSouth relied on him being all there."

"Let me assure you that he was *all there,* Mr. Rodarte. Foster was in full command of his faculties."

"I thought maybe his car accident had jarred something loose." He tapped the side of his head. "Maybe you hadn't even noticed."

"I would have noticed."

"Well, the signs could've slipped past you. You've been awfully busy."

He paused strategically. *Busy with your lover.* That was the implication. She refused to take the bait and only stared at him with a passivity she was far from feeling.

"Your husband took medication."

"Yes. Drugs to strengthen his immune system. Others for the health of his digestive tract, which was severely damaged in his accident. Sometimes a sleep medication."

"Along with those, he took prescriptions for acute anxiety. I'll spare us some more time here, Mrs. Speakman. I've already talked to your husband's psychiatrist."

Laura drew a deep breath. "As an adolescent Foster was diagnosed with OCD. Obsessive—"

"I know what it is."

"Then you also know that it can be controlled with medication."

"I believe you." He chuckled. "I'm a little obsessive myself. You poll a hundred people on the street, nearly all are crazy in one way or another."

Such an inane remark didn't warrant a response.

"Would you say your husband's OCD was under control?"

"Yes."

"Was he depressed?"

"No."

"Not even just a little?" the detective wheedled. "For instance, he might have been a little depressed over your affair with Burkett. The guy turns my stomach for what he did, but even I gotta admit, he's got a face the ladies go for. The height. The hair. The gladiator's body. To a man who's disabled, like your husband was, that in particular would be a slap in the face. Did he know about Burkett and you?"

She shook her head.

He cupped his ear.

"No," she said tersely. "He didn't. Not to my knowledge." She stood up. "Is that all, Detective?"

"Not quite. Did Burkett try to contact you after the breakup?"

She considered lying, then thought better of it on the chance Rodarte already knew the answer to this question, too. "A couple of times, he called the Sun-South offices and tried to talk his way past Kay. I never took his calls."

"You haven't seen him since that day you told him it was over between you?"

"No."

"Or talked to him?"

"The one time he reached me, I hung up on him."

"Did he ever issue threats against your husband?"

"Of course not!"

"Did he ever suggest to you that if your handicapped husband was out of the picture, you'd be free to come back to him? Instant divorce. That kind of thing. Did he ever suggest that he might remove your husband?"

She looked at him aghast. "If he had, don't you think I would have acted on it? Reported it?"

His smirk insinuated much.

She drew herself up straight. "No, Mr. Rodarte. Griff Burkett never posed a threat to either Foster or me."

"That you know of."

She was about to speak when she realized that it was a valid speculation. Hedging, she said, "He never threatened me."

"But he could have threatened your husband without your knowledge."

"Foster never said—"

"But Burkett *could* have."

Reluctantly, she nodded.

Rodarte glanced at his mute partner, his expression tongue-in-cheek. When his attention came back to Laura, he said, "Did Burkett ever mention a hideaway? Ever talk about a friend with a lake cabin, or a private getaway, someplace he may be laying low now?"

"Nothing like that. He didn't confide in me. We didn't talk much at all."

Too late she realized she'd walked right into that one. "No, I guess not," Rodarte said, leering and casting his partner another glance. "Mrs. Speakman, it goes without saying that if you hear from Burkett, you'll contact me immediately."

"Of course."

"I'm posting some men here at the house."

"Is that necessary?"

"Burkett may have come here last night for the two of you," he said quietly. "He didn't know you were going to be in Austin, did he?"

She shook her head slowly, stunned by the thought that Griff would want to harm her. "It wasn't decided that I would go until early yesterday morning."

"So when Burkett came here last night, he expected you to be here, too."

"I suppose." She closed her eyes, trying to imagine Griff in a murderous rage. His hands were large and strong, but they could be gentle. Were they also capable of violence? She couldn't imagine that. Could she?

"I advise you to keep someone with you," Rodarte said. "Actually, I'd rather you move to an undisclosed location until Burkett is apprehended."

"I'll think about it."

"Do." He looked around the room and silently consulted Carter, who closed his notebook and slid it back into his breast pocket. "I guess that's all for now. Unless you can think of anything else that might be pertinent."

She shook her head absently. Then she remembered a question she had wanted to ask him. "Who reported the murder?"

"Nine-one-one got a call."

"From Foster?"

Rodarte shook his head. "The ME said he wouldn't have had time. He wouldn't have been able. And there was no phone near him."

"Manuelo doesn't speak English."

"No, the caller definitely spoke English."

"So it was Griff Burkett."

Rodarte shrugged. "Looks like."

CHAPTER
24

GRIFF WOKE UP WONDERING WHERE THE hell he was.

And then he remembered, and wished he had remained asleep.

Foster Speakman's blood was on his hands. The man had died fighting for his life, blood gushing from his neck, his terrified eyes fixed on Griff.

Griff sat up and buried his face in his hands. "Fuck me."

If not already, then very soon, every cop in Texas and neighboring states was going to be looking for him. When the fingerprints on the letter opener in Foster Speakman's neck were run through databases and matched to Griff's, Rodarte would feel like he'd won the lottery. Better.

He hadn't got Griff for Bill Bandy. But this time there was so much physical evidence placing Griff in the Speakmans' library at the time of Foster's death, they probably wouldn't even bother with a trial.

Nor was there any question of motive. Rodarte knew about Griff's rendezvous with Laura and had determined they were for sex. All the elements stacked up. Griff Burkett would go straight to death row. He might just as well start swabbing his arm in preparation for the needle.

Rodarte would go on TV and say that Griff Burkett, already a convicted felon who had been implicated in one murder, had gone to the Speakman mansion, argued with the defenseless, cuckolded husband—who was confined to a wheelchair, for crissake—and savagely stabbed him. No doubt he would emphasize the savagery of the crime by throwing in a few more adverbs, like *ruthlessly, brutally,* and *heinously.*

The media would lick their chops. The story contained the juicy ingredients that make a reporter salivate: A victim already stricken with tragedy. Money. Sex. A cozy rendezvous. A ne'er-do-well who had seduced the beautiful wife into an affair that ultimately led to the violent death of her husband.

It was the stuff that could win a Pulitzer for a journalist who didn't mind wallowing in slime.

Griff sat on the edge of the sagging mattress and looked at the bloodstains embedded in the creases of his hands. He'd scrubbed them until the small bar of soap was a sliver, and the stains were still there, an indelible part of his handprint.

Things couldn't possibly get worse.

Well, actually, they could. Laura would be told that he had killed her husband.

Last night, after fleeing the Speakmans' estate, he'd driven to his apartment and hastily packed several changes of clothing. But he didn't tarry there, knowing that would be the starting point of the search for him. He'd been at home when he was arrested the first time, dragged out in handcuffs, shamed before his neighbors, his disgrace spotlighted in the media. He didn't want a repeat of that humiliating scene, so he left hastily, taking only what he could carry, knowing he might never set foot inside the place again.

He drove to a shopping center and abandoned the red Honda in the parking lot. Soon an APB would be issued. Every law enforcement officer would be on the lookout for it, so he had to put distance between himself and the car.

He'd walked for miles, keeping to dark streets, no particular destination in mind. Just walking. Trying to figure out what the hell he was going to do now. First order of business was to find a place to hole up until he could get his head on straight.

He'd reached the motel by coming up on the back side of it. It faced an interstate highway but was set well back from it on the access road, a low-slung row of rooms squatting between a pawnshop and a store that sold retread tires for as low as $14.99. The businesses were closed, their doors bolted for the night.

It was a low-rent, hasty-tasty motel with a flickering red-neon Vacancy sign in the office window. Actually befitting him. It was the kind of place his mother would have gone to with a man she met in a bar. The kind of place where Griff might have been conceived.

The clerk was glassy-eyed from the joint he was sucking on when Griff walked in. Griff asked how much for a night, laid cash on the counter, and picked up the key that was wordlessly slid toward him. He wasn't even required to sign a register. If the junkie noticed the bloodstains, he was indifferent to them.

Griff let himself into the room, dropped his duffel bag, and went directly into the phone-booth-size bathroom. The toilet was stained. It smelled of piss. The whole room stank of other bodies, mildew, lives in ruin. He stepped into the shower fully clothed, washing himself and his clothes, letting the water run until the red current swirling around his feet faded to pink and finally became clear.

The bedspread was stained, but he was too exhausted to care. The amorous grunts and groans coming through the thin wall from the room next door kept him awake, but the rhythmic knocking of the headboard lulled him into an uneasy doze just as the sun was coming up.

Now, though, he was fully awake. It was going on noon, and he had to know just how grim his situation was. He switched on the TV that was bolted to the wall. Local stations were beginning their midday newscasts, and, as expected, Foster Speakman's murder was the lead story on every one.

They showed live video pictures of the estate's perimeter wall, police cars blocking the gated entrance. One station had its helicopter circling the property, although there wasn't a good view of the house because of the trees. A file photo of "this prominent Dallas businessman and distinguished citizen" appeared on the screen. The picture of Speakman was several years old, taken, Griff guessed, before the car accident, when he was more robust.

The governor, speaking from her office in Austin, solemnly hailed Foster Speakman as a man who had been, and would remain, an inspiration to all who knew him. She commended him for the courage with which he had faced his personal tragedy. His murder was shocking. Her heart went out to his widow, Laura Speakman, who had demonstrated a courage and poise that matched those of her late husband. She vowed the full assistance of her office and every state agency in the apprehension and conviction of Speakman's murderer. "The perpetrator of this egregious crime will answer for it," she pledged.

A Joe somebody, whom Griff remembered from the SunSouth office parking lot, was identified as the airline's spokesperson. He resolutely dodged microphones and cameras as he waded through reporters on his way into the corporate building.

"He's promised a statement will be forthcoming shortly," the anchorwoman told her viewers. "We'll get that to you as soon as possible. Greg, you interviewed investigators at the scene. What have you learned from them?"

Greg, the field reporter, had taken up a position outside the ivy-draped estate wall. He said the police were reluctant to discuss the details of the case at this time. "One interesting aspect to this mystery," he said, "is that the victim's aide, Manuelo Ruiz, who was constantly at Mr. Speakman's side,

apparently wasn't in the home last night. His absence is unexplained."

"That is interesting," the anchorwoman said
without interest.

The well-coiffed anchorwoman didn't attach any
importance to Manuelo's disappearance, but it was
damn important to Griff that the aide hadn't yet
been found.

He continued to flip through the channels until
all the stations moved on to other stories. He hadn't
been named as a suspect, but neither had anyone
else. Only that one reporter had mentioned Manuelo. And Rodarte hadn't appeared in any of the
reports Griff saw.

"Has his nose to the ground looking for me," he
muttered, switching off the set.

Griff's involvement was still unknown by the
general public, so that bought him a little time. He
had a hiding place. It was unlikely the motel clerk
would remember the guest in room number seven,
even when Griff's face started appearing on TV
screens. So he had some breathing room.

His primary worry was finding Manuelo—Ruiz,
was it?—before Rodarte did. But in order to do
that, he needed a car.

He located a Dallas telephone directory under
the bed, along with a dusty Gideon Bible. The directory had seen more use, but not by much. It was
several years old, and bugs had left droppings on
the pages, but it had business listings as well as
residential. He used the motel's phone to place the
call.

"Hunnicutt Motors."

"Is Glen there?"

"Hold please, I'll see."

He was subjected to elevator music for several minutes.

"Glen Hunnicutt." It was a booming voice as large as the man who possessed it.

"Comfort Inn. You said it could just as well have been the honeymoon suite at the Paris Ritz."

Only another ex-con, even one incarcerated in a minimum-security facility, would recognize the tone and know what it signified, would know not to blurt out a name or say too much. Following a significant pause, the car dealer said, "Hold on."

Griff heard the receiver being set down, movement, a door closing, more movement. When he came back to the phone, Glen Hunnicutt spoke in a low rumble. "How're you doin'?"

"I was doing great."

"Was?"

"Now I'm screwed. I need to borrow a car, and nobody can know about it."

Glen Hunnicutt was a successful used-car dealer. By his own admission, he'd got greedy. For several years he'd cooked his books, fudging heavily on the income he reported to the IRS. He got caught and was sent to Big Spring to repent.

Being away from his wife had been torture for him. She was all he talked about. With every breath, he bemoaned his homesickness for her and their marriage bed. One evening Hunnicutt really got the doldrums, droning on and on about his celibate misery.

"And it's not just getting laid I miss. She's special. I mean it, really. She puts up with me, and that's saying a lot. I love her so much. That may sound sappy, but it's the God's truth. I don't know if I can take being away from her. I really don't. She—"

Griff, who'd been an unwilling audience for this lament, sent his chair over backward as he lunged toward Hunnicutt. "Jesus Christ, will you shut the fuck up?"

Then he hit Hunnicutt in the mouth as hard as he could, his famous throwing arm behind the punch. His knuckles connected with Hunnicutt's perfect caps, cleanly separating them from his gums.

Hunnicutt, spitting chipped porcelain and blood, was helped to his feet by other prisoners who rushed to his aid while hurling recriminations and insults at Griff. As one held a towel to Hunnicutt's bleeding mouth, he said, "Joke's on you, asshole. You've just done Hunnicutt here a favor."

Above the heads of the others, Hunnicutt and Griff made eye contact. Griff held it for several beats before turning away.

It was possible for prisoners in minimum security to obtain furloughs—temporary, unescorted releases from the prison. They were granted for limited and specific purposes, such as a family crisis, a funeral, or specialized medical treatment. Including dentistry.

The next morning, Hunnicutt filed a formal request for a release to have his teeth fixed. He met the requirements. He was given a form that cited all the rules and restrictions of the furlough. He affixed his signature to the bottom, promising to uphold them. A few days later the warden granted him the temporary release.

In between trips to the dentist's office, Hunnicutt and his wife kept the sheets hot at the Comfort Inn in Big Spring.

For slugging his fellow prisoner, Griff was reprimanded and his privileges were temporarily revoked.

When the car dealer returned, sparkling new caps well cemented, he'd sidled up to Griff and thanked him. "What the hell are you talking about?" Griff grumbled. "I just wanted you to put a lid on it."

Knowing better, Hunnicutt said, "I owe you one. A big one."

Griff hoped Hunnicutt remembered that IOU. He was cashing it now. "Nothing fancy or flashy," he said into the greasy telephone receiver. "Just a reliable set of wheels. Will you help me?"

Following another long hesitation, Hunnicutt said, "I've got a boy now."

Griff's shoulders slumped with disappointment. He could press the issue. He could remind Hunnicutt that while he and his wife had been screwing each other blind, he'd been doing a series of menial and unpleasant tasks as punishment.

But what right did he have to drag this likable guy, a husband and now a father, into the tub of shit he was in? Hunnicutt would be guilty of aiding and abetting. He'd be violating his probation. It was a lot to ask of him. Too much.

"I understand," Griff said.

"He just turned four."

"It's okay. Forget I asked."

"He was conceived at the Comfort Inn."

Griff's heart skipped a beat. He held his breath.

Hunnicutt said, "Last row of the lot. Third car in from Lemmon Avenue. Keys will be under the mat."

Griff gripped the phone, squeezed his eyes shut, and what came from his lips might have been a silent prayer of thanks. Then he said, "If you're asked, I stole the car, okay? Don't get into trouble over this. Tell them I stole it."

Hunnicutt said nothing.

"Did you hear me?"

Hunnicutt hung up.

On foot, Griff estimated it would take him a couple hours to walk to Hunnicutt Motors. He couldn't leave until after dark. Twilight came late this time of year. He had approximately nine hours to kill.

He was hungry, but his stomach would have to wait till he could use a drive-through and decrease the chances of being recognized.

Trying to ignore the hunger pangs, he lay on the bed and stared at the dirty ceiling. He thought about Laura, the hell she must be going through, the emotional pain, the guilt.

Because by now, she would know about his fingerprints on the murder weapon. Rodarte, in his insidious way, would have told her he knew about their affair. It was a classic case of jealous outrage, almost a cliché. Her lover had killed her husband.

And how would Laura have responded? How could she have responded? Would she tell Rodarte about their contract? No. Griff couldn't see her telling all for Rodarte's avid ears. She would omit that part. Not for Griff's protection, or even her own. But for Foster Speakman's. And the child's. She might be painted a scarlet woman, but at all costs, she would preserve Foster's reputation and secure the future of her baby.

If only he could talk to her . . .

But that wasn't going to happen, so he might just as well stop wishing for it.

He opened the telephone directory again and looked for listings under Ruiz. There wasn't one for a Manuelo. He hadn't expected that kind of luck. But maybe the Salvadoran had relatives. Using the motel phone, Griff dialed the first number.

"*Hola?*"

"*Manuelo, por favor.*"

His grasp of Spanish was limited to what he'd learned in two years of high school, but he gathered by what the woman said that he had the wrong number.

He went down the list, calling every Ruiz. No Manuelos. And even if he had run down the one he sought, Manuelo wouldn't have stuck around waiting for Griff to show up. He would've run like hell.

The man was no fool.

Without a car, there was nothing more Griff could do until dark. He had no choice but to wait out the long hours of the afternoon.

CHAPTER
25

IT'S NICE OUT HERE."

At the sound of his voice, Laura jumped and turned around suddenly. "Oh, Detective. Hello."

Rodarte had crept up on her deliberately, wanting to get an honest reaction out of her, not one she had time to rehearse. He climbed the steps and joined her in the gazebo. "You don't see many of these anymore." He pretended to admire the lacy woodwork trim on the circular roof.

"Foster's grandmother had it built even before the house was completed. Foster told me she wanted someplace where she could sit and watch the swans. They always had swans in the pond."

The gazebo sat on a rise overlooking a pond where a pair of honest-to-God swans were gliding across the mirrored surface of the water. *Rich folk,* he thought scornfully. If he had their money, he'd spend it on something better than gazebos and swans.

"You mind?" He nodded at one of the vacant wicker chairs. She shook her head, and he sat down. She was wearing sunglasses, so he couldn't see her eyes to tell if she'd been crying. He guessed she had because she was twisting a damp Kleenex between her fingers. *Tears of grief or guilt?* he wondered. He really didn't care. Not unless she'd plotted with Griff Burkett to kill her husband.

Now, *that* would be a story, wouldn't it? It would be written up in *People* magazine; *20/20* would do a segment on it. They'd make a movie of the week out of it. Maybe they'd cast him in a bit part, or he could serve as technical adviser to the producers, get movie credit.

But first he had to prove it.

"More peaceful out here than inside," he re-marked as he settled against the floral-print chair cushion.

Mrs. Speakman's assistant had been joined by Mr. Speakman's, a woman named Myrna some-thing, who vacillated between crying like a baby and issuing orders like a drill sergeant. Together with Mrs. Dobbins, the housekeeper, they were manning the telephone, finding places for the floral arrangements and fruit baskets that were delivered by the truckload, cleaning up after all the cops who had been in the house last night, and making lists. They made endless lists.

A homicide generated a lot of busywork for ev-erybody but the corpse.

"I had to get some fresh air," Laura Speakman said. "And away from the telephone."

"Who's called?"

Behind the opaque lenses he figured she was giving him one of her haughty, condescending looks. "People conveying their condolences."

"Anybody I should know about?"

"Griff Burkett. That's who you mean."

He grinned as though to say, *You know me too well.* "It's my duty to check. Has he tried to contact you?"

"No. He wouldn't."

"You sure about that?"

"He wouldn't." She went back to looking at the swans. One had buried its face beneath its wing.

"I got the autopsy report from the ME." Her only response to that was to roll her lips inward and compress them into a hard line. "Your car accident two years ago? Besides the obvious damage to his spinal column and legs, your husband suffered a lot of internal injury."

"I mentioned that this morning when we talked about his medication."

"It was pretty bad."

"Yes, it was."

"Some of his organs were friable. That's the word the ME used. Weak. Eventually he would have died from one of those organs giving out. Probably sooner than later. That also according to the ME." He paused on purpose. "But what killed him was a severed artery."

She swallowed. "How long would it have taken?"

"Hmm, not long. But there was blood on his hands, tissue under his fingernails."

She snapped her head around to look at him.

"That's right, Mrs. Speakman. Your husband fought for his life."

Rodarte actually enjoyed telling her that. Finally he got a reaction out of her. Her chest rose and fell on a quick little breath. She pressed the Kleenex against her mouth.

"He lived long enough to struggle with his attacker," he continued. "Have to admire him for that. Him, paralyzed from the waist down, battling a guy with Burkett's size and strength. He never had a chance, but he put up a brave fight." Leaning forward, he placed his hand over hers. "Are you all right?"

She yanked her hand from beneath his. "I'll be fine."

"I know this is hard for you."

"Is there anything else, Detective?"

"You can make arrangements for burial now."

"Thank you."

"Just contact the funeral home. They'll know what to do."

She nodded.

He stood up and moved to the railing that enclosed the gazebo. Staring out across the well-manicured landscape, he said thoughtfully, "Do you think Burkett attacked your husband suddenly, in a jealous rage? Or do you think they quarreled over the money?"

"Money?"

When he came around, she had removed her sunglasses and was staring up at him inquisitively.

"Didn't I mention the money to you?"

"What are you talking about, Detective? What money?"

"The cash. In the navy blue box. It was on your husband's desk in plain sight when the crime scene unit got here. They nearly shit when they— I'm sorry. Pardon the expletive." He gave her a feeble smile. "See? Just thinking about it rattled me. It's not every day you see that kind of money all heaped together. Half a million in one-hundred-dollar bills."

Her lips parted soundlessly. She stared into near space for several moments, then shifted her gaze to a shrub loaded with big blue flowers that looked like pom-poms. He didn't know what you called the flowers, but he knew how to define Mrs. Speakman's reaction. She was stunned to hear about the half mil. More specifically, she was stunned to learn he knew about it.

"Half a million dollars in cash," he said. "Sitting right there. It's under lock and key in the evidence room now. You'll get it back. Unless it turns out to be ill-gotten funds of some kind."

"Ill-gotten?"

"Drug money, something like that."

She turned back to him and stood up suddenly. "Listen to me, Detective Rodarte. My husband wasn't involved in anything illegal, and if you were to check his financial portfolio, you'd realize just how ludicrous that allegation is."

"You said he had a meeting with Griff Burkett here in your home. That's how you two met."

"What bearing does that have on this?"

"You said you didn't know what they talked about."

"I still don't see the relevance of—"

"Burkett was found guilty of racketeering, Mrs. Speakman. So I was thinking that—"

"Whatever you're thinking, you're wrong."

"Then how do you explain the cash?"

She folded her arms across her middle and tilted her head to one side. "Why are you just now mentioning this box of money to me?"

"With everything else, it slipped my mind," he lied.

Their mutual stare held for several seconds, then she shrugged. "Foster kept large amounts of cash in the safe here at home, and in another at his office."

"You don't say. Why?"

"He liked to pass it around."

"Pass it around?"

"It was a trait of his. An idiosyncrasy. He was a lavish tipper. He enjoyed leaving huge gratuities to waiters, hotel maids, the tollbooth attendant, anyone who did a service for him. Sometimes he would go out to the airport and hand out cash gifts to Sun-South ticket agents, baggage handlers, people who worked for him and were rarely thanked for the jobs they did. He did things like that often. Ask anybody."

He raised his hands in surrender. "I believe you. It's just a strange hobby. Never heard of such."

"Foster didn't advertise it. He did it for the pleasure he derived from doing it, not for self-aggrandizement."

"Thank you for telling me," Rodarte said, faking sincerity. "That could be one explanation for the box of cash. Except . . ."

"What?"

"Burkett's prints were on the lid of the box. How do you explain that?"

"I can't. But it proves that Griff Burkett isn't a thief."

He chuckled. "Well, the Department of Justice, gamblers nationwide, and the Cowboys organization would disagree. He took them for plenty every time he shaved points. I guess he didn't need your husband's half million."

She pounced on his remark as though about to contradict it, then closed her mouth quickly and put her sunglasses back on. Whatever she had been about to say, she'd thought better of it. "If that's all, I'd like to go in now and place that call to the funeral director."

"Sure," he said, waving her toward the steps. He walked along beside her as they crossed the expansive lawn. Whenever he got too close, she moved away, which amused him. "Oh, I forgot to tell you. We found two different blood types in Burkett's Honda. One, of course, was your husband's. Burkett must've had his blood all over him."

The sunglasses weren't large enough to conceal her grimace, but she didn't address the issue of her husband's blood being on her lover. "The other is probably his," she said. "If there was tissue beneath Foster's fingernails, he probably scratched him."

Rodarte said, "I would think that, too, except we've already tested it. Doesn't match Burkett's blood type. So what I think is, it's Manuelo Ruiz's blood. Because it's the same blood type as what we got off your library rug."

"Implying what?"

"That Manuelo Ruiz was bleeding, too." Rodarte tugged on his earlobe as though thinking it through. "The man's vanished. I got in touch with Immigration to try to track him down. Guess what?

Ruiz didn't have papers. Your husband hired him illegally."

"That's academic now, isn't it?"

This rich bitch was one cool broad, staring up at him through her dark sunglasses, her body language a dead giveaway to her contempt for him. He'd like to have done something to shake her up, something to crack that smooth mask she wore whenever she was talking to him. Twist her nipple, maybe. Push his hand between her legs. Something that would shock and frighten her.

"I guess it's beside the point now." He smiled amiably, even as he was thinking how much pleasure he would derive from humiliating her.

"Then what is the point, Detective?"

"Griff Burkett knocked off the wetback, too."

Well, at least that elicited an honest reaction. He wasn't sure if she flinched away from the racial slur or from his allegation that Burkett had committed double murder. It was hard not to look smug, but he kept his stoniest cop expression in place. "I don't know if he got rid of Manuelo before or after he killed your husband, but it's almost a certainty that he's responsible for Ruiz's unexplained disappearance."

She wet her lips, pulled the lower one through her teeth, and he understood why Burkett liked fucking her enough to kill for it.

"Maybe Manuelo was frightened away by what he saw," she said. "He ran."

"Without taking any clothes or personal belongings? Without a car? Without the half million cash? Unlikely, Mrs. Speakman. But, on the outside chance that he ran from something that scared him out of his wits, I've had cops calling on every Ruiz in the Dallas phone book. Fort Worth, too." He leaned forward and whispered, "Want to know something funny? We weren't the first to call those folks today, asking did they know Manuelo."

"No?"

"No. Come to find out, somebody beat us to the punch. A man has been calling the same people, looking for Manuelo Ruiz."

"Griff Burkett?"

He spread his hands at his sides and smiled.

She removed her sunglasses, carefully folded down the stems, and studied them for several moments before lifting her head and looking up at him. "Well, which is it, Detective Rodarte?"

"Which is what?"

"If Griff Burkett killed Manuelo, as you allege, then why has he been calling people named Ruiz, looking for him?"

She held his gaze for several moments, then turned her back to him and started walking toward the house.

Rodarte stared after her, trying to control the anger pulsing through him. All right, she'd got him on that one, and he had no one to blame but himself for the blunder.

Truth be told, he hadn't dwelled a lot on the fate of Manuelo Ruiz because he didn't give a flying fuck what had happened to him. Whether Burkett had killed him or was trying to chase him down because he had witnessed a murder and needed to be silenced, it mattered not in the least to Rodarte.

He would either find the wetback's body or run

him down and get him to testify against Burkett. Whichever, he had Burkett for Foster Speakman's murder. Burkett's ass belonged to Stanley Rodarte.

And so does the widow's.

Chuckling to himself, he thought of the payback he'd extract for her snooty condescension. After the funeral. After the folderol had died down. After Burkett was locked behind bars. Using the prison grapevine, he'd make sure Number Ten heard about his attentions to the lady. Every salacious detail.

Jesus, was that gonna be fun, or what?

CHAPTER
26

FOR THE REMAINDER OF THE AFTERNOON, Griff paced the dismal room, wondering how in hell he'd sunk so low. When had this unstoppable decline started? When he accepted Vista's first bribe? Or before that, when he began placing bets while at UT? Or had he been irreversibly ill-fated when his mother had abandoned him to run off with her boyfriend Ray?

Sometimes he thought he'd been doomed even before he was born.

During the weeks between his conviction and the day he reported to Big Spring to begin his sentence, he'd conducted a search for his parents. Wasn't it natural for a child to turn to his parents when he was in trouble?

Thanks to the Internet and websites dedicated to linking lost relatives, it hadn't taken him long to track down his father. After serving his jail sentence in Texas, he'd left the state, alighting several places but never staying anywhere for long, until he eventually wound up in Laramie, Wyoming. He died there in a local hospital at the age of forty-nine. Hospital records said he suffered from several maladies related to alcoholism.

It took more time to locate his mother. She had either committed bigamy and married men without first securing divorces or simply assumed the names of the various men she lived with.

As the day of Griff's incarceration approached, he frequently asked himself why he was bothering to try to find her, why he was even curious about her life now, when she'd left him without a shred of remorse. To his knowledge she had never tried to learn what happened to him, so why was reconnecting with her so important?

He didn't know what drove him. It was a compulsion he couldn't explain, even to himself, so he gave up and just went with it.

His doggedness paid off. On the day before he was to begin serving his sentence, he found her in Omaha. He obtained an address and a telephone number. Before he could talk himself out of it, he called the number.

It was a decision he came to regret.

Quite a send-off to prison, he thought now, caustically.

Why today, when he was in worse trouble than ever, was he conjuring up all this crap about his parents? Maybe because thinking about them reinforced what he strongly suspected: He had been on this path to self-destruction before he even left the womb.

Which didn't bode well for the eventual outcome.

Depressed, he lay down on the ratty bed and actually slept for a while. Perhaps that was his body's way of letting him temporarily escape from his reality. Even kinder was his subconscious, which let him dream about Laura. His hands were on her. He was moving inside her. She was clutching his ass, arching up to receive him, moaning his name. Heartbeats away from coming, he woke up, her name on his lips, soaked in sweat, sporting a painful erection.

He got up, showered, and turned on the TV in time for the local evening newscasts. As he'd feared, a smug-looking anchorman with bad hair announced that the police were seeking Griff Burkett for "questioning in the brutal slaying of Foster Speakman."

This came as no surprise, of course, but Griff sat dazed, immobilized by the sudden appearance of Stanley Rodarte on the screen. He was standing in the glare of video lights, which intensified his ugliness. "At this point, Mr. Burkett is only a person of interest. All we know at present is that he was inside the Speakmans' mansion last evening."

This statement of fact caused a feeding frenzy among the reporters, who began firing questions at him. Full of self-importance, Rodarte denied them answers, saying only "Burkett's involvement warrants further investigation. That's all I have for you right now." He turned his back on them and walked through the iron gates onto the Speakman estate.

Rodarte was there. Inside the ivy-covered walls. With Laura. She would revile Griff Burkett now.

Rodarte would stoke that, use it to win her to his side. The thought of her and Rodarte breathing the same air made his empty stomach clench as tight as a fist.

Darkness finally fell. Even with the temperature hovering in the low nineties, it felt good to be outdoors, away from the lingering odors in his motel room. But it took Griff nearly two hours to walk to Hunnicutt Motors, and by that time the heat was taking its toll. He hadn't dared stop to buy a bottle of water, so he arrived at the car lot gritty with dried sweat and dehydrated.

But the hike had been worth it. The car had been left as promised.

It was a nondescript sedan somewhere between brown and gray. The model name on the trunk lid was unfamiliar to him, and he couldn't even identify the car's maker. Pontiac? Ford maybe? The cloth upholstery gave off the musty smell of stale tobacco smoke when he warily opened the unlocked door. No alarm went off.

The keys were beneath the floor mat, the gas tank was full, and the engine fired as soon as he turned the ignition. Conveniently, the chain that was usually stretched across the driveway as a security measure was lying on the pavement. Hunnicutt had thought of everything.

Wyatt Turner, attorney-at-law, lived in one of the nouveau riche neighborhoods of North Dallas. Every house had a swimming pool in the backyard, golf clubs in the garage, and inside, an upwardly mobile couple trying to keep up with the Joneses. Pets were optional. Most had children.

The Turners had only one. Griff had never seen Wyatt Junior in person, but he'd seen his picture on Wyatt's desk. He was a fifty-fifty blend of his parents, which was unfortunate for the kid. Griff had met Susan Turner only once, at a social function long before he was in need of Wyatt's services. She was a pallid woman, virtually colorless, with a personality to match. She practiced law also, but not criminal law like her husband. Taxes, corporate, probate, something dull like that. And Griff bet she was good at it. She was uptight, unfriendly, and unattractive. Compared with her, Wyatt was the life of the party.

Griff cruised past their house and saw that there was only one light on inside. He hoped it was Wyatt burning the midnight oil and not Susan. He parked two streets over and conscientiously locked the car door when he got out. He had dressed in shorts and T-shirt, running shoes, ball cap. In a neighborhood of yuppies like this one, people ran at all hours, whenever they could wedge the workout into their busy schedules. He hoped that if he was seen, he'd be mistaken for a guy who had time to exercise only late at night.

He jogged the two blocks. One dog barked at him from behind a wood fence, but otherwise he went unnoticed. At least he hoped so. Someone inside one of these upscale homes could have spotted him and called a neighborhood security watch or the police. That was a risk he had to take.

He had noticed that the house next door to the Turners' had a For Sale sign out front. The property was dark, inside and out, which was to his advantage. When he reached it now, he detoured off the sidewalk into the shadows of the yard. He went around to the side yard that abutted the Turners' driveway. There he crouched in the shrubbery to catch his breath and plan his next move.

Through open blinds, he could see into the lighted room of the Turners' house. It was a home office, reminiscent of Bolly's except much neater. A stuffed deer head mounted on the wall. Framed diplomas. Law books on the shelves. A computer monitor was on, casting a bluish light onto the desk and several open files.

The lawyer appeared, coming into the room carrying a glass of milk and what looked like a sandwich on a plate. He was wearing a white T-shirt and a pair of pajama bottoms. The tail of the T-shirt was tucked into the elastic waistband of the pajamas. *Tucked in.* In spite of his situation, Griff had to smile at his lawyer's sleeping attire. But he shared a bed with Mrs. Turner, so that explained it. Griff would have sooner made love to a corn husk.

Turner sat down at the desk, took a bite of the sandwich, and as he chewed, he gazed into his computer monitor. Griff took a deep breath and stepped out of the shrubbery. He crossed the driveway and walked up to the pair of French doors that opened directly into the office. He tapped lightly on a pane of glass.

Startled, Turner looked in his direction. When he saw Griff, his face registered a series of expressions—astonishment, apprehension, finally anger.

Griff tried the door handle. It was locked. He jiggled it several times, making metal rattle against metal. He read the curse on Turner's lips as he got out of his chair. He glanced cautiously into what

Griff presumed was a hallway, then quickly came to the door and opened it.

Angrily he whispered, "Do you know that every cop within five hundred miles is after you?"

"Then you'd better let me in before one of them spots me on your doorstep."

Turner motioned him in, then stepped outside and looked down his driveway into the street. Satisfied that there were no wolves at the gate, he shut the door, after which he went around the room hastily drawing the blinds closed.

Griff picked up the sandwich and began wolfing it down. Between the car lot and here, he'd used the drive-through window to pick up a Whataburger and demolished it as he drove. It had taken the edge off his hunger but hadn't appeased it. Peanut butter and jelly had never been his favorite, but right now it tasted delicious. He drank the milk, too. Turner was watching him, seething.

"I need this more than you do," Griff said through a mouthful. Then, motioning toward his lawyer's paunch, he added, "A lot more."

"I want you out of here."

"I need information."

"I'm not CNN."

"You're my lawyer."

"Not anymore."

Griff stopped chewing. "Since when?"

"Since you—" Turner's loud voice startled even him. He froze, listening, then went to the door and looked into the hallway again. "Don't move," he whispered to Griff over his shoulder. "Don't make a sound."

The lawyer disappeared into the dark hallway.

Griff could hear doors—he assumed to bedrooms—being softly closed. Despite Turner's warning, he went to the French doors and separated the slats of the blinds to peer out, wondering if Hunnicutt's car parked two streets over had aroused a watchful homeowner's suspicion. Had anybody noticed a jogger at midnight suddenly disappearing into the dark shadows surrounding a vacant house?

Turner returned, walking on tiptoe. Quietly he pulled the door closed behind himself. "Susan's a light sleeper."

"Since when aren't you my lawyer?"

"Since you murdered Foster Speakman," the lawyer returned, matching Griff's angry stage whisper. "Christ, Griff. Foster Speakman! You could just as well have killed the president. Is it true you were screwing his wife?"

Griff held his accusatory stare for several seconds, then crammed the last of the sandwich into his mouth, muttering, "You should be so lucky."

"What?"

"Nothing." He finished the milk, then wiped his mouth with the back of his hand. "I didn't know a lawyer could fire a client."

"I don't want anything to do with you. You're too dangerous."

"Dangerous?" Griff spread his arms wide. All he had on him was the car key and his cell phone clipped to the elastic waistband of his running shorts.

"I'd call you dangerous," Turner said. "He said you stabbed Speakman in the neck with his letter opener. A paraplegic, Griff. He said Speakman tried to fight back, tried to protect himself from you, but—"

"He who? Who said? Rodarte?"

"Of course Rodarte. He and that silent partner of his came to my office this morning. Rodarte did all the talking. He asked if I knew where you were, and fortunately I could honestly say no." Turner frowned, unhappy over knowing Griff's whereabouts now. "Rodarte is having a field day. This time, make no mistake, he's got you."

"I don't get my day in court?"

Turner gnawed the inside of his cheek and cast a worried glance toward the closed door. "Make it quick." He sat down in his desk chair and tried to look lawyerly—a role hard to pull off in the pajama outfit. "How'd you meet the Speakmans?"

"I was invited to their home. Speakman proposed a business deal."

Turner looked dubious. "What kind of business?"

"We talked about me doing some ads for his airline." That wasn't exactly a lie. It wasn't exactly the truth, but he couldn't tell Turner the truth. Not yet. Foster Speakman's reputation be damned. As far as keeping his secret was concerned, all bets were off. But Laura shared that secret. Griff would keep it for her sake.

"That's nuts," Turner remarked.

"That's what I told him. But, come to find out, he had a lot of idiosyncrasies and weird ideas. Anyway, he told me to think it over, he would, too, so forth."

"The wife? Laura?"

"I met her that same night."

"Instant lust, Rodarte said."

"Rodarte said that?"

"Words to that effect. He said the two of you had a hot and heavy affair."

Griff wondered where Rodarte was getting his information. Probably he was merely speculating and making it sound like fact. "She and I got together. Four times to be exact. Over a period of months. The last time we saw each other, she called it off."

"Why?"

Disinclined to tell Turner more than that, he shrugged. "Typical reasons. Guilt mostly. I thought I'd never see her again."

"But you wanted to."

He didn't answer, but his expression must have given him away.

Turner groaned. "You just handed Rodarte motivation on a silver platter. To get the girl, you bumped off her husband. You don't even need a criminal law degree to see that, Griff."

"Besides motivation—"

"And opportunity."

"I didn't barge in on Speakman last night. I went to the mansion at his invitation."

"He *invited* you?"

"He invited me."

"What for? Did he confront you about the affair? Had the wife felt so guilty she confessed all?"

"I don't know. I don't know how much Laura told him about us." In all honesty, he didn't.

"Have you been in touch with her?"

He shook his head.

"I advise you not to try."

"As my former lawyer?"

Ignoring the sarcastic dig, Foster asked, "Can you prove Speakman invited you to the mansion last night?"

"Not yet."

"What does that mean?"

Losing patience, Griff said, "Besides motive and opportunity, what's Rodarte got on me?"

The lawyer hesitated.

"Come on, Turner. You owe me at least that much. What am I up against?"

Turner snorted. "Well, there's the murder weapon covered with your fingerprints. Your DNA will match the tissue they dug out from under Speakman's fingernails." He pointed toward the bloody scratches on the backs of Griff's hands. "Correct?"

"Correct."

"Hell, Griff," he said, wincing, "Rodarte doesn't need anything else to nail you for Speakman. But there's also this guy named Ruiz."

"Manuelo. Speakman's aide. Looks like a South American headhunter with a pleasant but empty smile."

"Nobody's seen him." Turner paused and looked at him expectantly. When Griff didn't say anything, he continued. "Rodarte checked with Immigration. No file on him. He was an illegal."

"You're using the past tense."

"Was he there last night?"

Again Griff refrained from saying anything.

"Don't bother lying," the lawyer said. "They found blood on the rug and in your car. My old

Honda. The blood wasn't yours or Speakman's. Rodarte surmises it's Ruiz's. He's searching for his remains."

Beneath his breath, Griff said, "Fuck!"

"Well finally, the oracle speaks. And isn't that an eloquent statement?" the lawyer said with asperity. "Was he alive when you left him?"

"Which?"

Turner rubbed his high forehead as though to smooth out the worry lines. "Either."

"Speakman was dead. Ruiz was *adiós*."

"He escaped you?"

"He ran."

"Did he see Speakman get stabbed?"

Griff didn't respond.

"Did you . . . Was Ruiz also injured? *Was* that his blood on the rug and in the Honda?"

Griff was about to answer, then checked himself. "Are you my lawyer or not?"

Turner studied him for a moment, than asked quietly, "What about the money, Griff? The half million. And don't play dumb, because your finger-prints were on the lid of the box. So, what was that about?"

"Beats me," he replied laconically, with a shrug. "Speakman says, 'Look in the box.' I looked in the box. I guess he was showing off how rich he was."

"It wasn't for you?"

Griff looked at him as though that was the most preposterous thing he'd ever heard in his life.

"Rodarte suggested that Speakman was paying you off for something."

Griff's gut tightened. "Like what?"

"Something you had delivered. Or a service you'd performed for him."

"Shit, Turner, where's your brain? Where's Rodarte's? If that money had been for me, I sure as hell wouldn't have left it behind. I'd have it and be living it up in some exotic locale, not bumming peanut butter sandwiches off you."

The lawyer wasn't fazed. "Lotta money, Griff. Large bills banded together. Stacked neatly in a box. Kind of like the take you got from Bandy for throwing the play-off game against the Skins."

"I'm telling you—"

"Okay, okay. For now let's say Speakman just liked keeping boxes of cash around and it had nothing to do with his murder. Rodarte doesn't even need that element to get a conviction." Turner stood, circled his chair, placed his hands on the back of it, as though he were about to address the court. "Listen to me, Griff. This is a prosecutor's dream case. They've got hard evidence. They've got your DNA. And if Ruiz is alive—"

"He is. Or was last time I saw him."

"And if he isn't already back in Honduras—"

"El Salvador."

"Whatever. If they can catch him, they'll have an eyewitness in addition to the incriminating evidence. But," he said, lightly slapping the leather chair back for emphasis, "on the positive side, you placed the 911 call, right?" Griff nodded. "So that suggests you didn't want Speakman to die. It can be argued that Speakman invited you there, and if the jury buys that, then the next step is their believing that there was no premeditation on your part. You went to Speakman's house at his invitation. He confronted you with the affair you were having—"

"Had."

"Had with his wife. You argued. Something he said lit your fuse, next thing you know—"

"I picked up the letter opener on his desk and plunged it into his neck."

Turner actually looked sad about it. "You've got a good chance of being charged with manslaughter, instead of murder one. That's probably the best you'll do on this one, and I'm telling you that both as counsel and as a friend." He paused to let that sink in.

"I hate to paint such a bleak picture, but that's how it is, Griff. And you're only making yourself look guiltier by running. Turning yourself in to Rodarte will be rough. I'm not saying it won't. But it'll be much harder for you if you don't."

"I'm not turning myself in."

"If you do—tonight, *now*—I'll represent you. I'll be right there with you every step of the way. Let them conduct their investigation, and then we'll see just how badly the evidence is stacked against you. Rodarte has been known to exaggerate, to insinuate that he has more than he actually does, but we *know* he has the weapon and, coupled with the motive, it's damn incriminating.

"It actually works in our favor that you left the money behind. You didn't commit robbery, so it's not a capital murder. I'll argue like hell for the manslaughter charge. I'll also file for change of venue. Get the trial out of Dallas.

"But wherever it's conducted, you can bet the prosecutor will hammer home how defenseless

Speakman was against you. He'll paint you as a brute who attacked a man who couldn't possibly fight back and win. He'll make the jurors despise you, and any argument you put forth won't change the indisputable fact that you were a football player and he was a paraplegic.

"Turn yourself in and let me take over your defense. The only time you have to speak is at your arraignment, when you plead not guilty. You don't have to breathe a bloody word to Rodarte, the jury, nobody."

Griff had listened patiently, but now he said, "And you think *not* talking will make me look innocent? Come on, Wyatt."

"I believe in jurisprudence, in our system of justice."

"Well, your perspective on it is different from mine. You promised me I'd get off with probation if I cooperated with the feds and told them what I knew about Vista's operation. Look what happened to that."

"That was different."

"Right. We were dealing with the federal grand jury and what-ifs. This time Rodarte's got my prints on the instrument that killed my lover's husband."

Turner's head dropped forward. He stood, a frown creasing his brow. Finally he raised his head. "I appeal to you once more, Griff. Give yourself up."

"That's the best you can do?"

"That's it."

Griff studied him a moment, then said softly, "You haven't even asked me."

"Asked you what?"

Snuffling a rueful laugh, Griff said, "Never mind. Have you heard from Jerry Arnold?"

"He called this afternoon. Kept saying, 'Why would he do something like this?' Stuff like that. You've lost another fan."

Griff wasn't surprised. "Well, thanks for the info. And the sandwich." He turned toward the French doors.

"Griff, wait."

"See ya, Turner." He opened the door.

He heard the squeal of brakes as though a car had taken a corner too fast. He heard gunning engines, the *whish* of rubber on hot pavement. And in the house across the street, the front windows reflected colored lights. Red. Blue. White.

CHAPTER
27

TURNER RAISED HIS HANDS IN SURRENDER. Self-defense maybe. "I had to call them, Griff. It's for your own good."

Griff sneered. "As counsel and friend, go fuck yourself."

Then he was out the door. He skirted the swimming pool and used a lawn chair to help him vault the privacy fence. His knees took the brunt of the eight-foot drop to the ground on the other side. Another swimming pool. This one had the underwater light on. It felt like a searchlight, directed on him.

A searchlight made him think of a police helicopter, and that gave him the impetus to bust through the gate without fiddling with the latch. He ran through that yard, across the street, into the front yard of another house, where the sprinklers were on. His thrashing legs got wet, and so did the soles of his shoes, making them slippery.

Another freaking fence. "Shit!" Didn't these people trust their own neighbors? He searched for the gate, which was hard to detect in the darkness. He found it, but it was locked from the inside. He backed up, threw himself against it. It didn't budge.

He heard tires screeching, close enough for him to smell the smoking rubber.

He ran through the sprinklers again to the neighboring house. Finally, a house with no fence, only a hedge. He plunged through it. The thorny holly plants clawed at his bare legs, tearing skin, but he didn't let that slow him down. He ran between that house and the one behind it, which put him on the street where he'd left the borrowed car.

He paused in the darkness between two houses, his lungs a bellows, his heart a jackhammer. He could hear shouting, tires squealing, car doors slamming. Hunnicutt's car was three houses from where he stood. Nothing here was moving. Yet. He couldn't delay. The search for him would soon spread to this street. He had to risk exposure.

He stepped from between the two houses, primed to sprint.

A police car, lit up like a Christmas tree, took the nearest corner on two wheels.

Griff ducked back into the shadows. Cursed Turner. Cursed his luck. Cursed his whole frigging life.

Then he ran.

Later, he would wonder how in hell he had got out of there. His escape almost made him a believer in divine intervention. Maybe for once in his life, God had suited up to play on his team.

He zigzagged through the neighborhood, moving from one patch of darkness to another. The chopper did appear with its searchlight, which was more powerful than the beam of any lighthouse. For hours he dodged it and the squad cars that either sped or crawled through the streets. Policemen on foot searched, practically going door to door.

He took a few minutes' refuge in an open garage, where he found a rag to blot the streams of blood off his legs. Sweat made the wounds sting mercilessly. Once, when he got trapped between the approaching chopper's searchlight and a policeman on foot, he slid into the deep end of a swimming pool. Luckily there was no underwater light, and the pool was one of the pretentious ones, designed to replicate a tropical lagoon formed by lava rock, so it was dark.

He held his breath until he thought his lungs would burst, but because of all the swimming he'd done recently, he was better conditioned than he would have been normally. Looking up through the surface, he could see the chopper's light sweeping the area. The policeman came so close, Griff could hear him muttering to himself.

Finally both the officer and the helicopter moved on. Griff's head cleared the surface, and he gulped oxygen. He climbed out of the pool, pruney but revived. His legs weren't stinging anymore. He didn't even attempt to return to the car. Cops would have been all over it once they ran the tag number through the DMV and discovered it didn't belong to anyone living on that street.

He still had his cell phone. Thank God he'd taken it with him. He thought about dialing Glen

Hunnicutt, asking him to meet somewhere and pick him up. But he didn't want to involve the man any more than he already had.

He had no one else to call. No one he could trust. No one who trusted him.

He felt safer when he was out of Wyatt Turner's neighborhood, but only a bit, because he still had a long way to go to reach the motel. Cops all over the city would now be on the lookout for a man of his description on foot. There would be a lot of harassed joggers in Dallas that morning. Those who ran before daylight were sure to be stopped and scrutinized.

When he walked beneath the freeway overpass and saw the neon vacancy light flickering in the motel office window, he wanted to weep with relief. It wasn't much, but it was the only hiding place he had. Dawn was just breaking.

He needed to lie down. Close his eyes. Breathe easily. Rest.

But as he neared the parking lot, he noticed that the dope-smoking night clerk was no longer on duty. His replacement was dressed casually, but he looked too clean-cut to work in a place like this.

Griff ducked behind the used-tire store's portable marquee. From that tenuous hiding place, he watched the guy come out from behind the check-in desk. He left the office and started down the breezeway. He was carrying a foam cup. Steam was rising from it. The aroma of freshly brewed coffee made Griff's mouth water. But his heart began to feel very heavy when he saw the guy stop at room number seven and knock three times on the door.

It was opened by a man who was as clean-cut as

the one manning the office. He took the coffee from his buddy and savored his first sip with a long "Ahhh." They had a brief exchange, then the office guy left the other inside the room and walked back to the office.

Griff crouched behind the sign advertising the special on retreads and bent his head over his knees.

How the hell had they found him? Was Rodarte fucking clairvoyant?

He remained hunkered down behind the sign for a while, until his overtaxed leg muscles began to cramp, his knees to grow stiff, and the eastern horizon to become limned with orange.

Knowing he had to relocate, he reached into his sock for the bills he'd tucked there before going to Turner's. The currency was wet from his time in the pool, but it was spendable. He'd hid his cell phone beneath the diving board of the swimming pool, out of sight, before he'd slipped into the water, then retrieved it when he got out. The battery still had juice.

That paltry amount of cash and the phone were the only resources left to him. He didn't even have a dry change of clothes. But he couldn't stay here. He had to move. He forced his aching legs to unfold and began walking, being careful to keep something between himself and the office of the motel.

As he walked, he flipped open his phone and placed one short call.

Glen Hunnicutt was in his office, drinking coffee and shooting the breeze with a customer, when the dealership's receptionist tapped on his open office door. "Excuse the interruption, Mr. Hunnicutt.

There's someone here to see you. A detective with the police department. He says it's important."

"Come in." Hunnicutt rolled his hand, motioning the man into his office.

"Stanley Rodarte, DPD." He extended Hunnicutt his card.

"Have a seat, Detective," Hunnicutt said expansively, pointing him toward a chair. "You want some coffee?"

"No thanks."

"You sure? Our coffee's as good as our auto-*mo*-biles."

"No thanks."

"Maybe a nice, cold Dr Pepper?"

"Nothing, thanks," Rodarte said, showing his impatience.

"You shopping cars this morning, Detective?"

"No." Rodarte nodded toward the other man in the room, who was seated across from Hunnicutt's desk. "Could we have a minute alone? This is a police matter."

"Meet James McAlister. Jim's my lawyer, so I have no secrets from him." The look on Rodarte's face was priceless. It was all Hunnicutt could do not to chuckle. The detective hadn't expected a lawyer to be present.

Hunnicutt had arrived at the dealership shortly after daybreak so he could replace the security chain before his employees began reporting for work. He'd been at his desk catching up on paperwork when Griff's warning call came through the main phone line. Fortunately, he'd answered.

Upon hearing his voice, Griff said, "It's hit the fan. I'm sorry. You'll be hearing from a cop named

Rodarte. Stanley Rodarte. He gives you grief, you say this to him. You listening?"

"I'm listening."

Griff had left Hunnicutt with the message, then hung up.

Addressing Rodarte now, Hunnicutt said, "Jim's here to buy a car for his daughter who's turning sixteen next week. He expects a discount from me. Like hell, I said. He never gave me a discount on legal fees. I told him—"

"We found a car belonging to you," Rodarte said, brusquely cutting in. "It was found abandoned on a neighborhood street a few miles from here."

Hunnicutt looked at McAlister, registering surprise. "You found it? Already?" He whistled. "I'm impressed. We only reported it stolen, when, Jim? Eight, nine this morning? You guys in the DPD are good!"

Rodarte had received his second blow. "You reported the car stolen?"

McAlister snapped open the briefcase resting on his lap and took a form from it. It had been filled out by the policeman who'd responded to Hunnicutt's call, reporting that a car was missing from his inventory. Rodarte yanked the form from McAlister, glanced at it, and verified its accuracy, down to the car's make and model, license plate, and VIN. Hunnicutt got the impression Rodarte was about to wad up the form and hurl it to the floor. McAlister rescued it just in time and replaced it in his briefcase.

"When was it stolen?" the detective asked tightly.

"Don't know. I didn't notice it missing until this morning. Cars get shifted around all day, every day.

It could have been missing a couple weeks, a couple days, or a couple hours. No way of telling."

"Griff Burkett's prints are all over that car," Rodarte growled, looking like a man barely in control of his temper.

"Griff Burkett? *The* Griff Burkett? No shit! You sure?"

"Oh, yeah. I'm sure."

"Well, I'll be. Imagine that. Hmm. Wonders never cease."

Rodarte's glower turned darker. "He left it parked two streets from his lawyer's house, where he went last night asking for information that would help him elude arrest for the murder of Foster Speakman. Turner called us instead."

Hunnicutt looked over at McAlister. "Lucky I've got you."

"Burkett managed to get away on foot," Rodarte said.

"The boy has talent," Hunnicutt said. "Fastest quarterback I've ever seen. That fancy footwork of his was something to watch, wasn't it?"

Rodarte looked ready to explode. "You gave that car to him, which amounts to aiding and abetting a murder suspect."

"That's an awfully ugly allegation," McAlister said calmly. "I'm hereby instructing my client not to answer any further questions, Detective."

Ignoring the lawyer, Rodarte kept his eyes on Hunnicutt. "When did Burkett call you? Yesterday? Last night?"

Hunnicutt said nothing.

"Obviously you admire him, but he's no hero. Yesterday he made a bunch of calls to area families named Ruiz. I had cops calling those same families, searching for clues into the disappearance of Manuelo Ruiz, who we believe witnessed Foster Speakman's murder. We compared notes. Same phone number showed up on several caller IDs. We traced that number to a fleabag motel out on 635. I've got men staking out the place, waiting for him to slink back to where his stuff's at.

"And when he does, I'm going to put him through the wringer. Your name's bound to come up. He'll give you up, Hunnicutt. Burkett doesn't have friends, only people he uses then shits on. He has loyalty to no one except himself. You talk to me now or face indictment later."

Rodarte paused, took a breath. "Now, where is he? If you know, and you don't tell me, you're obstructing justice. *Where is he?*"

Hunnicutt calmly lit a cigarette. "You sure you couldn't use a Dr Pepper?"

Rodarte banged his fist on Hunnicutt's desk. "Tell me, goddammit!"

"Detective Rodarte, you're harassing my client," McAlister said.

Rodarte stood up and leaned far across Hunnicutt's desk, thrusting his face close. "I can get your phone records for this place, prove he called here."

"You'd need a search warrant," the lawyer said. "I doubt any judge in the county would grant you one for such a flimsy reason, but if one did, and if you found a number belonging to Mr. Burkett on those records, it still wouldn't prove that he spoke with Mr. Hunnicutt.

"How many calls a day do you estimate come into this busy car dealership? Hundreds, right? My client can't be responsible for any of them. And if you did manage to prove that my client talked to Mr. Burkett, that doesn't prove that he provided him a car or assisted him in any way."

Rodarte, still ignoring the attorney, glared into Hunnicutt's guileless face.

"I think you've run out of ammunition to back up your threats, Mr. Rodarte." Hunnicutt placed his cigarette in the hollow belly of his armadillo-shaped ashtray and stood up. He moved to his office door and opened it.

Rodarte disregarded the blatant suggestion that he leave. He asked, "How'd Burkett get the key to that car if you didn't give it to him?"

Hunnicutt yelled through the open doorway, "Sweetheart, come on in here a sec."

The receptionist who'd ushered Rodarte in reappeared, asking brightly, "Did he change his mind about the coffee?"

"What's my pet peeve?" Hunnicutt asked her. "What do I get onto the salespeople about more than anything?"

"Letting customers leave without buying a car."

Hunnicutt boomed a laugh. "Second to that."

"Leaving the keys under the floor mats."

"Thank you, honey."

She left, and Hunnicutt turned back to Rodarte. "Leaving the keys under the floor mats. They do it for convenience's sake, always meaning to go back later and properly lock the cars they've taken out on demonstration drives. They plan to go back when they don't have customers stacked up. But—thank God, and I ain't complaining—sometimes they've got customers waiting. So they just slide the ignition key under the mat. Then they get distracted or busy and forget." He shrugged his burly shoulders. "I chew ass about it all the time, but what can you do? They're selling cars like hotcakes."

He shared a long look with Rodarte, who glanced over at the unflappable lawyer. McAlister raised his eyebrows eloquently. Rodarte stalked through the office door. When he pushed past Hunnicutt, he said in a malevolent undertone, "You haven't heard the last of me."

Hunnicutt said to his lawyer, "Excuse me, Jim. I'm gonna walk him out."

"Glen—"

"It's cool."

He moved quickly for a man his size and caught up with Rodarte as the detective was climbing into his car. Rodarte rounded on him. "I know you provided Burkett that car. You were jailbirds together at Big Spring. Next time, you'll go to Huntsville, and let me tell you, that ain't no country-club prison like the one you're used to. Your big white ass would be a turn-on to lots of queers I've put there." His eyes glinted with malice. "You've made an enemy today, Hunnicutt. Nobody makes a fool of me and gets away with it. You wait and see."

Hunnicutt leaned in. He was a head taller than Rodarte and seventy pounds heavier. "Don't threaten me. I know about you. You're a bully. The worst kind. You got a badge to back it up. But if you even think about hurting me or a member of my family, you remember what I told you today."

"Yeah, what's that?"

Hunnicutt leaned down even closer and whispered, "Marcia's got a lot of friends." As he straightened up, he had the pleasure of watching Rodarte's eyes turn wary. Griff had known what he was talking about. The name meant something to Rodarte, and so did the implied threat. It instilled, if not fear, at least reservation.

Hunnicutt held the detective's stare, then stepped back and flashed a wide smile. "If you're ever in the market for a used car, come see me." He walked to the front of the olive green sedan and kicked the tire. "But I'll tell you right off, I wouldn't take this for a trade-in."

What was he going to do?

Where could he hide?

Surrendering, as his turncoat lawyer had urged him to, wasn't an option. Even if he wanted to entrust himself to the legal system again, which he didn't, Turner had deserted him, and, by the sound of it, so had his probation officer. There was no one in his corner.

No, he could not turn himself in. But while dodging capture, he could be gunned down in the street, if not by someone wearing a badge, then by a citizen with a vigilante mentality.

Taking temporary shelter in a cement culvert, he flipped open his phone and punched in the familiar number, only because there was absolutely no one else he could call.

It rang six times before it went to voice mail. "Thank you for calling the Millers. Please leave a message." Griff hung up and immediately redialed, more from a desire to hear Ellie's cheerful voice than with the hope of his call being answered. He listened to the recording again, wondering where

Coach and Ellie could be this early in the morning.

But if one of them had answered, what would he have said? What could he say that they would believe?

He punched in another number he had committed to memory. Jason Rich answered. "Hey, Jason, it's Griff." He tried to sound like nothing out of the ordinary had happened. "I called to apologize for not making it to our workout yesterday. And looks like I won't be there today, either."

"How come?"

"I've come down with some kind of stomach flu. I think I got hold of some bad tamales. I've been puking my guts up." A short pause, then, "Is your dad around? I'd like to talk to him, please."

"You're sick?"

"Yeah."

"Then it's not true, what he said?"

"What who said?"

"That policeman."

Griff pinched the bridge of his nose, hard. "Was his name Rodarte? A detective?"

"A man with scars on his face. He came here yesterday and talked to my dad and me."

Griff had hoped that Rodarte would forget his tie to the Riches, but Rodarte never forgot anything. He had made a veiled threat to harm Jason. Yesterday he had questioned him, probably put pressure on the kid to tell him everything he knew about Griff Burkett. He would have frightened the boy. Griff could have killed the son of a bitch for that.

"He said you—" Jason's voice cracked. "He said you—"

"Jason!"

Bolly's voice, coming out of the background. Sharp. Intrusive. "Who are you talking to? Jason, *who is that*?"

Then Jason, in a pleading voice, said, "Dad, he's—"

"Give me the phone." Scuffling sounds. Then directly into Griff's ear, Bolly snarled, "I should have known better than to trust you."

"Bolly, listen, I—"

"No, *you* listen. The cops have been here twice. My wife freaked out, especially when this Detective Rodarte told her what you did."

"Bolly—"

"I don't want you calling here. I don't want you near my family. I trusted you with my son. Jesus, when I think—"

"I wouldn't lay a hand on Jason. You know that."

"No, killing your lover's paraplegic husband is more your speed."

Griff squeezed his eyes shut, trying to block out the accusation and the image it conjured. "I called to tell you to be careful of Rodarte. Keep Jason away—"

"Don't dare even speak my son's name."

"Listen to me!"

"I'm over listening."

"Don't leave Jason alone with Rodarte. Don't leave Jason alone, period. I know what you think of me—"

"You don't know the half of what I think of you. I hope this Rodarte finally nails your ass. And when he does, I hope they fry it."

CHAPTER
28

FOSTER SPEAKMAN'S FUNERAL BEFITTED A head of state.

Prestonwood Baptist Church had the only sanctuary large enough to accommodate the crowd, and the membership graciously offered it and their choir for the service. The auditorium was filled to capacity. The overflow were seated in annex buildings, where the service was telecast on closed-circuit TV.

Secret Service agents ensured the safety of the first lady, who attended on behalf of the president, who was out of the country. Several congressmen were also there. The governor of Texas delivered the eulogy. A notable clergyman delivered the homily. A Tony-winning Broadway star with whom Foster had attended prep school led the congregation in singing "Amazing Grace." To conclude the service, the Lord's Prayer was led by the senior pilot of SunSouth Airlines, leaving not a dry eye in the church.

The cortege stretched for miles.

The event was well documented by the media, from the arrival of dignitaries and celebrities at the church until the crowd at the cemetery dispersed. Most of the television coverage ended on a poignant image, the same heartrending tableau that was captured by a still photographer and published in the newspaper: Laura Speakman silhouetted against the cloudless sky, standing alone with head bowed beside the casket of her husband.

As Laura stood there, she didn't realize that cameras with telephoto lenses were clicking away fast and furious from a respectful distance. In fact, that was the first moment she'd felt truly alone since Foster's death, five days earlier.

Finding privacy in which to grieve had been near impossible because she'd been surrounded by people. There were duties and responsibilities that only she, as his sole survivor, could handle. Performing these tasks had, by necessity, kept her grief at bay during the day.

At night, when she retired to her bedroom, she was still aware of the other people inside her house. Kay had ensconced herself in one of the guest bedrooms, Myrna in another, both refusing to leave Laura alone overnight. Policemen were at the gate. Others patrolled the acreage within the estate wall.

Consequently, she hadn't yet indulged her sorrow or fully grasped that Foster was gone. Not until this quiet, solitary moment, when the reality came crashing down on her.

Kay had accompanied her to the funeral home to select the casket. She remembered going, looking at the choices, listening to the funeral director's recommendations. But she hadn't really looked at the casket until now. It was handsome and simple. Foster would have approved.

For the spray, she had ordered white calla lilies, a flower he particularly favored because of its clean and uncluttered form. She reached out and touched one of the blossoms, rubbing it between her fingers, registering both its creamy texture and what that tangibility signified. This was real. This was permanent. Foster was not coming back. She would never see him again. She had so many questions to ask him, so many things to say, but they would remain unasked and unsaid.

"I loved you, Foster," she whispered.

Her heart was convinced that he knew that. At least the old Foster had known how much she loved him. Strange, but since his death, when she thought about him, she didn't see the man in the wheelchair, behaving oddly, saying things he knew would wound her.

Instead she saw him as he'd been before the accident. She envisioned the Foster who'd been vital and bursting with energy, his body as strong and vivacious as his personality, his humor and optimism infectious to everyone with whom he came into contact.

That was the Foster Speakman she mourned.

By the time the limousine arrived at the mansion, the place was already packed with guests who'd been invited to eat, drink, and share memories of

Foster. It was expected that she host such a reception, but the very idea of enduring it had exhausted her. She'd delegated the planning to Kay and Myrna. In the formal dining room was an unsparing buffet. Waiters passed through the crowd with trays of canapés. People were queued at the bar. A harpist provided background music.

Laura mingled with the guests, accepting their condolences, crying with some, laughing with others, who told anecdotes about Foster. During the telling of one story, out of the corner of her eye, Laura noted that the double doors to the library remained closed. She had learned through Kay that the police had released it as a crime scene and that she was free to use it again. Mrs. Dobbins had arranged for it to be thoroughly cleaned.

Nevertheless, no one went near that room. Nor did anyone mention the circumstances of Foster's death.

Detective Rodarte was a grim reminder of them. He arrived late and kept to the edges of the crowd. Laura tried pretending he wasn't there, but she was constantly aware of him. She would turn and catch him disdainfully scanning the crowd, or staring at her with unnerving concentration.

The house was almost clear of guests when Laura drew Kay aside. "I want you to call a meeting for two o'clock tomorrow."

"What kind of meeting?"

"Executive council and board members."

"Laura, surely you're not thinking of coming into the office tomorrow," she exclaimed. "No one expects you to plunge right back in."

"Foster would," she said with a brief smile. "Two

o'clock. Please, Kay," she added when she saw that her assistant was about to protest. "Make my excuses now. I must go upstairs. Let me know when everyone's gone."

Half an hour later Kay tapped on her bedroom door. "It's me," she said, stepping into the room. "Everyone's gone except the caterer's crew. They're loading up their vans now and will soon be out." She glanced at the suitcase lying open on Laura's bed. "Explain to me again why you're being moved out of your own home?"

"Detective Rodarte believes I'll be safer in a hotel."

"Safer from whom? Griff Burkett?" Kay scoffed. "He's probably in Mexico or someplace by now. You've got twenty-four-hour guards here. He couldn't get to you if he wanted to, and he would be crazy to try."

"Well, the detective believes he might be just that crazy. And Burkett hasn't left the area. At least he was still around three days ago. He went to his attorney's house in the middle of the night. The attorney called the police. Burkett managed to get away. But on foot." She zipped the suitcase closed and pulled it off the bed. "Detective Rodarte is of the mind that he's desperate and dangerous, and until he's captured, he poses a threat to my safety."

And, she thought, *he's afraid I'll protect my lover from capture.* He hadn't said as much, but his insinuations hadn't required any guesswork.

Kay said, "I think it's criminal that you're being forced out of your home, particularly now, when you need a haven."

Laura looked at the beautiful surroundings wistfully. "Actually, Kay, I probably wouldn't stay here anyway. It's an awfully large house for one person. Anyway, it never really was mine."

She didn't explain the statement. She wasn't certain she could. Over the course of the past few days, she'd come to realize that she felt like a visitor here. A welcome visitor, but a visitor all the same. Foster had never treated her as such. In fact, he had encouraged her to change the decor to her liking, to make it her house. But she'd felt it would be improper to do so. It had been his family's home for much longer than she'd been a member of his family. He was her only reason for being here and her only connection to the house. His death had severed that connection.

Besides, she wasn't sure she could ever go into the library again.

Kay took the suitcase from her. "Let me carry that. You look like you're about to collapse. Did you eat anything?"

"A little," she lied. She'd thrown up the English muffin she forced down for breakfast. As for the carafe of coffee that had been on the tray, she couldn't bear the smell of it and had poured it down the bathroom sink. So far, no one knew about her morning sickness.

She and Kay descended the sweeping staircase. Rodarte was waiting at the bottom of it, leaning against the carved newel post, cleaning his fingernails with the tip of a pocketknife that he should have been using to pare them.

"Ready?" He closed the knife and slipped it into his pants pocket, pushed himself away from the banister, and headed for the front door. There was a squad car waiting just beyond the entrance.

When Laura saw it, she drew up short. "I'm driving myself."

"Are you sure you're up to it, Mrs. Speakman? The DPD would like to extend you the courtesy of—"

"Thank you, but I prefer taking my own car."

"You won't be needing it," Rodarte argued. "You'll be driven wherever you want to go."

"Are you placing me under arrest, Detective?" It was the first direct challenge she'd issued him.

"Nothing of the sort."

"Because if that's your intention, do it properly. I want to be read my rights, and then I want to call my attorney." Probably she should have sought legal counsel already, but doing so would have implied guilt. At least she feared that's how Rodarte would see it. It was equally possible that by not calling in an attorney she was playing right into the detective's hands. The car issue was a means of testing the nature of the "protection" he insisted on extending her.

Rodarte looked over at Kay and shook his head with regret, as though to say that Laura was becoming hysterical and that under the circumstances her fraying nerves were understandable. Looking back at Laura, he spoke to her as though she were mentally unstable. "These measures are for your protection, Mrs. Speakman."

"I'm taking my car," she declared, enunciating each word.

He tried to stare her down, but she didn't budge. Finally he heaved a theatrical sigh and said to one of the uniformed policemen loitering near the patrol car, "Go get her car."

Laura passed the policeman her keys. No one said anything until he returned driving the car. He climbed out, and Laura took his place behind the wheel. Before she shut the door, Kay leaned in.

"I'll finish here and help Mrs. Dobbins lock up. After that, you can reach me at home." She scanned Laura's face, looking worried about what she saw. "Order room service. Take a long bath. Promise me you'll get some rest."

"I promise. Don't forget to schedule the meeting. You should call everyone tonight."

"I will."

Laura closed the car door and reached for her seat belt.

Rodarte opened the passenger door and got in. Smiling, he said, "I thought you might want company."

Certainly not yours, she thought. But she said nothing as she started the car, drove down the long drive, and passed through the gate. A squad car that had been parked on the street pulled out in front of her. Rodarte's partner, Carter, was driving the green sedan, riding her rear bumper. The other squad car followed him.

She complained of the police escort. "We look like a parade."

Rodarte merely harrumphed, flipped open his cell phone, and reported to whomever he called that they were under way.

Their destination turned out to be a luxury downtown hotel where he'd registered her under an assumed name. Accompanied by Carter and two uniformed policemen, they went in through the service entrance and used the service elevator to reach the top floor.

"You have it all to yourself," Rodarte told her as they alighted from the elevator. Two policemen were waiting outside a room at the far end of a long hallway. Rodarte unlocked the door to the room and ushered her in. Carter remained outside.

It was a well-appointed, spacious room. Rodarte placed her suitcase on the luggage rack inside the closet, poked his head into the bathroom, checked the view of the Dallas skyline beyond the wide windows, then let the sheer drape fall back into place as he turned to face her. "I hope you'll be comfortable here."

"It's very nice."

"There'll be a policeman stationed outside your door, whether you're in the room or not. Another will be at the end of the hall, where he can monitor the stairwell and both elevators. They'll be in radio contact with guards at various posts downstairs, inside and outside the building."

"Is all this precaution necessary?"

"I'm making sure that nobody gets in."

And that I don't get out.

As though underscoring her thought, he extended his hand. "Can I have your car keys, please?"

"What for?"

"Safekeeping. We'll be watching your car, too."

Despite everything he'd said, this room was essentially a holding cell. Until he was convinced that Burkett had acted alone in killing her husband, she would remain under suspicion and, it appeared, under lock and key.

She folded her arms across her chest and assumed a stance. "I'd be interested to hear what my attorney has to say about your authority to confiscate my car keys."

He grinned, and with a wide sweep of his arm motioned toward the nightstand. "There's the phone."

His smirk, the challenge in his expression, said he knew she was bluffing.

"What if I need to go somewhere?"

"Oh, I'll leave the keys with the cop outside your door here. If you need to go somewhere, just ask him. He'll clear it with the cops downstairs. You'll be either accompanied in your car or followed." He touched her arm with the backs of his fingers, almost like a caress. "Your safety is our top priority."

She pulled her arm away from his touch, which made her skin crawl. "I feel well protected."

"Good."

She hoped he would go then. Instead, he sat down on the end of the bed. She remained standing.

He grinned, as though knowing how repulsed she was by his sitting on the bed she would sleep in. Then his smile inverted into a frown. He said, "You've been so busy with all the funeral arrangements I haven't wanted to bother you with the investigation. But just to give you an update, there's been no trace of Manuelo Ruiz. No leads, even."

"I'm sorry to hear that," she said, meaning it. "I'd like to learn what Manuelo knows about that night."

"I don't think we'll ever know what he saw or heard. I think Burkett made sure of that."

She turned away and moved to the window. Lights were just beginning to come on against a twilight sky. There was a lot of traffic on the expressway, moving in both directions. People were going about their lives. Having dinner out. Attending baseball games. Grilling burgers in the backyard with friends. She envied that normalcy. It had been missing from her life since the night of the car accident.

That fateful crash was the pivotal event of her life, even more so than she had realized at the time. If not for it, Foster and she might be going to a movie tonight. They would have conceived their children naturally, out of love for each other. There would have been no need to seek alternative methods. They wouldn't have met Griff Burkett. He wouldn't be a fugitive, Foster would be alive, and she wouldn't be wishing that this loathsome detective would go away and leave her in peace.

"So far, I've been able to keep your affair with Burkett out of the press."

She hadn't heard him move up behind her. He was standing so close she could smell his aftershave and feel his humid breath on the back of her neck.

"But I don't know how long I can keep it under wraps, Laura."

It was inappropriate and unprofessional for him to use her first name. Yet to correct him would only call more attention to it, and she preferred to appear indifferent. He wanted her edgy and uneasy, even fearful of him. So she let it pass and kept her back to him.

"Reporters want to know what business Burkett and your husband . . . late husband . . . had with each other. What was Burkett's motive for killing him? That's what they're clamoring to know.

"Now, strictly as a favor to you," he said, lowering his voice to an intimate pitch, "I haven't revealed that, haven't even acted like I know what could have possessed Burkett to do such a terrible thing. But when he's caught, well, that'll be another kettle of fish. When he's indicted, this thing is going to blow wide open, more than it already has. There's no way I can conceal your adultery."

That word brought her around. But unable to stand being that close to him face-to-face, she moved away. "I'm prepared for that."

"Really? Are you sure you're prepared for the beating you're going to take? Right now you're regarded as a tragic figure, the bereaved widow of a murder victim. The media is sensitive to your feelings, treating you with kid gloves. But I don't have to tell you how nasty reporters can get, especially when they feel like they've been deceived. They can turn on you." He snapped his fingers loudly. "Like that. You'll need protection from that onslaught."

"I appreciate your concern."

"Someone at your back, acting as a buffer."

"Thank you."

"You'll be glad to have me close. Protecting you like a . . ." He waited a beat, then said, "brother."

Inwardly she shuddered. "I'm very tired. If there's nothing else—"

"The car keys?"

She retrieved them from her handbag and reluctantly handed them over, being careful not to touch him. "Thanks." He bounced the keys in his palm and looked smug to have them in his possession. "Order anything you like from room service. The DPD is taking care of the charges."

"How long are you going to extend me this hospitality?"

"Till Burkett is in custody."

"That could be a while."

He grinned. "I don't think so. But you'll be our guest till then, whenever it is. In the meantime, don't worry. He can't get near you." Having made clear his message, he went to the door and placed his hand on the knob. "If you need anything, call me. Anytime." He glanced beyond her toward the bed, then his gaze slid back to her, and he smiled. "Nighty-night."

CHAPTER
29

A S SOON AS RODARTE WAS THROUGH THE
door, Laura turned the dead bolt. She heard
him confer with Carter and the policeman
outside, then the soft *ping* of the elevator when it
arrived.

But even after she knew he was gone, she stood
hugging herself. She would ask housekeeping to
bring her a can of air freshener so she could rid the
room of his scent. But later. She didn't have the
wherewithal to talk to anyone just now. She was
weary of words.

She unzipped her suitcase and began unpacking
it. But halfway through the chore, she ran out of
energy. Even the will to move deserted her. She lay
down on the bed. Tears came easily. They ran un-
checked from the corners of her closed eyelids,
trickled down her temples and into her hair.

Just as they had that day when Griff Burkett had
brushed her tears away, the day it all had changed,

the day—*face it, Laura*—he had reawakened her to feelings and sensations she hadn't experienced in a very long time. She'd told herself she didn't miss them, didn't yearn for them. How foolish she'd been. How wrong.

But she'd been particularly susceptible to tenderness that afternoon. Foster's indifference to her SunSouth Select proposal had cut her to the quick. It was worse than an outright rejection would have been. He simply had never acknowledged it again. He'd acted as though she'd never made the presentation. He'd killed the project with apathy, smothered it with his silence.

That afternoon, just before leaving to join Griff Burkett, she'd gone into Foster's office looking for something. What she'd found was the syllabus she had spent hundreds of hours preparing. It was in his wastepaper basket, along with the pieces of the airplane model. He'd disassembled it and tossed each component into the trash.

Even Griff Burkett had asked her about the model. He, a stranger, with no vested interest whatsoever in the airline industry, had been more curious about it than Foster.

Seeing the destroyed model had devastated her. It signified the death of her idea. Even though it was almost a certainty she would ovulate that day, she should have called Griff Burkett and canceled their appointment. She was too emotionally fragile to go, but she went, not wanting to explain to Foster why she had skipped a cycle and wasted an opportunity to make a baby for him.

While she lay beneath the sheet, waiting for their

hired stud to come into the bedroom, she felt like a sacrifice on an altar. And it occurred to her then that that was precisely what she was, a sacrifice on the altar of Foster's ego. She'd been crying over that when Griff came into the room.

Neither had expected what happened next. She was certain that Griff hadn't intended it any more than she. Indeed, her tears had made him angry at first.

And then, with surprising gentleness, he had whisked them away. His caring had soothed the hurt of Foster's rejection. Instinctually she had grasped at it, clutched it with a desperate need for validation and tenderness, understanding and affection. Griff had responded to this reaction as most men would, sexually.

She had never joined him in that house seeking sexual satisfaction. Quite the opposite. She had fought the very idea of it. She went through her days, and nights, telling herself that she didn't feel deprived, that fulfillment came from other aspects of her life with Foster, that she didn't miss the weight of a man on her.

But feeling him swell inside her had been powerfully erotic. She was seized by a longing so acute, wasn't it natural, even excusable, that her body responded, and that, almost in spite of herself, she had given herself over to it?

She could almost justify what had happened between them that day.

But how could she excuse the afternoon four weeks later? She couldn't. What they'd done had been wrong, and ultimately calamitous.

Now she pressed her hand against her lower abdomen and wept for the child who would never know his father.

Either of them.

The next day she presided over the meeting she had called. All the department heads were there, as were all the board members.

She cut straight to the chase. "I won't hold you to the terms of Foster's will, automatically appointing me CEO. Foster wrote the proviso to prevent leaving the airline without a specified executive officer in the event of his sudden death. You know how he hated leaving anything to chance. However, he also ran this corporation as a democracy. I intend to carry on that tradition."

She reached for her water glass and took a sip. "Foster's manner of death will result in a trial. If not a trial, then at least there will be a formal inquiry and legal entanglements that can't be avoided. One way or another, I'll have to get through them, unsure of how or when they will be resolved. I want to prepare you for some unpleasantness. Allegations will be made, and I'll have to address them publicly.

"There will be an ongoing melee with the media. I hope to protect SunSouth from the worst of it, but Foster's and my names are synonymous with the airline. I beg your cooperation. If anyone from the media asks you for a comment, please refer them to our legal department. No matter how harmless a reporter may seem, please don't reply to any questions or make any statements or speculations. Anything you said could be used out of context."

"What unpleasantness do you predict?" one asked.

"The nature of our relationship with Griff Burkett may come into question. I confess it was intensely personal and private." An awkward silence descended over the room. Everyone focused on something other than her.

When no one spoke, she continued. "That brings me to my next point. If at any time you deem me unsuitable or incapable of carrying out my responsibilities to SunSouth Airlines and its employees, if you don't wish me to represent the airline as CEO or in any other capacity, request my resignation and I'll tender it immediately and without argument. I want you all to understand that."

Finally Joe McDonald raised his hand. "I've been appointed spokesperson for this meeting."

"All right." She braced herself. Perhaps they'd already decided that a woman whose husband had died under unexplained but violent circumstances, who was involved with a felonious ex–football player in any way, wasn't fit to be their CEO.

"We discussed this in advance of the meeting," Joe told her. "And we're in unanimous agreement that we want you to remain in your present position. That is, CEO."

"I'm very pleased to hear that," she said, struggling to keep her emotions under control. "I would hate to lose my husband and my job in the same week. But what I told you remains in effect. The continued success of SunSouth must be your priority. If ever you feel the future of the airline is in jeopardy, it's your *duty* to replace me."

"It's our duty to support our leader," Joe said.

Several others said, "Hear, hear." Joe continued. "We stand with you, Laura. You have our complete trust in your integrity, as well as in your ability to run this airline."

"Thank you." She blinked away tears. "Now, with that matter settled, let's talk about Select." There were murmurs of surprise. "Are there still copies of the syllabus circulating?" she asked Joe.

"I collected them all. You told me that, for the time being, Select was tabled."

"For the time being, it was. I'm officially untabling it."

It was an exhausting day but a rewarding one. She accomplished much. The reintroduction of Sun-South Select had been received with the enthusiasm she had hoped for. Many commended her for moving ahead and focusing on the future, rather than dwelling on the unhappiness of the past.

Following that meeting, she had conferred with the senior partner of the law firm that handled Foster's personal affairs. In deference to her, the venerable gentleman had come to her office. They went over Foster's will, the various bequeathals he'd made to charity groups, and specifically to the foundation named after Elaine.

"I'd like to deliver that donation personally," Laura told him. "As you know, the foundation was very dear to Foster. In fact, once the estate is sold, I want all the proceeds to go to it."

"Sold?"

He was surprised that she wished to sell the estate and tried to dissuade her from making such a radical decision at a time when her emotions were running high.

She remained steadfast. "This isn't a rash decision. I've had two years to think about it. If Foster hadn't survived the car wreck, I would have put the estate on the market then. There are no surviving Speakmans. I don't want to live there alone, and it's too magnificent to stand empty. That would be a waste. So please make the necessary arrangements. I want the sale to be handled as discreetly as possible, with no fanfare, and no media. Those conditions must be specified in the contract with the realtor."

"Understood," the attorney said.

Rightfully, her unborn baby was heir to the estate. But she couldn't see herself bringing up a child in those vast, formal rooms. The child would never miss what he'd never known. No doubt the attorney would have argued the unfairness of her decision, but she didn't tell him she was pregnant.

He, as well as the SunSouth personnel, needed time to absorb the shock of Foster's death before being further shocked by his having left an heir. She needed time to absorb it herself.

Except for the police car following her back to the hotel, she felt more at peace than she had since Foster died. Her mood wasn't buoyant by any means, but she felt a sense of satisfaction for having endured the day without succumbing to the sorrow that had kept her inert the night before.

The police officer at the door of her room didn't forget to ask for her car keys. She relinquished them with a frown, which he pretended not to see. While she sipped a Coke from the minibar, she watched the six o'clock news. The manhunt for Griff Burkett was still the lead story.

Rodarte was on camera, talking about possible leads, but Laura didn't believe him, and the reporter interviewing him also looked skeptical. When asked about Manuelo Ruiz, he paused strategically, then said, "I'm afraid to speculate on Mr. Ruiz's fate, although we remain hopeful that he'll be found unharmed." His point was made by what he didn't say.

She switched off the TV and took a shower. She looked at the room service menu, because in spite of a mild residual nausea, she was hungry. She wondered how that could be. Nothing looked appetizing, but she ordered a club sandwich and asked that mashed potatoes be substituted for French fries. At least the potatoes and the toast on the sandwich might settle her stomach.

The food arrived. The policeman signed the tab, grudgingly adding the five-dollar tip she insisted he give the waiter in addition to the fixed service charge. She took the tray onto the bed with her and, while nibbling at the food, began making a list of Foster's possessions that she wanted to give to people who'd been special to him. There were items from his office, the house, and especially the library, that she knew he would want certain individuals to have.

That done, she started writing acknowledgments. Kay had already tackled that job, but some of the thank-you notes Laura thought it was only proper that she write personally.

The policeman knocked loudly on the door, startling her. "Mrs. Speakman? Are you all right?"

Setting aside the note cards, she got up, went to the door, and looked through the peephole. He almost filled the fish-eye lens, standing with his back to the door, arms extended at shoulder level, as though barring entrance.

"I'm fine, Officer."

"Good. Stay inside."

"What's the matter?"

"Don't open the door."

She unlatched the chain, unlocked the bolt, and opened the door.

The policeman turned and pushed her back into the room. He kicked the door shut with his heel at the same time he backed her into the wall.

"Never knew a woman yet who stayed put when told to."

It was Griff Burkett.

CHAPTER
30

"L ET GO OF ME."

"Un-huh."

She tried to push him away. He tightened his grip on her shoulders, which only caused her to struggle harder. "Stop that!" he said.

"Then let me go."

"Not a chance."

She stopped trying to fight him off, but her eyes threw daggers. "How did you get past the guards?"

"They're in the stairwell. One of them's missing his hat, shirt, and gun belt," he said, nodding down at himself. The shirtsleeves were several inches too short, the buttons strained against his chest, and the fit across his shoulders wouldn't pass close inspection, but it had fooled Laura enough to get her to open the door. He hoped it would fool anyone who saw him escorting her from the building.

"I didn't hit them hard. They won't be out long. I've got to smuggle you out of here before someone realizes they're not at their posts." He pulled her away from the wall. "Get some clothes on."

She dug her heels in and tried to wrest her hand free from his grip. "I'll scream this building down before I go anywhere with you."

He took her by the shoulders again. "I did not kill your husband, Laura."

She closed her eyes and shook her head, refusing to hear.

"Listen to me. Manuelo Ruiz stabbed Foster, not me."

Her eyes popped open. She gaped at him. "Manuelo would never—"

"He did. And I'll give you a detailed account of what happened that night. Later. Right now, we're getting out of here. Now, dammit, get some clothes on." He said it with an undertone of threat, playing on her evident fear. He would make amends later, but he didn't have time for niceties now.

Coolly, she said, "I can't dress as long as you're holding on to me."

Gradually he removed his hands from her shoulders but was poised in case she tried to get to the door. She stepped around him and moved to the bureau. She took several articles of clothing from a drawer, considered them, exchanged them for others.

Impatiently, he yanked the items from her hand and threw them onto the bed, then jerked on the belt of her robe, untying it. "Get into them, and make it fast." She turned her back and let the robe slide off her onto the floor. She was naked. He was running for his life, but it was a sight that momentarily stopped him from thinking about anything else. She stepped into panties and worked a T-shirt over her head, then started moving toward the door. He grabbed her arm, halting her.

"There's a tracksuit in the closet."

The closet was adjacent to the door. He went to it, slid open the door, and sorted through the clothes.

"That," she said.

"This?" She nodded. He peeled the tracksuit off the hanger and thrust it at her. "Hurry."

She stepped into the stretchy pants and pulled them on. "If you force me to go with you—"

"I don't have a choice."

"Of course you do!"

"Shoes." He took a pair of sneakers from the closet and dropped them at her feet.

"You'll be adding kidnapping to your other crimes."

He helped her balance while she worked her feet into the sneakers. "Where's your purse?"

"Griff, I implore you."

"Are you wearing the jacket?"

She pulled it on. "Rodarte—"

"Will be checking with these guys any minute."

"That's right. You'll never get me out of this hotel. He has guards posted downstairs, too. They've got my car keys."

He fished her ring of keys out of his pants pocket and jangled it at her. "You're walking out of here, Laura. You and your *police escort*. Anyone challenges you, you say you need some things from the store, you have a hankering for Taco Bell, your grandmother is sick. I don't care what excuse you give, just make them believe it."

She looked him over. "Despite the getup, don't you think they'll recognize you?"

"For your own safety, you'd better hope they don't."

She glanced down at the holster on his hip. Rather than frightening her, it seemed to embolden her. Taking a stance, she folded her arms and looked up at him. "You wouldn't hurt me. I know you wouldn't."

"You don't think?"

Slowly, she shook her head.

He moved in close and lowered his face to within inches of hers. "I'm not going back to prison. So if I'm caught, all bets are off. I'll blare to the whole frigging world that Foster Speakman couldn't get it up. He was no longer a man, the marriage was a sham, and, in order to have a kid, he hired me to fuck his wife." Her face went slack with dismay.

"Yeah," Griff said, "think about that. I saw the pictures of his funeral, watched the stories about it on TV, saw you posed so pretty at his graveside. I've read his obituary and listened to politicians singing his praises. Everybody thought he was bloody wonderful, didn't they? What do you think their opinion of Foster the great is going to be when I tell them he paid me to play stud for him?

"And don't forget, to prove it's true, I've got a hundred grand in the bank with his name on the signature card." He encircled her biceps, forming an unbreakable grip with his strong fingers, and shoved her toward the door. "Now move it."

"Hey, Thomas?"

Griff pulled up short, and Laura with him. The sound came from the earpiece he'd stuck in his ear after putting on the cop's uniform. Thomas was being paged by one of his counterparts downstairs. Giving Laura a warning look, Griff clicked on the transmitter clipped to the shoulder seam of the shirt. "Go ahead," he mumbled.

"Where's Lane?"

"At the elevator with Mrs. Speakman," he whispered, as though not wanting to be overheard. "He's bringing Her Highness down."

"What for?"

"She wants some carryout."

"Sick of room service food?"

Griff grunted a noncommittal reply.

"Yeah, she's got it really tough," the cop said sarcastically. "Even with Lane tagging along, Rodarte isn't gonna like it, her going out after dark."

"Then Rodarte can come babysit her."

The other cop laughed. "I hear that." He clicked off.

Griff looked through the peephole, then pulled open the door and checked the hallway. He pulled Laura behind him as he ran toward the service elevator. He'd placed a dolly in the open door to keep it there. When they were inside, he dragged the dolly in and pushed the button for the ground floor.

"Where's your car?" he asked.

"In the employee parking lot."

"Once we're out of the building, where?"

"To the right."

"How far?"

"Fairly close." His eyes drilled into hers, demanding more. She said, "Within steps of the entrance. But we'll never get past the guard at that door."

"He's napping."

The cop was still out cold, right where Griff had left him, behind a Dumpster, out of sight of any hotel employee who happened to use that entrance. Griff had come dressed in a set of navy blue work pants and shirt, carrying a stack of empty boxes. The ruse had worked long enough for him to get close to the cop and knock him out.

The policeman on the top floor, guarding the stairwell and service elevator, had reacted with surprise when the elevator doors opened and Griff stepped off. "Hey, you're supposed to clear it downstairs before—" Griff had thrust the boxes at him and punched.

Hearing the commotion, the cop guarding Laura's door had come running. He'd rounded a corner and got clouted on the head with the butt of his buddy's service pistol. Of the two, he was the larger. Griff had hastily stripped him of his uniform shirt, hat, and gun belt.

He'd handcuffed each of them behind their backs, also linking the pairs of handcuffs together, then put duct tape over their mouths. Even when they regained consciousness, they'd make an awkward, mute, four-legged animal that would have trouble getting out of the stairwell and raising an alarm.

He was guilty of assault on three police officers. That was the least of his worries.

He knew there was another cop posted at the corner of the parking lot. It was just dark enough that Griff hoped from that distance the cop would see only a uniform shirt and hat and would mistake him for Lane. As he and Laura emerged from the service entrance, Griff kept his face averted but raised his arm and waved. The cop waved back.

Laura led him to her BMW. He unlocked the driver's side. Thinking of the horn, he said, "Remember what I told you upstairs. If you want to uphold your late husband's reputation, you do not want me to be caught."

He closed the door and quickly walked around to the passenger side. Once he was in, he put the key in the ignition and started the motor. "Take the freeway to Oak Lawn. Exit and head north until it merges with Preston."

She looked at him with surprise.

"That's right, Laura. We're going to your house."

Getting past the policeman at the gate was going to be the next tricky part. While Laura drove, Griff formulated a plan.

"You won't get away with this," she said.

"I have so far, haven't I?"

"Policemen in five states are looking for you."

"But they haven't found me."

"Where have you been hiding?"

He didn't answer that. "When we get to your place, make sure your headlights are on bright. Pull in so that they're shining directly into the windshield of the patrol car that's parked in front of the gate."

"Are you sure the gate is still being guarded?"

"I'm sure."

"How did you know where to find me?"

"Followed Rodarte."

She looked at him with astonishment. "You've been following Rodarte? How?"

"What's the code on your gate?"

She turned her head back to the road, and her hands tightened on the steering wheel. "I can't think of a single reason why I should tell you that."

"Can you think of a reason why your husband would have had half a million in cash at your house that night, stacked neatly in a stationery box?"

"I explained that to Rodarte." In nervous stops and starts, she told Griff about Foster's heavy tipping practice.

"Half a million dollars' worth?" Griff said, laughing. "Nobody's that generous."

"Rodarte believed me."

"I doubt it. In any case, I could throw a shitload of doubt on that explanation. Or"—he paused for emphasis—"you could give me the gate code." She gave him the code, and then he told her how it was going to play out when they reached the estate.

As instructed, when she turned in to the private drive, she pulled in so that her headlights shone directly into the squad car. Griff opened the passenger door. Before getting out, he said, "I could make mincemeat of Foster Speakman's reputation. Remember that."

He stepped out of the car, leaving the door open, and walked toward the keypad on the column near the gate.

The policeman had got out of the squad car and was approaching him, his hand raised, shielding his eyes against the glare of Laura's headlights. Griff kept moving, asking over his shoulder, "How's it going here? Everything quiet?"

"Yeah. What's up?"

"Officer?" Laura called out to him.

The cop turned toward her. Griff reached the column, punched in the sequence of numbers she had given him, holding his breath until the double gate began to swing open.

"Is everything all right here?" Laura had alighted and was standing in the open door of her car, talking to the policeman.

"Yes, ma'am."

"This additional security is so unnecessary."

"Better to be safe, ma'am."

"I need to pick up some things from the house. I shouldn't be long."

By now, Griff was back at the car, sliding into the passenger seat. She bent down and addressed him. "You don't have to go inside with me," she said, following the script he'd given her. "In fact, I'd rather you didn't. I'll be perfectly safe inside my own home."

"I'm supposed to stay with you, ma'am. Rodarte's orders," he said, making sure the other cop heard it.

She huffed as though vexed and looked back at the officer. "Could you move your car please, before the gate closes?"

Quickly he returned to his squad car, started it, and rolled it forward far enough to clear the gate. Laura drove through.

Griff didn't start breathing again until the gate closed automatically behind them. But if that officer was any kind of sharp, he'd be checking with Rodarte to see if Laura's visit to her home had been approved. Or he would soon be receiving a call from the hotel telling him that Mrs. Speakman had been abducted. Griff hoped to be in and out before either happened.

"Go in through the front door, where he can see us."

She followed the driveway and parked directly in front of the house. Griff got out and approached the mansion's grand entrance, looked around, played the role of bodyguard in case they were being observed. Laura used her key and opened the front door. The alarm started beeping. She made no move toward the keypad.

Griff said, "The house on Windsor Street would become a tourist attraction."

She understood the warning and punched in the code that silenced the alarm.

"Lights?"

She touched a switch that seemed to turn on every light in the house. "Fancy," he said, impressed.

"Now what?"

"Now we go to the garage. Specifically, to Manuelo Ruiz's apartment above the garage."

She looked at him with incredulity. "Is that what this is about?"

"That's what this is about. How do you get to the garage?"

Looking like she wanted to argue, she turned instead and walked stiffly across the foyer. He followed, relieved that she was leading him in the direction opposite the library.

The kitchen was three times larger than the house Griff had grown up in.

On the far side of it was a door. Laura walked toward it. "Wait," he said. "That goes outside?"

"Through the mudroom, then outside."

"Is the exterior door visible from the front gate?"

"No."

Griff went around her, opened the door, and saw a utility area that deserved a more glamorous name than mudroom. He opened the exterior door and looked out. There were no longer policemen patrolling the estate grounds. They'd been pulled off when Rodarte had moved Laura to the hotel yesterday evening. Griff had been watching, and he knew.

Nevertheless, he felt exposed as he and Laura crossed the motor court between the house and the detached garage. Laura indicated a door at the side of the building. "Manuelo's apartment is through that door and up the stairs, but you won't find him there."

"I don't expect to."

There was a keypad on the wall adjacent to the door. "Another freaking code?" Griff motioned to it impatiently, and Laura punched in a sequence of numbers. The door opened with a metallic click. They slipped inside. Griff pulled the door closed behind them and heard the lock engage.

"No lights," he said, sensing that she was groping the wall for the switch plate. "You came to pick up stuff from the house, not the garage. The lights stay off."

He pulled a small flashlight from the policeman's belt and switched it on. He shone the beam down at their feet, but he could see her in the ambient light.

"Laura. Is there really a baby?"

CHAPTER
31

JUDGING FROM THE LOOK ON HER FACE, THE question had taken her completely by surprise. She stared at him for several seconds, then made a small motion with her head.

He felt an expanding pressure inside his chest. He'd never felt anything like it before, so he couldn't put a name to it. It was a strange feeling, and yet a good one. Like supreme satisfaction. Like the total opposite of what he'd been feeling the other day in the motel when he'd reviewed his life history.

He looked down at her abdomen but couldn't detect any change. Of course there wouldn't be any yet.

He wondered if she was thinking, like he was, about their last afternoon together, when he'd reached around her and closed the front door. How could they have foreseen the cataclysmic impact that simple motion would have? Because of it, one life had ended. And another had begun.

His gaze tracked back up to her face. Their eyes met and held. This warm, closed space in which they were standing seemed suddenly to be very small and airless. He didn't dare take a deep breath for fear of breaking the silence that pressed in on them, teeming with implication.

He knew there must be something appropriate to say to a woman who had your baby inside her, but damned if he could think of what it might be, so he didn't say anything, just continued staring into her eyes, until she finally looked away.

He touched her chin and brought her head back around to face him. "I'll go to death row unless I find Manuelo Ruiz. Do you understand?"

She shook her head, slowly and then more adamantly. "No, I don't. It's not possible. Manuelo worshiped Foster. He wouldn't—"

"But I would?"

She searched his eyes, then made a motion with her head and shoulders that could have meant either yes or no. But even if she had the slightest doubt, it was crushing to him.

He dropped his hand. "I don't know why I hoped you would believe me when my own lawyer didn't even bother to ask whether or not I had killed your husband. He just assumed I had. I didn't. Manuelo did."

"He couldn't."

"It was a bizarre accident. Seeing what he'd done, the guy wigged out. He bolted. He's scared and may be halfway to El Salvador by now. But without him, I'm sunk."

He shone the flashlight beam on his wrist-watch. They'd driven away from the hotel twenty-seven minutes ago. Thomas and Lane and the rest of them were probably catching hell from Rodarte by now. Soon a posse would be dispatched.

"My time's running out." He motioned her up the staircase.

On their way, she said, "If Manuelo is running, this is the last place he would be."

"Officially, there's no record of the man beyond a social security number, which was fake, and a Texas driver's license with a phony address."

"How do you know this?"

"Rodarte. He was quoted in the newspaper."

"If the police can't find him, how do you hope to?" By now she had reached the door at the top of the stairs. It was unlocked. Griff switched off the flashlight and followed Laura into the apartment.

"Where are the windows?"

"There aren't any. Only skylights on the back side of the roof."

Trusting her to be telling the truth, he turned the flashlight back on but kept it aimed at the floor. It was a spacious single room which, Griff estimated, covered half of the garage below. It was equipped with a small kitchen area with dormitory-size appliances, and a TV in a cabinet opposite the bed. The bathroom was compact.

The apartment had already been tossed by the police. Bureau drawers had been left open, the closet door stood ajar. The twin bed had been stripped. The mattress was askew.

"Hold the light." Griff passed her the flashlight,

then started his search with the TV cabinet. "How did Manuelo come to be Foster's aide?"

"He was a janitor at the rehab center. Foster was there for several months after he got out of the hospital. One day after a strenuous therapy session, he experienced respiratory distress. He was no longer hooked to monitors, he couldn't reach the call button. Manuelo happened by. He didn't summon help but came in, lifted Foster out of bed, and carried him to the nurses' station. Foster credited him with saving his life. I think Manuelo felt the same about Foster. His life improved dramatically when Foster took him in."

The drawers of the cabinet had yielded nothing except some loose coins, a broken pair of sunglasses, nail clippers, underwear, folded T-shirts. "In from where?" Griff asked. "Where had he lived before?"

"Foster may have known. I never did," she replied, following his movements with the beam of the flashlight. "Manuelo showed up here with a small duffel bag of belongings and moved into this apartment. Foster bought him new clothes. He paid for his training as a nursing aide, on how to care for paraplegics. Manuelo was devoted to Foster."

Griff snuffled. "Yeah. I know."

Although the bed obviously had already been searched, he felt the mattress and box springs, looking for bumps where something could have been stashed. He moved the bed away from the wall and motioned for her to direct the flashlight onto the floor beneath it. Low-nap carpet. No sign that it had been sliced to form a secret pocket. "Did he have family? Friends?"

"Not to my knowledge. Griff, Rodarte has already asked me all this. The police have been searching for Manuelo since the night . . . the night Foster died."

"The first time I saw him, Manuelo struck me as a survivor," Griff said. "Foster told me he'd walked to the U.S. from El Salvador." A small curtain hid the plumbing for the tiny kitchen sink. He parted it but found only pots and pans, some dishwashing liquid. He looked in the oven and microwave but came up empty. He checked the fridge but found nothing except a few canned drinks, condiments, three oranges.

"Walking through Guatemala and Mexico? That tells me that he was either very, very poor or running from something and didn't want to risk traveling on public transportation. Probably both."

In the bathroom, he looked in the tank of the toilet, then took the light from Laura and shone it down the shower drain.

She asked, "How do you know to do that?"

"Some things you learn in prison."

There was nothing in the medicine cabinet above the sink except shaving implements, toothpaste, toothbrush. He returned to the main room, hands on hips, looking about. The ceiling? He couldn't see any seams in the material where Manuelo might have cut out a section to form a hiding place.

Inside the closet were several pairs of black trousers, two pairs of black shoes, and a black baseball-style jacket. "Where's the duffel bag?" he asked rhetorically.

"The what?"

"You said he arrived with a small duffel bag of personal belongings. Where is it?"

"I suppose he took it with him."

"Trust me, he didn't stop to pack that night. He didn't take his clothes or his toiletries. It said in the newspaper that cash was found in his apartment. Nobody leaves money behind, unless they don't leave of their own accord."

"Which is why Rodarte suspects you of—"

"Killing Manuelo, too. I know. But I didn't. Laura, the man was hysterical. Out of his head. He ran like the devil was after him." He frowned at the look she gave him. "No, it wasn't me he was afraid of."

She didn't respond to that. Instead, she said, "He didn't pack, so you believe that his duffel bag is here somewhere. So what? What good would finding it do us?"

"Maybe none. But a top-notch rehab hospital wouldn't have hired even a janitor without immigration documents. If Manuelo sneaked into the country, he must have had help getting falsified papers so he could get work. He had to have had a contact. And I bet he would have stayed in touch with that contact in case he had to get the hell out of Dodge, quick. He would have—"

The wail of approaching sirens cut him off. "Shit!" He grabbed Laura's hand and pulled her through the door onto the landing of the stairwell. He switched off the flashlight, but just as he did, he noticed the door opposite the one to Ruiz's apartment. "What's that?"

"What? I can't see anything."

"That door. Where does it go?"

"It accesses the attic space above the other side of the garage. It's not finished out. Foster had talked about one day flooring it, but— What are you doing?"

Griff had pushed open the door, and the hot, contained air rushed out to envelop them. He switched on the flashlight and shone it into the large space, empty except for exposed insulation and joists, plumbing pipes, and electrical conduits.

About three feet in front of him, an air-conditioning duct stretched along the floor for the entire width of the attic; it was the duct that would have conveyed a/c and heat into Manuelo's apartment.

Griff aimed the flashlight beam on the silver tube and tracked it from the far wall forward.

The sirens were getting closer, louder.

He tried to block them out and concentrate on the duct, taking in every seam, every wrinkle in the material, looking—

He uttered a soft cry of elation when he saw the patch. "There it is!"

Wasting no time to think about it, he stepped out onto the two-by-four nearest him and inched along it toward the patch. If he slipped, he could drive his foot through the Sheetrock, which wouldn't support his weight. The only thing keeping him from falling through it and landing hard on the garage floor twenty feet below was his agility. And his will to find Manuelo Ruiz.

When he got even with the patch, he stuck the flashlight in his mouth, and, balancing on the balls of his feet, leaned across the emptiness toward the duct.

The sirens had stopped. Not a good sign.

He ripped away the tape forming the patch and plunged his hand into the hollow duct. His fingertips brushed something, but it was just out of reach. The flashlight fell from his mouth onto the Sheetrock floor several inches below the two-by-four on which he balanced. It rolled away, out of reach. He let it go.

He crabbed along the two-by-four until he could grasp the object inside the duct. The attic space was as hot as an oven. Keeping his balance while reaching into the duct was an extreme effort. His knees were screaming. Sweat ran into his eyes, making them sting. The policeman's shirt was too damn small. It was confining his shoulders, limiting his reach. He strained against it, ripping the shoulder seams but gaining a longer reach.

Finally he got two fingers on the object, clamped them shut, and pulled the object far enough forward for him to grab hold. He gave it a hard yank, ripping the skin of the duct as he pulled it out. It was a black duffel bag.

He stood up quickly and, with the deft steps of a tightrope walker, made his way back to the door at the staircase landing. "I've got it!" But he was talking to empty darkness. Laura had vanished.

CHAPTER
32

THE HOUSE WAS STILL ABLAZE, LIGHTS ON in every room. Through windows where the drapes were open, Laura could see uniformed policemen searching the rooms for her and Griff.

She was halfway across the motor court when her elbow was hooked from behind. "This way," Griff said.

She tried to throw off his hand, but his hold was tenacious and she had to run to keep up with him. "Griff, this is insanity. Turn yourself in. Talk to Rodarte. Tell him what you told me about Manuelo."

By now they were on the far side of the garage, out of sight of the house, away from the landscape lighting, running pell-mell through the darkness. They went around the pond and then plunged down a natural berm. She lost her footing and would have fallen if he hadn't kept his tight grip on her. She stumbled along after him.

The ground leveled off at the estate wall. It didn't appear this tall from a distance. Now its twelve feet seemed awfully high. The vines and shrubbery covering it were dense but well maintained. Incongruously, there was a cold drink can standing upright at the twisted root system of a wisteria that was in full leaf and completely covering a section of the wall.

"Griff!" She pulled hard on his hand.

He turned to her. "Listen and believe, Laura. Rodarte is convinced that I killed Bill Bandy five years ago. Now he's convinced that I killed your husband. If I turn myself in, I'll be at the mercy of a legal system I no longer trust. Especially since Rodarte's on the case."

"Then turn yourself in to someone else."

He shook his head stubbornly. "Not until I can take Manuelo Ruiz in with me, ready and willing to corroborate my story. I've got to find him."

"Okay, I can see that," she said, breathless from their run. "But let me go back. Let me tell your side of it and explain why you're reluctant to surrender."

"No."

"If I say—"

"Why did Rodarte have you under lock and key?"

"To protect me from you."

"Right. So if I get backed into a corner, as long as I've got you as my hostage, I've got something to bargain with."

"You wouldn't hurt me."

"*You* know that. Rodarte doesn't. Now come on." He dragged her forward, toward the wisteria.

"Do you expect me to climb that?"

"Don't have to." Still keeping hold of her with one hand, he used the other to clear away some offshoots of the vine, revealing a metal grate at the base of the wall. He shoved it aside with the toe of his shoe. "Drainage," he said.

"How did you find this?"

"I came looking." He put his hand on her shoulder, forced her down. "Crawl through. I'm right behind you."

Lying down on her stomach, she wiggled through the opening. The ground was damp, but because of the drought, it wasn't muddy. The wall was about a foot thick. On the other side was a twenty-acre greenbelt that served as a buffer between the elite private properties that backed up to it, like the Speakmans', and the commercial district on the far side.

By the time she was on her feet, Griff had pushed the duffel bag through the opening. It was a squeeze to get his shoulders through, but he did and sprang up on the other side. Taking her hand, he guided her across a rough and rocky creek bed. It was dry now, but when it rained, the runoff from the Speakman property would drain into it through the grate by which they'd made their escape.

Once across the creek bed, Griff took off running through the greenbelt. But as they approached the boulevard on the far side, he slowed to a walk. Across the wide street was a row of boutique shops and two popular restaurants. The shops were closed, but the restaurants were busy with the dinner crowd.

Pausing in the shadows of the park, he released

her hand long enough to take off the uniform shirt, leaving him in a white T-shirt. He removed the pistol from the policeman's holster, then tossed the gun belt, shirt, hat, and cold drink can into the nearest trash receptacle. He zipped the pistol into Manuelo Ruiz's duffel bag.

Taking her hand again, he waited until the traffic thinned, then struck off across the divided street. He didn't run, which would have attracted attention, but walked swiftly toward the parking lot of the Indian restaurant. He wove them through the rows of cars until they reached the back of the lot, where it was dark.

He fished a remote key from his pants pocket and used it to unlock a car. He opened the passenger door and motioned her in. He walked around and got behind the wheel, closed the door, and tossed the duffel bag onto the backseat. The dome light dimmed and then went out, leaving them in darkness.

They sat still and silent, trying to catch their breath.

Not until now that they'd stopped did Laura realize how breathless she was, and how fast her heart was pounding, as much from adrenaline as from physical exertion. The palms of her hands were dirty. The front of her tracksuit was streaked with loose soil.

"I'm sorry about that," he said, when he noticed her palms.

"I'm a fugitive, too. I'm not worried about a little dirt."

"You're not the fugitive, I am. You're my hostage, remember."

She smiled ruefully. "You asked why Rodarte had placed me under lock and key? He claimed it was for my protection."

"But?"

"He was afraid I would help you escape." His gaze remained steady, but she could read the unasked questions in it. "He never said that, but I sensed that was why he put me in the hotel, under guard. And I suppose I have helped you escape, haven't I?"

"Does that mean you believe I'm innocent?"

Before she could answer, a police car screamed down the boulevard, its lights a wild kaleidoscope. Griff turned on the car's ignition. Grinning, he said, "Rough neighborhood. We'd better move to a safer one."

He had to wait for another oncoming police car to roar past before pulling out into the street. "You're thumbing your nose at them," she remarked.

"Nothing that brave. They won't be looking for this car."

"Whose is it?"

He drove, saying nothing.

"The visit to your lawyer's house made the news."

"Yeah, I saw. The media failed to mention what an untrustworthy son of a bitch my *former* attorney is."

"He said by turning you in he was trying to help."

"Bullshit. He was trying to cover his own ass."

"They searched for you for hours."

"I got lucky."

"How did you get away?"

He gave her a wry grin. "It wasn't easy. Some-time, when you've got a lot of time, maybe I'll tell you all the adventures I encountered that night."

She gave his clothing a once-over. "The police were looking for a man in running shorts and sneakers."

"Which were barely holding together by daylight the next day. I was traveling light, but luckily, be-fore going to Turner's house, I'd put some cash in my sock. I used it the next day to buy some clothes at a big flea market." He glanced down at the T-shirt and work pants. "Selection was limited. I'm sure some of the goods were hot, so no one ques-tioned the customer who looked like he'd been dunked in a polluted river and then run through a shredder."

"Were you recognized?"

"Doubtful. The market draws a large Hispanic crowd. Typically they follow soccer, not American football. I tried to be inconspicuous."

Her eyes shifted up to his blond hair. "That couldn't have been easy."

"Especially not when I started asking around about Manuelo Ruiz, looking for someone who might know him. Those inquiries aroused more suspicion than my ragtag appearance. I didn't stay long."

"Where have you been hiding?"

He didn't reply.

"You're not going to tell me, are you?"

"The less you know, the better. Rodarte can never accuse you of collaborating with me. You're my hostage. Got that?"

"I've got it. I don't think Rodarte will be convinced. When he introduced himself, I recognized his name immediately. Before, when you warned me about him, you didn't say he was a policeman. You made him sound like a criminal. You said he'd beat up a friend of yours."

"He did. And sodomized her. Ruined her face. Broke—"

"A *woman*?"

"Yeah, and Rodarte nearly killed her."

Laura had assumed Griff was referring to a male friend. Learning that Rodarte had assaulted a woman filled her with repugnance and fear. "He attacked her because of you?"

"Because she wouldn't give him any information."

"What kind of information?"

"About my past and present business dealings. Not that she knew anything, but it did her no good to tell Rodarte that."

"He must have thought she knew something. Is she a close friend?"

"I guess you could call it a friendship. Actually, I'm her client. She's a prostitute."

That piece of news took her aback. Had he been using the hundred thousand she and Foster had paid him to buy the services of a prostitute? Of course the money was his to spend, it was just that she had never known anyone, of either sex, who admitted going to a prostitute. Maybe that was why it was so startling to her that he had in such a matter-of-fact way.

Curiosity compelled her. "What's her name?"

"Marcia. She's not a street hooker. She has a

penthouse. She's clean, classy, very expensive, beautiful. Or was. It's been months since the assault, and she's still recovering, going through a series of reconstructive surgeries on her face. She won't even talk to me about the other. Rodarte has a badge, but he uses it as a free pass to hurt people and get away with it." He shot her a glance. "You've been with him. Did he ever touch you?"

"Last night he stroked my arm. It made me shudder. I think he knew that, and that's why he did it. Behind everything he said was a sexual innuendo."

Griff's long fingers were flexing and contracting around the steering wheel as though preparing to pull it out of the dashboard. "It was only a matter of time before he hurt you. Which was another reason I wanted to get you out of there. Anything he did to you, he would have felt you had coming because of your affair with me."

She remembered Rodarte coming up close behind her, promising in an insinuating whisper to be her protector—or not—when her affair with Griff was exposed. Griff may indeed have rescued her. But there was still much he had to answer for. "So you had a car, and a hiding place, and you've been following Rodarte."

"You were my connection to Manuelo. I knew you'd be essential to finding him. But I also knew Rodarte would be keeping close watch on you, expecting me to turn up sooner or later.

"Yesterday evening, after the funeral and reception, I was parked on Preston Road, near where I left the car tonight. When I saw this caravan of police cars coming from the direction of the estate, I pulled out into traffic. So I was actually ahead of your police escort. I slowed, let you drive past, then followed you to the hotel."

"How'd you get the room number?"

"I didn't, but it was a logical guess that you'd be on the top floor."

"I had the floor to myself."

"I figured that, too. When I got up there tonight, I had a nanosecond to look down the hall and see which door the cop was guarding before throwing an armload of empty boxes at his buddy.

"Anyway, last night, once I knew where you would be when I needed you, I went back to the estate to try to find a way in. The guard never left the front gate, but the ones that had been patrolling the grounds were pulled off. No need for them since you were no longer there.

"I knew that the park behind the property was the only possible access. I combed every inch of that side of the estate wall, practically on hands and knees. In the dark, mind you. I was looking for a rear gate. Something. Took hours before I found the grate. I loosened it, crawled through."

"And left that drink can there so you could find it again from the inside."

"In a hurry. Just in case cops were in hot pursuit. The rest you more or less know." After a beat, he said, "Except this."

He turned in to the parking lot of a multiscreen movie theater and found an open slot between a van with a Garfield clinging to the rear window with suction cups on his paws and a pickup truck with tires taller than their car.

He cut the ignition and turned toward her. "The

night I got out of prison, I was desperate to get laid. I went to Marcia. Just that once. There's been nobody since."

She took a breath, held it for several seconds before letting it out. "I wondered."

"Why didn't you ask?"

"I didn't have the right."

He moved suddenly, stretching his arm across the space separating them, curving his hand around the back of her neck and pulling her toward him. He kissed her hard, stamping his lips firmly against hers, pressing his tongue deep into her mouth. Then he pushed her away as suddenly as he'd grabbed her.

Hoarsely, he said, "You had every right."

He let go of the back of her neck and returned to his place behind the wheel. For several moments they sat in silence, hearing only the soft popping sounds made by the car's motor as it began to cool.

Finally he turned to her. "He called me. Foster. The day the pregnancy was confirmed. He invited me to your house the next night so he could thank me and pay me in person. Did you know any of this?"

"No."

"He also said he'd figured out how I would be paid if I outlived you both. Remember that hitch?"

She nodded.

"He said he'd worked out a solution. He used that and the promise of the half million to get me there. And while I was there, Manuelo tried to kill me."

"*What?*"

"You heard me."

"*Why?*"

"Because Foster ordered it."

She inclined away from him until she was pressed against the passenger door. "You're lying!"

"No, I'm not. And you know I'm not, Laura, or you'd have put up a bigger fight before leaving that hotel with me. You're not a pushover and you're no coward. If you'd wanted to get away from me, you'd have been screaming bloody murder every step of the way, because, as you said, you know I wouldn't carry out any threat to hurt you. You're here because you want to be. You want to hear the truth of what happened. In any case, you're going to listen."

He paused for breath and to organize his thoughts. Also to see if she would, after all, open the car door and run screaming across the parking lot. She didn't, so he began.

"Over the last several days, I've spent the daylight hours, and a lot of the nighttime, thinking. *Thinking.* And remembering. In my mind I've replayed every word, every small detail, from the first meeting till those last horrendous moments of Foster's life, and I can see now how well he planned it. It was a masterful game plan.

"It even occurred to me that he'd lied when he called to tell me you were pregnant. I hadn't heard it from you. I thought maybe that was the juiciest piece of bait for the trap he laid. That's why I asked you earlier if you were really pregnant."

"It was confirmed the day before he died."

"So that much was true. Once Foster knew he had his child and heir, he wasted no time setting me up to be silenced forever. Only his plan backfired, and he died instead."

"How? How, Griff? What happened when you got to the house?"

"Manuelo let me in like before. Poured me a drink, then left Foster and me alone in the library, behind closed doors. We toasted our success. He started talking . . . well, bullshit. About how delighted the two of you were over the pregnancy."

"That wasn't bullshit."

"Yeah, but . . . but it was the way he was telling it. He got choked up, or pretended to. He told me you'd never looked so beautiful as when you said, 'We have a baby,' and how meaningful that word *we* was to a man in his condition.

"He told me your breasts were tender, that you wouldn't let him touch them and how embarrassed you'd be to know he'd told me that. He talked about the baby. Could I guess what it would be? Had I thought about what it might be when we were making it? He reminded me that I'd have to read in the newspaper whether it was a boy or girl. I wouldn't know its name until I read about it."

Griff gave a bitter laugh. "Looking back, I can see that he was goading me. He was saying things he knew would get under my skin. At the time I just wanted him to shut up about you and the baby. I didn't want to hear what a happy little family the three of you would be."

He gave her a significant look, wondering if she could read between the lines. He guessed she could. She lowered her gaze to her hands, which were clasped tightly in her lap.

"He showed me my payoff money. The sight of

it made me sick. Sick at my stomach, sick at myself. Marcia claims she never feels like a whore, but when I looked down into that box of money, I did. Our deal wasn't illegal, but I felt a lot guiltier taking Foster's money than I did taking the two million from Vista, and that's the God's truth, Laura.

"I didn't even want to touch it, and he sensed that. He said he was surprised by my restraint. I mumbled some excuse for it. Then he started laughing and said, 'Oh dear, you don't want it to end, do you?' "

Laura looked at him sharply. "What?"

"Something like that. He began gibing me about developing a taste for you like I had the gambling. He said I must have really enjoyed 'doing' you, and that's a quote. He was giving me this gloating smile. Thinking about it now makes me angry all over again."

At the risk of casting doubt on his innocence, he reined in his anger and stuck to the facts. "I called him a sick fuck. He wouldn't shut up about it and started saying over and over, 'Poor Griff.'

"The taunting made me irate, Laura. I admit that. I felt myself about to lose it. Wheelchair or not, I wanted to deck him. I wanted to so bad I had to turn away. When I did, I looked down at the desktop. Swear to God I didn't see the letter opener. Or if I did, it didn't register. What I noticed was this sheet of paper with official-looking writing on it.

"Foster backed down then. He stopped that hideous chanting. I don't know if he sensed how close I was to knocking him across the room, or if he saw what had caught my eye. But in any case, he said, 'Oh, that's why you're here, isn't it? That's my proposal for what should happen if both Laura and I die before you. Read it.'

"At that point, I just wanted to conclude our business and get the hell out of there before I did something I would regret. So I picked up the sheet of paper and began to read. Or tried."

"It was gibberish."

Surprised, he said, "You've seen it?"

"Rodarte gave it to me, asked if I knew what it meant."

"Okay, so you know it was a ruse. I'd belted the strong bourbon. And I was still seeing red over the things he'd said. I thought that was why I wasn't understanding what I was reading. I went back to the beginning and started over. And that's when I sensed movement behind me."

"Behind you?"

"Manuelo. I hadn't heard him return. Foster was probably doing that 'poor Griff' bit so I wouldn't. I caught a glimpse of Manuelo just in time."

Reflexes, honed by years of dodging tacklers, had kicked in. He'd moved sideways only a fraction of a foot, but it was enough to neutralize Manuelo's lunge toward him.

"Unfortunately, his reflexes were almost as quick as mine, and he was able to wrap his arms around me, one at my throat, the other around my rib cage. You know how wiry and strong he is."

She nodded.

"He began to squeeze. He felt like a python around me." Griff remembered struggling, clawing at the man's arms. He broke Manuelo's skin with his fingernails but achieved nothing else. For a man so short in stature, the aide had astonishing strength. His muscles had been conditioned to place pressure where pressure was desired, and to do so with absolute control.

They'd engaged in a macabre dance, going round and round, knocking over the end table, sending objects to the floor, breaking a lamp. "I tried like hell to break his stranglehold," Griff went on, "if only for a millisecond, long enough for me to take a breath. Nothing worked.

"Soon, I felt myself growing weaker. Black dots appeared in my field of vision. I'd had the wind knocked out of me and lost consciousness on the football field, so I recognized the signs and knew I was on my way under. But I could still see Foster sitting in his wheelchair, slapping the arms of it in sequences of three, muttering 'Do it, do it, do it,' also in sequences of three."

Laura pressed her fingertips against her lips.

"Are you believing any of this, or am I wasting my breath?" he asked.

"Go on."

"You're not gonna like what I'm about to say. I was on the brink of blacking out when I realized what I think I knew from the moment I met him. He was a lunatic."

"Don't—"

"No, Laura. You're going to hear this. He was insane. At least on some level. What man in his right mind, married to you, would ask another man to have sex with you? Pay him to. For *any* reason."

She didn't produce an answer, and Griff hadn't expected one. "I'm convinced now that doing away with me was his intention all along." She was about to protest, but he spoke before she could. "Think about it. He was fanatical about keeping our agreement a secret. In order to guarantee that, I had to die. Leaving me alive was untidy. For a compulsive cleaner, I was an unacceptable wrinkle in the bar towel, a water spot on the granite. He insisted on perfection, and for his plan to be perfect, I had to be eliminated." He paused, then said, "Him I could understand. But I wondered about you."

"Me?"

"Were you in on it, Laura? Was this your plan, too?"

"I'm not even going to honor that with a response."

"Why'd you go to Austin that day?"

He listened as she explained the circumstances. "Whatever happened that night, I wasn't a part of it," she said with heat. "I didn't even know you'd been to the mansion until Rodarte told me your fingerprints were on the murder weapon."

He dragged his hand down his face. "I didn't think you would plot my death, but when my lights were going out, the question did flash through my mind. Were you conveniently in Austin so you wouldn't have to witness my murder?"

"You truly thought that?"

"Uncanny how clearly you see things when you think you're about to die. You'd refused to talk to me after our last afternoon together."

"You know why I didn't, why I *couldn't,* talk to you, Griff."

"Guilt."

"Yes."

"So maybe the only way to rid yourself of your guilt was to do away with me."

She looked at him, her gaze unflinching.

He sighed. "Okay, I know better. But that's what went through my mind. But then, just as I was about to lose consciousness, a worse thought occurred to me. You were in on Foster's secret, too."

She looked at him without reaction for several seconds, then recoiled. "What are you saying?"

"After you gave birth to the child, what if he decided that you were a threat to his secrecy, too."

"Foster loved me. I know that. He adored me."

"I don't doubt it, Laura. But his mind was more twisted than his body. What if he began seeing you as a flaw to his perfect plan? If you were out of the picture, he would be the only one on earth who knew the truth about his heir's parentage. You would be a living threat and, as such, would have to go."

"He would never!"

"Maybe," Griff said without conviction. "But it was the fear he would that saved my life. It gave me renewed strength. I started fighting that Salvadoran son of a bitch like something just let out of hell. I bucked. I kicked. I clawed. Even tried to bite him.

"But I was starved for oxygen. My coordination was for shit. I could barely think. All I accomplished was to use up my reserves. It was then I realized that the only way I'd survive was to pretend to succumb. I went limp.

"'Good, good, good,' I heard Foster say. Manuelo let go. I had the presence of mind to fall face-first onto the rug so I could hide that I was breathing.

Foster said, '*Muy bien, Manuelo. Muy bien. Muy bien.*'

"I could hear Manuelo gasping for breath. He was standing close to me. I partially opened one eye and saw his right shoe inches from my head. I grabbed him around the ankle and yanked his foot out from under him. Gravity did the tough part."

Manuelo went down hard, landing on his back. Griff lunged on top of him and drove his fist into the man's nose, felt cartilage give way to the thrust, felt blood on his knuckles. But Manuelo wasn't dispatched. He placed the heel of his hand beneath Griff's chin and gave a push that could have snapped his neck if he hadn't averted his head in time.

Manuelo used that instant to throw Griff off. He sprang to his feet with the agility of a cat and kicked the side of Griff's head with his heel. Griff cried out as pain splintered through his skull. He felt a surge of nausea in the back of his throat but swallowed it as he staggered to his feet.

He managed to stand, but unsteadily. The room was spinning. To stave off the unconsciousness that threatened, he blinked rapidly and brought Manuelo into focus. The man's vacant smile had been replaced by a snarl.

"He had the letter opener in his hand," Griff told Laura. "Foster was saying, 'No blood, no blood, no blood.' But I don't think Manuelo heard him. He was past listening, past caring. The fight had become a matter of personal honor. He'd been ordered to kill me. To save face, that's what he was going to do."

Laura's eyes were wide. She hadn't moved or spoken in several minutes.

"When Manuelo sprang, I dodged." Griff had relied on his timing, the innate talent that had enabled him to throw a pass with a precision that defied physics a split second before he was tackled. He'd waited until Manuelo moved, then ducked, fallen to the floor, and rolled. "Manuelo couldn't stop his momentum. He broke his fall against Foster's wheelchair, landing hard."

"And the letter opener . . ."

"Yeah." It had been buried to the hilt in the side of Speakman's neck. "When Manuelo scrambled back and saw what he'd done, he screamed. Long as I live, I'll never forget that sound." Another sound Griff would never forget was the gurgling noise coming out of Speakman's mouth, which was opening and closing like that of a dying fish. But Laura didn't need to know the grisly details of how her husband had suffered before he died.

"It was a dreadful accident," he said to her now. "But to Rodarte it looks like the act of a jealous jilted lover."

For a long time, they sat in silence. Finally Laura took a deep breath, as though rousing herself from a sound sleep or a bad dream. "You're right. To Rodarte it looks exactly like that."

"What does it look like to *you*?"

CHAPTER
33

AFTER SEVERAL SILENT MINUTES, GRIFF said, "You must believe me, at least a little, or you wouldn't still be in this car."

Laura ran her fingers through her hair. She'd been trying to find words that would convey the doubts she'd been harboring without sounding disloyal to the husband she had just buried. But she wasn't sure that was possible.

"Foster was over the moon about the baby," she began, "but I begged him not to notify you until we'd had the pregnancy confirmed."

"He called right after you got the results of the blood test."

"That evening, he admitted speaking to you. He apologized for not waiting on me to be there when he called you but said he couldn't wait to share the happy news. He said that you wished us well, but that you were mostly interested in how soon you'd get your money."

"That's a lie. I—"

She held up her hand. "Let me tell it from my perspective. You can rebut it later." He nodded. "Foster and I celebrated that night. He'd had Mrs. Dobbins prepare a special dinner. He forced a second helping of potatoes on me, reminding me I was eating for two. He wouldn't let me out of his sight. He made me use his elevator rather than walk upstairs. He said the staircase was dangerous, that I could fall. I told him I would go insane if this was how the next nine months were going to be. But I was indulgent of his mood. We actually laughed about his overprotectiveness.

"When Manuelo had him settled for the night, I went to him. He held me and told me how much he loved me, how thrilled he was about the baby. Things like that." Her cheeks warmed with self-consciousness. "He was very tender and attentive, more affectionate than he'd been in months. I stayed with him until he was asleep." She was intensely aware of Griff's utter stillness, his unwavering gaze.

"His behavior being what it was that night, I couldn't understand his insistence that I go to Austin the following morning. It was an unnecessary trip. The incident could have been handled by the supervisor there, and should have been. It was an insult to him that Foster sent me as an overseer. That wasn't his usual style of management. Sending me didn't make any sense."

"It makes sense to me."

Reluctantly, she nodded. "We had wrapped up the problem in Austin by midafternoon. I could have been on an earlier flight back to Dallas, but, without consulting me, Foster had obligated me to have dinner with some of the key people in the Austin office. The meal dragged on forever. I barely made it to the airport in time for the nine o'clock flight, the last of the night."

"He didn't want you back before then. He wanted you out of the way. By the time you got back, I would be dead."

"I still can't believe that, Griff. I just can't. Despite what you think, he wasn't a lunatic. I'll admit he had grown increasingly obsessive. Doing things in sequences of three. The cleanliness. Did you notice the bottles of hand sanitizer?"

"Everywhere."

"Nothing could be soiled, nothing out of place, nothing left to chance. But it's unthinkable to me that he would order Manuelo to kill you with his bare hands."

"He didn't want my blood ruining his priceless rug."

She shot him a look. "You know what I mean. How did he plan on getting away with it?"

"He would claim I had stormed the castle and tried to kill him."

"Over what?"

"You. He would say that Manuelo had saved his life when I attacked him in a jealous rage."

"But Foster didn't know Rodarte. He certainly didn't know that he had discovered the Windsor Street house and had concluded we were having an affair. If you'd been killed instead, what motive would Foster have given the investigator—"

"Rodarte would have made damn sure he was

put on the case. He'd promised to witness my self-destruction."

"Then what reason would Foster have given him for your attempt on his life?"

Griff thought about it. "Money. I went to the mansion and demanded more."

"Foster wouldn't have told anyone about our arrangement with you, especially not someone as slimy as Rodarte."

"Maybe he'd have said he offered me a job in advertising, then changed his mind and withdrew the offer."

"Plausible, I suppose."

"Knowing Rodarte as I do, I'm sure he eventually would have played his ace, broken the news to the poor cuckold that I'd been sneaking afternoons with his wife. Of course, Foster would have let him go on thinking I had acted out of jealousy. Our secret affair would have made him look more like a victim, and me a likelier murderer."

Laura silently conceded that it sounded logical, but she wasn't yet ready to fully accept it. "Why would Foster have that phony document? And the box of cash? How would he have explained them?"

"If Manuelo had killed me," he said, "they wouldn't have been there. Foster didn't expect anyone but me to see them."

There was no disputing that. "All right, I see how he could have given Rodarte a credible explanation, and Rodarte would have accepted it, believing Foster to be in the dark about us. But what would Foster have told me?"

"Probably that the confirmed pregnancy had

made me greedy. I got to the mansion and demanded more than the half million. When he refused to pay more, I attacked him. Thank God for Manuelo. And thank God I'd done the job I'd been hired to do. You were pregnant. My death was a tragedy, but wasn't it lucky that I was no longer around, an ongoing threat to your secret and the well-being of your child." He paused, then added, "It would have been just as he wanted it, Laura. Neat and tidy."

They were quiet for a time. Movies ended. People trickled out of the theater and made their way to their cars. Others arrived. There was a line to purchase tickets. But the van and the pickup truck stayed, and no one paid attention to the couple sitting in the innocuous midsize car between them.

"Your fingerprints were on the hilt of the letter opener."

"So were Manuelo's."

"But he could have handled it at any time." She tried to make eye contact, but he avoided it. "Griff?"

"I didn't want you to know how he died."

"I have to know."

He looked away from her, out the windshield, his eyes following a family of four, mom and dad, two children, who'd just come out of a movie. The young son was rolling his eyes, flapping his arms, doing a disjointed jig, obviously imitating an animated character. They were laughing as they piled into their SUV and drove away.

"Why were your fingerprints on the letter opener?"

"I was trying to save his life," he replied in a quiet voice. "When I saw what had made Manuelo scream, I pushed him aside and shouted at him to call 911. But he was transfixed by the horror of what he'd done. So I placed the call. While I was doing that, Manuelo split.

"I bent over Speakman to see just how bad it was. My initial reaction was to try to pull the letter opener out of his neck. I took hold of it but almost immediately realized it would be better to leave the thing where it was. It was partially plugging the wound, and even at that it was gushing." He stopped, cursed softly. "Laura, you don't want to hear this."

"I must."

He hesitated, then continued. "There was nothing I could do but what I did, which was to apply pressure around the blade, try to slow down the bleeding."

She swallowed. "Rodarte said that there was blood on Foster's hands, tissue under his fingernails. That he had . . ."

Griff held out his hands to her, palms down, so that she could see the scratch marks on the backs of them. "He was trying to pull the letter opener out. I knew for certain he would die if he did, so, yeah, we fought over control of it."

He waited to see if she would respond to that, but when she didn't, he went on. "I talked to him, trying to calm him down and stop him from struggling. I told him that help was on the way. Told him to hold on, to hang in there. Stuff like that. But . . ." He shook his head. "I knew he wasn't going to make it, and I think he did, too."

"Did he say anything?"

He shook his head. "He couldn't articulate."

"Were you with him when—"

"Yes. I stayed."

"Thank you for that."

"Jesus, don't thank me," he said, sounding almost angry. "Believe me, as soon as he was gone, I was out of there. I knew what it would look like. I showed no more guts than Manuelo. I grabbed my ass and ran. And . . ." He stopped, looked away, toward the brightly lit entrance to the theater.

"What?"

He blew out a gust of breath. "There were plenty of times after that last afternoon with you when I wished he was dead." He looked directly into her eyes then. "Not dead specifically. Just . . . just *not*. In the depths of my rotten soul, I wished him away." He continued looking at her for ponderous seconds before speaking again. "But I didn't kill him. Do you believe that?"

She opened her mouth to speak but discovered she couldn't. His story was more credible than she wanted it to be. But she also remembered that afternoon of fevered lovemaking, the hunger and urgency of it. Her impassioned responses had unleashed from him a wild possessiveness. She remembered the way his large hands had moved over her body, claiming it, the intensity with which he had thrust into her, and how jealously he'd held her afterward.

She lowered her head and massaged her temples.

"Forget I asked," he said curtly. "You're not going to believe me until you have Manuelo Ruiz's sworn statement that he accidentally stabbed your husband. You and Rodarte."

She reached out and angrily grabbed his hand. "Don't you dare compare me to Rodarte. And don't give me attitude, either. You're asking me to believe in your innocence. I want to, Griff. But believing you also means accepting that my husband, the person I had loved and admired for years, was a madman who plotted your murder. It's a lot to absorb so soon after burying him. Forgive me if that's proving to be difficult."

She dropped his hand, and for several moments the atmosphere crackled. He was the first to relent. "Okay. No more attitude." He reached into the backseat and got the duffel, placed it in his lap, and unzipped it. "My only hope of exoneration—from anybody—is to find Manuelo Ruiz."

He rifled the bag, removing what appeared to be the aide's keepsakes from El Salvador. A rosary. A map of Mexico, with a red crayon line snaking up through it to a starred spot on the Texas border.

"His route," he said. There was an old photograph of a couple on their wedding day. "His parents, you think?" He passed her the picture.

"Possibly. Their age looks right."

That was it except for a few Spanish-language paperback books and an inexpensive wallet. Griff checked every compartment. In the last one he looked, he found a piece of stained paper. It had been folded so many times, the creases were dirty and almost worn through. Griff carefully spread it open on his thigh.

He read what was printed on it, then smiled and passed the sheet to her. Written in pencil were four digits and a name. She looked back at him. "An address?"

"Appears to be. It's a place to start looking."

"It could be right here in Dallas or in Eagle Pass."

"Yeah, but it's something." He seemed suddenly galvanized. "Do you have a cell phone?"

She reached into her handbag and withdrew it. Checking the readout, she saw that she'd missed several calls. "I had silenced it at the office and forgot to turn it back on. Kay called once. Rodarte's called three times. The last time was twelve minutes ago."

She handed the phone to Griff. He pressed the send button, so that Rodarte's number would be automatically dialed. It rang only once before he answered. "Mrs. Speakman?"

"Sorry to disappoint you, Rodarte. You've got me. And I've got her."

"You're a moron, Burkett. You're just digging yourself in deeper."

"Listen, I'm gonna make this quick, simple enough even for you. I did not kill Foster Speakman. Manuelo Ruiz did."

Rodarte laughed. "Right. The minion. The slave who idolized the guy. Yank somebody else's pod."

"It was an accident. Manuelo was fighting with me."

"Trying to protect Speakman from you."

"Wrong again, but we'll go into the details later. You and I both need Manuelo. You're right about him worshiping Speakman. That's why he was so horrified by what he'd done, he ran. Find him and all our problems will be over. I've got a lead for you." He read off the address. "We found it in Manuelo's belongings. He didn't have much, so this means something or he wouldn't have kept it."

"What city?"

"I don't know, but you've got resources."

"And he's got almost a week's head start."

"That's why you can't waste any time. If you find him, treat him kindly, and you'll get the truth of what happened that night. Nobody committed a murder. Manuelo will tell you that. He can tell you—"

Griff broke off suddenly, surprising Laura, who'd been following every word. One second he'd been speaking rapidly into the telephone, the next, he was silent, staring into near space. Through the phone, she could hear Rodarte saying, "Burkett? Burkett, are you there? Burkett!"

"Griff?" she whispered. "What?"

He focused on her sharply, then slapped the phone closed, abruptly ending his call. He opened the car door and dropped the phone onto the pavement. As he turned on the car's ignition, he said, "Rodarte's probably put a satellite track on your phone, so we've got to get the hell out of here."

"I don't understand." She clutched the hand grip as he backed out of the parking slot and wheeled the car sharply.

"Manuelo Ruiz can clear me."

"That's why you're desperate to find him."

"And why Rodarte is desperate *not* to."

CHAPTER
34

H E SPED OUT OF THE THEATER PARKING lot, wove through the commercial complex, and took the first ramp he could onto Central Expressway, heading north, driving as fast as he dared but not so fast as to invite being stopped. He drove with one eye on the rearview mirror, afraid that, at any moment, he would see a pursuing squad car.

"Why wouldn't Rodarte want to find Manuelo Ruiz?" Laura asked.

"Think about it. He hasn't exactly launched a full-out manhunt for him, has he?"

"He thought that you had killed him, that all they would discover was a body. He was more interested in finding you."

"So he could indict me for murder. Best-case scenario for Rodarte would be for Manuelo to be across the border, well on his way back to the jungle, never to be seen or heard from again. Shit!" he hissed, thumping the steering wheel with his fist. "Do you think he got that address? Do you think he understood it?"

"I—"

"Because if he finds Manuelo before I do, the man will never make it into a court of law, probably not even into an interrogation room."

"You think Rodarte would help him escape?"

"If Manuelo's lucky, that's what he'll do. What scares me is that Rodarte will make sure no one hears Manuelo's account of what happened. Ever."

"You mean . . . he would kill him?"

Griff shrugged.

"Griff, he's a police detective."

"Who's dedicated himself to putting me on death row. To that end, Manuelo's easily dispensable."

"So what do we do? Call one of Rodarte's superiors, tell them your side?"

He shook his head. "I don't know who his friends are. He recruited two of them to beat me up. I wouldn't know who to trust."

"Then what?"

"We find Manuelo before Rodarte does."

"How are we going to do that?"

Swerving in front of a truck to take an exit, Griff muttered, "Wish the hell I knew."

The pancake house was open all night. At any hour it was well lighted and crowded, and so was the parking lot. A car left there didn't attract attention. Griff parked, and they got out.

"Welcome to the glamorous world of a fugitive."

He took Laura's hand and led her around to the back of the building, where the odorous Dumpsters were open and overflowing.

"Where are we going?"

"It's a half-mile walk. Are you okay with that?"

"A half mile is a warm-up."

He smiled down at her, but his expression was grim. "I didn't say it was an easy half mile."

Leaving behind the commercial area, they entered a residential neighborhood. Over the past several days, through trial and error, he'd learned the safest route, if not the easiest. It took them through yards with dense shrubbery and large trees but no exterior lighting, fences, or barking dogs.

They came upon the house from the rear. Griff was relieved to see that no lights were on inside. Each time he came back to his refuge, he was afraid the owners had returned during his absence.

The backyard was enclosed by a stockade fence, but when they reached the gate, he opened the latch without difficulty. "It's never locked." He ushered Laura through the gate, then closed it silently.

"Who lives here?" she asked, speaking in a whisper. The houses on either side were obviously occupied. Lights shone through windows. Somewhere close a sprinkler was swishing. They could hear a television show's soundtrack.

"I used to." He led the way to a back door, opened it, and pulled her in behind him. The alarm system began to bleep, but he punched in a sequence of numbers and it went silent. "They never changed the code. All these years, it's been the same."

"This was your house?"

"My high school coach and his wife. They took me in when I was fifteen."

"The Millers." At his look of surprise, she added, "I read about you."

He didn't risk turning on any lights, but there was enough light from the neighbors' houses straining through the kitchen window curtain that he could make out her features as he searched her face. "You read about me?"

"When Foster recommended you to father the baby. I researched your background."

"Oh." He waited a beat, then said, "I guess I passed. In spite of the fact that my dad was a wife beater and my mother a whore."

"That wasn't your fault."

"People say the apple doesn't fall far from the tree."

"Generally speaking, people are unfair."

"Not in this case. I turned out rotten, too."

She shook her head and was about to say something when the refrigerator cycled on, creating a buzz that sounded as loud as a chain saw in the silent house. She jumped. He touched her arm. "It's just the fridge. It's okay. Come on." He took her hand and pulled her behind him as he made his way from the kitchen into the living area, where the drapes were drawn and it was much darker.

Still speaking in a whisper, she said, "So this is where you've been staying all this time?"

"Since my escape from Turner's house."

"They've been sheltering you?"

"Hardly. They don't know I'm here. I came to see Ellie not too long ago. She mentioned a trip to

Hawaii. I guess that's where they are. Anyhow, I showed up here, prepared to throw myself on their mercy. I didn't have to."

"You may when they return."

"I may," he said ruefully. "I'm sure Coach will kick me out. But at least they can't be accused of sheltering me. I'm sorry I can't turn on any lights. The neighbors know they're away and will be keeping an eye on the house. It's that kind of neighborhood. Careful. I've got to close this door." He shut the door between the living room and the hallway, plunging them into total darkness.

"Didn't Rodarte think to look for you here?"

"I'm sure he did and probably still has a car doing periodic drive-bys. But when he discovered the Millers were out of state, he figured I wouldn't be here. Besides, he knows Coach can't stomach the sight of me now. He'd think if I showed my face around here, he'd be the first person Coach would call. I've been hoping that all this would be cleared up before they return from their vacation and they'd never know that I'd used their house." He laughed softly. "Ellie probably would figure it out, though. I've tried to clean up after myself, but she's an excellent housekeeper."

"Is that their car we were in?"

"Their second car. Not used much. I sneaked it out of the garage in the middle of the night, drove it to the parking lot of that restaurant, and left it. I've been coming and going from there. As far as the neighbors know, the car is still in the garage."

He felt his way along the wall till he reached the doorway to his bedroom. "In here."

When they were inside and the door closed behind them, he released her hand and felt his way over to the desk. He found the lamp by feel and turned it on. They blinked against the sudden light. He motioned toward the window that overlooked the front yard. "Crude but effective."

He'd stretched a dark blanket over the window frame and secured it all around with tape, so that not even a sliver of light would shine through. "From the outside all you see is drawn blinds."

"Genius."

"More like desperation."

A laptop computer was on the desk. He switched it on. He'd found it in the spare bedroom. Coach had always cursed computers, saying they were "too damn hard to operate," so Griff supposed it was Ellie who'd joined the age of electronics.

While it was booting, he watched Laura as she moved around the room, looking at photos, trophies, clippings, and other memorabilia of his life—starting at age fifteen.

"You began early."

She was looking at a photo of him taken before he was old enough to shave. He was kneeling with one knee on the turf, wearing a football uniform with full pads, his helmet tucked under his arm, his expression as badass as he could make it. The photos and awards in this room chronicled his football career from those adolescent teams up to that fateful play-off game with the Redskins.

"You loved it, didn't you?" she asked.

"Yes."

"Do you regret what you did?"

"You have no idea." He glanced at the computer monitor. It wasn't a speedy, streamlined new model. Programs were still loading. Laura sat down on the edge of the bed and folded her hands in her lap, like she was settling in to listen.

Griff looked at a framed photo of himself caught in the motion of throwing a pass. It had been taken during the game that had won his high school the state championship. Coach's team. The school district had held a victory parade upon their return from Houston, where the game had been played in the Astrodome. Up to that point, it had been the highlight of Griff's life.

"You know from the day you start that it can't last forever," he said. "Even if you go all the way to the pros, it's short term. Thirty is old. Thirty-five is ancient. And that's if you escape serious injury. You're never more than one play away from the end of your career. Or even the end of your life. Each time the ball is snapped, it's a tempt of fate."

He turned his head and looked at her. "But I wouldn't trade a day of it. Not a single day. I loved the buildup that was part of each game. By kickoff time, I'd have a knot in my gut harder than a fist, but it was a good kind of anxiety, you know?"

She nodded.

"I loved the snap, getting my hands around that ball. I loved the adrenaline rush I got every time I called a tricky play and it was perfectly executed. I received perks and favors all along the way, a college education, millions in salary. But the truth is, Laura, I'd have played for nothing.

"Because even on the worst days, I loved the game. I loved it even on the Monday mornings when I could barely get out of bed for the aches and pains." He smiled. "Most mornings it still takes me half an hour before I can stand up straight."

He looked at the computer. It was still grinding. "I remember one Sunday afternoon in Texas Stadium, lying on the turf after I'd been sacked by a thousand pounds of Broncos in front of a capacity home crowd. I looked up through that stupid hole in the ceiling of the stadium, and even then, knocked flat on my butt and having lost seven yards on the play, I was so goddamn happy to be there I laughed out loud. Everybody thought I'd had my bells rung, got a concussion, or just plain cracked under pressure. No one could guess I was laughing out of pure joy over the game. The *game*." He shook his head and snuffled a sad laugh. "Yeah, I loved it. God, I loved it."

Several moments elapsed. He heard Laura draw in a long breath and let it out slowly. "And they loved you."

When he looked back at her, she was staring at a photo of him with the Millers. "You mean Coach? Ellie?" He shrugged uneasily. "Emphasis on the past tense."

She indicated the walls, the full shelves, and said softly, "It's all still here, Griff."

He held her gaze for a moment, then turned back to the computer. "Finally." He moved the cursor to the icon that would link him to the Internet. He felt Laura move up behind him and look over his shoulder.

"What's your plan?"

"Haven't got one. Go on some kind of search engine, I guess. See if I can find this address. Start with city of Dallas, move to Dallas County, expand to the whole damn state if necessary."

"Is that your top speed?"

He typed by hunting and pecking. He looked up at her over his shoulder. "Are you faster?"

They switched places. She sat in the desk chair. He braced his arms on the back of it so he could see the monitor. She was a much more proficient typist. "Manuelo didn't write down whether it was Lavaca Street or Road or Lane," she remarked. "We'll have to try them all."

"How many Lavaca Streets, Roads, et cetera do you think there are in Texas?"

"Hundreds?"

"That's my guess, too. And Rodarte's got better computers and more people."

"Can I make a suggestion?"

"Be my guest."

"Tax records. Every property is taxed."

"You think a person who provides fake documents to illegal immigrants pays property taxes?"

"The taxes would be assessed. Whether or not they're paid is another matter."

"Okay. Are there tax records online?"

"We'll try. Tax assessor records for Dallas County?"

"Knock yourself out."

She began searching for such a website. "Tell me about Bill Bandy."

The request surprised him, and for a moment he didn't say anything. Then, "What do you want to know?"

"How you met. How you got involved with him."

He gave her a condensed version. "When I got in over my head, he introduced me to a syndicate.

They canceled my debt, in exchange for a few interceptions, fumbles. Nothing that couldn't happen to any quarterback on any given Sunday."

"Bandy betrayed you."

"The feds offered him probation in exchange for setting me up, and I'll bet they didn't have to twist his arm too hard."

"There's a Lavaca Street in Dallas, but the addresses have three digits, not four," she reported.

"Try Lavaca Road."

"The newspapers said that Bandy delivered the two million to your Turtle Creek condo."

"True. He was wearing a wire. Second I took the box of cash from him, agents came busting through my front door, read me my rights."

"You were put in jail?"

"Yes," he said tightly, remembering the humiliation of that experience. "Wyatt Turner got me released on the condition that I give up my passport. Soon as I got out, I went looking for Bandy."

Laura stopped typing, turned and looked up at him.

"Right. It was a stupid thing to do. But I was furious. I guess I wanted to frighten him into thinking he was as good as dead for setting me up." He cursed himself under his breath. "What a goddamn fool I was. When I got to Bandy's place, the door was open. I went in. I almost walked out without seeing him. He'd been stuffed between the back of the sofa and the wall. His neck had been wrenched so hard his head was practically facing backward."

"Who killed him?"

"I'm sure the Vista boys were behind it. They

wanted him silenced, so he couldn't give them up like he had me."

"They could've killed you, too."

"I think they thought it would be more fun to keep me alive, let me be charged with Bandy's murder. I'm sure it was them who tipped off the cops."

"How did they know you were going to be at Bandy's place?"

"I guess they figured I'd go after Bandy, at the very least to tell him how disappointed I was in him," he said with sarcasm. "I was still kneeling beside the body when two squad cars showed up, responding to an anonymous 911 call from a pay phone, they said."

"Vista was watching you."

"Obviously. And if you could see this guy called Bennett, you'd think he could sit through a tornado without blinking. Anyway, here I was, facing federal charges of racketeering and illegal gambling, and there was my bookie, the one who'd ratted me out, dead on the floor.

"Enter Detective Stanley Rodarte, who'd been dispatched to investigate the crime scene. He came in and introduced himself, told me what a great ballplayer I'd been, and what a shame it was that I'd turned crooked. Then he looked at the body, looked back at me, and started laughing. It seemed that open and shut."

"No address like this on Tarrant County's tax records, either," Laura said.

"Denton? What's on the western side of Tarrant?"

She consulted a map on the screen, where the counties were delineated. "Parker."

"Try that, too. Damn," he said, looking at the map and realizing the scope of this effort. "This could take all night." He consulted his watch, wondering if Rodarte had already isolated the address and was speeding toward it.

"It wasn't the open-and-shut case Rodarte thought it would be," Laura said.

"Bandy's back room had been torn all to hell. Ransacked. My prints were on the sofa, the wall behind it—hell, I was kneeling beside his body when the police arrived. But they couldn't place me in that back room, hard as Rodarte tried. The grand jury found it impossible to believe that I would avoid leaving prints or other evidence while ransacking the place, then take off gloves before killing Bandy. And if I had, where were the gloves?"

"Why was his back room ransacked?"

"Rodarte is of the opinion that Bandy had money squirreled away in there somewhere and that I helped myself to it."

Again she turned and looked up at him. "But you didn't have any cash stuffed in your pockets at the time, did you?"

"No. But it wouldn't necessarily have been cash I was looking for. It could have been a bank account number. A combination to a safe. Something I could commit to memory. Later, when I was out of prison, I'd have a treasure waiting for me." He looked at her hard. "Just so you know, I never went into Bandy's back room. I didn't know what was or wasn't in there. As far as I know, he didn't have any funds stashed away for a rainy day."

Quietly she said, "I didn't ask." She turned back around and, after scanning the information on the monitor, said, "There's no Lavaca anything in Parker County."

Griff opened the duffel bag and removed Manuelo's map. "Pull up that map of the state again." She did. When it appeared on the monitor, he tapped a spot. "That red crayon star is here." He pointed to the southern tip of the state. "Somewhere between Mission and Hidalgo."

"We assume that's where he entered the country. Lord, how far is that from here?"

"Four hundred miles at least. Probably closer to five."

"Lots of counties."

"Yeah, but I'd bet his contact wouldn't be too far from this area. Say Manuelo came north through San Antonio and Austin."

"Basically following I-35."

"Basically. Let's concentrate on the counties immediately to the south of Dallas–Fort Worth."

"Hood, Johnson, Ellis."

"Check those and work your way down."

They found it in Hill County. "Griff! There's a Lavaca Road in Hill County. On the outskirts of town it turns into FM 2010. We thought it was a house number!"

He leaned over her, and she pointed it out on the screen.

"What town is that?" he asked.

"Itasca."

"Repeat that," Rodarte said.

"Itasca."

"Where the hell is that?" He was driving with

one hand, holding his cell phone to his ear with the other.

He'd had a desk cop back at the police station searching for the address Griff Burkett had rattled off to him before hanging up. Thanks to a satellite and technology he didn't understand, Laura Speakman's cell phone had been tracked to a movie theater. Before he could even get excited about it, they'd found the damn thing lying on the parking lot pavement.

From there the trail had gone cold because Mrs. Speakman's car had been left at the mansion, they didn't know what Burkett was driving now, and the moviegoers they'd questioned didn't know diddly. Rodarte had left Carter there to try to pick up the trail. Actually, Rodarte was glad he could assign his partner another task. From here on, he preferred working alone.

Rodarte became furious thinking about Griff Burkett and his adulterous lover—had she plotted her husband's murder with him?—laughing up their sleeves at him. The idiots he'd posted to guard her were going to be looking for jobs tomorrow. Then he was going to hurt them. And their wives. And their kids. They would come to regret the day they were born.

And that didn't begin to cover what he had planned for Griff Burkett and the poor, innocent, grieving widow. He wished he'd fucked her when he had a chance. *Who would she have told? The cops?* he thought, scoffing. *No way.* Not when he could turn it around and tell them about her illicit affair with her husband's killer. Yeah, he should have responded to the impulse he'd had there in her hotel room, bent her over and fucked her. His problem was he was just too nice a guy.

The desk cop was rattling off directions. "From where you're at, go south on 35 E till you get to I-20 and head west. Then out of Fort Worth, take 35 dubya south. Watch for the exit."

"So where's this Lavaca Road or whatever?"

"Runs out the east side of town and turns into farm-to-market 2010. We reckon that's where the numbers came from. It's not exactly a street address, but it makes sense."

"I guess," Rodarte said, unconvinced. "But stand by in case I need to call you again."

"I already called the local *po*-lice down there. Chief's name is Marion."

"First?"

"Last. Plus I alerted the Hill County SO. Marion's sending a squad car to scout out the area, see if his boys can pick up anything. When you get there, you'll have plenty of backup."

"Is there still an APB out for Manuelo Ruiz down there?"

"I asked Marion to jog everybody's memory."

"And one for Griff Burkett?"

"Considered armed and dangerous. Just like you said, Detective."

"He's got a cop's service weapon."

"Told Marion that, too. Pissed him off." After a pause, he added, "And to think we used to cheer the son of a bitch."

"Yeah, to think."

The best that could happen would be for Burkett to be spotted and plugged by an underpaid, over-anxious Hicksville cop, a Cowboys fan who bore a grudge based on principle.

Someone else killing Burkett would remove any suspicion from him. But there was a distinct downside: it would deprive him of taking down that bastard himself, and that was something he very much looked forward to.

"What's the number of the police station down there?" Rodarte asked the desk cop. Once he had it, he clicked off and called that number. He identified himself and was soon patched in to Chief Marion. "Rodarte, Dallas PD."

"Yes, sir," he said crisply.

"Just calling to follow up. What's happening down there?"

"There's nothing on FM 2010 except an old farmhouse. Vacant. Looks like it was abandoned a long time ago. My men said a strong wind would knock it down."

"No shit?"

"The place was deserted. We'll keep looking, but among my officers and the sheriff's deputies, they don't know of anything else out that way. Not for miles."

"Okay. Keep me posted."

"Sure thing, Detective."

Rodarte closed his phone and tossed it onto the passenger seat, cursing his culpability. Had Burkett sent him on a wild-goose chase? Given him some busywork to keep him occupied while he and his ladylove got away?

He pulled his car to the shoulder of the freeway, rolled down the window, and lit a cigarette. He kept the motor idling while he considered his options.

* * *

"Itasca," Laura repeated. "Ever heard of it?"

"No, but I'll find it." He gave her shoulders a squeeze. "Great work. Thanks." He moved toward the door. "Switch out the light till I'm gone. And remember not to turn any lights on unless the door to this room is closed."

"You're going now?"

"Right now. I just hope Rodarte doesn't have too much of a lead."

"But we don't know if that's it, Griff. And even if it is, Manuelo may be long gone."

"I've gotta try. He's my last hope."

"I'm coming, too," she said decisively.

"Un-uh. No way. I don't know what I—"

"I'm coming with you." She stood up, but when she did, a strange look came over her face and she pushed her hands between her thighs.

"What's the matter?"

She just stood there, looking at him with alarm. Then her face crumpled, and she groaned, "Oh, no."

CHAPTER
35

EVEN WHEN HE SAW THE BLOOD ON HER hands, saw the streaks of it on the legs of her tracksuit, Griff didn't comprehend what was happening until he looked into her eyes and saw the anguish in them. "Oh, Jesus."

In a keening voice she said, "My baby."

He reached for her, but she backed away. "Laura, I gotta get you to a hospital."

"There's nothing to be done."

"You don't know that."

"Yes, I do." Her eyes filled with tears. "It's lost."

"No, no, we'll stop it. We can. We will."

She looked around frantically. "Where's the bathroom?"

He got to the door ahead of her and reached inside to switch on the light. She slipped around him and closed the door behind her.

"Laura?"

"Don't come in."

He placed both palms on the door and, leaning into it, ground his forehead hard against the wood, never in his life having felt so useless. Miscarriage. He'd heard the word, knew what it meant, but had never realized that it entailed that much blood, or caused this much despair. He felt pointless, super-fluous, and helpless. The laws of nature had emas-culated him.

He stood outside the bathroom door for what seemed forever. Several times he knocked, asked how she was doing, asked if there was something he could do. She replied in monosyllabic mumbles that told him nothing.

The toilet flushed numerous times. Water ran in the sink. Eventually he heard the shower. Shortly after it stopped running, she opened the door. She was wrapped in a towel. His eyes moved over her from the top of her wet hair to her toes and back up, stopping on her eyes, red-rimmed and tearful.

"Is it hopeless?"

She nodded.

He assimilated that, marveled at the anguish it caused him. "Does it hurt?"

"A little. Like really bad cramps."

"Um-hmm," he said, as though he had any idea what menstrual cramps felt like.

"I need something to put on."

He looked beyond her. Her tracksuit was in a sodden heap on the floor of the shower. "I'll find something."

"Do you think Mrs. Miller has some pads?"

Pads? His mind scrambled. Pads. Right. Ask him about Tiger Balm or jock itch remedies and he was conversant. Athlete's foot? On it. But he'd never even walked down the feminine hygiene aisle of a supermarket. Not on purpose anyway. He'd never bought a product for a girlfriend, wife, daughter. His knowledge of such things was limited to the box of tampons his mother had kept beneath the bathroom sink. He knew they were necessary, but that's all.

"I'll be right back."

He didn't even think about the lights he was turning on as he went banging through the house, bumping into walls, flinging open doors he'd left closed the last few days. In the Millers' bedroom he opened the closet they shared. Coach's clothes hung on one side, Ellie's on the other, shoes lined up neatly beneath.

He yanked a robe off a hanger, then began rifling bureau drawers until he found her underwear. Not the skimpier, lacier kind he'd seen Laura in, but what he came up with would do.

Pads. Wouldn't Ellie be past menopause? Hell if he knew. He searched their bathroom but didn't find any personal products in any of the cabinets. The guest bath? Ellie had nieces who came to visit occasionally. Maybe . . .

In the guest bath closet he found extra toilet tissue, toothpaste and soap, disposable razors, even cellophane-wrapped toothbrushes. Pads and tampons. Thank God for Ellie. He grabbed the box of pads.

Laura was sitting on the lid of the toilet, hugging her waistline, staring into near space, rocking back and forth. He set the items on the counter, then crouched in front of her. She was still wrapped in the towel. He saw the goose bumps on her bare arms and legs. "I'm sorry I took so long."

"You didn't. It's all right."

"You're cold." He placed the thick robe around her shoulders. "Put your arms in." He guided her arms into the sleeves, then pulled the robe together over her chest, towel and all.

"Thank you."

"What else can I do?"

"Nothing."

He remained squatted down in front of her, staring into her face. "Are you sure . . . Maybe . . ." She shook her head, cutting him off, severing his hope.

Fresh tears spilled over her eyelids and rolled down her cheeks. "There was a lot. Too much for it to be a false alarm."

"You should go to the hospital. Call your doctor at least."

"In a day or so, I'll go to the doctor. I know they have to make sure that it all came out." She swallowed hard, he thought probably to hold back sobs. "I'll be okay. I have to get through this part. It's not pleasant, but . . ." She swiped at the tears on her cheeks. "This happens all the time. One out of every ten pregnancies. Something like that."

But it doesn't happen to you. And not to me. This was a sorrow they shared. He touched her cheek, but she yanked her head back and stood up. "I need privacy now."

"Can't I—"

"No. There's nothing you can do. Just . . ." She motioned for him to leave.

Her rejection made him feel like he had fangs and claws. His merest touch was a violation to her tender, feminine flesh. His size and sex suddenly felt incriminatory. He didn't know why that was, but he felt burly and awkward and blameworthy as he stood up and backed into the open doorway. He went out and pulled the door closed behind himself.

When she came out, Griff was sitting on the edge of the bed, his elbows on his knees, his head in his hands, his fingers making tunnels through his hair.

Hearing her, he looked up, his expression bleak. She felt self-conscious, wrapped from chin to ankles in the pink terry-cloth robe that belonged to a woman she'd never met. He'd found underwear for her. Sanitary pads. Even with her husband, she'd never shared moments as personal as the last few she'd shared with Griff Burkett.

He said, "It's my fault, isn't it?"

"Your fault?"

He came to his feet. "In the hotel, I was rough with you."

"No, you weren't."

"Yes, I was. I manhandled you. Then I forced you to run, made you crawl through a wall on your belly, dragged you—"

"It wasn't your fault, Griff."

"Like hell! It wouldn't have happened if I'd left you alone. You'd still have your baby if you were safe inside your hotel room, not on this damn fool's mission of mine."

"Listen," she said softly, hoping to calm him. "I've been feeling twinges for several days. I was spotting on the morning of Foster's funeral. That's normal during early pregnancy. I thought it was caused by stress, the shock of his death. I ignored it. But the cramps and spotting were signals. It would have happened no matter what, Griff." She could tell by his expression that she hadn't persuaded him.

"Are you still bleeding?"

"Some. I think I've already expelled the . . ." Unable to bring herself to say it, she ended with "I think the worst of it is over."

"So, you're going to be okay?"

"Don't worry about me. I'm sorry I caused you this delay."

"Delay?"

"Manuelo."

"Oh. Right."

"Do you know how to get to Itasca?"

He looked at her like he didn't understand the question, then said, "South on 35 out of Fort Worth. I'll find it."

"How long will it take you?"

"I don't know. Hour and a half maybe."

"And if you do find Manuelo, how are you going to convince him to come back with you? He doesn't even speak English."

"I'll make myself understood."

"He'll be scared. When he sees you, God knows what he'll do."

"I can take care of myself. Can you?"

"I'll be all right."

"Can I get you anything before I go?"

"I can't think of anything."

He turned his head away. "Yeah, okay." He was speaking in a clipped voice, lightly slapping his palms against the outsides of his thighs, anxious to be away. "I would stay, except—"

"No, you must go. Actually, I'd prefer to be alone right now."

"Sure. Understandable." He plowed his fingers through his hair and walked in a tight circle, then whipped the bedspread back. "Lie down. Sleep."

"I will. Be careful."

"Yeah."

He turned abruptly and left the room, pulling the door closed, not loudly but soundly. She heard the door connecting the hallway to the living room being opened, then shut.

Knowing she was finally alone, she sagged under the weight of her heartache. She lay down on the bed, turned onto her side, and drew herself into a tight ball. Then, burying her face in the pillow, she opened the floodgate that had been tenuously holding back her emotions.

Her sobs were so intense, they shook her whole body. So when the mattress dipped, she didn't trust herself to believe that he had come back. She didn't let herself accept it until she felt his hand stroking her shoulder and heard his whispered "Shh, shh."

He'd made it as far as the back door. He'd even taken hold of the doorknob. His future, possibly his life, depended on finding Manuelo Ruiz before Rodarte did. It was in his best interest to leave now, drive as fast as he could to that dot on the map, and rout out the only individual in the world who could save him from being convicted of murdering Foster Speakman.

Besides that, Laura had rejected his help. She'd practically pushed him out the door. No mystery there. It was his fault that she'd lost the baby. Earlier tonight, when she told him it was for real, that she was pregnant, he'd thought: *Finally.* For the first time in his life, he'd done something right and good.

He should have known that it wouldn't last, that he would somehow mess it up. Anyway, it was over. The baby was lost, and there was nothing he could do about it now.

Go! Go! Turn the freaking doorknob.

He was moving back through the living room before he fully realized he'd made an about-face. He heard her sobs when he opened the door into the hallway. The sight of her huddled inside the pink robe, weeping into the pillow, made his heart feel like something had pinched it, hard.

He lay down behind her and touched her shoulder. "Shh, shh."

"You need to go," she moaned.

"No, I need to be here with you. I want to be." Placing his arm across her waist, he scooped her back against him.

"You can't let Rodarte—"

"I can't leave you. I won't." He pressed his face into the nape of her neck. "I'm sorry, Laura. God, I'm so sorry."

"Please stop saying that, Griff. Stop thinking it. This wasn't your fault. It wasn't anyone's fault. It was nature's way of saying something wasn't right. I was only seven weeks pregnant. It wasn't even a baby yet."

"It was to me."

She raised her head. Her swimming eyes found his. Then with a long, mournful sound, she turned toward him and pressed her face against his chest. His arms went around her, drawing her to him, holding her close, tucking her head beneath his chin. He sank his fingers into her hair and massaged her scalp.

She wept and he let her. It was a female thing, a maternal thing. The tears were essential, cleansing, as necessary for healing as the bleeding. He didn't know how in hell he knew that. He just did. Maybe in times of crisis, you were graced with superior insight like that.

When her crying finally subsided, she tilted her head back against his biceps. "Thank you for coming back."

"I couldn't leave."

"I didn't want you to."

"You pushed me away."

"To keep myself from begging you to stay."

"Honestly?"

"Honestly."

He looked deeply into her eyes. "They're pretty."

"What?"

"Your eyes. When you cry, your eyelashes stick together in dark spikes. They're pretty."

She gave a soft laugh and sniffed. "Yes, I'm sure I look radiant right now. But I appreciate the sweet talk anyway."

"It's not sweet talk. I don't make sweet talk."

She hesitated a moment, then tucked her face back into his neck. "You've never had to. Have you?"

"I never wanted to."

"With Marcia?"

"She was paid to sweet-talk me."

"And with me, it certainly wasn't necessary. With or without it, you were being paid."

He placed his finger beneath her chin, forcing her to look at him. "Do you think that on that last day I was thinking about the money? Or making a baby? No. I broke every speed limit to get there for only one reason, to see you. That afternoon had nothing to do with anything except you and me. You know that, Laura. I know you do."

Slowly, she nodded.

"Well, good." They smiled gently at each other.

She was the first to speak. "You're not rotten."

He laughed. "We're back to that?"

"Did you ever look for your parents? What happened to them after they abandoned you? Do you know?" He didn't say anything for such a long time that she said, "Forgive the questions. You don't have to talk about it."

"No, it's okay. It's just ugly."

But she continued to look into his eyes, hers inquiring.

He supposed she was entitled to know just how ugly it was. "My old man died of alcoholism before he was fifty. I tracked my mother to Omaha. Right before I checked in to Big Spring to start serving my sentence, I worked up enough nerve to call her. She answered. I heard her voice for the first time in, hmm, fifteen years.

"She said hello again. Impatiently, like you do when you answer the phone and the caller doesn't say anything but you can hear them breathing. I said, 'Hey, Mom. It's Griff.' Soon as I said that, she hung up." Although he'd tried to form a callus around it, the pain of that rejection was still sharp.

"It's funny. When I was playing ball, I used to wonder if she knew I'd become famous. Had she caught me on TV, seen my picture on a product or in a magazine? I wondered if she watched the games and told her friends, 'That's my son. That Pro Bowl quarterback is my kid.' After that call, I didn't have to wonder anymore."

"Your call caught her off guard. Maybe she just needed some time to—"

"I thought the same thing. Glutton for punishment, I guess. So I hung on to that phone number. For five years. I called it a few weeks ago. This guy answered, and when I asked for her, he told me she'd died two years ago. She had a lot of pulmonary problems, he said. Died slow. Even knowing she was going to die, she made no attempt to contact me. Truth is, she simply never gave a shit about me. Not ever."

"I'm sorry, Griff."

He shrugged. "Doesn't matter."

"Of course it matters. I know how bad it hurts. My mother abandoned me, too." She told him about her father. "He was a real-life hero, like a character in the movies. His death shattered Mom and me, but eventually I recovered. She didn't. Her depression became debilitating, to the point where she wouldn't even get out of bed. Nothing I said or did made her better. She didn't want to get better. One day she put herself out of her misery. She'd used one of Daddy's pistols and left herself for me to find."

"Jesus." He pulled her close and kissed her hair.

"For the longest time, I felt that I had failed her.

But now I realize that she failed me. Even though this baby was infinitesimal, only weeks from conception, I felt fiercely protective of it, Griff. I wanted to guard it from being hurt, emotionally as well as physically. How could a parent, any parent, relinquish the parental instinct to nourish and protect her child?"

He drew a deep breath and let it out slowly. He didn't have an answer. He'd been asking that about his mother for as far back as he could remember. "I should have been up-front with you about my background. But I was afraid that if I was, you'd think I was the bad seed and choose someone else as a surrogate."

"I admit I didn't think too highly of you at first."

"Tell me," he said, a smile behind his voice.

"My opinion of you changed when you brought the lubricant."

"You're kidding."

"No."

"I didn't want to hurt you again."

"Hmm, and got very upset when you discovered I hadn't used it."

"Yeah, but what really made me mad was that you thought I wouldn't mind hurting you."

"So you said. Your angry reaction changed my opinion of you. You cared much more than you wanted to show. I saw that you weren't nearly as rotten as people think. As *you* think."

"Don't go pinning any medals on me, Laura. You were still another man's wife, but I started looking forward to being with you. I wouldn't admit it, even to myself. But I did. It was his idea, and every time you met me, it was because he insisted on it. But after that day you had the orgasm, I stopped kidding myself."

"So did I," she confessed softly. "I knew it would be dangerous to be alone with you again. That's why I told Foster I wouldn't go back. But I did. And, despite everything that's happened, I can't honestly say I'm sorry I did."

He came close to saying something then, making some kind of profession, the likes of which he'd never thought he would make to another human being. But the timing was off. Way off.

Instead, he took her hand and laid it against his chest, pressing it close to his heart. She wouldn't know, couldn't know—for him, who never invited a touch—how significant that small gesture was. But he knew.

She said, "I always wondered . . ."

"What?"

Looking chagrined, she shook her head. "Never mind."

"What?"

"What you used."

"Used?"

"To . . . you know. While I was in the bedroom, waiting. I always wondered what you did, what you used to get aroused."

"Oh," he said around a soft laugh. "I used you."

"Me?"

"The first time we met there, you had on a soft pink top under your ball-breaker's suit."

"I beg your pardon."

"You were wearing the kind of business suit that said you wanted to be taken seriously. Seen as an equal in the workplace, not as a woman. But it didn't work, because to me you still looked like somebody I wanted to have sex with. Especially that top. It was about the color of this robe."

"I know the one."

"So to get it up, I thought about your breasts under the top, all soft and warm. Thought about sliding my hands up under your top and touching them. And that did it."

"Just that?"

"Well, there may have been some flashes of tongue against nipple," he added, grinning unrepentantly. "And the times after that, I thought about you, lying in there, prim on the top, nothing on the bottom, waiting for me. Worked every time. Of course, that last day was different."

"Yes."

He touched her lips with the backs of his fingers. "The hardest thing I've ever had to do was let you leave and go back to him."

"I think he knew something had happened that afternoon. Something shattering for me. When I got home that evening, he acted strangely. I was undone, and he knew it. He was almost taunting me."

Easing him away from her, she turned onto her back and stared up at the ceiling. "I've come to realize that all this—you, the baby, all of it—was Foster's way of punishing me for being at the wheel when he was injured."

"How could he blame you? It was an accident."

"That's just it, Griff. He didn't believe in accidents. You have to understand his OCD. Everything had to be done in sequence and in a particular way. No deviation whatsoever. He believed that any change in the order of things resulted in calamity.

"He wanted to drive home that night because he'd driven us there. But I said no because he'd had more to drink than I had. I interrupted the sequence, and what happened was a consequence of that. He never blamed me out loud. But I think now that he did inside. He must have harbored a deep resentment that became corrosive."

Griff was glad she was talking this through. She needed to, more for herself than for him.

"I could have conceived a child by going the clinical route, using a donor. Foster used his OCD as an excuse not to. But that wasn't the reason. I see that now. I loved him purely and exclusively, and he knew that. Our marriage was sacred and precious to me. I valued it above everything. So he devised a way to weaken it, if not destroy it altogether."

"Like his legs."

"Like his legs. Morally, he knew how I felt about his plan. I told him time and again I thought it was wrong, but he wouldn't take no for an answer. He played upon my being an overachiever, never backing away from a challenge or task. I can see now how deftly he manipulated me. He appealed to what he knew would get me to agree."

"Then he put you in bed with me, a pariah, a man you couldn't admire and wouldn't like."

"No," she said with a sad smile. "There you're wrong. He chose you because you were handsome and strong, unquestionably masculine. You'd been abstinent for five years. I'd been for two. How could each of us not become attracted to the individual who was giving us what we'd been missing? He *wanted* us to be attracted. Especially me. So that, in my heart, I would be committing adultery, violating the marriage vows I'd held so dear."

What she was saying made sense. Or it would have to the twisted mind of Foster Speakman. "Once the child was conceived and I was dead, you would feel the loss, along with the guilt."

"I think that's what he had in mind."

"You believe me? Everything I told you about how he died? Without question?"

"It's hard to think this way about my husband, but yes, Griff, I believe you. Your death was part of his plan. The perfect punishment. I would never be able to look at the child without thinking of you and remembering my sin. My infidelity would never have been acknowledged as such, but I would have spent the entirety of my life trying to make up for it." After a long moment, she turned on her side again to face him. "We dragged you into a terrible mess. I apologize for that."

"You didn't drag me, I jumped in willingly, with far fewer scruples than you. I was after the easy money. Lots of it. Even Rodarte said that a hustler like me would—"

"Rodarte!" She sat bolt upright and gave him a shove. "You've got to go now."

"I can't leave you."

"You have to, Griff. I'm fine. But I won't be if you stay with me instead of finding Manuelo. You must go. You know I'm right."

He did know that. Regretfully, he got off the bed, then bent down to stroke her hair. "You're sure you'll be okay with . . . everything." He motioned toward her middle.

"I'll be fine."

"Stay in bed. Try to sleep." He kissed her lips lightly. "I'll be back as soon as I can." Before he could talk himself out of going, he turned.

Coach and Ellie were standing in the open doorway. In his loudest sideline voice, Coach bellowed, "What the hell are you doing in my house?"

CHAPTER
36

HERE'S THE THING, RODARTE TOLD HIM-self. Griff Burkett had successfully (a) lured or (b) kidnapped Laura Speakman from the hotel. He had escaped arrest at her mansion. He was driving an unknown vehicle. Basically, he was in pretty good shape to elude capture for a while longer, maybe even enough to get far away.

So why had he used the Speakman broad's cell phone to call him, knowing that Rodarte would be able to track the call and mark their location? Sure, Burkett had been smart enough to leave the phone in that theater parking lot, but why take such a risk in the first place?

Burkett wouldn't. Not unless he had something to say that was mighty important, something that he felt would get him off the hook completely.

Rodarte sat in his car on the shoulder of the interstate and smoked half a pack—fuck quitting—before determining that Burkett hadn't been play-acting. He'd sounded excited and definitive. Burkett believed that Lavaca Road in Itasca was a link to Manuelo Ruiz, whom he claimed had killed Speakman accidentally. Meaning Burkett was innocent.

It must be true. If Ruiz *had* witnessed Burkett murdering Speakman, Burkett would be racing down to Itasca to silence the man, not calling Rodarte and telling him where to find him.

Conclusion: Manuelo Ruiz was no longer a footnote in the case. He'd been bumped up to a principal player. His new status called for action.

Rodarte used the redial button on his cell phone. It rang only once before being answered. "Itasca PD."

"This is Rodarte again. Put Chief Marion on."

A few clicks, then, "Detective Rodarte?"

"Anything?"

"Nothing. I got two men still watching the house, though."

"Call them back and cancel the APB on Manuelo Ruiz."

Rodarte sensed Marion's surprise. "Why's that?"

"Somebody screwed up," Rodarte said, faking exasperation. "Dumb computer geeks. Looking for a house address and came up with a route number instead. Got y'all hyped up for nothing. I hope to God they never issue those guys guns."

The other cop chuckled. "Thanks for the call, Detective. I'll pull everybody in, including the sheriff's office. My officers will be disappointed. They thought they were going to get in on something big."

"Not tonight."

"What about Burkett?"

"Still at large."

"Big guy like him, you'd think he'd be easy to spot."

"You'd think."

"Well, we'll keep an eye out."

Rodarte apologized again for the mix-up, said he hoped he hadn't kept Marion and his officers up too late, and told him good-bye. He flicked his cigarette butt out the window, then, smiling, pulled his car onto the interstate and headed toward Itasca.

When he saw the Millers, Griff thought, *The surprises just keep on coming.*

Both had on sandals, shorts, and florid Hawaiian-print shirts. Ellie was wearing a straw hat. A wilted lei drooped from her neck. She looked flummoxed. Coach, in spite of his ridiculous attire, was seething.

Hoping to defuse the impending explosion, Griff said, "Coach, Ellie, this is Laura Speakman."

Coach nudged Ellie aside and bore down on Griff. "The widow? Yeah, we know who she is. We read about Foster Speakman's murder in *The Wall Street Journal* while we were in Hawaii." He shot Laura a look, then his hard gaze swung back to Griff. "Next thing I know, I'm getting a call from a Dallas detective, apologizing for bothering me while I was on vacation, but it was important, he said."

"Rodarte?"

"That's right. Stanley Rodarte. He asked if we knew where you were. Had we had any contact with you? Would we know where he should start looking for you? Why? I asked. Did this have to do with Bill Bandy? Oh no, he said. That's old news. He's looking for you in connection with the Speakman murder. Your fingerprints were on the murder weapon."

"Joe, your blood pressure," Ellie said quietly.

"I told him I didn't know anything about you, what you were doing, where you were, and I didn't want to know. Now I come home and find you all cozy *in bed* with the late millionaire's wife. And it doesn't look to me like she's in mourning."

"Well, you're wrong!" Griff shouted, going toe-to-toe with Coach's anger. "She's mourning the loss of her baby. *My* baby," he said, thumping his chest. "She miscarried it tonight there in your bathroom."

Ellie made a sorrowful, wounded sound.

"Laura was pregnant by me, but I didn't kill her husband." Griff looked beyond Coach at Ellie. "You've got to believe that." To Coach he said, "It's up to Laura how much she confides in you, but she can tell you that I did not commit murder. I'm on my way now to find the only man who knows that for certain and can keep Rodarte from putting me on death row."

Griff moved toward the door, but Coach planted his hands firmly on Griff's chest, stopping him. "You're not going anywhere. I'm turning you in."

"You can't stop me."

"Oh yeah?" Coach shoved him backward.

"He has to go, Mr. Miller." Laura swung her feet to the floor and got off the bed. "I'll tell you everything you want to know. But Griff didn't kill Foster. In order to prove it, he must leave now."

The older man divided a look between her and Ellie, whose expression indicated that, this once, she had sided against him. He came back around to Griff, who could tell Coach was warring with himself for reasons he believed to be right and just. "If you're innocent—"

"I am."

"Then turn yourself in."

"I can't. While I'm wading through the formalities, Rodarte might eliminate this other guy."

"Eliminate? What do you mean?"

"Exactly what you think I mean."

"Who is this other guy?"

"Speakman's aide, who's been missing. Coach, there's no time to explain it all now. I've got to go."

Coach stepped back and raised both his hands. "Dig yourself in deeper. See if I care. I wash my hands of you."

"You already did, five years ago."

"Long before that!"

The words hurt, but Griff couldn't dwell on them now. He picked up Manuelo's duffel bag. When he looked back at Laura, he didn't say anything, but he hoped she knew what he felt.

Then he brushed past Coach and left the house in a dead run.

Rodarte located the abandoned farmhouse while dawn was still several hours away. As described, it was the only structure he'd seen since he left town central, and it was practically falling down. He hadn't passed any patrol cars, and none were in sight. Chief Marion, good as his word, had called back the posse.

Rodarte slid his nine-millimeter from his shoulder holster and chambered a bullet, took a flashlight from his glove box, then cautiously got out of his car. He made a circuit around the house, shining the flashlight on the unstable piers holding up the structure and onto the roof, which not only sagged but had large holes. Most of the windows had been broken out. The place was a shambles.

It was surrounded by fallow cotton fields, the earth as flat and black as a griddle. The air was hot and still, and so quiet he could have heard a gnat fart. Neither the approach of his car nor his prowling had flushed out Ruiz or anybody else who might have been hiding inside. He didn't get the feeling that he was being watched through one of the busted windows, either, and his instinct for that kind of thing was excellent.

Minding his step for fear of falling through the rotted planks, he walked across the porch and tried the front door. It swung open on rusted hinges that squeaked. Standing on the threshold, pistol in his right hand, he shone the flashlight around the interior. It stank of mice, living and dead.

There was one main room, with a fireplace full of litter and old ash. Opening off this room were several doorways. He crept to them one by one. Bedrooms. One bathroom. A kitchen. All vacant. No sign of occupancy for at least a decade.

"Fucking waste of time," he muttered. So Burkett had been yanking his chain after all, sending him on a wild-goose chase while he was hustling the widow down to Mexico for some R&R, romance and rutting.

He switched off the flashlight, sat down on a windowsill, and lit a cigarette to smoke while he ruminated on his next move. He blew a plume of smoke through the vacant window frame. Without any wind, the smoke hovered in the air like a ghost.

Rodarte stared through it across a yard of hard-packed, parched earth.

There was a pen that probably had been home to a hog, a goat maybe. Too small for a horse. The posts of a barbed-wire fence either were listing or had already toppled. The wire lay in rusty coils on the ground. Thirty yards or so beyond the fallen fence was a barn that appeared in even worse condition than the house.

The barn.

Rodarte stuck the cigarette between his lips and squinted through the smoke rising off it. He checked his flashlight to see how the battery was holding out. Getting dimmer, but still working. He dropped the cigarette onto the bare wood floor and ground it out.

Outside, he could see well enough without the flashlight. But he kept it in one hand, his pistol in the other, as he went around the house to the back. The yard was an obstacle course. An abandoned wheelbarrow lay on its side. A tree stump obviously used as a chopping block still had the hatchet embedded in it. The shadowed hulk under an attached lean-to turned out to be a disemboweled tractor.

He stepped over the fence, carefully avoiding the lines of barbed wire, and walked toward the barn. The double doors were closed but held together only by a wooden latch that pivoted on a nail. He flipped it up and pushed the door open just wide enough for him to peer inside. The darkness was penetrating. The stifling air smelled of manure and soured hay.

Sensing no movement or sound, he opened the door wider and slipped inside. He switched the flashlight on and shone it around. His knowledge of barns was limited to what he'd seen in movies, but in his uneducated opinion, this one was fairly standard. A loft running the length of one side. Horse stalls. Tack and farm implements.

And Manuelo Ruiz.

Or somebody.

Instinctually, Rodarte knew he wasn't alone. And for one split second, he felt a pang of fear. *It could be Burkett.* Burkett might have set him up. Burkett might have sent him here to be ambushed. Had he been outsmarted by that cagey son of a bitch?

Before Rodarte could complete the thought, he sensed movement behind him. As he turned, a hard blow landed on his shoulder, numbing his arm and hand. He dropped the flashlight. With his other arm, he swung a wide arc that ended abruptly when his palmed pistol connected with the side of his at-tacker's head.

It wasn't Burkett. Too short, too dark, too thick through the middle. And Rodarte hated himself for the relief that came from knowing that.

But he still had a fight on his hands. The man was stunned and staggering but not downed. He ducked his head and lunged toward Rodarte. The detective got a knee up in time to catch the man beneath his chin and practically shoved it up his nostrils. Rodarte heard teeth clack together and figured that some of them had broken. With a grunt of pain, the man fell to the earthen floor.

Rodarte, his momentary fear now replaced by anger, grabbed the flashlight and shone it down, directly into the man's face. It was swarthy, broad, the features flat. The eyes blinking against the beam of light were inky black. They widened marginally when they saw the barrel of Rodarte's pistol aimed directly at them.

"*Hola*, Man-u-el-o."

The man showed a flicker of surprise.

"Yeah, I know your name. We've got a mutual friend. Griff Burkett."

At that, Ruiz rattled off a barrage of Spanish.

"Shut up!" Rodarte barked. Ruiz fell silent. "I'm not interested in anything you have to say. Anyhow, you should save your strength for the job you've got coming up."

Reaching down, he grabbed the man's shirtfront and hauled him to his feet. "See that shovel over there?" He directed the flashlight's beam at the pile of tools he'd spotted earlier. "Get it." Ruiz just stood there looking at him vacantly. "Don't pull that *no comprendo* bullshit on me." He hefted the pistol and clearly enunciated, "Go and get the fucking shovel."

Ruiz's obsidian eyes glittered in the flashlight's beam, but he did as he was told. "Don't even think of trying to clobber me with it," Rodarte said when Ruiz turned with the shovel's handle gripped in both hands. "I'll shoot you right now if you do."

He motioned for Ruiz to go ahead of him through the barn door. Rodarte followed at a cautious distance, the nine-millimeter aimed at the man's spine.

The eastern horizon was turning gray. "Get a move on, Manuelo." Planting his foot against the other man's buttocks, Rodarte pushed him hard enough to cause him to stumble and fall.

Ruiz rolled over onto his back and glared up at Rodarte in a way that made the detective glad he had a gun trained on him. "We'll see how feisty you're feeling after you've put that shovel to good use." Ruiz looked at the shovel, then back at Rodarte, seeming puzzled. "What?" Rodarte asked around a chuckle. "You didn't expect *me* to dig your grave, did you?"

CHAPTER
37

LAURA STARED BACK AT THE TWO PEOPLE staring at her.

She could smell the plumeria blossoms of Ellie Miller's wilting lei. The odor was heavy and sweet. "You just returned from vacation?" she asked.

Ellie replied. "We got into DFW a half hour early. Around four-thirty."

"I'm sorry you had to come back after a long flight to find a stranger in your bed." She gave a soft, humorless laugh. "Like the three bears. How was your flight?"

Ellie crossed to Laura and took her hand. "You're the one who's had a rough night. How're you feeling?"

"I'll be all right."

"Sure you will. But right now it's bad. Cramping?"

"Hmm."

"I know. I went through this four times."

"I'm sorry."

Ellie shrugged philosophically. "Wasn't meant to be." She patted Laura's hand. "I'll get you something for those cramps."

She went out, leaving Laura alone with Coach Joe Miller. He was an intimidating presence. He stared at her, his expression judgmental. Yet he also seemed curious about her, in spite of himself.

"I'm sorry about your baby." He nodded toward the door through which his wife had passed. "Ellie shrugs it off, but her heart broke each time."

"I'm sure it did."

"You're sure it was Griff's baby?"

"No question. My husband was incapable."

"Sterile?"

"Incapable," she repeated.

"Huh." He digested that, then asked, "Is that why you took up with Griff?"

Before she could answer, Ellie returned carrying a bottle of ibuprofen and a glass of water. "Take two."

Laura had already sworn off analgesics that pregnant women were advised not to take. Swallowing the capsules was a painful reminder that the precaution was no longer necessary.

"What are you doing?"

That from Ellie, whose voice was sharp, imperious, and directed toward her husband, who had picked up the telephone on the desk.

"Calling the police."

"You're going to sic the police on that boy?"

"He's not a boy, Ellie. He's a man. He has to be held accountable."

"Please, don't call Rodarte," Laura said. "He's Griff's sworn enemy."

"Because he's a homicide detective and Griff is a . . . a . . ."

"See?" Ellie said, planting her fists on her narrow hips. "You can't even bring yourself to say it because you know it isn't true."

"If it's not true, why's he running?" Coach asked. "Why doesn't he turn himself in?"

Ellie, having no answer, looked helplessly toward Laura, who implored Coach to hang up the phone. "Please don't make that call. At least not until I've told you about Griff and me. And Foster. All of it. Please, Mr. Miller."

He considered her for several moments, then reluctantly replaced the phone and folded his thick arms across his barrel chest. "Well?"

She began with the day Foster first told her of his plan and left nothing out except the most intimate details of the four times she and Griff had been together.

"I never heard anything so outlandish," Coach said. "You're telling me that your husband *paid* Griff to . . . to do that?"

"Regrettably, I went along, for reasons that are too complex to explain now. After I learned I was pregnant, I didn't expect ever to see Griff again."

While she was listening to Laura's story, Ellie's eyes had turned moist. "How did you feel about that? About never seeing Griff again?"

Laura hesitated, then said, "I was conflicted. And because I was, I would never have *allowed* myself to see him again."

Ellie nodded, understanding.

"I would have stayed with my husband forever," Laura continued. "Rearing the child as his, exactly as he wanted."

"So what made it all go south?" Coach asked. "Let me guess. Griff."

"Actually, Foster. I blame myself for not seeing how severe his OCD had become. I think I didn't want to see it. Anyway, it, coupled with the accident, had changed him. He was no longer the Foster I fell in love with. I hoped a baby would bring that Foster back.

"In any case, I was committed to our marriage and our life together. If he hadn't attempted to kill Griff, I would be with him tonight. And Griff wouldn't be a fugitive." She divided a look between them. "I swear everything I've told you is the truth."

She had no doubt that Ellie believed her. Coach was gnawing the inside of his cheek, apparently unconvinced. Suddenly he turned and picked up the telephone.

"Joe, didn't you hear a single word she's said?"

"There's nothing wrong with my ears, Ellie."

"Then how can you—"

"Because I know Griff," he said. "He's always looked out for number one. He's never given a damn about anyone except himself. You, me, his teammates. Nobody."

"You're wrong," Laura said.

"He may have been a little selfish before," Ellie said. "But he's different now. I saw the change in him when he was here. And if you weren't so damn stubborn, Joe Miller, you'd—"

"Mr. Miller, please," Laura said. "You'll regret—"

"I'm calling the police." He shouted it over their chorused protests, slicing his hand through the air. "Now that's all there is to it."

There wasn't much traffic to slow Griff down. Rush hour at its heaviest was a couple hours away. He made good time to the Itasca exit. The town still slumbered, but he crawled through it, heeding speed limit signs, not wanting to get stopped now.

It wasn't difficult to find Lavaca Road. He continued along it until it turned into FM 2010, a narrow, rutted road that seemed to have been traveled so infrequently as to have become completely overlooked.

After a couple miles, he began to fear that he and Laura had been wrong. But then he spotted a dilapidated farmhouse and barn, showing up as smudged shadows against a sky just turning pastel with the rising sun. But he knew he had the right place.

Rodarte's car was parked in front.

Griff slowed and turned in to the gravel driveway, spotting them instantly—two dark figures silhouetted against the glow in the eastern horizon. He rolled to a stop, turned off the engine, and opened the car door. The early morning atmosphere was soft and silent, deceptively benign.

Keeping the two men in sight, he reached into the duffel bag and took out the policeman's pistol. Impersonating a deliveryman, incapacitating the cops, his and Laura's madcap escape from the estate, all seemed a long time ago. Those recollections were blurred.

But vivid in his memory was the look on her face when she realized that the baby was lost.

If . . . if . . . if . . .

There were so many of them, he didn't even know where to begin regretting.

But one big *if* remained: if he didn't live through this, he hoped Laura knew that he loved her. Bad timing or not, he wished he'd said it when he'd had the chance.

He stuffed the pistol into the back waistband of the navy blue work pants he was still wearing. When he got out, he left the car door open, just in case he had to make a quick getaway. He walked along the exterior wall of the house toward the rear, realizing what a large and easy target his white T-shirt made against the faded clapboard. Rodarte and Manuelo Ruiz stood as still as scarecrows in the fallow field.

But then Rodarte raised his arm and waved. "Hiya, Griff."

Griff disliked guns. Didn't know much about them. Knew even less about police-issue pistols. But as he crossed the littered yard and walked toward the other two men, he was comforted by the weight of the pistol at the small of his back.

He had to step over a barbed-wire fence that had been knocked down. Dirt clods and fossilized tractor tracks made the ground uneven. But he didn't look down. He kept his gaze fixed on Rodarte. When he got close enough to make out the detective's features, Griff saw that he was smiling with amusement as he held his pistol aimed at Manuelo.

The tableau confirmed what Griff had feared— Rodarte didn't plan to use Manuelo Ruiz as an eyewitness. Even if Griff allayed Manuelo's fear and persuaded him to return to Dallas and tell the truth about Foster Speakman's accidental death, Rodarte would never permit it. Because Rodarte didn't want Griff to be exonerated. He didn't even want him locked away for good. He wanted him dead.

And now Griff understood why. He knew why Rodarte had been waiting for him outside Big Spring FCI. He understood why he'd been tailing him and monitoring his every move since his release. He'd thought Rodarte was trying to scare him into making either a mistake or a confession. Fact was, Rodarte was scared of him.

The ground at Rodarte's feet was littered with cigarette butts. At Manuelo's feet lay a shovel. Behind him were a mound of freshly turned dirt and a wide hole. The implication sickened Griff. The bastard had made the Salvadoran dig his own grave while he stood there, smoking and smiling.

Probably, Griff thought, he and Manuelo would share the grave.

Manuelo stood as still as a statue carved of teak. His eyes were as hard and impenetrable as polished stones. Griff couldn't tell if he was afraid, resigned, or waiting for an opportunity to pounce. He had no idea what his arrival would signify to the Salvadoran. He wished he had the Spanish-language skills to tell him that Rodarte was their common enemy, *not each other.*

"I was beginning to think you weren't coming," Rodarte said when Griff halted about ten yards away from him.

"You were expecting me?"

"Hoping. What kept you? Bet I know." He winked. "The widow's hot snatch. Hope you got a piece of it, 'cause it'll be your last." Leer still in place, he said pleasantly, "Hand over the pistol."

"Pistol?"

"You want a knee blown out?"

"You can't aim at both of us at the same time. If you take your gun off Manuelo, he'll be on you before you can blink."

"Okay. What say I shoot him first, then blow your knee out just for giving me lip?"

Griff reached behind his back.

"Easy."

With exaggerated slowness, Griff pulled the pistol from his waistband. He could kill Rodarte without remorse. Marcia was reason enough, not to mention the rest of it. But even with a fatal wound, Rodarte might have time to get off one shot. Griff couldn't risk Manuelo dying. He still needed the aide's testimony about Speakman. He held the pistol far out to his side.

"Toss it over."

Griff did as told. The pistol landed among the butts at Rodarte's feet. "Thanks. Now we can all relax."

Nodding in Manuelo's direction, Griff said, "Let him go."

"No, I don't think so."

"He'll head straight for El Salvador. You'll never see him again."

"Probably. But why should I lose sleep over it? He might develop a guilty conscience about running out on you."

"So you know he killed Speakman?"

"Must have, or you wouldn't have told me where he was at."

"I realized that mistake too late."

"Lost your famous timing, Number Ten?" The detective formed a sad face. "Gee, that's too bad. And just when you needed it most."

"Let him go. Your quarrel is with me, not him."

Rodarte chuckled. "Well, you've got that right."

"You want me to go down."

"What gave me away?"

"You want me to go down for Bill Bandy. But not because you think I killed him. You know I didn't."

Rodarte grinned. "You're getting warmer."

"You know I didn't because you did."

"And they call jocks dumb." He snorted. "Of course, it did take you five years to figure it out."

"The Vista boys hired you to muzzle him permanently."

"It was sort of an audition. There was word going around that Bandy's days were numbered. The Vista trio were afraid he was going to turn them over like he did you. I'd been wanting to do some moonlighting for them, but they're a tight little clique. It's hard to win their trust."

"So you seized an opportunity."

"I offered my services."

"Thinking that if you rid them of Bandy, they'd welcome you into their fold and put you on their payroll."

Rodarte beamed his ugly smile. "Who better to help out with problems like Bandy than a homicide detective who can steer murder investigations in the wrong direction?" He began to laugh, deep inside his chest, then out loud. "It was a great plan, and then it got even better. Swear to God, Burkett, when you showed up at Bandy's place, I nearly pissed my pants. I couldn't have planned it any better."

"You were there when I arrived."

"In the back room. Before I snapped his neck, he swore up and down he didn't have a secret stash, but have you ever known a bookie who didn't lie? If I returned some skimmed funds to Vista in addition to getting rid of Bandy, think how pleased they'd be.

"So I was back there tossing the place when I heard the door. You came barging in like a bull elephant with a grudge to settle. When I realized it was you, I could barely contain a fit of the giggles. While you were woe-is-me-ing over Bandy's body, I sneaked out back."

"And called in an anonymous 911."

"At a pay phone around the corner. Soon as it went out over dispatch, I radioed in, said I was in the neighborhood, volunteered to check out the alleged homicide." He grinned. "You know the rest."

"You had a golden opportunity to kill me, too. Why didn't you?"

"I was afraid to, afraid that would piss off the Vista boys. I thought they might have special plans for you, and it wouldn't sit too well if I robbed them of the pleasure. In hindsight, I should have taken you out."

"Those five years were awfully long for me, but they must have been torture for you," Griff said. "As long as I was alive, you were vulnerable. You've been scared shitless I would figure it out. That's why you've been hassling me, pretending you were acting on behalf of Vista, knowing all along I hadn't stolen from Bandy. You didn't find anything in his back room, did you?"

Rodarte shrugged. "Maybe he wasn't lying after all."

"You're still not in Vista's fold. Apparently they weren't impressed."

"Not yet."

"But you're hoping that killing me now will win their approval."

"It can't hurt. They don't like you."

"They like you even less."

"We'll see." He laughed abruptly. "You know what's really funny? I didn't even have to bring about your downfall. You did that all by yourself. Fucking a paraplegic's wife. That's low, Burkett. Even for the likes of you. The only thing," he said, pulling his face into a pucker of concentration. "What was that half mil for? Was he trying to buy you off?"

Griff just stood, glaring at him.

"Not going to tell me? Okay. Doesn't matter anyway." He leaned forward and casually picked the pistol off the ground, then turned and fired a bullet directly into Manuelo's chest.

Without a sound, the Salvadoran fell backward into the makeshift grave.

CHAPTER
38

GRIFF GAVE A STRANGLED CRY AND LURCHED forward. "You killed him!"

"Not me, Burkett. You." Rodarte pitched the pistol toward the open grave, where it landed in the dirt. "You ran the man down. By the way, remind me to ask Mrs. Speakman how you learned about this place. Anyway, you ran Ruiz down here, forced him to dig his own grave, then, using the weapon of a policeman you assaulted, you shot Ruiz in cold blood so he couldn't testify against you at Foster Speakman's murder trial."

Griff was still staring at the empty spot where Manuelo had been standing seconds before. He looked at the pistol, much too far away to retrieve. His gaze coming back to Rodarte, he held up his clean hands. "They'll know I didn't fire the pistol."

"Oh, you will. After you're dead. Don't worry. I'll set it up to look convincing."

"Laura knows the truth."

Rodarte winked. "I have ways that'll convince her otherwise."

Forgetting every rule of self-preservation, Griff lunged.

Rodarte reacted, getting off two shots before Griff grabbed the wrist of his gun hand and wrenched it. Rodarte screamed in pain and dropped the pistol.

Payback time, Griff thought as he slugged Rodarte hard in the mouth. He swung his left fist at the detective's cheekbone and felt the skin split. But his satisfaction was short-lived because of the pain in his left shoulder, like a branding iron being gouged deep into the flesh. Only then did he realize that he'd been struck by one of Rodarte's bullets. However, the pain only fueled his rage. He struck mercilessly.

Rodarte fought back with a vengeance. He landed a punch in Griff's gut, and when Griff staggered back, Rodarte sidestepped and threw another at his kidney. The angle wasn't good, so the blow didn't have full impact, but it was enough to cause Griff's knees to buckle.

He caught himself before he fell and, acting reflexively, kicked backward, connecting solidly with Rodarte's shinbone. That slowed the detective down long enough for Griff to come around to face him again and catch a fist in his ribs rather than his kidney.

They hammered at each other until Griff lost all sense of time and place, till his hands hurt almost more than the bullet wound, more than any other bleeding part of him. Rodarte's mouth was a ghoulish maw, from which he continually spat blood. His eyes were crazed with hatred. And Griff knew that Rodarte would fight till one of them was dead.

Not long ago, he would have thought, *Fine. I'll kill the bastard, or he'll kill me, and either way it won't matter much.* But now he wanted to live. He wanted to live for a long time, and with Laura. That hope kept him fighting even after the fight had gone out of him and every effort was tremendous.

The sweetest sound he'd ever heard was the wail of sirens. They were coming from far away but rapidly approaching. While they were a relief to Griff, they seemed to madden Rodarte and renew his flagging strength and determination.

He bared his blood-covered teeth and charged. Griff feinted left, then right. Rodarte plunged forward headlong, tripped over a deep rut made by a tractor tire, and fell face-first into a nest of coiled barbed wire.

He shrieked like a banshee, but later Griff wondered if it was from the pain caused by the vicious barbs, or from fury over being defeated.

Griff stood watching as Rodarte struggled to free himself, but his frantic attempts to escape the wire only increased its hold on him. The barbs became embedded in his clothing, his flesh.

The sirens were closer now. Griff shouted down at Rodarte. "Stop fighting it! It's over!"

"Fuck you!"

Miraculously, the detective managed to roll onto his back, but he was wrapped in wire. Strands of it were stretched taut across his face, the barbs digging deeply into his contorted features. Still his arms and legs thrashed. He managed to get a knee up, although his shoe was trapped in a snare of wire.

"Give it up, Rodarte," Griff gasped as he wiped his bleeding nose. "For God's sake."

The sirens couldn't have been more than half a mile away. Griff scanned the road for the approaching police cars. Across the flat, fallow fields, he saw the flash of colored lights. One minute, two at the outside and—

"Kiss your ass good-bye, Number Ten."

Rodarte was aiming a small pistol up at him; only now Griff could see the ankle holster beneath his pants leg. The detective was bleeding from countless puncture wounds, but he seemed unaware of them. The hand holding the pistol was scraped and bleeding. But the finger around the trigger was steady, and so was his aim. The wire across his face made his ugliness even more grotesque. Although it had pinned down one side of his mouth, he still managed a distorted smile.

Griff registered all this in a millisecond. He knew this was his last heartbeat. His final thought was of Laura.

And then Rodarte's smile went slack. He gave a short cry at the same instant Griff was knocked to the ground. Manuelo Ruiz was a blur moving past him, and so was the edge of the shovel as it arced down from high above the Salvadoran's head directly into Rodarte's cranium, cleaving it in two.

After talking almost nonstop for an hour, Griff settled tiredly against the hospital pillow and stared at the acoustical ceiling tiles. His new lawyer, who'd come recommended by Glen Hunnicutt, spoke from across the room. "Gentlemen, my client has an-

swered all your questions. I suggest you leave now
and let him get some rest."

The two Dallas detectives ignored the lawyer
and remained where they were. Griff supposed they
were waiting to see if he had anything to add. One
of them was gray haired, taciturn, and weary looking, a veteran. The other was younger than Griff.
More aggressive and edgy than his partner, he'd
done most of the talking.

Griff couldn't remember their names. He wasn't
real sure about the attorney's. Hunnicutt had made
arrangements with him while Griff was still in surgery to repair the bullet wound in his shoulder,
which had been nasty and painful but not too dam-
aging, certainly not life threatening.

After a lengthy silence, he asked, "Is Ruiz gonna
make it?"

"Seems so," the younger detective replied. "He's
a tough customer, I'll say that for him."

"He is that." Griff could remember how it had
felt having the life squeezed out of him. "He won't
be charged for killing Rodarte, will he?"

The detectives shook their heads in unison. The
younger said, "If he hadn't, Rodarte would have
shot you."

Griff acknowledged that with a small nod.

"That old barn is used as sort of a halfway house
for aliens coming in. When he entered the country,
Ruiz was directed there, told he could obtain false
documents from a guy who'd meet him there. The
papers cost him all the money he had, but with them
he could get work immediately. Immigration officials
are looking for the guys who run that operation."
He paused, then added, "Through the interpreter,

Ruiz also admitted to killing Foster Speakman."

"It was an accident," Griff said.

"That's what he claims."

"It's the truth."

"He said you and he were fighting. Is that correct?"

"Yes."

Since Griff and McAlister—that was his name, Jim McAlister—hadn't had time to confer privately before this interrogation, the lawyer cautioned him now with a soft clearing of his throat. Not that Griff would have blurted out the truth, the whole truth, and nothing but the truth.

The younger detective continued. "Ruiz was a bit sketchy about the cause of that altercation."

Manuelo was being loyal to his late boss. He wouldn't incriminate Speakman by telling the police that he had been ordered by him to kill Griff. Griff saw no point in telling them, either. He kept his poker face.

"You want to shed any light on that, Mr. Burkett?" the younger detective prodded.

"I can't."

"Was there some kind of *thing* between you and Speakman?"

"Before that night, I'd met him only once, and it was a friendly meeting."

"You had no cross words that night?"

"No."

"Did you provoke Ruiz?"

"No. Not intentionally anyway. He attacked me from behind."

"He admitted that," the older detective grumbled. He was frowning, as though confused. Or highly skeptical. "Still doesn't explain why he attacked you."

"I don't know why."

"Come on, Burkett," the younger detective said. "Of course you know. What were you doing there?"

The lawyer cut in. "I'd like a private word with my client before he answers that."

"No, it's okay, Mr. McAlister. I can answer." Griff was betting that the police didn't know about his relationship with Laura. He was gambling that Rodarte had kept that like an ace tucked inside his sleeve, waiting to play it when it would be most advantageous to him and most detrimental to Griff and Laura. He said, "The meeting that night was a second job interview."

"Job?"

"To do endorsements for SunSouth." It was an implausible claim but also impossible for them to disprove.

"What about all that money?"

"Beats me," Griff lied, speaking before McAlister could stop him. "The box was sitting on the desk in plain sight. Speakman told me to open it and look inside. I did. About that time is when Ruiz attacked me. Maybe he thought I was about to steal the cash from his boss. As I said, I don't know what set him off. Whatever it was, he'll regret it for the rest of his life. He worshiped Speakman."

Clearly the detectives believed there was more to it, but that was all they were going to get from him.

Grudgingly, the younger detective said that Ruiz had told them the same story. "He admitted to killing his boss accidentally during his struggle with you, and said that when he ran from the house, you were trying to save Speakman's life. All of which clears you."

Jim McAlister sat back in the vinyl chair, looking complacent.

"Did he also corroborate everything I told you about Rodarte?"

The younger detective nodded. "He didn't understand what the beef was between you and Rodarte, but everything else he told us matches what you said went down at the old farm."

"What about Bill Bandy's murder?" McAlister asked.

"What about it?" asked the older detective.

"For five years suspicion has been cast on my client. He has steadfastly denied any involvement beyond discovering the body."

The detectives glanced at each other in silent consultation over how much they should tell. Finally the younger detective said, "We're inclined to believe Mr. Burkett's allegation against Rodarte. He's been under investigation by Internal Affairs for a while. Many complaints have been filed against him and some of his pals within the department. Too many to ignore. Serious stuff, like harassment, brutality, corruption. One woman suspect claimed Rodarte fondled her while she was in his custody and then got rough with her when she protested."

"Sounds like him," Griff growled. He had hoped to keep Marcia's encounter with Rodarte out of the fray and was now glad to know she could be left in peace.

The younger detective was saying, "Anyhow, Bandy's murder case will be reopened and investigated from a different perspective."

"Am I under arrest?" Griff nodded toward the door of his hospital room, where a uniformed policeman had been posted.

"For the assault on the three police officers in the hotel, as well as for impersonating an officer."

"There were mitigating circumstances," McAlister said.

"Save 'em for the judge at his arraignment," the older officer said. He seemed to hold defense attorneys in no higher esteem than he did the lawbreakers they represented.

"Just be glad you're not being charged with kidnapping," the younger detective chimed in. "According to Mrs. Speakman, when you explained to her that Rodarte was impeding justice, she went willingly to help you locate Ruiz."

Three pairs of eyes were fixed on Griff, waiting to see how he would respond. He said, "Without Mrs. Speakman I would never have found him, and without him I would have been falsely charged with murdering her husband. I'll never be able to repay her trust in me." He paused, then asked what was in store for Manuelo Ruiz.

"Soon as we clear things up with him, and he's well enough to travel, he'll be sent back to El Salvador. He faces charges there. Killed a guy who'd allegedly raped his sister. We figure, let the authorities down there have him. They've got first dibs."

"I wish him well," Griff said, almost to himself.

"Generous of you," the older cop said. "If he hadn't attacked you, you wouldn't be in this mess."

"He also saved my life." Taking a deep breath, Griff closed his eyes and asked tiredly, "Is that it?"

CHAPTER
39

H IS NEW LAWYER TOOK IT FROM THERE.
McAlister ushered the detectives out. He instructed Griff to stay in contact and not to
answer any further questions without him present,
told him to rest, and then he too left.

Griff closed his eyes, but rest eluded him. Although his body was battered and he was exhausted,
his mind wouldn't shut down. Yesterday, he, along
with Manuelo, had been transported by helicopter
to the trauma center at Parkland Hospital, where
both had undergone surgery.

He had vague recollections of being prepped and
a few drug-blurred memories of the recovery room.
This morning he had awakened in this private
room, a little more than twenty-four hours after he
saw Rodarte's skull split open with the sharp edge
of a shovel.

James McAlister, attorney-at-law, had shown up
only minutes ahead of the Dallas detectives. He'd

barely had time to introduce himself and tell Griff that as soon as Glen Hunnicutt had heard about the events in Itasca, he'd called him on Griff's behalf.

Now Griff was relieved to have the interrogation behind him. But it had left him more exhausted than before. His body ached from his fight with Rodarte. His shoulder throbbed. But his mind was unsettled over Laura.

As Foster Speakman's widow, she would once again be in the spotlight while the police and media sorted through the legal detritus left by Burkett, Ruiz, and Rodarte. The speculation that would swirl around her was inevitable. He could only hope for a bigger story to come along that would supplant them as the lead on the nightly news.

But in the meantime, how was she bearing up? Was she well? Beyond the obvious, had she suffered from the miscarriage?

He blamed himself for whatever suffering she had to endure. Things might have turned out differently, her heartbreak might have been avoided entirely, if not for their last afternoon together. If he hadn't stopped her from leaving, as she'd been about to, could everything that had happened since have been prevented?

But—and now was the time for brutal honesty—if he'd had it to do over, would he have let her leave? Or, acting on her hesitation, would he have reached around her and closed the door as he'd done? Thinking back on it, he wondered, would he have let her go? Even knowing what he did now, would he?

He closed his eyes and let his mind drift back to that afternoon, to the sick disappointment he'd felt when she told him she was leaving and never coming back. He hadn't tried to persuade her otherwise. How could he? He had no rights to her. None.

He'd had to stand by helplessly, hopelessly, and watch as she pulled open the door and said, "Depending on circumstances, this could be the last time I'll see you."

"Could be."

"I can't think of anything to say that seems appropriate."

"Small talk seems smaller." Her smile told him she remembered when she'd said those same words to him. "You don't have to say anything, Laura."

"Then, good-bye."

They'd shaken hands, and he'd got the sense that she was as reluctant to let go of his as he was of hers. But she did let go and turned toward the door. When she made no move to go through it, he reached past her and pushed it shut.

He left his hand there for several seconds, giving her time to protest, giving her time to say, *What the hell do you think you're doing? Open the door. I'm leaving.*

When she didn't, he drew his hand back and placed it beneath her chin. With the merest pressure, he brought her around to face him. He looked deeply into her eyes and saw in them the same unspoken, desperate longing he felt, and when he did, he fell on her hungrily, pressing his open mouth against her neck, pinning her to the door with his body. She gave a low moan and reached for him. They kissed wildly, recklessly, with abandon and without finesse.

They brought one month of mental foreplay to this moment.

Her skirt was tight fitting, but he managed to work it up over her hips. He pulled down her panties as far as her knees; then she took over and got rid of them while he dealt with his belt and fly. Cupping her bottom in his hands, he lifted her and positioned her open thighs over his. He touched her. She was ready. In one fluid thrust, he was buried in her completely.

She wrapped her arms around his head and held fast as he fucked her, as much with his mind as with his body. Because of their position, it was impossible to move much, but he rocked against her, pressing as high and hard as he could. *Thinking about* what they were doing, *knowing* that he was at last inside her again, made him burn. And the angle was perfect for her. With each stroke, he grazed the erogenous spot. When he came, so did she. And it was crashing.

For what seemed endless minutes, they clung to each other, their breathing loud in the empty house, their bodies giving off incredible heat. Finally he withdrew and gently set her on her feet. Her arms remained wound around his head, his mouth on her neck. Slowly he kissed his way up to her chin and then let his lips hover above hers for agonizing seconds before settling against them. Her lips parted, accepting his tongue.

It was their first real kiss. It was a perfect kiss. Silky and wet and sweet. Intense. Very sexy. When finally they drew apart, he placed his palms on the door on either side of her head, and rested his fevered forehead against hers. "The past thirty days have been the longest of my life," he said, his voice raspy. "I lived in fear of you calling and saying we wouldn't need to meet again. I was afraid I would never get to kiss you."

She placed her fingers lengthwise over his lips. "If we talk, I have to go," she whispered. "You can't say anything. I can't hear anything."

He pulled back, about to argue, but her expression begged him to understand. And he did. They had to pretend this wasn't personal. Each knew better. They weren't fooling themselves. What had just happened had nothing to do with making a baby or anything else except raw desire. But they could not acknowledge it out loud. The only way she could stay was to pretend that she was doing this because her husband demanded it.

Saying nothing more, they went into the bedroom and began removing their clothes. By the time she got out of her shoes and had taken off her top, he was down to his skin. Unwilling to wait another moment to lie down with her, he stretched out on the bed and pulled her down beside him. Gathering her against him, he held the back of her head in his palm and kissed her until they were breathless.

He undid the front fastener of her lacy bra. Her breasts were lovely, soft, natural. He took the weight of one in his palm, brushed his thumb across the nipple until it was very stiff, then caressed it with his tongue. When he drew it into his mouth, she arched her back and whimpered with pleasure.

Blindly he sought her hand and guided it down. He sighed raggedly when her fingers closed around him, then her thumb, discovering a drop of moisture in the slit, spread it around the glans in slow, mind-blowing circles that were nearly his undoing.

Reaching around her, he unfastened her skirt and pushed it past her hips and down her legs. Naked now, she modestly lay back with her thighs closed, forming a perfect, enchanting V. He leaned down and gently blew on her, then pressed a kiss into the damp curls, teasing, teasing until her thighs relaxed. He moved between them and made slow love to her with his mouth.

It was she who drew her knees back and tugged on his hair until he was lying on top of her and his sex was deep inside her again. This time it was un-hurried, more emotional than passionate. He savored each sensation and made certain she did. When he felt himself getting close, he took her face between his hands and looked down into her eyes, wanting there to be no question that it was he, only he, making love to her, and for only one reason.

He lost count of the number of times they made love that afternoon, because it was one long act, one erotic exchange melding into the next. Though they weren't free to speak, they allowed each other unlimited access.

His lips touched each feature of her beautiful face again and again. He was at liberty to stroke every inch of her skin, to kiss the backs of her knees. He slid his thumb down the groove of her spine all the way to the cleft of her hips, then lay with his cheek resting in the small of her back.

Equally curious, she examined his large hands, tracing the heavy veins on the backs of them, suck-ing his crooked little finger into her mouth. She seemed to like his chest hair. A lot. She nuzzled it frequently. He loved the feel of her breath ruffling through it, loved feeling her fingertips exploring his navel and her knee tucked snugly under his balls, loved feeling her mouth's wet tug until he thought he would die of pleasure.

They were lying quietly, fondling and kissing idly, as satiated lovers do, when she looked at him sadly and pulled away. And he'd had to let her go. There was so much he wanted to say, but he was forbidden to. He wanted to tell her that, for the first time in his whole, misbegotten life, he was in love. He loved, period. He loved her.

"God help me," he whispered now to the walls of his hospital room, "I did from the start."

He must have slept. A slight shift of air roused him. He opened his eyes. Coach was standing just inside the door. He said, "Were you asleep?"

"Just resting my eyes."

He hesitated, then walked to the side of the bed and looked Griff over, his gaze settling on his bandaged shoulder. "How is it?"

"I'll live. Hurts like hell."

"They don't have any pain medication in this hospital?"

"I'm getting it." He raised his hand with the IV port. "It still hurts."

"Any permanent damage?"

"The surgeon says there shouldn't be. If I do my physical therapy."

"Yeah, well, I wish him luck. You always shirked on that."

"She."

"Huh?"

"The orthopedic surgeon is a she."

"Oh." Coach looked around the room, took

note of the TV suspended from the ceiling, the wide window. "Nice room."

"Can't complain."

"Food okay?"

"All I've had is beef broth and lime Jell-O."

"You hungry?"

"Not really."

Having run out of small talk, they were quiet for a time. Then Griff said, "Thank you for not calling the cops on me the other night."

"I did."

Griff looked at him with surprise.

"Despite Ellie's yammering, I put in a call. But not to Rodarte. After being passed around to several detectives, I finally landed one who sounded like he had some sense. I told him what was what, where you were headed, and that the situation had all the makings for becoming dangerous, possibly lethal to somebody. He got in touch with the police department in Itasca and mobilized them immediately."

"So you believed me."

"I believed her."

"Laura."

"I believed every word out of her mouth. You, I still know to be a liar."

"I was not lying! I did not—"

"Hell, I know you didn't kill Foster Speakman or that Bandy lowlife. That's not what I'm talking about."

"Then give me a hint."

"You lied about that game against Washington."

Griff's heart skipped a beat or two. He hadn't seen that coming. He stared at Coach for a moment, then averted his head and mumbled, "What are you talking about?"

"You know goddamn well what I'm talking about." His face red with anger, Coach bent over him until Griff was forced to look him in the eye. "That pass to Whitethorn. That game-throwing pass that got you sent to prison." Coach jabbed the edge of the hospital bed with his index finger. "I know the truth, Griff, but I want to hear you say it, and then I want to know why."

"Say what? Why what?"

Coach fumed. "I've looked at the video of that play till I'm cross-eyed. From every possible angle. In slow motion and fast forward. Time after time after time. A thousand times."

"So has everybody and his grandmother."

"But everybody and his grandmother don't know the game like I do. And not everybody knows *you* like I do. Nobody taught you and coached you like I did, Griff." His voice had turned husky, and if Griff hadn't known better, he would have thought he saw tears starting to form in the older man's eyes. "You couldn't have thrown a better, more accurate pass. You practically walked the football to the two-yard line and laid it in Whitethorn's hands. You put it right between the numbers on his jersey."

He straightened and turned away for a moment, and when he came back around, he said simply, "He didn't catch it."

Griff remained silent.

Coach said, "Whitethorn didn't catch it, but not because you threw a bad pass. He simply dropped the damn ball."

Griff, feeling the pressure of his own emotions, nodded. "He dropped the damn ball."

Breath streamed out of Coach's mouth, sounding like a plug had been pulled on an inflatable toy. It even seemed to Griff that he deflated. "So why in God's name did you lie about throwing that game? Why did you admit to a crime you didn't commit?"

"Because I was guilty. I was guilty as hell. I had every intention of screwing up and losing that game for my own profit. For two million dollars, I was gonna see to it that we lost. But . . ."

He broke off, unable to continue for several moments. When he did, his voice was gravelly. "But when it came right down to it, I couldn't do it. I wanted to win that game. I had to." His hand formed a fist as though trying to grasp the unattainable. "The only hope I had of saving myself was to win that game."

He lay back and closed his eyes, placing himself there on the field. He heard the roar of the crowd, smelled the sweaty jerseys of his teammates as they huddled, felt the tension compressed into a stadium of seventy thousand screaming spectators.

"We're down by four. A field goal won't do. The clock is running out. No time-outs remaining. It's the worst-case scenario, and if that isn't enough, the Super Bowl is riding on this game. We've got time for one more play.

"To cash in from Vista, all I really had to do was let the clock run out, and Washington would have had it. But, coming out of that last huddle, I thought, Fuck those Vista bastards. Fuck their dollars. They may break both my legs, but I'm going to win this championship.

"It all came down to that one play, Coach. One pass. One *choice* that would make me better than the sludge I'd come from. What I did on that play would define my character. My life, actually."

After a moment, he opened his eyes and laughed at the irony. "Then Whitethorn dropped the pass. He *dropped* it!" He scrubbed his face with his hand as though to rub out the memory of seeing his receiver lying on his back in the end zone, his hands empty as the game clock ticked down to double zeros.

"But it really didn't matter. I had sold my soul to the devil anyway. After the loss, I figured I might just as well get paid for it. So when Bandy showed up with my cash, I took it.

"Sometimes I think that maybe the shrink at Big Spring was right, that maybe I wanted to get caught. Anyway, after I was busted, people assumed I'd thrown a pass that was impossible to catch. Whitethorn let them think it. And I let them think it. I was guilty of everything else. I had lied, gambled, cheated, broken the law, pissed on the rules and ethics of professional sports." He smiled wryly. "But I didn't throw that game."

Coach dragged his fists across his damp eyes. "I've waited a long time to hear you say it."

"It feels good to say it. Because the worst part of it, the very worst thing of the whole experience, prison, everything, was knowing how badly I had shamed you and Ellie."

Coach cleared his throat and said gruffly, "We lived through it."

He said it in an offhand manner, as though this moment didn't have any significance. It did, though, and it was huge. Griff hadn't begged his forgiveness, and Coach hadn't granted it. Not in so many words. But that was the understanding that passed between them without it getting sloppy and sentimental. He was in Coach's favor once again. He had his pardon. Maybe even—dare he think it?—his love.

"It would mean a lot to Ellie if you came around more often, let her cook you a meal, fuss over you some, sneak you money she thinks I don't know about."

Griff smiled. "I will. I promise. If I'm not in jail."

Coach frowned. "Over what you did to get Laura away from Rodarte?"

"She told you about that?"

"Yeah, and it's all over the news today. But I don't think the assault charges will stick. Not when it comes out what a threat Rodarte posed, and she'll make sure everyone knows."

Mention of her name brought Laura into the room with them, an intangible but conspicuous presence. Griff looked hard at Coach, who read the unasked questions in his eyes. "She can't come to see you, Griff." He spoke in as soft a voice as he could manage. "Press would be on it like flies on dogshit. There's already been speculation. Raised eyebrows. You know what I'm talking about. Nothing specific, just the suggestion that something between the three of y'all was a little shady.

"Don't forget, it's only been days since she held a very public funeral for her husband. Joe Q. Public doesn't know that Speakman had gone off his rocker, and, for the future of the airline, she'd like to keep it that way. She certainly doesn't want anybody to know what you were hired to do for them."

"She told you about that, too?"

"All of it." Coach shook his head in bewilderment. "Hell of a thing. Never heard of such."

"It's in the Bible."

"Yeah, but Moses also wore a beard to his navel and ate locusts."

"Abraham."

"Well, anyway, Laura said you would understand why she can't come to you now."

"I do understand." Then after a beat. "I love her, Coach."

"I know." At Griff's surprised look, the older man nodded. "The other night, when your whole future depended on chasing down Rodarte and Ruiz, you stayed with her. That wasn't like you, putting somebody else's welfare ahead of your own. You've got to make another sacrifice now, Griff. If you truly care about this lady, you've got to give her time. Distance. Absence from you."

Griff knew that. He understood the necessity. But that didn't make it any easier to accept. "Is she all right?"

"Doing fine. Her worst problem is Ellie."

"Ellie?"

"She's in her mother hen mode. Practically smothering the girl."

Griff smiled and closed his eyes. "She's in good hands."

He must have dozed off again, because when he woke up, Coach was gone. The room was empty. He was alone.

EPILOGUE

GRIFF ANSWERED HIS CELL PHONE ON THE second ring. "Hello?"

"One o'clock today?"

His heart stopped before stuttering into a dangerously rapid beat.

"Can you be there?"

"Uh, yeah. Yes. Yes."

"I'll see you then."

He held the phone to his ear for another thirty seconds before snapping it closed. Then he stood there in the shopping mall, letting other shoppers eddy around him while he reassured himself that he was awake, that he wasn't dreaming, that it had actually been Laura calling.

As with the first time, he arrived at the house easily twenty minutes early. He drove around the neighborhood till twelve fifty-eight. When he got back, her car was in the driveway. He parked behind it.

It seemed a long walk to the front door. He was reaching for the bell when the door opened and she was standing there.

"I heard your car."

For a long time, he didn't speak, just stood there, taking in the sight of her. Finally his joy pushed its way out of his tight chest in the form of a light laugh. "You look terrific."

"Thank you."

"No, I mean it." She was wearing a pink, body-hugging sweater and a pair of black slacks. Simple, elegant, sexy as hell. "Really terrific."

She blushed at the compliment and stepped aside, motioning him in. He walked into the living area that was so familiar, yet completely altered since the last time he'd been here. The house had been transformed into an inviting home.

The armoire he recognized, but the sofa was new. There were additional pieces of furniture, art-work on the walls, magazines and books and an area rug, a bowl of white tulips on the coffee table. For the first time, the shutters were opened, letting in sunlight. It wasn't that cold out, so the low fire in the fireplace was more for ambience than for heat.

He turned to Laura, knowing what she was going to say before she said it. "I live here now."

"I read that you'd sold the mansion. Do you like it here?"

"I love it."

They exchanged a long stare, finally broken when she motioned him toward the sofa. "Would you like some tea?"

"Sure."

"Hot or cold?"

"Cold, please."

He sat down, and she disappeared into the kitchen. Curious, he leaned forward and opened one of the doors to the armoire. There was a TV, some reading material, and recent movies on DVD. Nothing X-rated. He closed the doors and settled against the sofa cushions in what he hoped looked like a relaxed position. In the two hours and eighteen minutes between her call and his arrival, he hadn't known a moment of easy breathing.

She returned carrying a tray with a pitcher of tea and two glasses. She set it on the coffee table and filled a glass for each of them. "Sugar?"

"I'm okay."

She passed him a glass, then carried hers to an armchair where she sat down facing him.

He sipped his tea. She took a sip of hers. But they drank in the sight of each other. He was afraid of starting the conversation, afraid of saying the wrong thing. He didn't know why she had invited him here today. The familiar manner in which she'd called, and the time of day she'd specified, couldn't have been coincidental. Yet she'd done nothing to suggest that this would end the way their past meetings in this house had. She may have simply invited him over for tea.

Eventually he said, "Your airline is going gangbusters. That new Select thing sounds interesting."

"It's scheduled to launch in three months." She laughed as she shook her head. "It's hectic and crazy. So much to do. A million decisions. Daily deadlines."

He smiled over her apparent exuberance. "But you're enjoying it."

"Every minute," she admitted. "I'm very optimistic for its success. We've already sold seventy-eight percent of our membership goal. Through the industry grapevine, I've heard that our competitors are scrambling to initiate similar services."

"Imitation is the sincerest form of flattery."

"Absolutely. But it's still *imitation*. We'll be first."

Her enthusiasm was evident in the way her whole face lit up. Her eyes sparkled. Her smile was so beautiful and uninhibited, it made his heart ache. And he realized this was the first time he'd ever seen her look really happy. Ever.

He raised his glass in a mock toast. "Good luck to you and Select. Not that you need luck. Sun-South's stock is at an all-time high."

"You're monitoring the stock?"

"I'm an investor."

"Truly?"

"Yep. Whatever you're doing, keep it up. It's working."

"I'm very busy and working hard, but I'm also maintaining some balance in my life. I give myself Wednesday afternoons off."

That explained her casual outfit. She wasn't going back to work later. He tried not to read anything into that. Tried but failed.

She watched him closely as she said, "Those Wednesdays off allow me time to devote to other things that are important to me. Like the Elaine Speakman Foundation."

He shifted in his seat. "The foundation. Right. I saw your picture in the newspaper recently. At some black-tie fund-raising event. How'd it go?"

"Very well."

"That's good."

"Beyond the money raised that night, the foundation recently received a sizable donation."

"Oh, yeah?"

"One hundred thousand dollars."

"You don't say."

"Hmm, but it was a rather unusual donation."

"In what way?"

"For one thing, it was made in cash. Hundred-dollar bills deposited directly into the foundation's account."

"Huh."

"Anonymously."

"Huh."

"And the bank handling the deposit said the donor insisted on remaining anonymous."

Griff kept his expression impassive.

"I respect him for keeping such a generous donation private," Laura said. "I only hope he knows how much his gift is appreciated."

"I'm sure he does."

After what seemed to Griff an endless suspension in conversation, she relented with a gentle smile and changed the subject. "You've been staying busy, too."

"You heard about the program?"

"I saw you interviewed about it on TV."

"It's catching on, working out really well."

"You sound surprised," she remarked.

"I am. It just sorta dropped into my lap."

Upon his discharge from the hospital, he had appeared in court and pleaded guilty to the assault charges. Jim McAlister got him released on bail and at his sentencing hearing argued brilliantly on his behalf. His arguments were supported by Laura Speakman's deposition, presented in her absence by her attorney, as well as by the testimony of Internal Affairs officers who had been investigating Stanley Rodarte.

Griff received a stern reprimand from the judge and had a year of probation tacked onto the ones he was already serving. Jerry Arnold remained his probation officer. McAlister and Glen Hunnicutt, who had proved to be a true friend, took Griff out for dinner to celebrate what they considered a victory.

Shortly after that, Bolly Rich had surprised him by inviting him for lunch. He apologized for refusing to listen when Griff tried to warn him about Rodarte. He said he was sorry for refusing to give Griff aid when he most needed it, but mostly for not giving him the benefit of the doubt. "It was two weeks before Jason would speak to me again."

Griff waved off the apology. "Don't worry about it, Bolly."

"You're letting me off the hook too easily."

"I've been let off easily, too."

Then Bolly told him of a program he and other sportswriters across the country had been discussing for a long while. They felt the time had come to implement it. "We're tired of the negativity surrounding sports, college and professional. As much as we write about slam dunks, touchdowns, and home runs, we're forced to report on drug abuse, steroid use, guns and violent behavior, rape—"

"Gambling," Griff said.

"Gambling. We're sick of all that crap. We want

to turn it around, put honor and the ideals of good sportsmanship back into sports. But we're just a bunch of wordsmiths, and I'm the most colorful of the group, if that gives you any idea. What we need is a spokesperson." Uneasily, he added, "And somebody who is squeaky clean wouldn't have much impact."

"You need a poster boy with a catchy slogan like 'Don't fuck up like I did.' "

Bolly grinned. "That sorta captures the gist of our thinking."

"They needed a bad boy like me to talk to young athletes," he explained to Laura now. "With the voice of experience, I warn them against common pitfalls. Bolly and his colleagues rounded up some corporate sponsors to fund the program. The NCAA has lent its full-fledged support. Fellowship of Christian Athletes. Alumni organizations. Sports associations all over the country have scheduled me to speak." He shrugged. "Maybe the talks I give are doing some good."

"You're being modest, Griff. I read just this week in Mr. Rich's column that already they've collected thousands of pledges signed by athletes swearing off steroids, et cetera. Including his own son."

"Jason's a good kid. He probably wouldn't get into all that anyway."

"But others would. Your speeches are making a huge impact."

"We'll see." He grinned at her. "At the very least, I'm chalking up a hell of a lot of frequent flier miles on SunSouth."

"You should sign up for Select."

"Can't afford it. My expenses are covered, and I get a more than decent salary, but I'm not going to get rich, Laura. Ever." He would never be rich like Foster Speakman. Like her. That was what he was telling her. "But I'm working in sports, on the periphery at least. And I'm doing something worthwhile." He smiled. "Sometimes, after I give a speech, they even ask me to toss the football a time or two. Give them pointers. Stuff like that."

"I'm sure those young athletes are dazzled."

"I don't know about that. But I enjoy it."

They were quiet for a time. She glanced out the window, into the fireplace, at the bowl of tulips. "Would you like some more tea?"

"No thanks."

"How is your friend Marcia?"

He was surprised she remembered Marcia. "Doing good. I saw her just last week."

"Oh."

At that Laura's polite smile wavered just a bit. Or maybe he imagined it. "She's got one more surgery scheduled, but it's only for fine tuning."

"The operations were successful, then."

"She looks fantastic. Better than ever."

"That's good. Is she . . . has she returned to . . . work?"

"Full-time."

"Really."

"Yep. Business as usual."

"Hmm."

If she was wondering about the nature of his visit to Marcia, why didn't she come right out and ask? He was hoping she would. He could tell her they were strictly friends now, but at least Laura's asking would indicate she cared about whether he was satisfying his sexual urges with a professional.

Instead, she said, "How were your holidays?"

"Fattening. Ellie cooked like there was no tomorrow. Yours?"

"I went away. Stayed in a bed-and-breakfast in Vermont, drove back roads, read a lot."

"Sounds nice." Sounded lonely.

"Would you like some more tea?"

"You asked me that already, and I said no."

"Sorry. How is your shoulder?"

"Fine."

"All healed?"

"Laura, why did you call me?"

His abruptness surprised her, then she looked chagrined for being caught stalling. She took a deep breath and said quietly, "I wanted to thank you."

His heart plummeted. She really had invited him just for tea. "What for?"

"For keeping our secret. You had so many opportunities to tell the whole sordid story. You didn't. You protected Foster, as well as me. He certainly hadn't earned your confidence. I wanted to tell you how much I appreciated it."

"Well, I didn't exactly want the world to know I'd been your stud for hire."

"Whatever your reason, thank you."

"You're welcome."

He didn't want her goddamn *gratitude*. He had honored his promise to Coach and to himself not to contact her, although not a day had gone by that he hadn't wanted to. So today, after months, when she'd called, he'd thought maybe . . .

But no. While he was sitting here making polite conversation, aching to touch her, wanting to taste her mouth, all she'd wanted was to say *thank you*. He couldn't take any more.

Agitated, he rubbed his palms against his thighs, then abruptly stood up. "Look, I need to run. I've got a . . . thing."

"Oh, I'm sorry." She stood as well. "I didn't mean to keep you."

"No, it's okay. It was good to see you."

"It was good to see you, too."

"Right. Thanks for the tea."

As he turned toward the door, he lightly slapped his side, which served as a reminder. "Oh, I almost forgot. I brought you something." Reaching into the flap pocket of his sports jacket, he took out a small box.

She looked at him quizzically as he passed it to her. "What's this?"

"One way to find out."

She held it, hesitating a moment before pulling the end of the ribbon to untie the bow. He realized he was holding his breath as she removed the lid. Lying on a bed of satin was a tiny gold star with an infinitesimal diamond in its center. She kept her head down, staring at the charm, so he couldn't see her reaction. But she remained so still he began to think this had been a lousy idea.

When another moment passed and she still didn't say anything, he tried to justify himself. "It wasn't very far along, I know. Probably no bigger than that diamond. But . . ." He ran his fingers through his hair. "But there's no marker, you know? Nothing to show that it ever existed. And it did. At least for a few weeks."

She kept her head down, didn't move. *Shit! Bad idea. Really,* really *bad.* He should just shut up about it and leave. Instead, he said, "I thought you might like to have something to remember it by."

When she finally raised her head, her face was wet with tears. "I'll always remember it. I'll hold it in my heart for as long as I live."

They moved simultaneously. His arms enfolded her, and he held on like he would never let her go. He might have vowed as much. Afterward, he couldn't remember for sure what declarations he'd made at some later time and which ones he'd made right then, just before cupping her face in his hands and lifting it to his. He did remember telling her he loved her, repeating it as he kissed her lips, her eyes, cheeks, and brow. Finally their lips met and they kissed deeply and ardently.

And then for the longest time, as afternoon turned to evening, they sat on the sofa together, enjoying the fire, holding hands, and talking. They talked about nothing that was too serious. They swapped anecdotes. They exchanged frivolous information. They laughed often.

It was their first date.

Pocket Books
proudly presents

RAINWATER

SANDRA BROWN

Available now

Turn the page for a preview of
RAINWATER. . . .

PROLOGUE

B Y ANY CHANCE, IS YOUR POCKET WATCH FOR
sale?"

The old man raised his head. The woman
asking about his watch was leaning across the glass
display case separating them. Inside the case were
snuffboxes, hatpins, razors with bone handles, salt-
cellars with their dainty sterling silver spoons, and
various pieces of jewelry recently acquired at an
estate sale.

But the woman's focus was on his watch.

He guessed the woman and her husband to be in
their mid-forties. To them the gold timepiece probably looked dapper and quaint, Rockwellian. The
couple were dressed in the preppy fashion of country
club members. Both were trim and tanned, and they
looked good together, as though they had come as a
set, the man as handsome as his wife was attractive.

They had arrived in a sleek SUV, which looked
out of place on the dusty gravel parking lot in front

of the antiques store. In the half hour they'd been there, several items in his inventory had attracted their interest. The things they had decided to purchase were of good quality. As their appearances indicated, they had discriminating taste.

The old man had been listing the items on a sales receipt when his customer posed the question about his pocket watch. He laid a protective hand over it where it rested against his vest and smiled. "No, ma'am. I couldn't part with my watch."

She had the confidence of a pretty woman who was accustomed to beguiling people with her smile. "Not for any price? You don't see pocket watches like that these days. The new ones look . . . well, new. Shininess makes them appear phony and cheap, doesn't it? A patina, like that on yours, gives it character."

Her husband, who'd been browsing the bookshelves, joined them at the counter. Like his wife, he leaned across the display case to better inspect the watch's workmanship. "Twenty-four-karat gold?"

"I would imagine so, although I've never had it appraised."

"I'd take it without having it appraised," the man said.

"I wouldn't consider selling it. Sorry." The shopkeeper bent over the case and continued to painstakingly write up their purchases. Some days the arthritis in his knuckles made handwriting difficult, but what place did a computer have in an antiques store? Besides, he distrusted them.

He did the arithmetic the old-fashioned way, carrying over the two and arriving at his total. "With tax, it comes to three hundred sixty-seven dollars and forty-one cents."

"Sounds fair enough." The man pinched a credit card out of a small alligator wallet and slid it across the top of the case. "Add two bottles of Evian, please." He went to the sleek refrigerated cabinet with a glass door. It had no place in an antiques store, either, but thirsty browsers stayed to browse longer if drinks were available, so the refrigerator was the shopkeeper's one small concession to modernity.

"On the house," he told his customer. "Help yourself."

"That's awfully nice of you."

"I can afford it," he told them with a smile. "This is my biggest single sale of the weekend."

The man took two bottles of water from the refrigerator and passed one to his wife, then signed the credit card receipt. "Do you get a lot of traffic off the interstate?"

The store owner nodded. "People who're in no particular hurry to get where they're going."

"We noticed your billboard," the woman said. "It caught our attention, and, on the spur of the moment, we decided to take the exit."

"The rental on that billboard is expensive as all get-out. I'm glad to know it's working." He began carefully wrapping their purchases in sheets of tissue paper.

The man took a look around the shop, glanced out at the parking lot, which was empty except for his own gas guzzler, and asked, somewhat doubtfully, "Do you do a good business?"

"Fair to middling. The store's more a hobby than anything. It keeps me active, keeps my mind sharp. Gives me something to do in my retirement."

"What line of work were you in?"

"Textiles."

"Were antiques always an interest?" the woman asked.

"No," he admitted sheepishly. "Like most things in life, this"—he raised his hands to indicate the shop—"came about unexpectedly."

The lady pulled forward a tall stool and sat down. "It sounds like there's a story."

The old man smiled, welcoming her interest and the opportunity to chat. "The furnishings from my mother's house had been in storage for years. When I retired and had time to sort through everything, I realized I didn't have any use for most of the stuff, but I thought other people might. So I started selling off china and doodads. Gradual like, at weekend flea markets and such. I wasn't all that ambitious, but, as it turned out, I was a pretty good merchant.

"Soon friends and acquaintances began bringing me items to sell on consignment. Almost before I knew it, I'd run out of space in the garage and had to rent this building."

He shook his head, chuckling. "I just sort of fell into becoming an antiques dealer. But I like it." He grinned at them. "Keeps me occupied, keeps me in spending money, and I get to meet nice folks like y'all. Where's your home?"

They told him they were from Tulsa and had been to San Antonio for a long golf weekend with friends. "We're not on a deadline to get home, so when we saw your sign, we decided to stop and take a look. We're furnishing our lake house with antiques and rustics."

"I'm glad you stopped." He passed the woman a business card with the shop's logo on it. "If you change your mind about that Spode tureen you spent so much time considering, call me. I ship."

"I just might." She ran her finger over the name embossed on the card as she read it aloud. "Solly's. That's an unusual name. First or last?"

"First. Short for Solomon, after the wise king in the Old Testament." He smiled ruefully. "I've often wondered if my mother had second thoughts about that choice."

"That's twice you've mentioned your mother." The woman's smile was warmer, even prettier, when she wasn't using it to try to finagle her way. "You must have been very close to her. I mean, I assume she's no longer living."

"She died in the late sixties." He reflected on how long ago that must sound to this couple. They would have been babies. "Mother and I were very close. I miss her to this day. She was a lovely woman."

"Is Gilead your home?"

"I was born here, in a big yellow house that had belonged to my maternal grandparents."

"Do you have a family?"

"My wife passed on eight years ago. I have two children, a boy and a girl. Both live in Austin. Between them, they've given me six grandchildren, the oldest of which is about to get married."

"We have two sons," the woman said. "Both are students at Oklahoma State."

"Children are a joy."

The woman laughed. "As well as a challenge."

Her husband had been following their conversation while examining the selections in the bookcase. "These are first editions."

"All signed and in excellent condition," the

shopkeeper said. "I picked them up at an estate sale not long ago."

"Impressive collection." The man ran his finger along the row of book spines. "Truman Capote's *In Cold Blood*. A Steinbeck. Norman Mailer. Thomas Wolfe." He turned to the merchant and grinned. "I should have left my credit card out."

"I also take cash."

The customer laughed. "I'll bet you do."

His wife added, "For everything except your pocket watch."

The old man slipped the fob through the buttonhole on his vest and cupped the watch in his palm. It hadn't lost a second since he'd last wound it. Time had yellowed the white face, but the slight discoloration gave it a richer look. The black hands were as thin as the filaments of a spider's web. The long hand had a sharp arrow point. "I wouldn't take anything for it, ma'am."

Softly she said, "It's invaluable to you."

"In the strictest sense."

"How old is it?" the man asked.

"I don't know for certain," replied the shopkeeper, "but its age isn't what makes it meaningful to me." He turned it facedown and extended his hand to them so they could read the inscription on the back of the gold case.

"August eleventh, 1934," the woman read aloud. Then looking back at him, she asked, "What does it commemorate? An anniversary? Birthday? Something exceptional?"

"Exceptional?" The old man smiled. "Not particularly. Just very special."

ONE

WHEN ELLA BARRON WOKE UP THAT morning, she didn't expect it to be a momentous day.

Her sleep hadn't been interrupted by a subconscious premonition. There had been no change in the weather, no sudden shift in the atmosphere, no unusual sound to startle her awake.

As on most mornings, sleep released her gradually a half hour before daylight. She yawned and stretched, her feet seeking cool spots between the sheets. But catching another forty winks was out of the question. To indulge in such a luxury would never have crossed her mind. She had responsibilities, chores that couldn't be shirked or even postponed. She lay in bed only long enough to remember what day of the week it was. Wash day.

She quickly made her bed, then checked on Solly, who was still deep in slumber.

She dressed with customary efficiency. With no

time for vanity, she hastily twisted her long hair into a bun on the back of her head and secured it with pins, then left her bedroom and made her way to the kitchen, moving quietly so as not to awaken the others in the house.

This was the only time of day when the kitchen was quiet and cool. As the day progressed, heat was produced by the cookstove. Heat seeped in from outside through the screened door and the window above the sink. Even Ella's own energy acted as a generator.

Proportionately with the thermometer, the noise level rose, so that by suppertime, the kitchen, which was the heart of the house, took on a pulsating life of its own and didn't settle into cool repose until Ella extinguished the overhead light for the final time, most often hours after her boarders had retired.

This morning, she didn't pause to enjoy either the relative coolness or the silence. Having put on her apron, she lit the oven, put the coffee on to brew, then mixed the biscuit dough. Margaret arrived right on time, and after removing her hat and hanging it on the peg inside the door, and gratefully taking a tin cup of sweetened coffee from Ella, she went back outside to fill the washing machine with water for the first load of laundry.

The prospect of buying an electric-powered washing machine was so remote that Ella didn't even dream about it. For her foreseeable future she must continue using the one with the hand-crank wringer that had been her mother's. Suds and rinse water from the tub were drained into a ditch that ran alongside the shed where the washer was housed.

On a summer day like today, the washing shed

became stifling by midmorning. But wet laundry seemed heavier when one's hands were raw and numb from cold during the winter months. In any season, laundry days were dreaded. By nightfall her back would be aching.

Solly, still in his pajamas, wandered into the kitchen while she was frying bacon.

Breakfast was served at eight.

By nine o'clock everyone had been fed, the dishes washed, dried, and put away. Ella set a pot of mustard greens on the stove to simmer all day, cooked a pan of Faultless starch, then, taking Solly with her, went outside to hang up the first basket of laundry that Margaret had washed, rinsed, and wrung out.

It was almost eleven o'clock when she went inside to check on things in the kitchen. While she was adding a little more salt to the greens, someone pulled the bell at her front door. As she walked along the dim center hall, she dried her hands on her apron and glanced at herself in the wall mirror. Her face was flushed and damp from the heat, and her heavy bun had defied the pins and slipped down onto her nape, but she continued to the door without stopping to primp.

On the other side of the threshold, squinting at her through the screened door, was Dr. Kincaid. "Morning, Mrs. Barron." His white straw hat had a natty red cloth band, striated with generations of sweat stains. He removed it and held it against his chest in a rather courtly manner.

She was surprised to see the doctor on her porch, but still nothing signaled her that this would be an extraordinary day.

Dr. Kincaid's office was in the center of town on

Hill Street, but he also made house calls, usually to deliver a baby, sometimes to keep a contagious patient from spreading his infection through Gilead, their town of two thousand.

Ella herself had summoned the doctor to the house a couple of years ago when one of her boarders fell out of his bed during the middle of the night. Mr. Blackwell, an elderly gentleman who fortunately had been more embarrassed than injured, protested even as Dr. Kincaid agreed with Ella that he probably should be thoroughly examined just as a precaution. Mr. Blackwell no longer lived with her. Shortly after that incident, his family had moved him to a home for the elderly in Waco. Mr. Blackwell had futilely protested his involuntary relocation, too.

Had one of her boarders sent for the doctor today? Little in the house escaped Ella's notice, but she'd been outside most of the morning, so it was possible that one of the sisters had used the telephone without her knowledge.

"Good morning, Dr. Kincaid. Did one of the Dunnes send for you?"

"No. I'm not here on a sick call."

"Then what can I do for you?"

"Is this a bad time?"

She thought of the clothes piled into baskets and ready to be starched, but the starch needed a while longer to cool. "Not at all. Come in." She reached up to unlatch the screened door and pushed it open.

Dr. Kincaid turned to his right and made a come-forward motion with his hat. Ella was unaware of the other man's presence until he stepped around the large fern at the side of the front door and into her range of vision.

Her first impression of him was how tall and lean he was. One could almost say he looked underfed. He was dressed in a black suit with a white shirt and black necktie, and was holding a black felt fedora. She thought his clothes looked severe and out of season for such a hot morning, especially compared to Dr. Kincaid's seersucker suit and white hat with the red band.

The doctor made the introduction. "Mrs. Barron, this is Mr. Rainwater."

He inclined his head. "Ma'am."

"Mr. Rainwater."

She moved aside and indicated for them to come inside. Dr. Kincaid allowed the other man to go in ahead of him. A few steps into the foyer, he stopped to let his eyes adjust to the relative darkness. Then he took in his surroundings as he idly threaded the brim of his hat through long, slender fingers.

"In here, please." Ella stepped around her two guests and motioned them into the formal parlor. "Have a seat."

"We thought we heard the doorbell."

The chirping voice brought Ella around. The Misses Dunne, Violet and Pearl, were standing on the bottom stair. In their pastel print dresses and old-fashioned shoes, they were virtually interchangeable. Each had a nimbus of white hair. Their veined, spotted hands clutched matching handkerchiefs, daintily hemmed and hand-embroidered by their mother, they'd told Ella.

With unabashed curiosity, the two were looking beyond Ella to catch a glimpse of the visitors. Having callers was an event.

"Is that Dr. Kincaid?" asked Pearl, the more

inquisitive of the two. "Hello, Dr. Kincaid," she called.

"Good morning, Miss Pearl."

"Who's that with you?"

Miss Violet frowned at her sister with reproof. "We were coming down to play gin rummy until lunch," she whispered to Ella. "Will we disturb?"

"Not at all."

Ella asked them to use the informal parlor and led them to it. When they were situated at the card table, she said, "Please excuse us, ladies," and pulled together the heavy oak pocket doors that divided the large room in half. She rejoined the two men in the formal side, which overlooked the front porch. Despite her invitation for them to sit down, they had remained standing.

Dr. Kincaid was fanning himself with his hat. Ella switched on the fan on the table in the corner, directed the stream of air toward him, then motioned the men toward a pair of wingback chairs. "Please."

They sat when she did.

This being summer, and wash day, she hadn't put on stockings that morning. Embarrassed by her bare legs, she crossed her ankles and pulled her feet beneath the chair. "Would you like some lemonade? Or tea?"

"That sounds awfully good, Mrs. Barron, but I'm afraid I have to pass," the doctor said. "I've got patients to see at the clinic."

She looked at Mr. Rainwater.

"No thank you," he said.

Returning to the kitchen would have given her an opportunity to remove her apron, which had a damp patch where she'd dried her hands, and to pin her bun more securely. But since her guests had declined the offer of a drink, she was stuck looking untidy for the remainder of their visit, the purpose of which hadn't yet been stated. She wondered what Solly was up to and how long this unexpected meeting was going to take. She hoped Mr. Rainwater wasn't a salesman. She didn't have time to sit through his pitch, only to say no to whatever it was he was peddling.

The smell of simmering mustard greens was strong, even here in the front parlor. The doctor withdrew a large white handkerchief from his coat pocket and used it to blot sweat from his balding head. A yellow jacket flew into the window screen and continued angrily to try to go through it. The hum of the electric fan seemed as loud as a buzz saw.

She was relieved when Dr. Kincaid cleared his throat and said, "I heard you lost a boarder."

"That's right. Mrs. Morton went to live with an ailing sister. Somewhere in eastern Louisiana, I believe."

"Quite a piece from here," he remarked.

"Her nephew came to escort her on the train."

"Nice for her, I'm sure. Have you had anyone speak for her room?"

"She only left the day before yesterday. I haven't had time to advertise."

"Well then, that's good, that's good," the doctor said and began fanning himself enthusiastically, as though in celebration of something.

Discerning now the purpose for their call, she looked at Mr. Rainwater. He sat leaning slightly forward with both feet on the floor. His black shoes were shined, she noticed. His thick, dark hair was smoothed back off his face, but one strand, as straight and shiny as a satin ribbon, had defiantly flopped over his broad forehead. His cheekbones were pronounced, his eyebrows as sleek and black as crows' wings. He had startling blue eyes, and they were steady on her.

"Are you interested in lodging, Mr. Rainwater?"

"Yes. I need a place to stay."

"I haven't had a chance to give the vacant room a thorough cleaning, but as soon as it's ready, I'd be happy to show it to you."

"I'm not particular." He smiled, showing teeth that were very white, although slightly crooked on the top. "I'll take the room as is."

"Oh, I'm afraid I couldn't let you have it now," she said quickly. "Not until I've aired the bedding, scrubbed everything, polished the floor. I have very high standards."

"For boarders or cleanliness?"

"For both."

"Which is why I've brought him to you," the doctor said hastily. "I told Mr. Rainwater that you keep an immaculate house and run a tight ship. To say nothing of the excellent meals your boarders enjoy. He desires a place that's well maintained. A peaceful and quiet house."

Just then, from the direction of the kitchen, came a terrible racket followed by a bloodcurdling scream.